Reading by Lightning

JOAN THOMAS

Edited by Bethany Gibson.
Cover illustration composed with images from iStockphoto.
Cover and book design by Julie Scriver.
Printed in Canada on 100% PCW paper.
10 9 8 7 6 5 4 3

Library and Archives Canada Cataloguing in Publication

Thomas, Joan
Reading by lightning/Joan Thomas.

ISBN 978-0-86492-512-1

I. Title.

PS8639.H572R43 2008   C813'.6   C2008-902745-0

Goose Lane Editions acknowledges the financial support of the Canada Council for the Arts, the Government of Canada through the Book Publishing Industry Development Program (BPIDP), and the New Brunswick Department of Wellness, Culture, and Sport for its publishing activities.

Goose Lane Editions
Suite 330, 500 Beaverbrook Court
Fredericton, New Brunswick
CANADA E3B 5X4
www.gooselane.com

For Caitlin

The oldest preserved maps of the world originate from Babylonian times, that is, from the third millennium before Christ. On these maps, the Earth is depicted as a flat disk floating on the ocean. Babylon is at the centre of the disk. To make a centre of power the centre of the world, just because it is one's own, is essentially a religious act.

Gerhard Staguhn, *Das Lachen Gottes*

If God did not make us then we must make ourselves.

Leon Rooke, *The Fall of Gravity*

Book One

A brilliant summer day, and an early version of me steps out of the general store in town. I'm wearing a yellow dress with tiny blue flowers on it, not a hand-me-down but a dress made especially for me from a proper bolt of cloth. My mother, who's behind me, has on a white cotton dress faintly patterned with grey worms (black and white daisies, this dress once was, although you would have to have known her for five years to know that).

I run down the wooden steps and there's Charlotte Bates standing beside the ice chest with a boy. Both of them are drinking root beer from bottles. Hello, Lily, says Charlotte in her warm way, and the boy looks up. He's dark haired and strongly built, not tall but taller than both of us. A cottonwood grows so close to the street that the boardwalk was built out around its massive trunk, and this tree drops moving green shadows onto his face and Charlotte's in the bright sunlight.

We're off for a drive, Charlotte says. Russell has Dad's car. Lily, this is my brother from Toronto. You meet at last! Lily Piper, Russell Bates!

Charlotte gestures prettily from me to Russell and smiles to acknowledge my mother, but my mother (who is unacquainted with the formal introduction) just keeps walking, one shoulder lower than the other because she's hauling a jug of vinegar for pickling. She doesn't even say, Come on, Lily, and surprise flits over Charlotte's face.

Come for a drive in the country, the boy says, looking at me.

Lily's *from* the country, says Charlotte.

My mother's climbing into the truck by then, but I stand on the boardwalk in my tie-up farm shoes, pinned down by their attention. I'm outlined in black by Charlotte's words, by *from the country*, I'm struck mute. But still I see everything. The fine texture of Russell's white shirt and the way the sun picks out individual dark hairs standing up from his forehead and shows the red in them. The geometrical framework of his cheekbones and temple, the way friendliness livens his face, as though it's nipping at his cheeks here and there from the inside. I see him solid in the sliding patterns of shadow and sun, and I also see myself, a girl pretty enough to stand there being looked at by this boy from the east: with a lift of gladness I see that I'm all right, I'm the best thing anyone could patch together with the ingredients I had at hand.

That was seven or eight years ago, and when I look back it seems to me that this boy from the east was a sign that life might drop something *real* into my lap, that I might not have to make it all up myself, like the girl in the fairy tale wearing herself out trying to spin straw into gold. So you'd think I might remember every single thing about that day (which by some sort of miracle I did spend with Russell Bates). But actually I recall only parts of it, and all of those memories are a little ragged now from being played over and over in my mind. I also hung on to a lot of irrelevant detail, the way you do. I remember a woman in a farmyard as we rolled by, a thin woman in a brown dress standing halfway to the barn as though she'd just come to herself with no idea of what she had in mind to do. And a turtle broken like a saucer on the river road, its white eggs spilled out into the dust. I remember also the way rain smacked against the windshield of Russell's father's big car while we were parked up at the Lookout, the clean circles the raindrops made on the dusty glass.

※

I wonder how you choose what you're going to remember. *That's what happened*, I say about any particular event. But of course we recall only a tiny fraction of everything that occurred. If every day that went by I'd saved a whole other set of details and impressions, my life as I tell it to myself would be completely different. This is a rather crucial human limitation. If your situation changes dramatically (if, for example, you're walking down a road and are suddenly scooped up in a whirlwind and deposited somewhere else, like that man in the Bible was), you may need to start thinking about your life in a whole different way. But how can you do that when all you have for information is what you chose to remember at the time?

I've tried to understand this. I remember talking about it with George when I was in England, far from my prairie home. While we were out walking one day, rain falling on the shoulders of our mackintoshes in the noiseless way it always falls in England, I asked him why you remember what you remember.

It's all electronics, George said. His hair was plastered to his forehead in clumps from the damp. He launched into an explanation of how the brain stashes everything away, and then an electrical impulse homes in to retrieve what you want. I just read a novel, he said, in which people wore *helmets* with electrodes attached to various parts of their brain. Every time an electrode lit up, the wearer of the helmet would think he was somewhere in his past. He would feel the things he felt back then. But there was no special importance to those moments.

Do you notice me wearing a helmet? I believe I said to that. We were walking along the hedgerows into town, our shoes

13

squelching wet. The narrow walls of privet were like a maze we had to navigate, and in the dim light his thin face gleamed — he had the sort of mushroomy skin that goes pale with exercise instead of flushing.

Or think about epileptics, George said. When an epileptic has a fit, everything happening at the moment feels familiar, dead familiar. That's because the fit fires up the part of his brain where his memories are kept. Everything feels *momentous*. But it's not, it's just the usual detritus.

The hedgerows ended abruptly just then — this was where the motorway sliced across the countryside at a diagonal. George climbed up the gravel bank of the motorway and shouted back over his shoulder: *And others when the bagpipe sings cannot contain their urine.*

Oh, that was George.

⚸

At Ward Street Grammar School in Oldham, Lancashire (where for several years I impersonated an English schoolgirl), we looked at the memories in rocks, limestone sliced open so the ammonites inside made two beautiful coiled snakes. I learned that a whole civilization, Phoenicia, was built on a passion for *indigo*. I learned the French words for *umbrella* and *nightmare*, and I saw a coloured plate of a fetus in a woman's womb. Occasionally details from the farm would float into my mind like strands of spiderweb and cling there. I'd be swinging up the street in Oldham with my book satchel over my shoulder and I'd see a flypaper slowly twisting against the cloudy sky. Or the pitchfork from the barn, straw and manure drying into wattle on its tines. I hated it all, I wiped it off with a shudder. That was me sitting on a polished bench in the library in a navy pleated skirt, my coarse brown hair falling over my eyes, but as the world nudged its way into my brain, I was *changing*, my skin smoothing, the poison ivy scabs dropping off, the dirt and raspberry juice scrubbed out from under my fingernails, the sins that stained me fading with my tan. While my desk partner muttered in Latin, I propped my history book up in front of me and let it fall open at random and my eyes slid onto the words Elizabeth I etched onto a window with a diamond when she was held prisoner as a girl: MUCH SUSPECTED OF ME, NOTHING PROVED CAN BE.

It was a new future I was glimpsing, not at all the future I'd pictured when I was growing up — which was not on this earth at all.

1

Straw is piled on one side of the loft and hay on the other. Our church is an open space between the two piles. The people sit on rough benches made from planks, and Mr. Dalrymple has a pulpit at the front where he stands with his back to the loft opening while he preaches. I'm nestled with other children in the hay under the eaves. We can't all fit on the benches so we're allowed to sit up there, from where we watch barn swallows plunge into the loft just over Mr. Dalrymple's ear, and the frantic beaks of their chicks strain up out of the row of mud nests plastered to the centre beam. *Some glad morning, when this life is o'er*, we sing, *I'll fly away. To a home on God's celestial shore, I'll fly away.*

With his back against the only light, Mr. Dalrymple's a cut-out figure, his outline soft where fat bulges over the waistband of his trousers. The sky is grey with dust, and he's a darker grey. *I'll fly away, oh glory*, he sings in a flat, dogged voice. The grey in the air around Mr. Dalrymple could be his distaste for this world, a distaste he shares with God, who is about to abandon the whole mess, pluck out the handful of people he wants and leave the rest behind. Not a glad morning, as Mr. Dalrymple pictures it, but a fearsome day. You can see the earth gearing up for it, the sky darkening and lightning flashing without a drop of rain ever falling, grasshoppers rising up like a spray of bullets when you cross the yard, the sunsets daubed with blood.

The hay is fresh and springy and not well packed. As the sermon starts I'm not even trying to sit still — I'm wallowing along the haystack in my blue cotton dress and tie-up shoes. Who knows why I'm working my way towards the front of the loft? Even I don't know. Without warning the hay surrenders and I sink down onto something awkward — a leg, attached to my cousin Gracie. Her mouth turns down in an eager apology (everything is her fault). Or my shoe scrapes an arm — my brother Phillip's. His hands dart up (it's a reflex, if I don't move fast he'll give me a snakebite).

Now I'm above Mr. Dalrymple. I can see the oily black hair smeared across his skull like molasses, and the adults sitting motionless in front of him. The front of the loft is open for light and for the easy removal of Christians, who will be snatched any minute from where they hunch with their heads sunk into their shoulders and carried up to heaven — not flying like birds, but carried upright with their arms at their sides, as though pulled by wires under their armpits. Mr. Dalrymple prays for the Rapture to come during church, when the Lord's chosen are gathered together in this humble abode for beasts. *In a moment*, he cries hoarsely, *in the twinkling of an eye, at the last trump. For the trumpet shall sound, and the dead shall be raised incorruptible. And we shall be changed!* There's a practised excitement in his voice, but underneath he sounds naggy: this is a threat, not a promise.

There are those who long for the Second Coming and those who dread it. Although (I think, reaching a furtive finger behind me to dig at the hay caught in the elastic of my under-pants), isn't it possible that even those who are born again will dread it? They'll hear the trumpet, and they'll feel a stab of fear and disbelief. They'd rather keep on weeding the garden, or whatever it is they're doing, but they'll be sucked up anyway, up over the shelter belt, their houses and barns and the parched earth falling away, the cattle in the pasture lifting big heads in surprise. But then as they fly they will be *changed*. They'll discover that they're dressed in beautiful white robes. They'll peer through the clouds to see who else made it — spying their friends, calling in astonishment, He *came*! We were *right*! — not thinking about the ones left behind, because (and I reach for a rafter to steady myself) this is *heaven* they're going to. Worry will fall from you — your heart has to change too, become the unthinking heart of a baby.

And I looked, Mr. Dalrymple reads out, his voice going up a notch, *and behold a pale horse. And his name that sat on him was Death, and Hell followed with him!* He prods at the text on the page with his index finger: these are God's very words. *And I looked* (I breathe as I inch my way towards the opening), *and behold a pale horse!* All I can see of my dad is his two long legs stretched out straight and crossed at the ankle. My mother's between me and him. She's taken her hat off, it's on her lap. She's lifted her face to Mr. Dalrymple with a listening expression, but her eyes are moving steadily along the haystack, looking for me, filled with helpless fury. The rope of her fury zigzags through the air towards the haystack, probing for me, and Mr. Dalrymple's voice fills the loft like oily smoke coming off the burn barrel, and I climb unsteadily, just out of their reach, working my way clumsily towards the loft opening.

On a weekday there's a special, quiet air to the loft, as though the prayers trapped in people's hearts on Sunday finally escaped and are hanging now in the dusty golden air. I sit up there, my legs dangling out the opening, and watch my mother out in the big garden we call the field plot, picking the tasteless pale yellow melons she and Mrs. Feazel cut into chunks and can for winter desserts. Citron, they're called. She's dragged the washtubs out there and she's filling them. Phillip is working, he's out snaring gophers. If my mother knew where I was, I'd be helping her.

From above like this, God has a clear sightline to my mother where she works in the field plot. She stretches her back, standing on the shrivelled vines, the only upright figure on the flat earth that God made the first Monday morning. The sun's right above her, she casts no shadow. She's wearing her green dress with a shirt of my dad's over it to keep the sun off her arms.

Joe Pye is at the other end of the garden, where the garden meets the field. Joe Pye, my father's friend who came with him from England. He's crouching beside the harrow, hard-edged with light, fiddling with the grease gun. I watch him ease his way gingerly down into the shadow of the harrow, his back-bone sticking out like a mountain ridge on a topographical map. How're you feeling, Joe? I asked him at breakfast. Aw, everything's agin me today, even me underwear, he said. Joe Pye never goes to church. He pulls his mattress out of the bunkhouse every Sunday and lies sleeping under the cotton-woods all morning. When the congregation flies past him up into the sky, they'll see him curled like a cutworm on his side, sound asleep.

I inch along the loft opening, picturing what happened on Sunday during church: the way a pit opened in the hay and I dropped into it, whooshing down, clutching at straws, at the sharp edge of the loft opening (last chance to stop myself). A giddy moment in the air before the ground zoomed up and hit me with a whack. Faces peering out of the loft above and breaking into laughter as I sat up. My mother flying around the corner of the barn, her furious hands clutching at me. Then I see a white-faced, chastened girl back in church sitting between her parents. Something has shocked them, her fall from the loft and something else. They sit weighted down with it, all three of them. The girl sits with her thin back straight, her hands cupped and all ten nails biting into her skin. Why didn't you at least *faint*? I say to her.

Our Ford truck bounces along the edge of the field and stops by my mother. My father gets out and they start to load the citron. My mother staggers a little under the weight of the second tub and it tips, and three or four melons fall to the ground and roll away. One of them's under the Ford. After she's picked them up, all but the one under the truck, she walks across the yard and calls me. I pull my feet up into the loft and lie back away from the opening and wait for exasperation to sharpen her voice.

⚒

By the middle of the afternoon the sick-sweet smell of cooked citron fills Mrs. Feazel's kitchen. Come here, says my mother. Sit down. You're going to break something. They're taking a rest in the living room, where it's cooler, Mrs. Feazel and my mother. I'm standing between the curtain and the window, flicking away the dead flies lying on the window ledge with their legs in the air. This window ledge is Mrs. Feazel's china cabinet, where she keeps her treasures lined up in a row. A clamshell with *Delta Manitoba* written on it in scrolled letters. A little brass dinner bell. Mr. Feazel's pin from the war, a tiny Union Jack. And the gallstone Dr. Ross took out of her, a flattened, yellow-green egg, not polished like a stone but with an irritating surface, like the scale on the inside of a kettle.

Come here, Lily, my mother says again.

Mrs. Feazel reaches over and nudges the side of my face with her knuckle, the way a man would. Oh, she's always been a restless one, she says. What a shock! My stars! We're sitting there worrying about our dinners and all of a sudden *this* one

21

goes shooting out of the loft right in front of our eyes! Oh, my stars — what a shock! You could of broke your neck! And that *man*! She leans forward, clenching and unclenching her eyes the way Mr. Dalrymple does. She makes her voice oily and accusing: *I don't mean any offence to the Piper family*, she says in Mr. Dalrymple's voice, *but Satan will sometimes take hold of a little child and use that child to distract listeners from the Word of God*. She shakes her head, shock at her own daring on her big, frank face. Satan! she laughs in her jolly way. Oh, my, my, my. My mother crimps her lips together and doesn't say a word. I step back and the rope my mother sends out pulls at me. It's caught me, it's coiled around both of us, a rope of secret fear.

※

My mother has only Phillip and me to think about. All around us are families with gangs of children, like the Stallings and the Abernathys. On Sunday mornings they ride into the yard on a hayrack pulled by plow horses, or, if there's a car and the gas to run it, they're crammed into the back seat and clinging to the running boards. Our family, the object of pity and envy, begins with Phillip and ends with me (because of me, because of what I did to be born). But it's our yard they come to, our barn, which had a church in the loft when we bought it.

When I was a baby we lived in a rented house in Burnley. Then my dad bought this farm. I remember riding out in a truck with all our things in the back, sitting squeezed against Phillip, riding out of the rust-coloured mist of babyhood (where all that I knew of myself was told to me by other people) and into the brown and grey world of my dusty childhood. A man with a shy, lashless face (a rabbit's face) is standing by the house. It's Mr. Pangbourne. His wife has just died, his second wife, and he's buried her by the first in the plot intended for himself, and is going back to the old country. The barn smells of freshly sawn wood. He built this barn because his old one fell down.

He never used it for animals. While his wife was sick, he offered it to Mr. Dalrymple to use for a church.

The house is old and has a summer kitchen tacked to the back of it. Its unpainted boards are silvered with age and shrunk down from the size they used to be. The minute Mr. Pangbourne drives out of the yard, my mother finds a book on a shelf in the pantry, *The Pilgrim's Progress*. It's just a stack of soft, thick pages tied up with string because the spine and covers have come off. In our new house in the evening she reads the story to us, about a man named Christian who has a heavy burden on his back that he can't lay down, and so sets off on a long journey to the Celestial City, where he will be free of it. Crouching in the living room while my mother reads aloud to us, I peer through a crack below the windowsill and see a chicken walk by outside.

When my mother finally puts the book down I tell them about seeing a chicken through the wall. This house was built by an eight-year-old boy taking instructions from a blind man, says Joe Pye, who that very afternoon walked up the lane from nowhere and sits now at the kitchen table chewing on a matchstick.

When winter comes my dad and Joe haul the stove in from the lean-to kitchen and install it in the living room. Dad pulls off the pie plate that was nailed over the chimney hole to keep mosquitoes out of the house. They keep a miniature inferno going in that stove, my dad and Joe, burning wood cut down by the river. They nail shingles over the cracks in the walls, but the wind finds new cracks every day.

In the barn our new cows sleep standing up. Down the road the Stalling girls sleep three to a bed and two beds to a room. I sleep in my own bed in my own room in our leaky house. All night I revolve over the mattress, dreams peeling off me. It's dark when I wake up to the cows moaning about the painful weight of their udders. My mother comes in and pries me out into air as cold as knives. Last year a house up the road burned down, killing four sleeping children while their parents did chores in the barn. Would you leave children alone in a house with a fire burning in the stove? people asked one another in low voices. Every dark morning my mother drags me and Phillip whimpering to the barn to be sure no neighbour will ever have cause to say such a thing about her.

When I turn six it's Phillip who takes me down the long dirt road to school. I wear a blue dress and bloomers made from a flour sack. We stop and examine a massive badger hole at the first corner. Goldenrod blooms among the thistles in the ditch. I manage to break off a tough stem of it and hold it up to my blue dress. I wish I had a pin, I say. Phillip walks backwards, watching with delight while I pull up the bodice of my dress and gnaw a little hole in the fabric to stick the stem through. You will get such a licking, he says.

At school I copy mottoes written on the chalkboard in Miss Fielding's large, childish hand while Miss Fielding stands against the windows with a burn mark in the shape of an iron on her skirt, placidly watching. I learn the times tables, and every morning we recite them, standing in a wavering row across the front of the schoolroom, breathing in the smell of wet mittens baking on the stove. *Two* is pale and silver-haired, overworked but willing. *Five* is a domineering, round-faced girl, her hair cut severely into a black fringe. When it's Five's turn she hauls the other numbers with her to Fifteen, Twenty, Twenty-five, Thirty, she puts up with no argument. (At Twenty-five, she gazes in delight at her twin and they drink tea together.) I stand between Betty Stalling and my cousin Gracie, chanting along with them, stories flickering through my brain. Stand up straight, Lily, says the teacher, but I slump against the blackboard, exhausted by the affairs of generations of numbers.

We have no chalk, there's no money to buy chalk, but there's a fancy table map donated by a rich lady named Mrs. Alexander. Its mountains are built up in plaster. The peaks of the Andes and the Alps are all chipped off — the exposed plaster is flat, but it could be snow. The Rockies are intact but black from children rubbing at them. England is a little island like a misshapen cucumber. The *old* country. I have cousins there: Lois and Madeleine and George (although George is not quite my cousin. He's not really their boy, my mother says in the disgruntled voice she uses for people she knows nothing about. He's an orphan they took in).

In England my father lived in a house made of brick, Joe Pye in a house made of stones. Here, in Nebo, Manitoba, everything is made of wood, and flimsy. This world is not our home. We'll be leaving any minute — nothing the drought can do to us matters, the cracks it's opening up in the fields (so wide and deep that Joe Pye loses his wrench down one of them), the Russian thistle taking over a corner of the prairie that should never have been broken. These are *signs*, they mean Jesus is coming soon. They're intended to fire up our faith, like a girl seeing a dust cloud on the horizon and knowing it means her boyfriend is driving up the road. *Even so, come, Lord Jesus*, Mr. Dalrymple cries in the loft, lifting his arms. I sit on the bench between my parents and reach inside and touch my memory of what he shouted that day (about Satan, about me), touch it delicately to see if it still throbs, and it does. I turn my eyes up to the rafters. I can see the frail stretched necks of the swallow chicks, their wide beaks reaching up, up from the mud nest towards something none of us sitting below can see.

I have inside me my own private picture of what lies ahead, the other world. I come across it sometimes when I'm lying in bed, halfway to sleep. I come across it in the dark, in a dark alcove of my mind, like a shrine lit up with guttering candles. It's from a place too far back for memory. I'm in the middle of the yard. Orange light blazes in the sky, flames fill the windows of the barn. The barn door is wide open and men come out, carrying something heavy, a body, sagging like a grain sack. They're stooped, they're trying to be gentle, carrying him. His head lolls. One limp arm drags on the ground, like when they took Jesus down from the cross, and a man scoops it up and drapes it across his chest. They prop him against the side of the barn and bend over him. I can see his white shirt, his body drooping back against the barn. I'm very small, just eyes and exhausted, shallow sobs that batter my chest like hiccups.

⌗

While everyone waits for Jesus, I persist in growing. My mother's cutting an old dress of hers down for me. I stand by the chesterfield in bare feet on the cold floor and she tucks and pins the bodice. I am ten or eleven, much smaller than she is. There will be fabric left over, and she'll stitch it into squares for potholders.

I shrink from her touch, from the prickling touch of the wool, clench my stomach and arms. Being close like this draws confidences from her. She tells me the story of her school friend who died after she breathed in a popcorn kernel and it festered in her lung. And about Felix Macdonald, the villainous farmer she worked for on the Bicknell road. And the harrowing story of my birth, when she first saw me folded and slimy like a calf, so small they pulled a mitten over my head to keep me warm. She winds backwards into this story — soon she'll get to *placenta*, a word she has a special, privileged knowledge of. *Afterbirth*, other people say, but my mother has reason to know better. She crouches, reaching blindly for the pins, her eyes half closed with the largeness of it, the way she was led down, down, into the Valley of Death. Five more minutes and they would have lost me, she says.

While my mother bends over the hem, my father comes in

26

and stands in the kitchen doorway drinking water from the dipper. A new frock! he says. You'll be fending off the lads in that. He has his cap on. I can't see his eyes, but I know he's looking at me.

The screen door slams behind my father. I feel warm where his eyes touched me, hope blooming in patches on my arm and shoulder. Sudden hope for this dress, which is brown wool, with deep notches in its too-big lapels and cuffs, different from the dresses other girls have. The *lads*, he says, because he's English. Jimmy Thrasher, he must mean, at the blacksmith shop. One day I was outside by the wagon, measuring the space between the spokes of the wheel with my bare foot, when Jimmy Thrasher came out and dumped a shaft in the wagon and reached over to pull on a string of my hair. You got a sweet box there. Any chance me getting into it? he said. I gave a little laugh. You never know, I said cluelessly. You never know, eh? he said. Well, I'm always here. My father came out then and we climbed onto the wagon and set off for home, and when I looked back over my shoulder Jimmy Thrasher was still standing there watching us.

Hand me the pincushion, my mother says. She's behind me now, tugging on the skirt. Even Dr. Ross was scared, she says. He came out to the waiting room when your father got to the hospital, and he told Dad it looked pretty bad. *I doubt I'll be able to save the both of them*, he said. *Short of a miracle.* She's nudging me to turn around so she can pin the front, but I stand stubbornly away from her, resisting the story. It was going to be one or the other of us, she says. That's what he figured. Finally she takes me by the elbows and cranks me round to face her. She's crouched in front of me, her head bent, her part a *path* worn down the middle of her orange hair. She doesn't look at me while she talks. She believes in a world that existed without me. Everything in it is shrunken down to the way she sees things.

I look over her head at the back wall of the living room where light from the kitchen window wavers. I'm immune to this story. She thinks this story is hers, but it's mine. I've seen the inside of it, its true meaning: the way I came to myself on that fateful morning, my face squashed and my arms and legs folded like a lizard's. It's a cave I'm in, like the inside of a pumpkin (although it's filled with water), and I am very small, only the thought of a nail at the ends of my tiny fingers. Nevertheless I dig and gouge, I locate a flap in the fretted walls and work my fingers under it. Membranes rip in a pleasing way as I pull, and blood swirls into the sea water around me, turning it the watery red of fish blood. And so I chose the day of my own birth, two months before my mother had in mind to bear me. And this is not something that ever occurs to my mother at all.

The threshing gang is finishing up at our place. In the middle of the afternoon my mother and I walk out to the field with a pail of lemonade and plates of bread and butter. There is just one stack left, and Chummy's in a barking frenzy, ferreting under it with her brown muzzle. My father is nowhere to be seen. Where's Will? my mother asks, but nobody knows where he's disappeared to. Back at the house we find he's somehow come in ahead of us — we can see his legs and feet through the bedroom door. He's lying face down on the bed with his boots on. My mother pushes me back and goes in and pulls the curtain across. I sit down on the step between the kitchen and living room. I can hear her talking to him in a low, urgent voice.

My dad was thirty-one when he met my mother. He lived all those years without knowing anything about her. It was her red hair that drew him to her, no doubt, the hair she's cut only once, after a boy at school poured rubber cement into it. In my mind I see my younger parents walking down a cow path in the pasture, both in their Sunday clothes. My dad is following my mother; he can't take his eyes off the bun peeping out from under her straw hat, like an animal emerging from its burrow. They come to a barbed-wire fence. But before they can stoop to crawl through it, I see her reaching for him, lifting her face to his, her eyes eager and determined. *This is what's done*, she's saying to herself. Or, *Begin as you mean to go on.*

I picture my parents out walking and the next thing I see my mother's a married woman standing in her own kitchen, the kitchen of a little house near the railroad tracks in Burnley. She's done what she was supposed to do: Phillip is a big-headed little boy at her feet, and a version of me is inside her. A preposterous predicament for both of us, but as I listen to the murmur of her voice in the bedroom I see this part perfectly. She's just as I know her now, perils snatching at her at every turn. Don't move too fast, don't reach above your head, don't drink too-hot liquids, don't breathe in fumes from the stove.

The thing is, when I announced myself with a show of glistening blood and water, there's nothing she was doing wrong. She still had two months to go, and it was an ordinary morning. She was standing in front of the wardrobe in the bedroom when she felt something letting go inside her and saw a scarlet stream sluice down the inside of her leg. They were living in town then, my father still working at the store, and in those days there was no such thing as a telephone or a car. She ran to the linen chest and reached with shaking fingers for a towel, plowing through the pile for something dark that wouldn't show the stain afterwards. She used it to wipe her leg and then she slid it into her underpants.

She had plunked Phillip into the sandbox just a few minutes before and told him not to move until she came for him. Not because she had any sense of what was coming, but because she wanted to start the laundry. It was a cloudless day, and outside her neighbour Mrs. Dempsey knelt by a flower bed in a little bubble of ordinariness, transplanting petunias from a plum case. Mother turned towards her and then turned back because she would have had to tell her why. The doctor's office was just two streets over. She would walk there. On the edge of her vision she saw Phillip playing in the sandbox, as if in the distance, as if he were someone else's responsibility. She walked quickly, although her knees had begun to shake. By the time she reached the corner she'd lost her grasp of where she was going. Then I picture darkness coming from the sides of her vision, closing off the light the way a camera lens closes. No one thought about Phillip sitting in the sandbox until hours later when Mrs. Dempsey found him, his little face swollen from crying and pee-soaked sand moulded under his backside. There is no end of children I can be compared to, quiet children, children who wait.

Because of me, because of the trouble I caused in church, our neighbour Mrs. Weedon becomes a Sunday-school teacher and leads the children out under the trees during the sermon, stopping at their truck and taking out a grey wool blanket for us to sit on. We'll sit in the shade, she says. But crossing the yard with all of us trailing after her she spies Joe Pye sleeping under the trees and she veers off in another direction, leading us to a patch of worn grass and weeds in the shade of the house. We sit in a circle and sing a song about a fountain flowing with blood. Flies bite at our ankles. Mrs. Weedon takes up a stick and shows us how they pounded the spike into Jesus' hands because of our sins: she shows us the place below the third knuckle where it went through.

I squirm off the blanket and thistles touch my legs and I begin to rub them and fuss. Mrs. Weedon reaches over and hauls me back onto the blanket. What about you, Lily? she says. She has dark tangled eyebrows and a shot of white across the iris of one eye. Have you asked Jesus to come into your heart and take away your sins?

I feel a lurch of fear that I've so successfully distinguished myself. Yes, I whisper.

In the dead of winter it's dark in the house all day from the thick frost coating the inside of the windows. One day it's too cold for Phillip and me to go to school. My father sits with his jacket and cap on and his boots up on the fender of the stove. Joe Pye's got a blanket over his shoulders. Joe's pounded a nail into the door frame and he's braiding string from it to make bootlaces. He has a piece of copper wire wound around his wrist to draw the arthritis out of his body. There are white beans boiling on the stove, their skins peeling off into the froth rising in the pot.

My mother sits on the chesterfield, turning the pages of *Pilgrim's Progress* over like cards in a deck. We've read the first part more than once, but we don't always make it to the end. We're near the beginning now, where Christian meets a man named Worldly Wiseman, who tries to warn him against the journey. *You are likely to meet with weariness, painfulness, hunger, perils, nakedness, sword, lions, dragons, darkness, and in a word, death*, Worldly Wiseman says. *Why, sir*, Christian answers. *This burden on my back is more terrible to me than all these things which you have mentioned.*

The beans start to boil over and my mother gets up to move the pot to the edge of the stove. I kneel against the back of the chesterfield and scratch at the frost on the window. My dreams in the night left a murky feeling in my chest, and Christian is making it worse, with his haunting dreams of his wife and children being burned up by fire from heaven and his constant blurting out his misery to anyone who comes along. I pick at the frost with my fingernail and listen to a familiar scratching sound behind me. It sounds like a mouse in the walls but it's not. It's the clock, scratching its own yellowed face with a bent hand. Then I hear my mother sliding the globe off the kerosene lantern to light the wick.

Imagine, she says. At three o'clock in the afternoon!

Can ye picture spending a winter in a sod house? asks Joe Pye from the doorway. No one answers. If somebody as much as grunts, Joe will tell about his first winter in Canada. Like living in a burrow, he'll say. Like being a badger in a hole. No windowpanes to be had for love nor money, so we emptied three pickle jars and worked them into the walls. Picture that, he'll say, bringing his bent hands together to show us the size of the jars.

But I don't say a thing, so Joe doesn't tell us. Instead, I press the heel of my hand against the window until its heat melts a hole in the frost. As I work I think about the calf I discovered behind the barn last spring, born too early, flat and white as though it were melting into a snowbank. I think about my father lying on the bed with his boots on. The frost refreezes as clear ice and I melt that too, I melt a clean circle, and in the melting frost I smell dust. My hand burning from the cold, I patiently melt a porthole as wide as a pickle jar. From time to time I press my stinging hand against my sweater.

Three pickle jars, Joe Pye says from behind me. That's all we had for light. That and the odd candle.

Suddenly another voice, my dad's. The windows of our house in the old country, he says. The glass in those windows was *wavy*. From being so old.

Wavy? I say, cranking my head around and sliding down on the chesterfield to look at him.

2

My father came to Canada from England in 1903. I believe he
thought of it as a temporary thing. Having little solid information, I thought of it in the nature of a fairy tale — he was
the eldest of three sons, sent to seek his fortune. To Nebo,
Manitoba, as it turned out, to a weathered frame house where
the wind blew all the freezing long winter and topsoil drifted
across the roads instead of snow. He never returned, but they
didn't send the younger sons after him, the way families do.

He came in a party of two thousand led by a minister
named Isaac Barr. When I was in England, when we cleaned
out my nana's house in Salford, I found, stuck at the bottom
of a box of jam and Marmite jars, the recruiting brochure that
brought him over. I had spent my early years wondering about
all this, and it was a huge relief to be given material to work
with. *There is the world as the world will be*, it said on the first
page, which I think must be a quotation, the rest of the
pamphlet not having quite the same literary flavour. The
brochure had clearly lain in water. I saw rain, a dark evening
in fall, gaslights gleaming yellow-green in the puddles. My
granddad, Percy Piper, stepping out of the public house and

spying the paper in one of those puddles, a brochure that had been making the rounds in the Woolpack. I pictured him plucking it out and taking it home and hanging it over a wire in front of the fire, prying its crinkled pages apart as it dried. At the time they called my dad a "nipper." This didn't refer to his size (he was seventeen, he must have been tall) but to the fact that he worked as a carter's helper. I imagined him coming home from work to find his brother Roland reading to their mother in a shrill voice. All the characters in these scenes have the Lancashire turn of phrase and eyes the colour of wet slate, a shade I'm partial to but did not inherit myself. My grandmother was exactly twice my dad's age at that time. I pictured her as a great overgrown girl with a wide, freckled face (she was still a great overgrown girl when I knew her in her seventies). She wore a dark serge skirt, a blue pinny, streaks of dried bread dough on it where she'd impulsively wiped her fingers while she was mixing, and wooden clogs. Above her head was a motto printed on cardboard in Gothic script: HOME IS THE NEST WHERE ALL IS BEST. "Here, Willie, you read," she said.

"'Let us take possession of Canada!'" my father read. "'Let our cry be *Canada for the British!* . . .' What's this, then?"

"Your da found it," said his mother. "Boris has one too. It's free land in Canada. Boris is dead set to go."

I imagine my dad's cousin Boris coming over that night and all of them studying the pamphlet together. This was the year after the Boer War ended, when the English were all fired up to hold on to their colonies and it looked as though Canada was about to be taken over by types who ate garlic and prayed to plaster statues of the Blessed Virgin. Not that it was prejudice or politics that inspired my relatives, not that they ever thought about it that way. They had their own reasons. Boris, for example, was a stableman for the tram, and Manchester had started laying down electric tramlines.

There was a voice behind the pamphlet, a minister named Isaac Barr. His tone was candid and respectful. He was addressing himself to a superior type of colonist, however poor. In a section headed "Programme of Action for Men of Small Means," he declared that a resolute colonist can, in a week's time, erect a small house to shelter himself for the winter. My dad fetched a pencil and they noted each mention of money: the steamer fare, the train fare, a registration fee for the land. My dad sat down to do the sums: eleven pounds, eighteen shillings, nine pence. This before living expenses, a horse and plow.

"The blighter's out to line his pockets," my granddad cried in dismay.

"Nay, Percy, the man's a reverend," said Nan.

"*I'm* doing it," said Boris (a fleshy youth with black hair standing up in clumps fortified by the grease from his scalp). "I'm signing on," he said. "I'm that afraid of electrification."

No one asked my father what he wanted. Every Saturday his mother opened his pay packet and slid six pence spending money across the kitchen table — that's the sort of boy he was. Canada must have seemed to him like something made up.

His parents talked into the night, but when Boris left, my father climbed the stairs and crawled into bed beside his brother Roland. In my version of events, he lay awake for a long time, breathing in the marshy smell of Roland's scalp and watching a wavy moon slide down the ancient glass of the bedroom window. In the other bed his little brother Hugh ground away at his teeth, and the voices of his parents drifted up the stairs. My father couldn't make out what they were saying, but he heard his mother laugh, a careless, happy laugh, and he rolled over and pushed his face into the pillow. He was someone I could hardly imagine, a boy who loved home.

I know from the minute I see my mother making coffee in the morning what sort of day we will have. Some days sadness and anger come off her like a smell, and something in my chest begins to hurt. My jobs are spelled out and I do them: I pick and peel vegetables, dry the dishes and set the table for the next meal, haul wood and water, clean the outhouse and carry ashes from the stove to pour down the holes, feed the chickens and gather the eggs. I do my work properly as an act of resistance: if she's wanting to punish me, she won't have a chance. Then I do extra things — carve petals out of the sides of the radishes, put jars of brown-eyed Susans on the table, arrange flowers in the outhouse between the two holes.

My mother finds the flowers in the outhouse and shoves them down a hole. Satan finds work for idle hands, she says. She puts me to work sifting through the milled oats to pick out grasshopper legs, which are not welcome when they turn up boiled in our porridge. She sits me down on the veranda to do it so she can keep an eye on me while she does the laundry. It's Monday and her hands are spongy and reeking of bleach. I strain the oats through my fingers, picking out the desiccated legs, shapely like miniature frogs' legs, or women's legs. Why are there legs and no bodies? I call down the veranda. What happened to their bodies? My mother, bent over a tub of grey wrung-out clothes, doesn't answer. She moves hunched from the washtubs to the wringer, not bothering to straighten her back. Someone might imagine that we've been taken prisoner by the same ogre.

Days he's not plowing or seeding or mowing my father cuts wood down by the river — that's how he uses his spare time. One night at supper he says suddenly, Saw a lynx today. Up in a spruce.

In a tree? Phillip says. Lynx don't climb trees.

My father doesn't answer. We're eating cold chicken, a laying hen that stopped laying. My father's working at taking the bones apart. Could the lynx have been up in the tree when he arrived with his axe? Strange it didn't take off! Could it have crept towards him as he worked? That would be stranger — lynx are very shy. While we pull his story apart, my father works on the hen, prying bits of tough flesh out from between its ribs. He never does explain.

After supper I walk down to the riverbank. The land falls in three gentle, giant steps as though a carpet were laid over a huge staircase. The tallest trees are on the lowest bank. I can see where my father was working: he cut down seven or eight poplars, and he started skinning the branches off them. I can see the spruce tree where the lynx must have lain. There's a bed of pine needles under it, and wood chips and shattered bark littered around. I picture the lynx on the lowest spruce branch, up near the trunk, its secretive, ornate face tipped to watch my father.

Where exactly was my father? Suddenly I understand. My father was sleeping. He lay down to sleep in that fragrant bed, and so there was no movement or noise to alert the lynx. I think of him lying drowsily under the tree, slowly opening his eyes and seeing the lynx, my father's grey eyes and the knowing eyes of the lynx connecting for an electric second before the lynx clenched its muscles and sprang away. He didn't tell us because he's ashamed to have been sleeping in the middle of the day. This happened in *Pilgrim's Progress*: Christian was overtaken by slothfulness and lay down to sleep and got into no end of trouble because of it.

I walk back filled with intention. In the shade of the granary, King and Dolly stand nose to tail swishing each other's flies. My father will be in the barn milking. I walk down the aisle to where he's perched on an overturned milk pail. His head is tipped against the cow.

You were sleeping, I say. When the lynx crept up.

He doesn't answer for a minute. No, he says finally, over the sound of the milk thudding into the bottom of the pail. I was looking right at her the whole time. It just didn't dawn on me what she were.

I don't understand how this could be. So what did you do? I finally ask. When you realized?

I rolled out of the way, he says. She jumped down and took off.

The cats are pacing around calling to him, switching their tails, furious with desire. He seems not to notice. Dad, I say. Finally he turns his head and sees them and then he stretches a tit in their direction and squirts out a white arc so they forget their dignity and rise up on their haunches, showing the crimson inside of their mouths.

***

I sit beside him at the table. Joe Pye and Phillip are across from us, and my mother is at the end near the stove. My dad's arm lies on the oilcloth beside mine. It looks darker because of the hair curling on it — but really, my arm is a darker tan.

Smoked whitefish again. I position a chunk of it on the back of my tongue and wash it down untasted with a mouthful of milk. My mother can't stand this performance. She swallows her last bite and stands up and goes out to the garden without stopping to pull her apron off — she's trying to avoid evidence that a woman like her has raised a child like me. The porch door slams and I gag and regurgitate onto my plate, tears springing from my eyes. We've been eating smoked fish for a month — a man came through in a wagon and sold my mother a crate of it.

Joe Pye looks at me with sympathy. You think that's foul, he says. You shoulda tasted ling fish. Remember, eh, Willie? He leans back and plucks at his moustache, ferreting for crumbs.

Ling fish? I ask.

Ling fish, says Joe. Yella. We et it every bloody meal on the ship. Eh, Willie? Remember ling fish? Just about caused a riot. They grabbed ahold of Isaac Barr one night and drug him down to steerage and held a flap a that stinkin' fish up to his face. Wouldn't open his mouth, the canny bugger. Remember, eh, Willie? Wouldn't taste the fish. So a chap hucks a piece a hardtack at him. It clips him right on the beak and he claps his hand like this over his face and the blood's leaking out from his fingers. And then he yells at us: *You're a pack of god-damn savages!* (*Goddamn* — my mother has gone outside, but Joe Pye still swallows that word with an apologetic laugh, so it sounds like *gom savages*).

Were you there, Dad? I ask. When he called them gom savages? Phillip gives me a sharp kick under the table.

I don't rightly recall, my dad says. He ignores the *gom*. He sits there in his overalls drinking milky tea. His voice sounds rusty, as though those words have been sitting inside him for a long time. He has more of England in his voice than Joe Pye has. There, now, chuck, he says. Eat your fish. His eyes are fine and kind and evasive. Things happen to him, but he never speaks of them. I feel a fierce longing to pry him open and see what's inside.

※

He did not tell me about their journey. It was Joe Pye, our arthritic little hired man, who found a chance to talk about the Barr Colony in every small event that happened around the farm. I pretended ignorance to keep Joe Pye talking. I knew the stories, but I had to work at casting my father into them. The huge, resolute act of getting on the ship, that's something I had trouble making him do.

He fell under a spell was my theory for a while, the spell of Isaac Barr. Isaac Barr, wearing a shiny beaver hat and a black

frock coat over his neat, stout, proud body. A great soft moustache and a dapper head, a head like a badger's, planted into
a soft thick neck. The way I imagine him, he had at his centre
a testiness that he tried to cover with civil speech. Rather like
Mr. Dalrymple. The day they steamed off from the Albert
Docks at Liverpool there was a whole settlement in Isaac
Barr's head and under his hat: a school and lending library,
musical and theatrical societies, a hospital, a commercial
syndicate. It was all there, worked out in amazing detail. He'd
spent the winter of 1902 in a rapture of creativity, writing a
novel in his mind, the story of a perfect world.

But in the flesh his characters turned out to be a problem.
Like God, who would take only born-again Christians in the
Second Coming, Isaac Barr would take only the English to
the Dominion. His reasoning was the same, he wanted a
perfect world. He'd gathered them up from all over England,
and they weren't farmers — a rather fundamental short-
coming, you'd think, but he was operating on the principle
that a Manchester umbrella vendor will in every instance
make a better Canadian than a Ukrainian grain farmer. He'd
flattered them into joining, and by the time they boarded the
ship they thought they were doing the New World a favour.
So they were demanding, even belligerent, and the most
belligerent were armed ex-soldiers just back from the Boer.

They were too savage for my father. He dropped out while
they were crossing Manitoba, somehow he escaped Isaac Barr.
He ended up farming among the very people Isaac Barr had
set out to protect him from. He settled in a district that was
half Eastern European farmers — Ukrainian mainly, but also
Polish, Czech, Russian. *Galicians*, we called them all, said it
the way the English said *Krauts* in the war, or *Huns*. The
Galicians have an epistle in the Bible written to them, I
remember pointing out, but my mother said it wasn't the same
people (although from what I learned in history at Ward Street

Grammar School, I believe she was wrong). When we ventured into their yards or kitchens we were cautious. Any question about the old country — their old country — was bound to produce something appalling, like the time Mary Kulyk offered to show us a picture of her grandmother, and it turned out she was *dead*, her mouth a straight line as though it was sewn shut and all her family with their heads tied up in black shawls standing behind the open coffin. The Galicians did not really belong in our district. Whereas my father was one of Canada's natural settlers: he was brought over on purpose, he spoke English, he ate normal food.

That's what I told myself, but even then I knew it wasn't true. Our neighbour Mr. Kulyk looked like something cobbled together out of the prairie, fine lines of dirt etching the wrinkles fanning out from his eyes, his eyes bright and his legs wiry, his hard little belly a storehouse of food for the winter. My father looked glazed, preoccupied, an undeveloped idea of a farmer, sleepwalking through the day.

One night, an ordinary night, my dad is alone finishing chores in the barn. Joe Pye is not with us just then. It begins to get dark and Dad doesn't come in, so finally Mother sends Phillip to see if he needs help. We're in the living room and Phillip comes back in and stands in the kitchen and says, *Mother.* He has the look on his face of a much younger boy. Dad's in the pigpen, he says. But by then Dad is at the window, walking unsteadily towards the house. One side of his hair and face is smeared with mud and pig manure. Mother says, *Will,* in a voice of consternation and blame. She says to me, Put water on.

While we work, Dad sits on a kitchen chair. I want him to talk to me, but he just looks at me once apologetically and says, Quite a mess, eh? and then he sits with his eyes to the floor as if he is trying to draw a curtain around himself. So without

41

being asked I go into the living room. All the while he bathes, Mother stays with him. I can hear her questioning him in a shrill whisper. Now and again he answers in a low voice. Then he walks through the living room wrapped in a quilt, chalky white, looking as though someone has whacked him between the eyes and he has just come to, and goes to bed.

In the morning it is Phillip who wakes me up, banging his boot on my door. There is no fire lit, and one of the barn cats stares boldly from the arm of the chesterfield. Dad's work-boots are by the back door, but Dad and Mother are not there. Phillip is sitting in the living room lacing up his boots. Get going, he says. We have to do the chores on our own. Where are they? I cry. Gone, he says. There is a queer expression on his freckled face. Dread clamps my chest. This is just as Mr. Dalrymple said it would be. While I slept I was thrust into a different life.

I run to the window. The sky is an eerie brown. But the Ford is gone! They have left by natural means, this is proof of it. My chest contracts in a sob of relief. I turn to talk to Phillip, but the porch door slams, and I'm left alone in the cold and watchful house. Over the sideboard hangs a flour sack of raspberries, luridly stained. It hangs by a cord from a hook in the ceiling, dripping methodically into a crock for jelly. Letting fall the evidence of the truck, I sink into the scene: They are gone forever and I am left. Left with the dripping jelly bag and the clock running down with no one ever again to wind it up. The oatmeal on the table abandoned to the mice. Empty jelly jars in a row on the sideboard. And the Bible. I reach for the Bible and open it to the inside back cover. The three words faintly pencilled there in my father's handwriting are stranger than ever:

> *Nitawagami*
> *Missinabi*
> *Nipigon*

I steal into their bedroom and sit on the edge of their bed. The window is open, but the animal smell of their sleeping breath still hangs in the air. In her haste to leave, my mother didn't take time to make the bed, and the bottom sheet has worked its way off the mattress. All their secrets are there, and all their ordinary things, looking shabby and secret now too, the stains on the mattress exposed and the enamel rim of the bedpan peeping out at the end of the bed, my mother's flannel nightgown drooping from the chair, her panties on the floor. My face in the mirror, my hair uncombed and my eyes knowing. I draw in my breath and look dartingly to the side, trying to catch a glimpse of myself not looking at myself.

After I've dressed and driven the cat from the living room, I drag the slop pail outside. At the pigpen I stand watching the pigs grubbing with their faces in the slop, lifting up their snouts with potato peel hanging from them. Most of the pen is dry. He would have to have rolled in the wallow the night before to be that covered with muck. I picture my parents in the wan light of dawn, hurrying to the truck, my mother's hair streaming down from under her hat. But where were they going, what drove them away? Above me the cottonwoods sway hugely against the sky, and the sense of some despairing act, brave and futile, hangs over the yard. The pigs crowd up to the rail fence, turning their rubber noses up to see what else I have for them, but their small, red eyes give nothing away.

Back in the house I run out to the kitchen when the porch door slams. What's going on? I cry before Phillip can step inside.

How would I know? he says. He slides the milk pails into the separating room and then comes back to the washstand and pours cold water into the basin. He washes his hands and drops his sullen face into the water.

When you found him, I say when Phillip has dried his face, what was he doing?

Just laying there.

Were his eyes open?

I don't know. He tosses the towel expertly at the nail and it catches.

Wasn't he trying to get up?

No. I told you. He was just laying there.

Well, why didn't you climb in and help him up?

Phillip's voice seesaws between a girl's and a man's, and he hates anyone who makes him use it. He grabs my forearm and twists the skin hard. Blah, blah, blah, blah, he shouts. Shut your blabbing mouth! Tears burn my eyes. I swat at him but don't dare to really provoke him. A pit of fury yawns between us — if we fall into it, there is no one around to pull us out.

We don't bother making a fire for porridge but smear two-day-old bread with butter and brown sugar and sit eating while the wind rattles the chimney cap and dried-up hollyhocks scratch against the window. With every glance I steal at Phillip my loathing grows. After a minute I get up and drag the stool in from the separating room and move over to sit at the sideboard beside the scarlet jelly bag. But when he has worked his way through six slices of bread he suddenly turns talkative. If you must know, they went to Winnipeg, he says. To see a doctor. Mother wouldn't wake you up. She didn't want to have to listen to all your nosy questions.

To see a doctor? I cry, breaking my vow of silence. Why didn't they go to Dr. Ross?

They don't want him to know.

To know what?

What do you think? Phillip's face turns crafty. He was *drunk*, he says.

Dad? I say, Drunk? Drunk?

Phillip's eyes dart to my face and then away.

What makes you think he was drunk?

I could tell.

Did he have a bottle with him? Embarrassment slides down over Phillip's face like a transparent eyelid.

No, he says belligerently. Not *with* him.

So why did you think he was drunk?

I could just tell, nincompoop, he says.

It's clear to me then that he's making it up. He gets up and at the door he says, Get the separator started. Somebody's got to take the cream can to town. And then the screen door slams.

⊗

It was on the Sunday-school blanket that I heard the story of the man who was suddenly taken away in a whirlwind while he was just walking along a road minding his own business. I listened intently because I immediately recognized my father in this story, but in fact on the day my parents vanish, I learn for myself that the world is as flimsy as tarpaper nailed over a window, that you can slip through a crack in it and find yourself somewhere else.

In what feels like late afternoon, I find myself alone on a road on the north side of Burnley, near the blacksmith shop. The wind's pulling earth layer by layer up into the air, and the trees that border the blacksmith's yard are black lines etched onto a brown sky. It's like being on the bottom of a pond looking up through dirty water. With every step I stir up silt. Off to the side Jimmy Thrasher, the blacksmith's son, is splitting wood, and at the edge of the road lies a dead raccoon, meticulously coated in dust, its long, curious nose pointing to the road.

Hey, I call. Jimmy Thrasher looks up.

I found a raccoon.

He comes walking out to the road. He doesn't say hello to me or acknowledge that he knows who I am. He goes up to the raccoon and turns it over with the toe of his boot. Its little human hands are folded as though someone laid it out for burial, and its eyes are open and coated with dust like two grey-brown buttons chosen to match its coat. That's a big bugger, he says. Then he walks back to his shed, and I think he's not coming back. But in a minute he does, carrying a couple of sacks and a long, curved knife. He kneels beside the raccoon and slips the point of his knife under its chin. Its neat coat parts to show a glistening red body. I've often watched chickens and pigs being gutted, but I have to turn away. I glance back just once to see him shoving the carcass like a naked baby into one sack and sliding the bloody skin into the other.

What're you gonna do with it? I ask, meaning the carcass.

Give it to the dogs, he says.

Are you gonna sell the skin?

Might. Might make myself a hat. He wipes his hands on the sack and then he stands up and grins at me. His skin is the colour of toast and blackheads are bedded like polka dots around his nose. My old man's off drinking at Kulyk's, he says. I'm going to the show when I've split this cord. It's *Tarzan*.

I wish I could go.

What's stopping ya?

After he's tossed the sacks into the shed he picks up his axe and goes back to his chopping. I trail after him into the yard and stand against the side of the house, gradually edging along to the curtainless window, and peer inside. The glass is filthy, and a piece of furniture with a rough, unvarnished back is pushed up against the window. I turn back to watch Jimmy Thrasher. No one knows where I am. Perhaps I'm a different girl entirely, perhaps I can do what I want. When Jimmy Thrasher finishes splitting his cord he sinks the axe into the chopping block with a grunt and turns towards the road, jerking his chin at me to follow.

Don't you want to wash your hands? I ask.

Don't you want to mind your own business? he says, not unpleasantly. He pulls a handkerchief out of his pocket and blows his nose, and with a quick, impudent gesture he shows me the black dirt that came out of it. Then he starts up the road towards town and I follow him.

※

That's my first movie, and I don't come back to earth, really, until I'm a good mile from town, until I find myself out on the section road, with the prairie dark all around me, its edges marked with yellow light. I come back with a lurch at the thought of my dad. The events of the morning have been ripped away from this dark night — there is no stitching morning and evening together into the same day. I'm seized by the terrible realization that my father and I are not at this moment in the same world.

Dust clots my nostrils so I can hardly breathe, but I begin to run, feeling under my shoes the soft dust that drifted across the road in the storm. A row of trees, the shelter belt from someone's farm, drops behind me. And suddenly in front of me is the sun, a *changed* sun, full of blood, a huge, crimson globe squatting on the edge of the field to the west as though the sky and the earth are being pried apart to reveal the fire of the firmament. As I watch it wobbles free of the horizon — it has reversed direction, it's *rising*, lifting itself ponderously into the black sky. I stand transfixed for one wild moment and then, with a lurch of sorrow and relief, I know that it's not the sun at all. It's the moon, the ordinary rising of a moon stained red by the dust in the air. To the north is a tiny square of bleary yellow light. I must already be at the Feazels' — that will be their window, the lantern burning on their kitchen table.

Phillip sits in the yellow cave of our kitchen with a lamp on the table and his gopher tails spread out in lots of ten. What do you think you're doing, taking off like that for hours? he says in his ugliest voice, and I know it's a miracle he hasn't gone to Aunt Eva's to tell them. Just as I'm floating off into sleep I hear the truck drive into the yard. Phillip won't tell — he'd be blamed too. My mother's everyday voice drifts down the hall and I hear the iron scrape of the stove door. My father is there, he's starting a fire to make tea. Tomorrow Mother and I are going to the Feazels' to pick and can peas. I remember this, and the weight of the commonplace world settles down on me.

⚒

The next day the wind has dropped — it would be a sunny day but dust the grey-brown of an old bruise still hangs in the air. Walking to the Feazels' I try to find out from my mother where they went, but she won't say. In any case the whole business of my father is fading, the idea of him lying like the prodigal son in the pig wallow, staggering across the yard smeared with manure. Other visions hang over me now, worlds outside my powers of imagination. It wasn't *Tarzan, the Ape Man* I saw with Jimmy Thrasher — it was Bette Davis and Gene Raymond, living in a shining silver city. Tall, beautiful buildings, with awnings that cars drove under in the rain, gleaming stone streets. All of it unbearably lovely and exciting. Bette Davis's satin gown with no fabric at all over her thin back, her shoulder blades sprouting like the wings of a baby chick below the shining cap of her hair. Gene Raymond with the same silver hair, as though he and Bette were made as a matched set. Bette's rooms with their silver carpets and curtains. All of it real, and not real, and not from my own mind. And yet in the light of it I can hardly make out my mother and Mrs. Feazel, stooping over the dry dusty rows, their hair tied up in kerchiefs.

48

Just after we get home in the late afternoon, our fingers green from shelling peas, my dad drives into the yard with the little wagon in the Ford. He picked it up at the creamery, where I'd left it, and he found out that I'd been to the show with Jimmy Thrasher. I'm sent to my room, and about an hour later, Mother comes in and sits on the bed beside me. She's not carrying the fly swatter they use for lickings, she's carrying a story. Something Aunt Eva told her, about a girl who died, in Burnley.

This girl wasn't a Christian, says my mother, her voice weighted with intent, but she was a well-brought-up girl. But one night she went to the show with a boy, a boy who just wanted one thing from her. In any other place she would have said no to him. But that night she forgot who she was. It was being with him in the dark like that, with those filthy pictures playing. And then afterwards, when she finds out (here excitement breaks through the hush of my mother's voice), when she realizes she's been caught and all the world will know what she's done, she can't bear to tell her parents. She can't bear the disgrace. For her whole family.

My mother waits for me to ask a question, and when I lie in silence she finally just says it.

She drank a bottle of lye, that's what killed her. Her and her baby. Her voice drops into a hush when she says *baby*. This is it, the crack of the whip, not lye or killed but *baby*.

I slide down on the bed and turn my head into the pillow. It's a good pillowcase, with flowers embroidered on its hem, pink daisies pulsing pinkly under my open eye. The last two days have been too much for me to take in — I feel the vertigo of an overextended traveller. You're a foolish, selfish girl, my mother cries. She weaves her fingers into my hair and cranks my face around to make me look at her. You don't know what it would do to your father, she says. It would kill your father!

I remember so clearly the body I had in those years. My thin arms, my hip bones jutting up from my stomach when I lay in bed, my thin legs that I think of as always in motion — running, hopping, skating, scrambling under barbed-wire fences, walking miles over the pasture and along the dusty roads. Dirt bedded in cracks in my heels, a boil in the fold of my arm so I couldn't bend my elbow all the way. Sties swelling like seedpods on my eyelids. The understanding growing inside me that I was not just one thing any more. I had entered the second stage of my childhood: I was now a child who had a memory of being something different.

Had a memory of summer evenings, for example, and climbing the maple tree beside the bunkhouse. The earth below me dark and the sky evening blue, as bright blue as a delphinium, moving swiftly to green a few inches above the horizon. The crickets starting up their chorus, the house and the barn sinking to nothing, merging with the dark, flat fields. I'd sit in the tree waiting for my dad, up against the trunk, bark digging into my backbone through my blouse. When he finally came out of the barn he'd be a shadow moving in and out of the yellow circle of light cast by his lantern. He'd go into the house and the screen door would slam — he'd go in without knowing I was there. I'd sit on in the tree, above the yard, above the perilous fate that bound me to my mother. Not a child and not a small animal, just *thought*, a nub of heat and longing, a point of view, above being born and above dying.

3

I kneel in the box of the bouncing truck and peer through the window into the cab. My mother sits on the passenger side in her white daisy-print dress clutching a plate on her lap, on which is stacked a mountain of egg sandwiches under a tea towel. She made mayonnaise that morning, beating oil into eggs, while a film of oily sweat glistened on her forehead. I was watching and saw the moment when the eggs and oil in the bowl turned into something completely new, something thick and creamy white. My mother rides beside my father, not looking at him, although I can tell she's still arguing. *Tractor* is the word on her lips. My father is not speaking. He made his comment at breakfast: I can't see myself buying Hughie Parrot's tractor out from under him. To which my mother said (and is no doubt saying again, although I can't see her lips): It's not Hughie Parrot's tractor. It belongs to the bank and it has from the beginning.

When the truck swings off the Burnley road and starts the long climb to the Lookout, I turn around and sit down. I want to be watching when we crest the hill and catch our first glimpse of the Parrot farm at the bottom of the rise, a barn that still has traces of red paint on its planks, a brick house with hollyhocks softening its corners. There is a goat in the yard, which I've seen only from the road. (You can make a good cheese with goat's milk, my dad said. Cheese! my mother said. Not likely! Bertha Parrot just has to be different. She always has to try to be different.) Today everything will be outside in the yard for the selling-up sale, beds with weeds poking up through the springs, the sock stretchers and chamber pot put on display, who knows what other different things.

Phillip squats in the other corner of the truck box, not holding on. That's the way he likes to ride, proving he can keep his balance in the back of a moving truck. I sit watching the road spool out from under the truck and think about Jimmy Thrasher, with that shock of black hair that like a dog he didn't bother to push out of his eyes. The way he suddenly spit towards the weeds by the road as we walked to town and said, Girls aren't worth the dirt they're made of. I'm not made of dirt, I said. Girls are made from Adam's rib. Then he squatted right in the road, the way Phillip is squatting now. Can a girl do this? he said. When I squatted beside him he dared me to lift one leg, and I showed him I could and then he let out a shrill, exultant laugh. Ha, ha, dog taking a piss, dog taking a piss, he shouted, and gave me a shove so I toppled over.

When we get out of the truck at the Parrots' my mother says to Dad, If you can't get the tractor, at least go in with Jack on the harrow, and then she takes the sandwiches over to the lunch table where a group of women stands. The sale is well underway. Mrs. Parrot is there, bending the brim of her straw hat down to shield her eyes. Her baby is hanging on to one of her legs, his diaper — a yellow towel — sagging down past his knees. My mother sets the sandwiches on the table. I better leave them covered, she says. All this dust.

Mrs. Parrot laughs. She laughs so no one will feel sorry, so my mother won't have to say anything about what is happening. The big kids are down at the creek, she says, looking at me.

Your furniture is sure going fast, Mother says.

Some of it's still in the house, says Mrs. Parrot. We're taking a lot of it with us. I sold the sideboard, though. It was too big anyway.

Will you be taking the piano? says Mother, as though she's just interested. At home she talks about the piano, about how, when he had his bull out on sire, Uncle Jack was in the Parrots' yard once and heard piano music coming from the house at ten o'clock in the morning.

I couldn't take it even if I wanted to, says Mrs. Parrot. It's part of the chattel mortgage. So is that, she says, watching the men lift the cream separator up to the wagon the auctioneer is using as a platform. That's the bank's. It's all the bank's from here on.

Hey! she shouts suddenly. The cream separator is covered with a sheet to keep it clean, and the auctioneer's helper has just pulled it off. I'll have that, she calls. That's not the bank's. The man folds the sheet neatly and hands it through the crowd to her and everybody laughs, and Mrs. Parrot laughs too, showing the gap between her front teeth and the little bud of skin growing down into it.

Just then a dark blue sedan drives up past all the cars parked in the lane and pulls right into the yard, as though the driver owns the place. The driver gets out and slams the door, and I see it's the new banker, Mr. Bates. He has a boy with him, a brown-haired boy about Phillip's age in a store-bought white shirt and gabardine pants. Mr. Bates walks through the crowd as though he has just dropped in out of interest, and the boy follows him, and then the auctioneer's chant starts up and people turn their attention back to him.

While they're bidding on the separator I go to look for the goat. It stands with a rope around its neck, tied to the back of the auctioneer's wagon. It is *different* beyond anything I've ever imagined. It has an old man's bearded face and sweeping eyelashes and a miniature oblong udder with two pointed tits sticking out of it. Its ears hang down like wide ribbons, and two narrow, fur-covered ribbons dangle from its neck. At the sight of its white eyes and their golden centres I feel a little thrill go down the back of my legs. I pick up a stick and touch the wavy hair on its back, and it flips a snowy flag of a tail and lets out a petulant protest. Phillip and our cousin Donald come along, and I do it again to show them.

Keep back from him, says Donald. He'll try to eat your dress.

That's not a billy goat.

It's a boy who says this, the boy who got out of the banker's car. He's standing right beside me.

Look, it's a nanny. He reaches a hand towards me — he wants the stick. I give it to him and he taps the udder, once above each tit. Anyway, he says, a billy goat would have horns.

We drop back from the goat and stare at the boy, and he looks easily back. He has his white shirt and a barbershop haircut, a belt holding up his trousers instead of braces, his knowing about different animals. What we have is one another and our joint silence. Here, he says. He hands the stick to me and walks away.

I see the boy again when they sell the piano. We're in the house then, and I'm standing right beside the piano, and as everyone crowds round I reach one finger out and press down on the end key, in the slow way you can press a piano key so that it goes all the way down without making a sound.

A Baldwin, says the auctioneer, standing with his hand on the polished top. One of the best. That's cherrywood! You don't see much of that around here. Made down east and brought in special by the national railroad. Look at the date on her, 1917. Those pedals are solid brass! *Perfect* condition. This piano will be a family heirloom one day. Who's going to show us how she sounds? How about it, Bertha?

54

People look cautiously around, but Mrs. Parrot seems to have vanished. Then Mr. Bates cocks his head at his son, and without any further persuasion, the boy walks up to the piano. There's no stool to be found so he just stands, his sturdy back inclined over the keyboard. He puts his hands on the keys and pauses for a minute as though he's listening to a song in his head. Then he launches in and plays a song I know from school, "Country Gardens." He plays straight through without mistakes but very choppily. At the end he shrugs and backs away from the piano, his mouth lifted in a rueful smile.

Mr. Stalling (who still has five daughters at home and a new wife with a bit of her own money) buys the piano. John Leslie, another man from our church, buys the tractor. My dad will pay Uncle Jack for a half-share in the harrow, but he doesn't bid on the tractor — it was out of his reach from the beginning, he says. Nobody buys the Parrot farm, nobody has the money or the credit. A Pentecostal from Burnley buys the goat for $6.50 and loads it into the back of his wagon. As it's being led to the wagon it looks right at me with its weird eyes and says, *Blah* in its woman's voice.

I meet the piano-playing boy's sister a few months later, which must mean I have been chosen out in a special way to know them. I meet her in the winter, when I skate to town. Phillip and I both have skates and so do my Aunt Eva's children, a legacy from my grandparents' big family, from a richer time. I learn to skate with my cousins on the slough behind Aunt Eva's. Then we start skating on the river, climbing down the bank from Aunt Eva's place, mostly me and my cousin Gracie. There is so little snow those winters that the river freezes clear, sometimes clear to the sandy bottom, sometimes with golden leaves suspended in the ice, and you can skate over this beautiful patterned carpet all the way to town, although from

Aunt Eva's it's still a long way because the river winds back and forth like a whip being cracked. No one but me wants to do it.

I'm amazed the first time I make it as far as town, coming around a bend and seeing tiny figures like the children skating on a pond in our Christmas jigsaw puzzle. On the bank fire burns in a barrel, and people stand around it warming their hands. There are girls skating hand in hand who stare at me, and boys who glide up behind me and pretend to shove me by accident, and sometimes ask me to skate. One of them takes his mitts off and tells me to as well and we clasp naked hands, bits of red fibre from our mittens stuck in the sweat of our palms. When he's gone a town girl skates up to me. You shouldn't take your mittens off when you skate with a boy, she says kindly, making a pretty little turn to stop. It's fast.

Fast, I say.

People will talk about you. Besides, you're going to freeze your hands. Come on. She holds out her gloved hand to skate with me and I take it.

Her name is Charlotte Bates. She is fourteen. She wears a wine-coloured felt hat and gloves and a scarf in matching wool. I'm wearing a coat with a strip from a wool blanket sewn around the hem to make it longer. I ask her where she's from, knowing from her hat and her confident ways that it's somewhere else. She says London.

London! I say. My grandparents live in England, and three of my cousins. Lois, Madeleine and George. (I pronounce *Lois* the way we do at home, to rhyme with *choice*.)

Charlotte looks at me with amusement. No, she says, It's London, *Ontario*, we come from.

She asks me where I live, and I tell her on a farm, knowing it to be a lesser thing. She asks me what we grow and whether we keep chickens or cattle or pigs (as though there are varieties of farms, as though what livestock we keep is an expression of our personal interests). She asks if I have brothers and sisters. I have two half-brothers, she says. Stephen and Russell. They live in Toronto.

Half-brothers, I say, thinking of Phillip and intrigued by the concept.

They have a different mother, she says. My father was married before. She says this in a voice that knows it is not quite ordinary. But she turns her face towards me and her calm brown eyes look directly into mine. I see Russell sometimes, she says. He comes down every summer.

Then she starts to hum, and she tucks my arm under her elbow so that I have to skate in rhythm with her, swaying from side to side. Two town girls skate towards us and past. They act as though they haven't seen us. Charlotte stops humming. Helen Hildebrand, she says softly in my ear. She stole my comb. Right out of my desk. And that's Alice Pratt with her. She stole my bow.

There's mischief on Charlotte's rosy face. Bow? I think. No, *beau*.

Time to go, Charlotte says then. Someone's standing on the riverbank in a sleek fur coat and a hat made of matching fur. It's Charlotte's mother. She's shocked to hear I've skated to town. You can't intend to go home on the river at this hour! she says. It'll be dark in a minute. It's twenty-four below. Do your parents have a telephone?

No, I say.

Well, Mr. Bates will be along any time now with the car and he can run you home.

So this is the banker's family! It's only when she says *Mr. Bates* that I put it together. I've learned the name of the boy who played the piano at the auction sale: it must be Russell Bates.

Charlotte takes off her hat and smoothes her hair. She has a low forehead with a pretty, wispy hairline. Don't, dear, her

57

mother says. Your ears will freeze. There's a nervousness in Mrs. Bates's eyes and at the corners of her mouth. The light is failing by then, most of the skaters are leaving. Only a few shouting black shapes are left on the river. The only colour anywhere is a stretched-out heart of lipstick the colour of raspberries on Charlotte's mother's mouth. What about you, Lily? she says. Are you certain you don't have frostbite?

No, I say. I'm fine. I turn towards Charlotte. I went to a Bette Davis movie, I say. Did you see it?

I don't care for Bette Davis, says her mother before Charlotte can answer. So *hard*. Then the blue sedan pulls up on the road and Mr. Bates puts his head out the window.

I want you to run this little girl out to the country, dear, says Mrs. Bates. She's skated in all this way on her own. Charlotte and I will walk home.

I try to protest, but I don't have the social presence to carry it off. Mr. Bates insists on holding my arm as I hobble to his car, and shows me how to swing my legs around once I'm seated inside so I don't scrape the floor with my blades or damage the seat. He doesn't say anything else except to ask me who my father is. When I tell him William Piper, he turns up our corner without having to be directed. I watch him covertly all the way home, this man who has two wives.

You won't be able to turn around in the yard, I say when we get to the end of our lane. It's all drifted in. Of course this is nonsense, but he stops on the road as I asked him to, and it's just bad luck that at the very moment I'm climbing out of the blue sedan my mother comes across the yard with a milk pail in each hand. She takes one look and then turns her head as though the question of whose car I'm getting out of is a matter of complete indifference to her. By the time I've hobbled into the porch and taken my skates off she has the separator going and is bending into her turning of the handle, and when I step into the doorway she looks up at me with an expression so savage that a shock of fear moves down the back of my legs.

⋇

I've prowled my parents' room and I know its secrets. Her drawers are lined with yellowed newspaper. She keeps a recipe tucked up along the side of her underwear drawer, a recipe in the bedroom, where recipes do not belong. *Family Planning Aid*, it's called, and it's written in a woman's round handwriting (not her own).

> *1 lb. cocoa butter*
> *2 oz. tannic acid*
> *1½ oz. boric acid*
>
> *Heat in top of double boiler and pour into large cake pan to set. Cut into squares the size of a postage stamp. Place as far in as possible ten minutes before.*

In the mornings my mother comes out of that bedroom as though a long night lying next to my father affords her no rest or joy. She walks out to the outhouse with a jacket over her flannel nightgown and her long hair hanging down her back in the bent waves her braids have imposed upon it. She's the opposite of Samson: her long hair saps her strength. Her stomach is still saggy from where her babies were, all those years before. She's haggard with her worries — her worries are like the puppies rooting into poor Chummy when she lay by the bunkhouse with her brown fur mangy and her tits stretched out, sharp-teethed little puppies sucking their mother to death. It's not us feeding on my mother, me and Phillip: it's her own unhappiness.

59

A sense of possibility is growing in me, a cold, crackling energy — I feel it in the long muscles of my thighs when I dig my skate blades into the ice. Little hard lumps have begun collecting under my nipples. When I first feel them I'm stung. I never asked for this, it's not prompted by any secret aspiration I have to be a woman. But I've announced myself. The day I went to the show with Jimmy Thrasher I threw down some sort of gauntlet. I examine my mother's reply, the story of the girl who drank lye. I've got a farm child's grasp of reproduction, but certain elements of that story elude me. The practical matter of how they managed it in a theatre seat, for one. And the character of the girl herself, who seemed furtively, recklessly bad, and yet was prepared to kill herself in a hideous manner to spare her family — although surely her drinking lye would only deepen the disgrace?

I'm helpless in all this, carried forward like a piece of bark on the creek in the spring. I sense that my mother's being carried along too, playing a part she might not have chosen to play. Satan finds work for idle hands, she said, and then seemed immediately sorry, as though he's too close, he's a family member we've decided never to mention. Jimmy Thrasher's busy, dirty hands come to me, boldly slicing open the raccoon, sliding its skinned body into a sack. And then in the movie, his hands grabbing at me, trying to worm their way onto the bodice of my dress, sliding up my leg. Quit doing that, I had to say all through the show, until finally I sank my nails deep into the flesh of his forearm and he called me a word I had never heard before and went to sit somewhere else.

It was sordid, I can see that. I sit in the church listening to what Mr. Dalrymple has to say about sin. In a real church, not the loft. The Nebo Gospel Chapel, a new church the men built a summer or two ago, when a letter from Mr. Pangbourne arrived, Mr. Pangbourne who had come into his money in the old country. I'm too old for Sunday school. *She's* too old,

I think, considering myself sitting in a pew with other girls my age, noting my thoughtful expression. She sits in a navy wool skirt, her legs gracefully crossed above her clumsy galoshes. *The heart is deceitful above all things, and desperately wicked*, reads out the minister. The girl savours the words: *desperately wicked*. She thinks of Bette Davis, when her parents came to the door (sober, respectable people with foreign accents like the Galicians') and Bette's father saw the giant shadow of Gene Raymond in his daughter's bedroom putting his clothes on. *I don't believe what you believe*, said Bette Davis. She spoke so strangely, as though the concept of speech was foreign to her, as though she'd rather just cast her eyes up and down under their heavy, shiny lids. It is her desperation, possibly, slowing her movements, weighing down her eyelids.

In the new, whitewashed church the signs of the Lord's coming are not so obvious. Maybe the girl will be here to grow up after all. She's more than she was (they were right to forbid movies), but she has no conception of what she can be. She's sent to her room to change her dress after church and she lies back on the bed and reaches up to feel the lumps on her chest (softer and bigger every week). She thinks about Charlotte's funny, wry face, and Mrs. Parrot laughing as her things were sold. She toys with the possibility that she can be something wholly unconnected to her mother.

Other places exist, my father is proof of it. He's a changeling, you might think: he has a changeling's ways. He's fitting a pane of glass into a window in the barn, and I go to help him, to hold everything steady while he presses a narrow bank of putty into the frame. He's so close through the glass that I can see the dots of his whiskers, the fine lines of white at the corners of his eyes that the sun never reaches because he's always squinting. He doesn't speak.

It was my dad who sent me to my room after I went to the show with Jimmy Thrasher. After Mother and I got back from picking peas at the Feazels' I was out in the yard when he drove in. He got out of the Ford and stood for a minute looking at me over the hood. After all that had happened, he was *himself*, with his faded overalls and his mild eyes, and the points of his shirt collar frayed and curling. But when he took the little wagon out of the truck and came over to talk to me, I was stunned to see that he was angry. He asked me if it was true I'd gone to the show the day before. Mr. Gorrie, he said. Mr. Gorrie was on the street when you come out. He seen you. With the blacksmith's lad. Hurt flared up in me — at the unfairness of it, that I should be held accountable to ordinary rules on such a night.

Your mother's going to be upset, he said.

Why do you have to tell her? I cried. My chest quaked and a sob, a single, hard sob, burst out. We stood together beside the house, where drought and constant traffic had pounded the grass to nothing. I was choked by pain. I'd have been glad if he'd gone into the kitchen to get the fly swatter and given me a licking, I'd have been glad for the sting and the familiar voluptuous crying, the machinery of crying taking me over entirely. But he just stood there. He took his cap off and wiped the sweat from his forehead with his sleeve, and then he dropped his eyes to me. For an instant I saw into him, I saw his love and his bewilderment. You better go to your room, Chuck, he said, and I went.

In 1902, Salford, Lancashire, my father's home, was a warren of narrow cobbled streets — just as it is today. They say Friedrich Engels navigated those streets every month in a buggy on his way to oversee his mill in Manchester. George claimed, in fact, that Engels wrote, *The proletarians have nothing to lose but their chains* with a bit of charcoal while being driven down Eccles Old Road. My grandfather, whom I never met, was a toll man on the turnpike. He had worked in the mill until the mill took off his left hand and then sacked him as unfit for the job. He knew nothing about farming.

I wanted especially to imagine my dad leaving home, taking hold of his fate and getting on a ship. My mother scorned imagination, I went where she couldn't go. It was hard — all I had for material was what Joe Pye said and the gleaming stone streets of a Bette Davis movie. Once I went to England, once I sailed into the port at Liverpool and met my nana with her big rag-doll face, I had something more to go by. But in a way it was even harder then to understand. Those mild-mannered, incurious people, exactly how did they do it? Did they dream of Canada the way I dreamt of England?

This is what I finally figured: that, as with most things, there was no real moment when my grandparents decided to send their son away forever. They started talking about it, and then excitement took over, and they couldn't bear to go back to ordinary days. Ten pounds spent on curtains and pots would have raised their stock in the street, but not the way it rose from just talking about sending Willie to Canada. And then Boris's friend Joseph Pye, a farm boy, committed to go and mailed away his fare and homestead fee. When my grandparents walked out onto Kersal Moor on Sundays they could see the Pye property on the other side of a drainage ditch: a square house of whitewashed stone. The Pye barn and the important cluster of outbuildings around it had the force of an argument.

How can you ever separate all the strands that make up a motive? "'Goodbye, Dolly, I must leave you,'" Nan sang as she knelt cleaning the flagstones with a donkey stone from the rag and bone man, and then she lifted her flushed face and said to my father, "You must take Duke. You'll want a dog on a farm."

"Nay, I'll leave her with the kids," my father said. I imagine a queer feeling going through him: he would know they had just crossed the line between dreaming about it and planning it.

By the end of February his name was on Isaac Barr's list and his fare was booked on a ship sailing from Liverpool. Those without a stake — like my dad — could work for a year in a nearby city called Winnipeg, where jobs were going begging, and for a fee Isaac Barr would undertake to register their claim. They discussed farming, a mysterious process to all of them. The thin face of Joseph Pye, newly graced god of agriculture, hovered over all their conversations. "Do they make machines for seeding wheat, do you suppose?" my father asked. He had seen grain being cut down in the fall but never seeded. "I believe they do, but Joe Pye will be able to say for sure," my granddad answered. Then added, "I wonder if you'd be best off going to cattle or sheep. Best ask Joe Pye." When it came time to strap up his trunk they found that one of the buckles was bent. "Happen Joe Pye can fix it," said his little sister Lucy.

It was April 1 when the Barr Colonists set sail from Liverpool, which might have told them something. My father and his parents rose very early that foggy morning to catch the train. He and his father put on celluloid collars, and Granddad put on his bowler hat (what they called a billy pot) and his white muffler. My father had said goodbye to his friends and the children the night before, a scene that he bore calmly because there were still several hours between himself and his leaving. I think that only Lucy got up in the morning and stood in front of the house, the curls on the back of her head matted and the corners of her mouth turned down.

My father and his parents walked to the station carrying the tin trunk that by then bore a label reading MASTER

WILLIAM PIPER, SALFORD, COUNTY LANCASHIRE and a red and blue sticker from the Beaver Line. In the trunk were all the things the mother of a prospective colonist would think to pack for a life in the All-British Colony where (as Isaac Barr assured them) the weather was favourable and the Red Indians were almost civilized. My granddad used his hook (this was the sort of job it was good for) to lift one end of the trunk by its leather strap. They walked by Willie's friend Robert's house, where Robert was asleep in an upstairs room, and by the house of Basil Milgate, who owed him two shillings and had not come down the night before to say goodbye. When they reached the rise at the end of the street my father did not look back. I'll see it again soon enough, he said to himself.

Boris was already on the platform, along with Joe Pye and his border collie, Chum.

"Will she sail for free?" my granddad asked.

"I'll pay what it takes," said Joe Pye, cupping one hand affectionately over her muzzle. "She's that good with sheep."

"Me and Willie are getting us-selves wolves," said Boris. "That's what they use where we're going."

The fog melted and sun flickered through the trees as they sped towards Liverpool. They clacked through Warrington and my father gazed for the first time at a town made of golden brick. Boris and Joe talked more and more and my granddad less and less. Nan had a gay moment at the station, but after that she did not speak at all and did not look at my father. She kept her shawl over her head and stared at the window. She was wearing her Sunday shoes instead of her clogs, and they were famous for hurting her feet, but my father had never seen her like this and thought she was angry about something.

At Edge Hill they went into a long dark tunnel and then they pulled in to Lime Street Station, under a high glass and iron ceiling, with clumps of fern growing from cracks in the brick walls. They disembarked and claimed their luggage and stood baffled among the throngs of people. Each of them felt a little squeeze of private disappointment that Isaac Barr was not there to meet them. Eventually they made their way up off the platform and Joe thought to walk out to the street to look and came back to tell them that a big wagon bearing the sign BEAVER LINE stood in the street. They dragged their gear outside. "Is this for Reverend Isaac Barr's ship, then?" my granddad asked, and the driver said, "It's the Beaver, ain't it?" In a few moments they set off through the stained stone buildings of Liverpool, on streets that descend to the sea.

When they got to the pier head the driver pointed out the SS *Lake Manitoba* moored out in the Mersey, a trim black and white steamship but not large. She had only one stack, unlike the other ships that loomed over the quays.

"Will she carry them all?" asked Granddad doubtfully. Isaac Barr had advertised for five hundred, but a man on the wagon said two thousand were going.

"They've fitted her out special," the driver said. He let them off at the Beaver Line baggage area, where massive carts were piled with crates and barrels and trunks and trunk-sized wicker baskets. A lad handed them a grease pencil and told them they must write on all their luggage WANTED, NOT WANTED.

"We wants it all," Boris said to him, "or we wouldn't of brung it."

"If you don't want it before Saint John it must go in the hold," said the lad firmly.

My dad was handed the grease pencil and printed NOT WANTED on all three trunks and they hoisted them up onto a cart. Boris pointed out six crates labelled PIANOFORTE SET UPRIGHT and two huge crates of oblong shape with no label.

"Them's coffins," he said. "Some navvy's takin' his coffin to Canada."

"Them's bathtubs," said Joe.

The long floating pier was crammed with parasols and women's hats as wide as the horizon. My father'd never been to Blackpool like certain of his friends, he'd never seen the sea, and he was dazed by the brightness of the air and the smell of salt and sewage and horses, the wild squabbling and swoop of gulls and the thunder of freight wagons trundling over the cobblestones. They saw two parrots and numerous cages of canaries and possibly some sparrows. They noted that patent-leather shoes were highly favoured as colonial wear. A brass band stood on the edge of the pier playing "Rule, Britannia!" My father looked eagerly at a girl with a pretty, sharp face sitting on a trunk. She wore her hair down, and he judged her to be somewhat younger than he was. Her mother was heavily pregnant. "They're never putting the poor dear on a ship in her condition!" cried Nan.

Excitement rose as the SS *Lake Manitoba* was moved up to the pier. They were soon separated from Boris and Joe. "Ne'r mind, you'll track them down on the ship," his father said. "You'll have nowt else to do for a week." Nan had bought some ship's biscuit and helped Willie tuck it into his knapsack under the Bible that she insisted the night before should come out of the trunk so he could read it on the ship. Granddad gave him the guinea he would need for expenses on the journey and watched Willie pin it into his pocket. "You don't want your knapsack pinched," said Granddad. "You must take care to sleep with it under your head." They acted as though they were preparing him for a week's voyage instead of for his whole life.

As no one was boarding they made their way into a pub. It was crammed, but Granddad managed to work his way over to the bar and came back with three pints, one in his one hand and the others held against the front of his jacket. "Here, lad, get that down your neck," he said. There was no place to sit so they stood and looked out the salt-etched window. In front of them was the Mersey full of steamships and tugboats of all sizes and across the water the miniature town of Birkenhead. As soon as she took a sip of her ale, tears began to stream down Nan's cheeks as though they were dislodged by her swallowing. She hung her head and the tears dropped in dark circles on the front of her dress. "There now, pet," said Granddad. They watched the baggage being loaded onto the SS *Lake Manitoba*, trunks and crates dangling from huge ropes and skidding across the deck. Just as Nan looked up a tin trunk like my father's swung wide and banged against the hull, splitting open. Everything inside fluttered silently through the air and fell into the water. Nan let out a little cry. "There now, pet," said Granddad.

"There's a thousand trunks on this dock just the same as that 'un," said my father gamely.

When they got back to the pier a voice was calling, "All aboard steerage" through a megaphone. There were throngs of men on the pier, but none of them recognizable as Isaac Barr. The band began to play Nan's very song, "Goodbye, Dolly, I Must Leave You," and she cried harder. My grandfather shook my father's hand, and Nan pressed her wet face into his neck and sobbed. "I'll do me best to send home," said my father. If any of them had any other last words they were lost in the din.

I know something about this kind of goodbye. It was impossible for my father to feel anything equal to the situation and so all he thought about was getting a spot on the portside deck so he could wave at his parents as the *Lake Manitoba* moved away. He was on his own and quick and he managed to work his way through the press of bodies to the railing, but by then his parents had been swallowed up by the crowd on the pier and all he could see was a flock of waving handkerchiefs. As the gangplank rose he felt a chasm of panic open at his feet, but he stepped back from the edge of it, telling himself that if he handled this bravely he'd be allowed to come home. But in this respect I know more about my father than he knew himself: I know the whole shape of his life and I know that he never will.

4

Aunt Eva starts to climb the ridge and Gracie trails after her.

You better watch! calls my mother. There's poison ivy up there!

My mother goes back to picking berries like a steam-powered machine. King stands under a basswood tree, lifting his tail and swinging it elaborately from side to side. It's horseflies — they're bothering us too, landing on our legs and digging in with a sudden malicious pick. My mother's got the honey pail on a string around her neck and she picks with both hands. It was just a disagreement about where to pick, but any argument with Aunt Eva energizes my mother, and she's been in a good mood anyway from the time she woke up.

I'm *so* thirsty, I say.

There's lemonade, says my mother. We'll have a drink while it's still cold.

Aunt Eva brought the lemonade. It's in a vinegar jug under the wagon, and there are four tin cups. Guiltily we unscrew the jug and fill two cups, and then we sit in the shade of the wagon. Without discussing it, we sit where Aunt Eva can't see us from up on the ridge. The horseflies find us, and my mother reaches up and locates the pins in her hair in four unerring stabs of her fingers. Her bun collapses and slides down her shoulder, and she clutches the hair in a tail and swishes it from side to side, her face crumpled in helpless laughter.

I glance down and there's a yellow jacket floundering in my cup. I dash the lemonade on the grass.

Lily! my mother cries. I thought you were thirsty! You'll end up like Bertha Parrot. Her mind always goes to Mrs. Parrot when she thinks of waste. Those people, she says, pressing her tin cup to her forehead to feel the cold. They had *toilet paper*! Did you go to the outhouse during their sale? They were going broke and they were buying toilet paper! And they were getting the *Family Herald* mailed out. It was in their outhouse. (The corners of her mouth go down — a confidence is coming.) I had to go to the toilet during the sale and I started reading a story in the *Family Herald* and I couldn't stop. I read the whole thing! I was holding the door open a little ways with my foot so I could read. And then when I was almost done, somebody came down the path! I was so busy reading that I didn't notice until he was right there. (Her voice drops to a whisper.) It was *Felix Macdonald*.

What did you *do*? I ask.

Well, I knew he had seen me! So I couldn't go out. I just shut the door tight and turned the latch. I sat there until he left. He kept thumping on the door. Finally (she mouths the words at me), *he peed in the bushes*.

Any mention of Felix Macdonald, the farmer she used to work for, signals an intimate interlude, knowing looks. Unwelcome pictures, my mother sitting in the dark on the toilet hole with her underpants down, listening to the start-stop hiss of an old farmer peeing. I pull my skirt down over my legs to discourage the horseflies. I tuck it tightly under me. Above me a bird sings the same two notes over and over. Finally I ask.

What happened to Dad? The day he fell in the pigpen.

There's a little silence while she takes a last swallow of her lemonade. Nothing happened, she says then. She rips off a handful of grass and uses it to wipe out her cup. Can't your father slip and fall?

☒

Joe Pye goes away for months at a time, and then he comes back. Phillip and I come home from school and he's sitting at the kitchen table nursing a cup of tea and there's a little celebration, not in the way of food or drink, but in the way of talk. Not about where he's been lately. He's been at another farm that had the cash to pay him for a while, there's nothing to tell.

If his arthritis is giving him a rest, he'll fall into talking about his great adventure. Find a way to ask about how they got to the colony — that's how you can always get him started. He'll always tell it, that amazing part, how they pulled in to Saskatoon one cold April afternoon, two hundred miles from their claims, and were told to get off, they were at the end of the line! They'd woken up excited, expecting to roll in to the settlement by nightfall, eager to see the hospital (St. Luke's — it even had a name) and the British Canadian Settlement Store that some of them had invested fifty pounds in, and the school and lending library. Instead the train ground to a halt at Saskatoon and they were dumped off on a muddy field. This is where Joe Pye dissolves into chuckles. If he's outside smoking at the time he'll be in danger of swallowing his cigarette.

Phillip, teetering on a chair tipped against the wall, interrupts. That's not what Dad says, he says. Dad knew from the beginning that the line stopped at Saskatoon.

Dad wasn't even there, I say. He got off at Winnipeg. I keep my eyes on Joe Pye. His cigarette is down to a flattened shred clamped between his stained thumb and forefinger. He takes a last pull on it, his eyes gleaming. What is coming is talk about that wicked man, a wicked minister, Reverend Isaac Barr. It's a strange kind of wickedness, not to do with liquor or murder or stealing. Well, stealing of course, but the real wickedness was his imagination, the way he created something beyond this world and lured them all into it.

⚔

The first sign of trouble, Joe said, was long before they got to Saskatoon. It was the way he refused to talk on the ship. As soon as they boarded they clamoured to see Reverend Barr. There was always a stir when he appeared — they wanted him to talk about what lay ahead. But he pushed on to his cabin, answering questions in a flat voice that said he was tired of repeating the obvious.

He had put another leader in place for all that, Reverend George Exton Lloyd. Reverend Lloyd was a tall man in a flat black hat, thin in all his aspects (legs, nose, fingers, smile). Joe Pye saw Barr and Lloyd together only once, standing in a passage talking. They talked for a long time and never once looked at each other. This was because Reverend Barr did not like to look up to anyone and Reverend Lloyd did not like to look down. Reverend Lloyd was a real-life hero. He had fought with the Queen's Own Rifles and defeated the rebel Louis Riel. In the middle of the battle he'd gone back to rescue a fallen comrade and been wounded and left for dead himself, and later had a bullet cut out of his back without gas or morphine. But he had a melancholy face. He was no threat to Isaac Barr — visions were not his department. His department was the mundane reality of homesteading, supply syndicates and crop rotation. Every afternoon he gave a lecture on the cabin-class deck, on a topic posted on a slate at breakfast: INDIANS. AGRICULTURE. CANADIAN LIFE AND PROBLEMS. Most of the passengers attended, although they didn't know

73

what to do with all these details and they were distracted by Reverend Lloyd's lisp.

As one of a handful of actual farmers on board, Joe was eagerly sought out (though when it came down to it his expertise was confined to sheep). After the lectures a crowd of plasterers and publicans and bookbinders and estate agents would gather around the farmers, listening gravely to their talk and risking the odd question. Boris didn't bother coming to the lectures. He had his own business to conduct. Someone had asked him about harnesses and he sprawled against the bulkhead sketching horses. Colonists who dropped five pence in his hat could buy a diagram of how to harness a horse for a Lancashire tram.

Meanwhile Isaac Barr kept to his cabin. Finally the rumour spread through steerage that they were all to go to meet him and be assigned their homesteads. My dad and Boris were not going directly to the colony, but they lined up with the others. Joe went first. In a large stateroom, a desk had been unscrewed and moved towards the door to serve as a wicket. At the desk sat Isaac Barr with his huge drooping moustache and his small head bent over a chart. When he looked up and raised his eyebrows Joe said, "Joe Pye, sir. Can ye point me to a claim with stones on it?" Joe had in mind to build a stone house, but he didn't say that part and Isaac Barr didn't ask. He just pressed his pen to an ink-soaked sponge and wrote PYE on a square near the bottom of the chart. After that he gave Joe a slip of paper on which was written 36SW-49-2 and said, "Mind you don't lose that." Next Boris stepped up to the desk and said, "Me cousin and me sent you ten pound to save our claims for next year, and we wants to know if we can pick them out now," and Isaac Barr said, "No, you can't. Move on now," and so they did.

When Joe and the others were told to get off the train in Saskatchewan, they still didn't quite get the picture. It took a while to dawn on them that if there was no railway line west from Saskatoon, there was likely no settlement either. Most of them (although not Joe Pye) had given Isaac Barr six pounds for a tent and groundsheet, but the tents were apparently in the train carrying their excess luggage — and that train had vanished. The Dominion Immigration Department set to work pitching a village of army tents for them, but they resisted settling in, they resisted being obliged to Canada in any way.

I'd always felt I understood Isaac Barr — how fascinated he was by his own notions, to the point that he lost track of whether he had done the work of making things happen. If I were making this story up from scratch, though, I would not have him carry on all the way to Saskatoon. I'd have him pretend to be called away on some important errand when they crossed the border out of Manitoba (called to Regina, to discuss settlement affairs with the governor). I see him galloping south on a tall black horse, glee on his face and a leather satchel over his shoulder stuffed with banknotes.

But that's not what happened. According to Joe, Barr stayed with them all the way, sitting among the eager colonists, riding towards his downfall. Was he completely crazy? Maybe he *wanted* to see the whole thing collapse into rubble. Maybe he wanted to be tested, to find out just how special he was, to see for himself what he would come up with next. What he did come up with, Joe said, was a fine duck tent with rooms, in which he lay day and night with a revolver under his pillow while outside the colonists milled around and planned the suits they would file against him as soon as a proper King's judiciary was set up in the North-West.

They made it to their claims eventually. Joe Pye got his stony field, others ended up with land so light it would blow away overnight if they had a dry spell. But they broke it anyway, and there *was* a drought, and now most of Saskatchewan looks like the wilderness where the Children of Israel wandered. When I was little it made me proud to know how much worse things were in Saskatchewan and that my father had been clever enough not to go there. We and most of our neighbours ended up having to help Saskatchewan out, feeding cattle and horses that came east in a boxcar. We agreed to board them because their owners had no feed and they'd die of starvation in Saskatchewan. We never knew the names of their owners — the elevator agent arranged it all, and one day the cattle were delivered in a truck.

Keeping livestock is not as much work as people think. In summer the cattle feed in the pasture, and in winter we put hay out on the river. The spring morning the ice goes out, all those smeared cow pies thawing and starting to stink, all that wallowing mess with the hoofprints of the cattle frozen into it, slides silently away down the river, and a few days later (close to Picou maybe, where the French farms are) it finds a home at the foot of someone else's yard.

One day in the fall I walk with my father all the way down to a field in the southeast quarter to fetch those cattle. He's put them out to graze in a wheat field that wasn't worth harvesting. My father strides along, his head bent into the wind. There are no earflaps to his cap, and he's pulled it down over his ears so that he seems to have no forehead at all — his face is just bony nose and jaw. I run along beside him, saying things to try to get him talking. Hmm, he says. Or, I s'pose.

When we reach the wheat field there are no cattle to be seen, and we cut across to the south side. Three rotten fence posts hang at crazy angles, and the barbed wire is trampled down. The cattle will be down at the river.

Stay here, Dad says. I'll drive them back towards you. He whistles for Chummy. In a minute he is behind the bluff on the other side of the fence and I can't see him.

I walk over the broken fence and a little ways into the bluff and then I stand and wait. Poplar leaves lie rotting under my feet. The willows in the bluff are bare wands a colour between green and orange that no one can name. The birds are gone. I stand alone under the low sky, a dull sky slung like a wool blanket over the earth. Nothing except me seems to be breathing. Just before the sun sets, it breaks through a rip in the grey blanket and picks out the seed ends of scrub maple in the bluff and the tufts of Russian thistle in the field and touches them with yellow light. Then they fade to grey again and the colour leaches out of everything. But still he doesn't come back, and I begin to get cold. I start to think about the lynx he saw down by the river, not here but on the other bend. I stand trying to recall a memory that was never mine in the first place, the way the lynx lay along a spruce branch, its fur the very colour of the prairie before it is broken, the way my father looked right at it without knowing what it was.

And I think, He never talks to me. There is the little laugh he always gives, as though any question you ask is just to hear the sound of your own voice. There is the way his eyes dart away to the side when you try to catch them. He's never once told me anything about himself. But I will ask. What's wrong with you? I whisper and feel how indecent the words are, hear them coming out and tearing the air, going through him like an electric shock. I'll ask, I tell myself, and I stand at the edge of the bluff until the sky turns to navy and he doesn't come and I begin to truly understand what it will be like when the Lord comes, an ordinary day when you least expect it, and my father scooped up with all the others, Mr. Dalrymple and Mrs. Feazel and my mother, the outhouse door swinging open, the chickens unfed. I see then what it will really mean to be left on the edge of a dark woods, just me with my insolent heart, a girl who thinks she knows better than her mother. I pace along the broken fence, dread growing in my stomach. Then

I know he's not in heaven at all but is lying on the cold earth staring at the sky, not dead and not asleep. Dad, Dad, I hear myself screaming, hating my cowardly voice. I start to run farther into the bush. As soon as I do I hear the lowing of cattle and see them coming in single file. I can see the broad white face of the first heifer and the narrow white face of Chummy running low alongside. Dad will be behind. I run back to the fence and stand with my feet planted on the barbed wire so the cattle won't get tangled in it, and the huge dark frame of the lead cow lumbers by me.

That heifer with the dark face, Dad says when he catches up to me. What d'you call her, she was halfway to Burnley. I thought I was never going to find her.

Tears bulge under my eyelids, stinging, and I turn my face so he won't see me knocking them off my cheeks. Now it is really dark, and we make our way by following the shape of the last cow. My father is breathing hard. We cross the wheat field and then a fallow field, stumbling over the stubble, dodging stalks of Russian thistle the plow has broken and folded into the furrows.

Another month and we'll be feeding them in the yard, my dad says. Just hope the hay lasts the winter.

Then we are at the pasture and walking along the wagon trail, feeling its grooves with our feet. If we had rain I'd get out of cattle altogether, he says at the gate to the yard.

It won't always be like this, he's trying to say to me. But my heart hurts and I can't respond.

What difference would it have made if he had talked to me? If I'd been able to ask him and he'd been willing to tell me? The way he learned to put it to himself, that's what he would have given me. And I would have taken what he said and made something else of it anyway, the way we do.

And of course no one talked back then, except about things that happened a long time ago. When I try to tell about our life I'm struck by how thin and poor my words are. The dog's dish, with its chipped enamel rim, battered by being driven over when I left it out in the yard. The chair with the broken back. The clock, our clock, with the hand that struggled to cross over the top of the hour. The goat. Things have just one word for them — dish, chair, clock, goat. The biggest crime you could commit against your neighbour was aspiring to anything fancier, especially words. The Parrots' goat might have been made especially to show how poor and mean words are.

But what if I'd known through all of those years that I would go away: that my silent childhood would be a preface to something else? What if I'd known that I'd be scooped up and carried across the sea to a red-brick city where people were profligate with words, squandered them without a thought on teasing and silly sayings and stories told over and over like singing a favourite song. Would knowing that have made a difference? Yes, it would have.

⁂

On a hot July day I lie on my back in the river and turn my face up to the sky and let the current carry me away. The sun is hot on my face, and the water is a fresh, cold band around my hairline. It's the day of the fair, but we're not going. We've been allowed to go before, but this year some old lady in the church caught the smell of sin on the air and managed to dig up a verse from Leviticus, something forbidding wheels fixed in the air, maybe, or calves and pigs feeding from the same trough. We've been sent instead to swim in the river, to Lynch's Bend, where the Nebo Gospel Chapel holds its baptisms, sent to the river to take our minds off the fair, my cousin Gracie and me and a lot of smaller children from the church. Joe Pye hitched up the hayrack and drove us there and let us off on the road, and we fought our way into private dens deep in the willows and there we changed into our bathing suits. My bathing suit is made from a dress from my mother's girlhood, plum-coloured.

I stay with the kids until the boys start pulling clots of clay up from the bottom and chucking them around, and then I float away on my own. The splashing and yelling of the others fades to nothing. I can smell salt on the air, and gasoline fumes — my sharp longing for the fair brings its smells to me. I lie in the water and the pantaloon bottoms of my bathing suit puff up like flotation devices strapped to my waist, and I think about meeting Russell Bates outside the general store that morning. I go over everything, how he showed in every detail and gesture that he was from somewhere else, just as he had when he came to the auction sale. Want to go for a drive in the country? he asked, and Charlotte said, Lily's from the country. And I thought how obvious that was, if you compared me to the two girls who sauntered in their careless town way out of the store just then, eating ice cream, both of them wearing slacks. How obvious in the way they put their tongues to their ice cream when Charlotte introduced us (Kay and Laura, they were called), in their insulting lack of curiosity and in the awkward way I turned in my cotton dress and tie-up shoes to follow my mother. I let myself float, I will myself to drown, I spread my arms and legs and let my body rise up into the blue sky, where a hot wind has blown off any wisp of cloud. And then I'm suddenly afraid I've drifted out over my head (I *will* drown, I think), and I put one leg under me and feel the mucky bottom and stand up to see Gracie motionless on a sandbar gazing up at the bank, where a figure is silhouetted against the sky. And I am presented then with astounding proof of the power of my imagination: it is Russell Bates standing on the riverbank watching us.

Hey! he calls. Lily!

Gracie raises an arm and waves up at him. She's smiling vacantly, a half-inch of pink gum gleaming at the top of her teeth.

How's the water?

Who *is* that? Gracie says.

It's Charlotte Bates's brother, I say, wading dripping towards the bank. I'm just going to talk to him for a minute. You stay here with the kids.

I scramble through the wolf willow on the edge of the water. Gracie is following me. *Stay*, I say sharply in the voice I use with Chummy. I start to climb, digging my toes into the soft sand. He's leaning against the passenger door of his father's car with his hands in the pockets of city trousers, watching as I scramble awkwardly up over the turf at the top of the bank, sand clinging to my wet feet and legs like high brown boots.

You're not at the fair? he asks. When I don't answer he opens the car door and says, In that case, how about a ride? Out of the corner of my eye I see Gracie's head rising over the edge of the riverbank like a sentinel gopher. I climb into the car, swiping at the sand on each calf with the opposite foot. Oh, don't worry about that, he says. I'll sweep it out. Give me something to do. He talks like his father and like announcers on the radio: in a knowing way. Worldly, confident, *eastern*.

He starts the car and puts it into gear and drives out onto the river road. I studiously do not turn my head to look back at Gracie. Water drips from my hair onto my shoulders.

Well, *I've* been! he says. I've done the Burnley Agricultural Exhibition, the whole shebang. The Ferris wheel, the barns, the ladies' pavilion. Checked out all the pies and quilts. What else is there? Oh, there's the merry-go-round. I *tried* to ride the merry-go-round, but the bastards threw me off.

We follow the curving river road, with bush on the left side and scorched fields on our right. He talks all the way up to the

Lookout. About going through the barns at the fair, looking for the two-headed calf Charlotte promised him, about the Exhibition in Toronto, the way their dad came into town and took them on a streetcar when they were little. This somehow takes him to working for a man who owns a moving van, and the rich in Toronto with their glass cabinets of ornaments, antique birdcages with finches in them, and then to stray cats, to him and his brother putting sardines down in the alley for the cats. He talks as though we're in a two-way conversation and he, just for the moment, happens to be carrying more than his share of it. In profile his face looks a bit humourless, like a *man's*, like a head on a coin, but then he turns to look at me and it's a different face, younger, with bent dark brows and a smile so open and friendly that I can hardly look at him. He takes a hand off the steering wheel and leans forward and pulls a metal flask out from under the seat. Undo this for me? he says. I unscrew the cap and a medicinal smell wafts out of the flask and stings my nostrils.

Just a bit of cough medicine, he says, making his lips flat and pressing the mouth of the flask to them. You've got a cough, I noticed.

No, I'm fine, I say.

Whatever you say. He smiles and winks at me and then he points the flask in my direction and I screw the cap back on. I love driving, he says. I'd like to drive out here from home. I'd take the north route, around Lake Superior.

How did you come? I ask.

Train, he says. If Steve comes next time maybe we'll drive. That's if my dad's still here by next year. If the pinko bastards don't get to him.

I've got no idea what he means. We've reached the Lookout and he pulls over onto the edge of the road and stops. You can see for six or seven miles, the whole district sagging below us and then lifting at the horizon, as though it's tacked to the sky.

You can see both the Burnley and the Nebo elevators. Our place in the middle distance, a farm belonging to shiftless strangers. Our barn, an ordinary barn now, and the bunkhouse and six-sided silo and the leaning, unpainted house. I point our section out to Russell and I mention the six-sided silo because no one else in the district has one. I'm finding a way to talk. I can be a simple country girl, a Hutterite girl, maybe, with a high white forehead and my hair in plaits.

Your house looks *crooked*, he says.

It was built by an eight-year-old boy taking instructions from a blind man, I say.

He laughs. That's a lot of land for one family, he says.

We have a hired man sometimes, I say. Joe Pye.

Joe Pye, he says and laughs again. Joe Pye's a weed where I come from.

He is a weed, I say recklessly. In a way.

Who lives there? he asks, gesturing to the Parrot farm at the bottom of the rise.

Nobody, I say. It was the Parrots'. They went broke.

I went to an auction sale with my dad once, he says. A long time ago. The first summer I was out here. Well, actually I went to a few of them. My dad always had to have a stiff drink first. He was scared they'd have a go at him.

He shades his eyes with his hand and studies the Parrot farm. I think that's the farm, he says. It is, I remember that house. My dad made me play the piano. The auctioneer was going on about the piano, how it would be a family heirloom one day, and he kept calling for the lady who owned it to come and show us how it sounded before they sold it out from under her, and she wouldn't come and finally my dad made me get up and play.

The outer folds of my bathing suit are drying, cooked plums turning brown. My hands are brown in my lap. I look at him and remember the way he shrugged and backed away from the keyboard at the end of the song, stumbled backwards onto an iron bedstead propped against a barrel, and stood working his fingers around its painted iron spokes while the last chord of "Country Gardens" hung in the air. They had a goat, I say, gathering up my wet hair in one hand and lifting it off the nape of my neck.

That's right, there was a goat, he says. He keeps his eyes on me while he pulls out his flask and has another drink. It's funny the farmers have never organized here, he says. The way they do farther west. In Saskatchewan the banks don't even try to foreclose. All the neighbours show up at the sale and then they won't bid more than a dollar for anything.

If people pull tricks like that the bank will just close up and leave town, I say, quoting my mother.

So much the better, he says. You could start your own credit union. Why should eastern banks be getting fat off prairie farmers?

I don't have an answer to this, especially as it's coming from the banker's son.

Will you look at that! he says suddenly. His eyes are on the rearview mirror. It's going to *rain*, he exclaims. I turn to look. The sky is still blue, but navy clouds are swelling in the west like bulbous balloons. The wind's come up, and along the road willows are turning their leaves to show their silver undersides. The astonishing prospect of rain fills the car with an eerie light, and I sit there galvanized by the thought that the same invisible shred of the past nestles in our two separate brains. Light shines off the chrome knobs on the dashboard of the blue sedan. I clasp my hands together (they're close to trembling with the glamour of it). A tiny bead of the past, but in both our memories: enough for Fate, like God's cousin in work clothes, to slide into the car and reach out his hands and draw the two of us together. The clouds mount as high as the sun and it's as though someone turns a lamp off, and the front seat of the car becomes a little room, a private room at dusk. I cross my legs, and feel the sand coating them, and reach down to brush at it. I can't look at him — I don't need to look at him, I'm so aware of him sitting a few inches away from my bare leg that I can hardly breathe. He lifts the damp hair off my neck and slides his hand under my chin, nuzzling at my ear, his lips starting up a tingling all along my face and down my neck. *Sweet*, he says. He traces a line along my cheek with his tongue (he'll taste the river, I think), and his hand is on my thigh then, just below my bathing suit. Raindrops freckle the dusty windshield, and he runs his fingers along the fine skin at the cuff of my bathing suit.

Hell, he says suddenly and sits up straight. There's a truck moving up the road towards us from the east. Our Ford. My chest squeezes fiercely at the thought of my father's face.

He'll never be able to get past us, Russell says. We'll have to go back the other way. He hands me the flask and starts the car. Before I know what he's planning to do, he's turned the wheel to angle the car around on the road. On his second try the right front wheel goes off the road. You have to go easy and rock it, I say, but he's floored the pedal and I can hear the wheel spinning and in a second the car has sunk into the sandy soil like a boat.

We climb out and stand in the rain and look. The wheel's buried up to its axle — the car's in sand up to the wide running board. The farms on the plain below have withdrawn behind a screen of rain. The whole sky is alive, immense clouds jostling across it. Wind flattens my bathing suit against my legs. The willows bend in our direction, confused sparrows tossed up and faltering and vanishing — none of us remember rain. I reach out one hand, I touch him shyly on the side, his fine white shirt plastered to his ribs by rain.

My mother is reduced to lying on her bed, apparently ill, and they can't banish me to my room because there are so many chores to do with her out of commission. The rain is a huge relief, but my father is silent, and it hurts me so that I can hardly breathe when I point something out, an early ripe tomato that I've brought in for supper, and he just nods shortly. Phillip stares at me across the table with what I first think is disgust, but then I see a sort of admiration in it.

It wasn't actually my dad who came up the road that day. It was the Tandys, a childless couple who live on the Bicknell road. Mr. Tandy could see there was trouble before he got to us, so he turned around in the Parrots' lane and backed up towards us. He got out and walked slowly over to the car without saying a word, the rain turning his grey work shirt black in big patches and his lips pursed as though he were a tradesman called in to do a job. He didn't ask who Russell was and how he ended up in this pickle. How he ended up there was evident by one look at him, by his linen shirt and polished shoes. Gonna have to jack her up, Mr. Tandy said when he'd had a good look. His wife stuck her head out the window of the truck and then pulled it back in.

There was a jack in the trunk of the blue sedan. Mr. Tandy found a plank in his truck to stand the jack on and set Russell to work pumping. Then he got out a chain. Slide over, I heard him say to his wife. That chap's in no condition to be driving. So she slid under the steering wheel of the truck and Mr. Tandy got into the car and they pulled the car off the jack and up onto the road while Russell and I stood in the weeds at the side, rain running off our hair and onto our shoulders.

Tell that girl we'll be taking her home, Mr. Tandy said to his wife as he walked back to the truck. I remember steam rising from our wet clothes and the cab of the truck filling with the smell of whisky. Mrs. Tandy leaned forward to look at me while we rode, and the whole high swelling of her chest moved up and down with excitement. She was a little woman with a pigeon chest (it must have been shaped by antiquated undergarments because you don't see women with chests like that any more). I'm frightened you'll catch cold, she said, her eyes glittering.

Washing and scalding all the little discs and funnels of the cream separator every morning I think of all the things Russell Bates appeared to know, things I couldn't even guess at. He told me a long story about Steve, his brother, who was working for the summer in the accounting office of KIWI boot polish, and who was asked to pose for an illustration of a young soldier polishing his boots. Take a look at *Maclean's* in October, Russell said. You'll see my brother in a full-page KIWI advertisement. The artist gave Steve the original and they hung it in the front hall, and now their mother was afraid Steve would join up, just from the effect of seeing himself in uniform! I feel myself peering through a knothole into this alien household, with a *divorced woman* in it. I see her, straightening the picture in the hall, an older version of Charlotte's mother, with the same anxious eyes, as though she's taken worry on as her vocation.

He could have spent the afternoon at the fair with Charlotte and Kay and Laura (Kay, I think it was, who came out of the store holding the change from the ice cream loosely in her left hand and coolly dropped the money into his pocket, touching his hip, standing close to him but not meeting his eyes). He could have spent the afternoon with her. Had he spent it with me because there was something about me he liked or because he was amused to see such an ignorant country girl? I think of the way he said certain words, *Maclean's, university, history,* in a tone of studied casualness, but the idea that he might have felt the need to impress me is preposterous. I think about him pulling out his flask, saying, This is whisky-flavoured cough syrup. Unknown in these parts but highly efficacious. Efficacious for your gout and your sciatica. Wonderful for your maidenly inhibitions (going to hand me the flask and then reaching around me to unscrew it himself and in the process circling me with both arms). The way we tussled around and he pressed the mouth of the flask to my mouth and I resisted or pretended to resist, whisky meanwhile sliding hotly in through my lips and dribbling down my chin and onto my bathing suit.

I force myself to haul the potato sack up from the cellar and spend the morning sprouting the potatoes, snapping off the lewd white tentacles reaching blindly through holes in the sack. Sinking into my penance, I carry a basin of warm water outside and scrub out the chicken coop, scraping at the dried white droppings with a knife, breathing in ammonia while the chickens peck at my toes. By rights a child should have drowned in the river that day because of my neglect, or Mr. Tandy should have contracted pneumonia from the drenching he got digging us out. But neither of these things happened. If I set aside the flask of whisky, my sin was my pleasure at Russell's hand on my leg and his nuzzling his face into my hair. My body is a danger, like a bomb wired up to a clock. My mother lies on her bed for most of three days, as an object lesson in how I can kill her if I keep this up.

5

Our horses both die of equine encephalitis in 1934. King dies first, unable to stand up one morning and dying the next. We have to use Dolly to drag his body out to the edge of the pasture where Dad and Phillip have dug a great hole, and there we bury him. People talk about the close bond between domestic animals, but she just puts her muscles into pulling the load in her usual willing way and doesn't seem to think anything of it. Then three days later she dies as well and we have no other horses to help so Uncle Jack comes over with the tractor to drag her away.

Something happens to my father again, this time away from the yard, and it's Mr. Feazel who brings him home in a wagon. Mr. Feazel helps him down from the wagon as though he's an old man, and he walks through the living room with a face the colour of porridge. After he's in the bedroom my mother follows Mr. Feazel into the yard and talks to him. I kneel on the chesterfield and look out at their two small figures under the cottonwoods, standing on a carpet of fallen yellow leaves. The sky is a delicate, perfect pale blue, like a ribbon. The yard is full of warblers that day, passing through on their way south. My mother's bun has begun to loosen and her hair hangs in a low chignon above her collar. She turns to face Mr. Feazel and they talk for a long time. Her face is unusually animated and composed, as though she is explaining a procedure in which she has a particular expertise. In the other room my father lies face down on his bed, and I kneel at the window and watch this mute conversation that could give me words to explain everything.

⚒

That winter I walk alone to school, two miles each way, wool socks pulled over my shoes and then my feet shoved into galoshes, my scarf wrapped around my face turning wet from my breath and freezing into a pliable board, my lashes iced together at the corners. Going to school I lower my head and see only the ground at my feet. I walk bent into the wind, as if all of nature is trying to keep me from an education and I am determined to get one. By the time I get to school and stomp into the vestibule, the breath torn out of me, my face is frozen and I have to talk slowly as though I am thick in the head.

The school goes only to Grade Nine, so this will be my last year. Gracie finished the year before and Phillip the year before that. I'm the only student older than twelve. I've read every book within the four walls of the school, most of them five or six times. One day Miss Fielding brings me a hair wreath she is working on, lying in a hat box. You might want to learn this, she says as I stare at the revolting little flowers in shades of mouse brown and grey. It's one of the handicrafts from my grandmother's day. It's not that hard to get hair. Miss Fielding and I want something from each other we are not going to get.

I last in school through most of the cold weather, until a cold snap in early March. At recess Betty Stalling and Mabel Feazel and I put on our coats and go out to the pony shed, a couple of the younger girls following us if we let them. This is the winter after rumours went around about my being drunk and half dressed in a car with a boy from the east. Sometimes they ask me dutifully about him, sometimes I just work him into the conversation, although we've worn out all the details about him, some of which were invented in the first place. Words rattle around in my head, but when they come out they are thin and feeble from overuse and fall into the silence around me with no effect. October has come and gone, the month when Russell's picture was to be in *Maclean's* magazine (*his* picture, it has become in my telling and almost in my mind), and by now the wealthy people in cities in the east will have tossed it into the kindling bin and their servants will have twisted its pages into tapers to start the fire.

If it's very cold and my dad has to start the Ford up anyway he drives me to school, but he's trying to make one tank of gas last through the winter, so this is rare. One day when we're bundling up we see his truck through the window of the school and everyone who lives out in our direction gives a cheer. We cram four of the Stalling girls into the cab, and the rest of the kids ride in the back, sitting up against the cab with their faces buried in their arms because the wind is so bitter you could freeze your nose off even with a scarf.

My dad drops the Stallings and the Pylandes at the end of their lanes. Long, pointed tongues of drifting snow lie across the road even though my dad drove that way just an hour before.

It's drifting fast, eh? I say.

He doesn't answer. He seems preoccupied, staring straight ahead. Then, as though the Ford is encouraged in its own purposes by his failure of attention, it leaves the snowy tracks and drives straight into the ditch. The ditch is shallow, and the truck tries to mount the little rise into the field and founders in the snow. My father seems powerless to stop it, so in a panic I reach my leg across the seat and hit the brake with my left foot. The truck lurches to a stop and stalls. And now my father is banging himself against the steering wheel. I grab his shoulder and cry, What are you *doing?* but he pays no attention. His body trembles and thrashes, back and forth, back and forth in an ecstasy of concentration. His eyes are open and a grin is on his face like the grin on the face of a dog, a mindless sound being forced out of him. His hand jerks in my face, protesting senselessly, and I sink back to avoid being hit. Finally the sound stops and his moving slows and he sags forward and lies with his head on the wheel.

We sit in silence. That animal sound sorrows on in my head, but in the truck cab and in the field around us is silence. The headlights poke into the darkness, lay their yellow shafts over the gentle low waves of drifts. The snow isn't deep, but under it is sand. We'll never get the truck out on our own. I reach over and turn the lights off to save the battery. Then there is nothing but the windshield and the white clouds of our breath. It takes a few minutes for light from the sky to seep back. But gradually the stars drill through the frost and grow brighter and brighter until the hood of the Ford and the field before us are bathed in silver. I risk a glance at my father. His face is shadowed by his hat, expressionless, lying against the wheel like on a sickbed. His mouth and eyes are closed. He's shared his secret with me; this is the private moment I longed for. But he did not choose to share it. It chose him. His body acted alone, took him over for its own rude, ridiculous purposes.

I know now, in fact I know more than he does because he went away and I stayed watching. It's mine to enter and understand. He still doesn't speak, doesn't ask me what I saw. Why should he ever talk about anything? My love for him wells up and I take his hand where it lies in his mitt on the seat and he squeezes my mitten. I'll get the shovel, he says then in a tired voice. There's relief in the sag of his shoulders and along with everything else I feel relief too, that it's over and he is still himself.

But he doesn't move, he lies there with his head against the wheel. We sit for another long time without talking. Then truck lights come along the road towards us. There's room for the truck to pass, but I know they'll see us and stop. I step out of the cab and walk with my mammoth shadow through the headlights and around to the driver's door. It's Mr. Stalling, Betty's dad, rolling down his window, turning his shy smile to the cold night.

That's us in the ditch, I say before he can speak. Can you run us home? My voice is ordinary, cheerful. I jump a bit to warm myself. Dad'll bring the tractor out tomorrow to get the Ford, I say. Then I go back to help Dad.

How'd you manage that? Mr. Stalling asks as I climb into his truck and slide across the seat. Driving off the road is what he means.

I guess he fainted, I say. My dad is climbing slowly into the truck after me and I reach across to help him close the door. As I lean over him I smell pee.

Everybody at our place is getting the flu, I add.

⚒

The week after my dad drives into the ditch I don't go to school because there is no let-up from the cold. In the dark of morning and early evening we trudge out to the barn carrying a lantern. It's so cold that the snowdrifts sound hollow. I haul the slop pail out to the pigs (who winter in the barn) and then I tramp to the henhouse and feed and water the chickens. The chickens despise one another in ordinary weather but are persuaded by the cold to sit in a tight row in the coop, warming the air around them with their chicken-smelling heat. They've stopped laying months ago.

In between chores, in that short winter day with the frost so thick on the windows that the house is dark, we all sit around the stove in the living room, the wind a constant

93

electric whine. My mother puts me to ripping old clothes from the rag box into strips, Phillip's woollen trousers worn so thin they won't hold a patch and my skirt that was Mother's and then Gracie's and then mine. These I braid into a long serpent that coils into a pile as high as my chair, and my mother winds it into a rug and sews the coils together flat. Then I am put to work unravelling sweaters, amazed at how eager the wool is to slip out of its rows and turn itself back into yarn again, although it still keeps the memory of what it was, the way my mother's hair does when it is unbraided. I unravel Dad's navy sweater, Mother's light blue sweater, and a red sweater my nana in England sent for me when I was little, collecting the short broken pieces from the worn elbows into a nest to be used for stuffing pillows and winding the long pieces of yarn into big balls. There is a sombre companionship to our days: our silence has a joint knowing within it. Mother says she will teach me to knit, but before she can, we all fall sick with a cold and flu. When I am better three weeks have gone by and I have lost the will to go back to school and no one makes me.

What I had to consider was the possibility that he was like this all along. That was why they sent my father to Canada, that was the missing piece in the jigsaw. It was the right shape, it snapped into place. But the colour was wrong. It was a sinister patch in the story of the kindly grandparents, did not fit with my father as a young man in England getting out of bed in the morning with unthinking confidence in what the day will bring him, knowing that he'll groom the carter's shaggy horses and take pleasure in it, that he'll bend effortlessly into lifting crates and rolling barrels, that there might be shepherd's pie for tea and a pint of cider after, and larks reeling in the sky in their evening roost when he walks out to Kersal Moor with his mates.

I did not invent this version of my father's life. I picked it up the way you pick a shell up off a beach. Polished, shapely, unlike anything you've seen or thought of before. *Sui generis.* When I learned this Latin term in school in Oldham I understood it immediately. There are things that are not cobbled together from something else, that have the authority of their own existence. Like the times tables that came to me intact in Grade Three, the numbers with their ready-made personalities, *Nine* a tall, responsible boy with thick brown hair, standing at a corner (at *Sixty-three*), waiting for *Seven* to ride eagerly up on his bicycle. No arguing with these stories.

Of course when I finally saw England I was able to elaborate the whole thing — I could slide what I'd pictured earlier into the endless uniform row houses of Lancashire mill towns. Walls took on the lavish designs of English wallpaper, all stained with pipe smoke and soot. Shelves appeared in the living room, crammed with ornaments from Blackpool. There was the fryer of lard sitting on the cooker shelf, and the oily smell of coal. The way the women dressed — lace collars and artificial flowers pinned to their blouses. But my father himself, as he lived in my stories and my heart, did not change when I saw his home, so I believe that I was always right about him.

I know what he must have felt the first morning on the ship, with the green hump of Ireland sliding evenly past the railing, how hard he would have found it to call up a sense of home. He would spy someone looking at a pocket watch and ask, "Do you have the time in Liverpool, sir?" and he would try to think what they were doing at home at that hour and he never could. He could trace his way down the passage and into the kitchen and then up to the boys' bedroom, but he could never call to mind whether you could see over the fence and into the ginnel from the back window. He could conjure up only the vaguest outline of his parents' faces, expressionless like dolls. All that existed of the world was a circle of ocean and the throbbing ship with its eager, pacing passengers.

The day it first happened, the day that swallowed up all his previous days — I'm irresistibly drawn to imagining that day. There are days that drain the meaning out of whole months before them. Joe Pye knew that sort of day — when his dog disappeared, when Dad and Joe climbed up on deck one morning and found that six or eight of the bigger dogs were gone, their yelping silent, the deck swabbed, and none of the crew willing to answer questions. That was the only day Joe did not like to talk about, although he would, when he was in a black mood. There are days that turn other days into a jumble of underexposed photographs you can hardly look at for the pain it gives you to recall your former, naive self. The day the dogs died and the day my dad's troubles began have merged into one day in my mind, and as time has passed I have been able to picture that day from beginning to end.

What they noticed first was that the deck was clean, as it had never been clean since they boarded at Liverpool. Five or six small dogs sniffed at their hands, but Chummy herself and the pack of dogs she ran with, the pack that had lain on the foredeck and bulkhead like a motley herd of sheep for the first four days of the journey, were nowhere to be seen.

"Someone's locked them up," my dad said.

A bony-faced woman from cabin class was there, clutching her lapdog to her like a life preserver. "Listen," she said. All they heard was the rumble of the engines and the roar of the sea, sounds they had stopped noticing days ago. William ran to the aft deck with several of the others and looked with dread into the churning wake. A lone sailor was swabbing close to the railing with his back to them.

"Hey, you there," one of the colonists called. "What the

bloody Christ have you done with our dogs?" The sailor turned
and lifted his shoulders to say, I haven't a clue.

"You lying swine," the colonist shouted. "Get me the
captain."

It was the first mate who eventually appeared. "This is
nothing to do with us," he said. "You were responsible from the
first day out for your own dogs."

"Ought we to have set a bleedin' armed sentry on our bleedin'
dogs, then?" they shouted.

A chemist from Leeds tapped the ebony tip of his walking
stick on the deck. "You have misjudged the calibre of man in
this enterprise," he cried. "The Beaver Line will never carry
another colonist, not when we're finished with you."

There was another meeting, an indignation meeting, they
had begun to call them. All afternoon sitting in steerage Joe
and William heard distant argument, shouts and the scuffle
of shoes on the deck. Some thought Reverend Barr should take
the captain to task, but those who had turned against Isaac
Barr were prepared to believe that he had come up during the
night himself and tossed the dogs methodically over the side,
although to William it seemed an unlikely undertaking for a
portly man.

"It were the crew," he whispered to Joe Pye. "They couldn't
abide the barking."

Joe declined to attend the meeting. "I'm that bloody sick of
bickering I'm ready to throw meself overboard," he said. That
night he bought a pint of gin from Bantam Bradshaw and gave
William a couple of nips. The skies began to pour rain in the
late afternoon and the men spent a long evening on their
bunks, exhausted by the effort of breathing in the thick air.
Someone tapped haphazardly on a tin drum, and an irritating
boy named Tommy Blecker roamed through the rows of
bunks, pulling bootlaces loose, trying to provoke a fight. Most
ignored him, but Boris had never been one to suffer fools; he

kicked out with his hobnailed boot as though Tommy were a pesky cat. "Git," he growled. "Git to your own bunk. I'd fight me own sister before I'd fight you."

"Your sister, eh?" said Tommy. "She the one I seen on the quay with a sailor?" He giggled his manic giggle.

Boris leapt from his bunk. "You wants to fight?" he yelled. "Fine, then. Let's see you take our Willie, then. If you wants to fight let's see you take a Salford lad." With one of his wicked smiles, he turned to the bunk where William and Joe were playing cribbage and laid hold of William's arm. William tried to twist free, but he was lying right at the edge of his bunk and he lost his balance and slid to the floor.

"Leave me be," he said to Boris. "I'll pick me own fights." He was aware of amused eyes watching from the bunks around and of the gin humming in his blood, and he felt his heart beginning to thud, for he didn't like fighting. The man who was tapping on the drum sat up and delivered a theatrical roll, and William braced himself to the lift and drop of the ship. He saw Tommy Blecker turn eagerly, and he took a step back and felt disgust for Boris and for himself, for his timidity.

And then a strange electric sensation seized him, the notion that he had been there before, exactly there at an important time of his life, seeing Boris with his peaked black eyebrows pasted onto his face, Boris waving his bulging arm, seeing Boris's open mouth and his big teeth with the black spots of rot between them, seeing Tommy Blecker's foolish face framed between the bunks, something of terrible significance coming out of Tommy Blecker's mouth, his voice bouncing back and forth through William's head. Time was winding back on itself and he was caught in its gears, he had been held in this moment before, a long time before when everything had a grand and terrible meaning. It was close,

close and familiar, as familiar as the secret intake of his breath, and he surrendered and felt himself swaying forward and let the voices and that terrible insistent meaning pull him in.

Later, it seemed a long time later, he was aware of faces above him, although he would not have been able to say whose they were. From their moving lips and the urgency of their expression he knew they were speaking, possibly asking him questions, but their voices meant nothing to him, and he longed to sink back into the darkness. There was something in his mouth, a stick shoved in crossways like a bit, and he spat it out and found that he was spitting blood. Some of them helped him over to a lower bunk and someone, it was Joe, he realized, helped him pull off his trousers. Soon after that the lights went out and he lay still, feeling terribly ill. He tried lying with a hand on the rough planks of the lower deck to root himself in the darkness, but still he felt himself floating giddily on the endless furlongs of water and the hours of the night until finally the two blurred in his mind and became the same thing.

Then he realized that it was morning. Strange images from the night before came vividly to him. He saw the drummer's stick rolling on the floor between his bunk and the wall and he recognized it as the stick that he had found in his mouth, left behind from his nightmare like the token in a fairy tale. He was terribly stiff and sore and his tongue was raw and he thought the fight must have gone on for a long time and that he had been hit on the head. He found his trousers, but they were damp and smelled of urine. Joe was standing by the bunk watching him.

"Did he beat me then?" he asked.

"Nay, lad, you fell down before he hit you," Joe Pye said.

Did it have something to do with the dogs? He could never say. He and Joe never spoke about it, or about Chummy. But Joe stayed with William every minute of the rest of the journey except when he went to the loo. Boris no longer joked with him, and he thought that maybe the other colonists looked at him strangely as he passed and talked to him less than they had before, although he couldn't be sure because how much they talked to him was not something he had taken note of in the past. In any case he kept his distance because of the shameful smell of piss. He was tired. He felt relieved of a kind of tension, as though something had exploded out of him and left him spent and exhausted. When he tried to think of what had happened he could only see himself from outside himself — although that is not where he had gone, he had not gone outside his body but rather into some cramped black place inside his mind, down some trap door he had not even known about before. But now in his mind he could see his abandoned self from above, the men bending over him, his thrashing arms and legs (he must have been moving around in order to be so stiff and sore), and the thought that his body had performed in this way on its own and that others had witnessed what he was denied knowing about himself filled him with humiliation. ·

It was then he saw the girl he'd watched on the Liverpool pier. He had watched for her daily but saw only two small, well-dressed boys he judged to be her brothers because they had the same high forehead and sharp, sweet face. But that day the girl herself appeared on deck with the two boys and with a toddler in her arms. She walked back and forth patting the toddler's back with a practised hand, looking out to sea the whole while at the clouds piling up on the western horizon. She wore black leather boots with shiny black buttons. Little loops of gold seemed to penetrate her earlobes, and the wisps of hair along her hairline gave her the look of a composed child. Afterwards he couldn't recall the device holding her hair back from her face or what she was wearing, but he recalled a general air of smartness, and himself pressed back against the bulkhead not daring to move when she walked by.

After that there was a day of moving in and out of fog and brilliant sunshine. Passengers looked at schools of porpoises through their telescopes. They saw flying fish and vessels with cod heaped on their decks in nets. By night the sea was so calm that the stars were reflected in white blotches on the water. Something cool and solid in the air made them feel they were near land. At the coolness William's chagrin lifted a little, but with every movement the smell of pee rose from the wool of his trousers, a smell he could not escape because his second pair was in the trunk and he had nothing to wear while he washed these.

On the last evening a lopsided moon spilled a narrow trail of light over the water and he leaned with Joe against the bulkhead for Joe's evening pipe. The lavatories were unusable by then, even the crew agreed, and the men had taken to relieving themselves directly into the sea as soon as there was a semblance of darkness. Boris preferred to pee from the rail. "Give us a hand, lads," he called. Someone hoisted him up and the whole gang held him by the knees. "Land ahoy!" he hollered. "It's England, by heck! I can see darling old England from here."

"Get on with it," one of his pals said, giving his leg a shake.

"What's that in the water?" Boris yelled. "Hey, Joe! Where are you, mate? Git over here! I can see your old Chum! By heck, she's swimming after the boat. There she is, I can see her likkle head in the waves." He fumbled with his crotch buttons. "Chummy, me darling," he called, directing an arc of piss over the waves.

Joe stood against the bulkhead giving no sign at all that he heard. He stood and smoked, moving only to bring his pipe to his mouth. "What work will you look for, then?" he asked my father eventually.

"Don't know," said William. He ran his fingers along the bulkhead and dug at a blister of paint. "How long did you take to save up your stake?" On the western horizon, opposite the moon, lightning trembled in the clouds, showing where the sky divided from the sea.

"Didn't save it," said Joe. "Me uncle give it me. He's a good man, is me Uncle Samuel. The farm's to go to our Alfred, so me uncle give me me stake."

William kept his eyes on the moonlight dribbled like silver paint across the waves. He could hear the sucking sound as Joe drew on his pipe, but he could not turn his head to look at Joe, could not bear to see Joe's mild eyes and the long slide of his nose, his high forehead and the thick, sandy hair curling over his neat ears. *Can I come with you to the colony, Joe?* Those were the words that came into his mind every time they were alone together, but he could not find the courage to open his lips and say them, especially not now.

The rim of the moon slipped into the sea and they turned to go below. Joe stopped to tap his pipe on the railing. "She did hate water," he said. "She were a queer 'un that way."

William had seen the last speck of England and he vowed to see the first of Canada, but when he woke up the next morning the engines were silent and they were floating in the Bay of Fundy with land on either side and the town of Saint John before them. With Boris and Joe he squeezed into a narrow space against the deck rail and stared at the shore.

"By heck, look at them trees," Boris breathed. "That's some blight."

"It's winter yet, ya thick git," said Joe.

I can imagine my father's response to the east coast because I've made the same journey and have seen the rocky shores of Canada with eyes softened by England. I can see the dark and barren forest and the rocks along the waterline and I can imagine how squat and makeshift the buildings looked to him.

They were loaded into five trains, into huge cars three feet off the ground, my father and Boris into the "bachelors' train" that would terminate in Winnipeg and Joe into Train Number Three, bound for the colony. There were no compartments in the rough cars but benches in rows like on a tram and bunks hanging on chains from the wall. The train ran along a high bank, lurching around bends and hurtling through rock canyons that looked as though they'd been blasted out earlier that morning.

The rail line was single-tracked, and the specials had to pull off for every regular train that came along. There was a stove at one end of each car for people who wanted to cook, but on the advice of Isaac Barr the single men were not carrying food. As soon as they sensed the train begin to slow for a stop, the men raced to get off at the front of the pack, because within ten minutes the local store would have nothing left but a few wizened potatoes and carrots. This meant push-ing your way into the doorway and leaping from a moving car onto the embankment, leaping because if you were at the front of the pack and didn't leap fast you would certainly be pushed. On those occasions when my father was at the front he bought bread and a wedge of cheese, a can of sardines and once some bologna with little spots of white blooming under the skin. The farther west they went the higher prices were. Most of the families on the other trains would be carrying provisions, but my father worried about Joe Pye.

It was farther across to Winnipeg than any one country had

the right to be. In the first few days they passed through some decent, hilly farmland, but that was soon finished and my father judged that no one could farm in most of this country. The railway stops were not yet villages, but they had names, strange names with consonants poking out of them, not like the names at home (Salford, Altrincham, Oldham) that sounded as though they'd been worn smooth by being often spoken. He began to feel an urgent desire to look at a map. As he had never seen anyone with a map in the bachelors' train he inquired at stores. In one store he saw a box of chalk and bought a piece. He walked up the line to a rock face and wrote JOE PYE on it so Joe would see his name on the rock as he sped by. He also bought a pencil and a tin cup. With the tin cup he caught cold water where it dribbled down the wet red rock face behind the depot. With the pencil he began to keep a list of place names (in the back of his Bible because he had no paper and in any case someone had already used his Bible to keep cribbage scores). He wrote,

Nitawagami
Missinabi
Nipigon

but didn't bother to note what happened at each stop because he believed he'd always remember. (At Nitawagami, Bantam Bradshaw bought a set of buckskins with fringes off the back of an Indian boy by the track. At Missinabi, a deer showed itself briefly on a rocky rise beside the track and the colonists took to propping their loaded rifles at the open windows, shooting at any movement in the forest. At Nipigon, when the train was almost at a stop, his challenger Tommy Blecker slipped while leaping to the platform and fell under the wheels. He was surrounded by men who lifted him and carried him to the station, holding the leg that was crushed close to his body so that they didn't have to see just how much of the thigh was attached. By the time a doctor arrived Tommy Blecker was unconscious. He would die the next day, news that didn't catch up to the bachelors' train and so never reached my father during the journey. But it didn't need to — he saw Blecker sink under the wheel and turn his face eagerly up to the men, crying, "I'm all right, I'm not hurt"; my father was standing right there and the damage had been done.)

After that he more or less abandoned notions of eating and gave himself over to sleep. All the telegraph poles were the same height, and their wires rose and fell with the terrain like a drawn-out strand of music. By now the earth was covered with snow and ice, as though they were travelling backwards into winter. The light changed and then changed again as the train hurtled along, but the forest was always the same; every time he opened his eyes it was to see, like a persistent dream, the same rock face and the same ragged column of spruce. Then, when even the trees fell away for a time and there was only rock, something began to squeeze his chest. The feeling did not go away when the forest resumed but squeezed tighter and tighter. When they stopped at Port Arthur he walked down the cinder track and into the woods and knelt on the snow (something he had never done before, he'd never knelt on snow) and coughed out some tears as though a nasty bit of phlegm had caught in his throat. It was clear to him that he was not equal to this country and he couldn't imagine how his parents could have chosen to send him.

The train station in Winnipeg was a vaulted cathedral. The men abandoned the train in a rush, leaving behind a litter of sausage rinds, whisky bottles, rabbit pelts, cigar stubs and spent shells, and pestered the staff for their luggage. But all the luggage was on the fifth train, they were told. Boris, with shockingly bloodshot eyes, came down the platform to tell my father that he was going off with some of the others to see the town. My father stayed at the station because he wanted to see Joe. The next two trains came in one after another about four hours later and stopped only briefly. There was a huge press of people, not just the colonists bound for the Britannia Colony who wanted to get off to stretch their legs but regular passengers boarding other trains going east and west. My father searched up and down the platform, but he did not see Joe. He did see the girl he'd watched on the ship, standing on the little stage between two cars as the third train pulled out. She was wearing her green travelling costume and as she was carried past my father she absently collected her hair with her hands, lifting it and twisting it into a knot on the back of her head. Her eyes slid over him and her expression didn't change.

Close to nightfall porters dumped the luggage from the last train onto the platform. My father spent several hours digging through it, moving methodically from one end of the platform to the other, turning tags from tin trunks up to the yellow light from the windows of the station. Boris appeared and said, "Give it up. We'll look in the morning." They walked through the station and out onto the street. The conductor had given them the name of a hotel down the street from the station, the Occidental, and Boris had already secured a room. At the hotel Boris asked for the key and they climbed three flights of stairs and went down a passage to a little room with two cots. "I'll be in the beer parlour with the lads," he said, dumping his knapsack on one of the cots. "Don't you go havin' one of them fits."

The next morning the cold in the room woke him. Boris was lying on his back on top of the blanket, breathing heavily, still wearing his boots. My father tied up his knapsack and closed the door quietly and went down the three flights of stairs to the lobby. At the desk he asked to pay his bill. Then he walked out onto the street. He turned south onto a wooden sidewalk, stopping two or three times to read notices in windows and on lamp poles. The streets were full of people, and the unfamiliar hats they were wearing and the babble of languages they were speaking told him that Isaac Barr's cause was already lost. When he got to the corner of Portage Avenue and Main Street he turned west. If he went east the sun would be in his eyes, so he went west.

6

In the summer an evangelistic crusade rolls into town. It's a
tired remnant of the tent revivals in the States, leftover stock
being sold off cheap in Canada. I am ripe for the plucking. I
fancy myself daring and audacious, I have broken my mother's
heart. But half the things I say and think come out of the
books on the one narrow shelf at the Nebo School (*My life is
a graveyard of buried hopes*, *You don't know how utterly wretched
I am*, etc.), books I no longer have access to, and when it comes
right down to it, on the day of my most dramatic transgression
I left Russell Bates and climbed into Mr. Tandy's truck without
a word of protest. I am neither one thing nor the other, and
something in me has been weeping since the day the cattle
were lost down by the river. I long to be sprung from the trap
of who I am. *Born again* might be a term for it.

At the same time I am appalled at the thought — of it
happening to me on their terms. And so of course it is bound
to, isn't it, or how would it be what it needs to be: renunciation,
capitulation, surrender, all my righteousness as filthy rags? My
being saved is bound to be as banal as it can be, bound to
happen in a tent set up at the fairgrounds and at the hands of
a West Virginian named Wesley Moore, who has had a call

directly from God, which in his particular case happened one day when he was riding on a ferry in New York harbour and took up a pair of binoculars to look at the Statue of Liberty and saw tears coursing down her stone cheeks, tears for the stench of sin that rose from that great land. A middle-aged man with blurred features and the suit and shoes of a gangster and a way of adding a syllable to the end of every second word (*Prayin-ah, and testifyin-ah, and bearin' witness to God-uh*), and a way of seeking out individuals and fixing them with a hooded gaze while we all hunch on backless plank benches in front of him, benches so raw the sap is oozing from the knot-holes.

There I am in my yellow dress in a row of girls, the Stalling sisters and my Gilmore cousins. During the hymns I stand looking around to see what Burnley boys have come to the crusade, looking for things to mock. All the hymns are about blood, lamb's blood: wading through fountains of it, or being washed in it. My mother is directly behind me, her anxiety drifting forward and settling damply on the back of my neck. Not just about me. She is rigid with fear that the Pentecostals will take it too far, disgrace us in the eyes of the town by falling into babbling fits, or hobble up on stage and mention some unspeakable disease to do with their inner organs, or try to cast the devil out of one another. During the sermon Wesley Moore paces back and forth, fondling the fine leather cover of his Bible, moving his hand intimately through its pages the way he might when he reads alone at night, building to his climax. He is a dab hand at the bait and switch, first getting people to slip their hands up privately if they want him to pray for them (*You there, I see that hand, bless you, God bless you*) and then, while his otherworldly wife at the piano diverts us seamlessly into the altar call, cajoling his victims out into the aisle. Mr. Gorrie the druggist stands at the side also facing in the wrong direction, watching the crowd through his dark glasses, like a marshal hired to prevent people escaping. The endless verses of "Just As I Am" run slower and slower and I crank my head right around and look shamelessly behind me. I want to see the faces of people coming up the aisle, I want to see the horror of their secret sins: how people look when they say, *I'm not who you think I am*, say it to the whole town. But on their faces is only resolve and caution, embarrassment, as though they've been called up to the stage as volunteers and can't see an easy way out of it. Betty Stalling slips past me and goes forward, her curtain of shining hair hanging down her back. She's done this once before, she was saved in church last summer. I recall this and a superior smile takes hold of my mouth.

⁂

Women come and hold a prayer meeting in our living room. I am not invited — it is clear they mean to pray for me. What Mr. Dalrymple said about me so long ago, it is still there in everybody's mind. I begin to feel eyes on me all the time: not Wesley Moore's, or God's, but my mother's, always on me with a fervent look, even when she is turned away kneeling in the garden. Bugger off, I whisper, and a small dark figure in my imagination creeps up and sinks sharp fingers into the white of her throat, into her skin white as a puffball, and then runs off into the bush, wiping the stink of her off its fingers. Standing by the bunkhouse witnessing this scene I think I will faint.

The fact is, I am ill and frightened that summer and have been for some time. I have started to *bleed* intermittently, my private parts are bleeding, or, more accurately, it is coming from inside me, at first just a little but lately profusely, so that I have to use a ripped-up towel to keep blood from seeping into my clothes. I've started having pains in my stomach as well. When I am having one of these spells the terror of my impending death fills me and I throw my blankets off in the night and will myself out of bed to tell my mother, but in the face of all that appalling blood I never can. Even when it goes away the dark knowledge of it lies like a stone in my stomach.

During the tent meetings I sense I am in for another bout of it. Night comes and steals away my daytime way of seeing things. A flaming scene materializes against the wall of my bedroom, cast there in shadows by the crocheted border of my curtain: roiling human figures in hell, thin, anguished creatures with arms and legs grotesquely stretched. All the talk about blood, I understand then, is a code meant specifically for me. On the path to the outhouse I am clamped by a fit of crying. Oh God, oh God, oh God, I cry as though I've just burned my hand on the stove. They all have a truth I can't deny: something is deeply wrong with me. It isn't the way I behave, it isn't the movie or Russell Bates with his flask of liquor, nothing as simple as that. It is the sin of being who I am.

⚏

In the meeting I sit between Gracie and Betty Stalling. Gracie has a pencil. She writes in the front of the hymnbook and tips it towards me: *His wife wears the same dress every night.* I push the hymnbook back at her and she closes it, hurt. On my other side Betty turns her face towards me. Tears swell in her eyes. My restless prickling legs have stilled. A familiar pain has started in my back, risen up from the hard, rough plank and seized hold of my legs and hips, clamping me to the bench.

And why have you come to the Lord's tabernacle tonight? Wesley Moore cries. *Why are you sitting among the Lord's anointed? You have come to mock! You have come to sneer! You sneer at the precious love of Jesus-uh. Do you think God is blind-uh? God is not blind-uh! God knows your heart!* I half close my eyes, so that his pacing figure blurs. I would plug my ears if I could do it without drawing attention to myself. Since the

Crusade began I've been thinking about Christian, of his brave and honest heart. *I am weary of my inner sickness,* he said. Where is *The Pilgrim's Progress?* I asked my mother that afternoon. Oh, she said. I threw it out a long time ago. It had all fallen apart.

Betty sits too close to me. The music starts up, Sister Adele's soft, lavish playing. I wish I could see my dad — I don't know where he's sitting. *The Lord knows your heart, your selfish heart. Bring it up and lay it on the altar-uh!* Betty looks at me with her lashless, red-rimmed eyes. Go on, she says. I'll go with you. They begin to sing. *Softly and tenderly, Jesus is calling, calling for you and for me.* Sobs shake my chest. Suddenly I'm standing. We push our way down the row, past Gracie, getting briefly tangled in someone's crossed legs. At the aisle I feel a huge up-swell of revulsion and terror and I jerk my arm free of her hand. I turn, turn and run towards the back of the tent. Faces lift, eyes open. *Come home, come ho-o-ome,* they sing with dreadful tenderness. I scuttle out of the tent, dodging the guy ropes, and stumble across the field, across the soft dirt of the racetrack to the grass on the other side. Goddamn, goddamn, goddamn, I moan, casting myself on the ground, feeling the prickly weeds under my bare palms, working my fingers into a crack the drought made in the earth. Oh no, no, no, I cry. Tears pour from my face onto the dust. I seem to see smoke issuing from a crack in the ground. I'm blind with humiliation and longing and self-disgust.

Someone's bending over me, someone has followed me. Not Betty Stalling. It's Mr. Gorrie, his knees creaking and his thighs bulging like saddlebags when he crouches beside me. I roll over on the grass and sit up. I see eyes behind his tinted spectacles, small round eyes looking at me knowingly, like fish through glass.

You might as well get it over with, he says. The Lord is not going to leave you alone until you do.

The roof of the tent has disappeared against the dark sky: the only light anywhere is the shining yellow band from the kerosene lamps hanging along the sides of the tent. I pull back from his outstretched hand and get up on my own. The air is cool on my wet cheeks. I wipe my face with the back of my hand and brush off my skirt. By then they're singing, *Just as I am without one plea but that Thy blood was shed for me, and that Thou bidd'st me come to Thee . . . Oh lamb of God, I come, I come*, the voices of people I know, each one lifting alone and all of them swelling together. I hear loveliness and longing in the simple melody.

Mr. Gorrie takes me by the elbow and I let myself move with him. We walk slowly towards the figures of the singers silhouetted against the light. We are pilgrims approaching the Celestial City. At the edge of the tent we duck our heads to enter and start up the aisle, where other feet have worn a path in the grass. He drops his hand, but he stays with me all the way to the front. We walk side by side all the way up the long aisle between the rows of singers and then across the open space before the stage, where the ground is littered with the bodies of moths that have battered themselves to inevitable death on the lamps strung across the front of the tent. There we stand among all the other penitents who have come forward, stand with our heads bowed while everyone sings, *Oh lamb of God, I come, I come.*

And so she is born again. Mr. Gorrie hands her over to Mr. Dalrymple, who is the one who leads her to the Lord. They sit on a bench set for that purpose on the grass behind the stage and Mr. Dalrymple reads her a few Bible verses, although afterwards she can't remember which ones. He's indifferent to the impulse that drew her forward — he's not interested in anything particular she might say, he knows young girls. Her voice is thick and stupid and when he says, Let's bow our heads and pray, she sits stupidly until he says the first line of a prayer and asks her to repeat it, Dear Lord and Saviour Jesus Christ (*Dear Lord and Saviour Jesus Christ*), I come to you tonight admitting I am a sinner (*I come to you tonight admitting I am a sinner*), a whole long prayer line by line like marriage vows. Perhaps she should know how to pray after all those years in church, but she feels as though her mind has been wiped clean. That, she suddenly understands, is as it must be.

Her parents and brother are waiting for her outside the tent. Phillip looks stonily in another direction, her father smiles at her quickly and then calls a comment to another man, one of his rare, nervous, overreaching efforts at jocularity (not about his daughter going forward but about the prospect of getting the Ford out of the parking lot), Betty and the other girls watch her shyly. Her mother clasps her waist in such a tender way that the girl sees that it was her all along, her own rebellion and outrageousness that made Mother the sort of mother she was, and that this surrender now frees her to be the sort of mother she can be.

When they drive into the yard Joe Pye is sitting by the side of the house smoking. He gets up and he and Dad go to the barn. Mother follows her into her bedroom as though that room and everything the girl is are now open to her. She is carrying the Bible and she sets it down on the bureau and gazes at the girl and says, Oh, you don't know how hard I've been praying for this day!

Then she smiles glowingly and says, Just a minute, and darts back down the hall. When she returns she's carrying the inkpot and pen. She sits down on the bed and opens the Bible to the front page, where someone in England has written, *The Lord Watch Between Me And Thee While We Are Absent One From Another.* She passes the inkpot to the girl to hold, and steadying the Bible on her knee she writes, *Welcomed into the fold, July 6, 1933,* and signs, *Lily Piper.* She shows it to the girl and the girl is astonished to see above it the inscription *Welcomed into the fold, May 14, 1931. Phillip Piper.*

Then she says, Let's pray together, Lily. There is so much true gladness in her voice, her face is so happy that the girl feels something breaking deep inside her stomach, shards of ice or spun sugar, and she begins to cry and turns her face into the front of her mother's dress, into a place where she has no memory of it ever being before, although it must have been there often when she was a little child. Her tears magnify the white bone of her mother's buttons and splash down in dark stains onto her mother's dress and a light, bright place opens inside her. This is the joy they talk about, flowing like a river.

Around her mother Lily is safe, for Mother knows exactly what she should do. On Saturday afternoons when the cleaning is done they bake angel food cake, for if there is something they have it is eggs. Mother measures out the flour and sugar, and Lily beats the egg whites by hand into glossy peaks, beating until the muscles in her arm burn. Mother knows when the eggs are stiff enough, she knows exactly what Lily should do, task by task. God is their commander and Mother is his lieutenant. Or Lily is a tightrope walker and Mother is her partner, standing on the other side of the tent and holding Lily's eye intently to keep her from looking at her feet, to keep her from falling. *You are one of us now*, Mother's expression says.

At church people smile at Lily. Mrs. Feazel clasps her hand and says, I'm so happy, and Lily likes her for it. Then Mrs. Stalling, Betty's stepmother, her eyeglasses glinting and the smell of raw onion on her breath, comes and clamps one arm around Lily and says, Well, at last! Thank the Lord! By then Lily's smile has frozen on her face and she knows that

Mrs. Stalling is testing her and sees her smile for what it is, false. Oh, it is so hard. Her good self is a starved little creature, she can hardly call up a sense of it. It's like tuning the dial of Joe Pye's radio to find KLS in Salt Lake City or WHP Des Moines, patiently combing for a break in the static, for the tiny voice you hope is out there somewhere.

Her dad sends her to the drugstore to get liniment for Joe Pye. When she walks up to the counter Mr. Gorrie looks at her and up close like that she can see through his dark glasses a keen proprietorial eye. Every time he says, in a voice that speaks of the hidden depths within his question, How are you, Laura? He doesn't even know her name! It is strange that Wesley Moore, whom she sees to be a charlatan, and Mr. Dalrymple, whom she sees to be a sour and nasty old man, and Mr. Gorrie, whom she sees to be a misfit in any society he chooses to associate himself with, were the ones God used to speak to her. But then she understands that God chose it to be this way: he can discern the intents of her heart and he knows that what she needs most is to humble herself.

All she has from her old life is her love for her father, and around him she fears her misery will swell up inside her and burst out, blowing a ragged hole in her chest. Secretly she questions whether God is doing his part. She thinks about when Vera Stalling was baptized, her wading to the shore holding Mr. Dalrymple's arm, the way her drenched skirt clung to her legs and her standing-up nipples showed right through her bodice. When thoughts like that come Lily knows she should pray: *Oh, Lord, cleanse my thoughts.* But instead despair stirs inside her. Nothing is different for her. As the days go by, her mother's expression turns from jubilation back to anxiety. Lily says something mean to Gracie in the churchyard and her mother overhears. She takes Lily back into the church and says softly, Jesus expects better of you now. Lily sits alone in the church for a while and digs her fingernails into her calves and leaves a little row of half-moons on her skin, but this is wrong too, this is *dramatic*.

On the morning she is to be baptized they are driving down the river road, Betty and Gracie and various people from the church in the back of the Ford, trying to get to the baptism before the water dries up, but she is still wearing her nightgown, branches from both sides of the road whipping against the windshield of the truck, the shame of her unpreparedness filling her. Later she has the Ford, she has turned back on her own to get her dress, she's the one driving when someone standing by the side of the road flags her over. She follows him into the bush, walking then, almost blind with the dread of being late. He is wearing a white shirt and she follows it, and there in the bush against a scrub oak is her mother, suspended against the tree, her pale hair tangled in the branches like vines of wild hops, her bloodless face hanging, her soul there but her spirit divided from it by some terrible event, some ritualistic visitation. Then nausea seizes Lily, and she struggles up from her bed and runs out into the bright morning. She is almost at the outhouse before she vomits in the weeds beside the path.

Later her father pumps a pail of water and dashes it over the spot where she vomited. She's just putting it on, says Phillip, tipping his chair back from the kitchen table to look into the living room where she lies on the chesterfield with the basin on the floor beside her, floating on her nausea, thinking it better to make a public display of her illness.

We don't want her throwing up in front of everyone, says her mother. When it's her turn.

It's only the river, says Phillip.

Her mother walks through the living room to get her hat. Without Lily to help with chores they are late and there isn't time to talk about it. If you're not coming I want you in your bed, she says. A few minutes later Lily hears the truck doors slam and hears them drive away. Tears drizzle down the sides of her face and into her ears. She tries to pray. I was willing to do it, she tells the Lord. But something inside her says that this is a lie.

※

The next winter is a winter of deep snow, the first Lily has known since she was a tiny girl. The drive to town is through an alien landscape, for snow has drifted over the fencelines. Lily is not going to school and seldom thinks about it.

In the spring Dr. Riske, the vet, asks if she can come to Leithwood to be a hired girl to his wife, who has just had another baby, but Lily's father says no, it's too far away. That is the year the Bates family moves away (Charlotte is not to be her dear friend after all and Russell is gone for good). And when she finally understands about the blood, when someone, Lena Haywood, a ramshackle girl of fourteen with a distinct dark moustache, announces that she is not going on a picnic to the river. I've got my rags, she says in her boy's voice, and Lily understands immediately. No doubt there were other clues, and she needed just this last one to put it together. She stands by the hitching rail at the church, not marked out after all, cursed but only in a normal way, a way she shares with Lena Haywood.

※

One June day her father comes into the house and says, I never seen the potato beetles this thick. They been sitting in the furrows since we planted, just waiting. How about taking a crack at it this morning, Lily?

118

After breakfast she gets the kerosene from the tool shed and squats down at the far end of the garden. The potato vines crawl with yellow and black striped beetles. She shakes each plant over the kerosene bucket and beetles fall in and swim in little circles until their legs stop moving. Some fall wide and she picks them up off the grey earth like fallen buttons and drops them into the kerosene. But this is only part of the job. Bending a plant over, you find a bright secret world on the backside of the leaves: clusters of perfect yellow eggs standing on end, tiny naked babies, glistening, monstrous, pumpkin-coloured larvae. She has to crush the eggs and scrape the orange larvae off with a stick, although they always end up on her fingers, where they cling like snot.

She is halfway down the third row when she feels too sick to go on and lets herself drop into the furrows between the rows. On Sunday Mr. Dalrymple preached about the Unpardonable Sin. It is an unspecified sin, unspecified either by Mr. Dalrymple or the Apostle Paul, and so each struggling Christian is left to cut the cloth to fit his own coat. As Mr. Dalrymple preached, Lily sat in the pew and felt the pieces falling into place to complete her despair. It was the explanation, the key: in one of her low moments of wicked thought God took umbrage and decided that there was no way in for her. It made sense of everything: why she'd failed to be baptized, why her heart is still so dark, why she tosses and weeps in her bed at night and has no peace, why her body burns with fury when her mother touches her, why her legs want to walk and walk and keep walking, over the curve of the earth and into a different self.

She lies on her back with her hands folded over her chest, ignoring the beetles and the dirt working its way through her hair to her scalp. A cluster of black dots moves unsteadily across the white sky above her. She can't tell whether these are birds or something swimming inside her eyeballs. She tries to formulate a prayer, but the words and sentences break up into thin scarves of smoke. Then Chummy comes bounding down the row towards her and she raises her head. Phillip is standing at the edge of the garden. Dad's back from town, he says. There's a telegram from England.

The bedroom curtain is pulled. When it opens she sees Dad's legs in his trousers and house shoes, lying on the bed. Mother comes out. Your granddad in England died, she says.

※

I was sixteen when Dad sent me to England to look after his mother. God saved me from my salvation and sent me to my backsliding, and for that one act alone I know there is a God.

Book Two

George spent the summer before the war digging up fossils, at Charmouth in Dorset. At one time fossils lay all over the shore for curiosity-seekers to pick up, but when George was there the shore had been picked clean and they had to dig in the humpbacked shale and limestone cliffs. But it was still easy, you could lift the shale off in thin sheets, like paper. Those cliffs were a book about evolution and you read it back to front. *The blue lias*, it was called, from the Dorset way of saying *blue layers*. Some of the pages were blank, and on others the fossils were just carbon scrawls on the page, flat as pressed flowers. But then you'd lift a sheet and a creature from two hundred million years ago would be sunk into the page, a slimy little bottom-feeder transformed cell by cell into a stone amulet.

That summer George's paleontology class collected ammonites, belemnites and crinoids, which put them handily by alphabet into three crews. George was in the B crew, where he wanted to be. Belemnites were common fossils all over England — people used to pick them up in sheep pastures and put them on their mantels for luck. They looked like slender, stony cigars, smooth and a warm brown in colour, with one end tapered. Before he went to Charmouth, George sat on the stool in his shed and made himself a chart about belemnites, listing all the things people thought they were: *Elves' candles. Fairy fingers. Porcupine quills. Starfish points.* Cigars? I suggested. *Narwhal teeth*, George printed, ignoring me. *Stalactites. Petrified twigs. Petrified lynx piss.* Finally: *Mollusc shells.* It turned out the belemnite was a mollusc that went extinct in droves along the Dorset coast. A preposterous creature, with ten rubbery arms where you expected whiskers, and a beak, and gills, and an ink sac — the sort of animal you might invent in a parlour game. But someone had dug one up intact in the Oxford Clay, so there it was, with a Latin name attached to it: *Lapides lyncis.*

At Charmouth they worked to the constant moan of the sea and the cry of gulls. The coast would hang dreamily in the haze on either side of them, and then would gather colour and substance as the sun climbed. Estuaries would open up along the gleaming shoreline, the buildings on Lyme Bay would take on chimneys and mouldings and painted doors. When the war took George up he moved out of my imagination like a ship gliding out of the range of radar. But I can see the shore at Charmouth perfectly, and Mrs. Slater's boarding house, where he stayed: dusty silk pansies on the mantel and a worn Persian carpet that they swept the crumbs from with a broom. I see the crew sprawled in the gaslight after supper, smoking and talking, talking about the war while mutton grease turns to lard on their plates. All *chaps*, as the English say, all chaps of a certain type. Ellen clearing the table, Cornish Ellen, who worked for Mrs. Slater all the time George boarded there. I can see things George's letters never mentioned: Ellen's pilly sweater the colour of tinned tomato soup and her touching efforts at glamour (grease pencil around the eyes, curls lacquered in a line to her forehead). Afterwards I follow George up to his room, see his narrow, sunken bed, watch George lean in to study the diagram tacked to his wall for a long, skeptical minute (the Oxford belemnite with a flat, haddocky eye). Watch him drop onto the bed and take off his boots and swing his legs up, draw a heavy book to his knees to use as a desk, and settle himself to write. To me.

1

For what we are about to receive may the Lord make us truly
thankful, said Uncle Stanley before anyone was properly
settled. We passed our plates down to him and he carved us
each a slice of the roast. Uncle Stanley had a morose, handsome
face, like an important person come down in the world. He
wore a jacket and bow tie in his own house.

And the voyage, then? How was that? asked Aunt Lucy,
my plump Aunt Lucy with wavy, fair hair and a rose-coloured
dress with gored panels in the skirt.

It was fine, I said.

Oh, she's a lovely gurl, my nana cried in a high false voice.
Nan was sitting beside me at the table, and she turned her big
rag-doll face in my direction and squeezed my cheeks between
two flat palms and planted yet another kiss on my imprisoned
lips. Oh, she's a bonny, bonny gurl, she's the image of her nana!
she cried. By the time she got to the end of this, her voice was
the voice of a gruff old man.

Not seasick? Aunt Lucy asked when this little display was
over.

No, I said.

We've never really been to sea, but we went to the Isle of

Man once on holiday and I was that sick I begged Stanley to throw me overboard. Remember, Stanley? Oh, I wanted to die. Your Uncle Roland lives in Belfast and every year he writes and says, *You must come over.* But I can't face the thought of the voyage.

My two English girl cousins sat side by side across the table from me, each one prettier than the other. Lois, the eldest, had hair that shone like a petal, clipped back from her smooth forehead with a shell clip and falling to her shoulders, where it turned under neatly. As Uncle Stanley carved the roast, Aunt Lucy spooned potatoes onto each plate and sent them back. Lois tried to pass the first plate on to Madeleine, and when Aunt Lucy said, That's yours, love, she pointed sulkily at a wide vein of gristle in her slice.

Over in Altrincham they've roasted a goose for their dinner, said Uncle Stanley. That's all gristle, a goose is nothing but fat and gristle.

His name is Archie, he's from Altrincham, and he lives on acorns, said Aunt Lucy mischievously. Green light fell on her face and hair from the screen of vines over the one high window in the dining room.

No, no, Ma. He lives on artichokes, said Madeleine. *Ar-ti-chokes*, she said precisely, in an English accent that was different from her mother's.

Lois's eyes gleamed and she lifted her chin. She picked a potato off her plate with her fingers and nibbled it, as though she were alone in the kitchen.

Now, there, none of that, said her mother, leaning over and swatting her. Did I ever tell you girls about the rich boyfriend I had in the war?

No, Ma, never, said Madeleine and Lois, looking at each other.

Well, Lily hasn't heard it, Lily hasn't heard any of my stories, that's the advantage of family from abroad. She mashed her potato with her fork, working a vast quantity of butter into it. Lily, love, she said, drizzling her whole plate with gravy and casting me a smile. Lily, at the beginning of the war I was working in a linen shop in Broughton Park, where all sorts of wealthy ladies and gentlemen used to come, and I met this lad. He came in one day to buy a present for his mother. Ooh, he was handsome, and a fine talker, not like the lads from Stott Street. I did fancy him — all the girls did. When he asked me to go out with him I didn't want to tell him where I lived! (He knew the minute you opened your mouth, love, said Uncle Stanley, cutting his own beef neatly into squares with the carving knife.) So I told him to pick me up at the shop, Aunt Lucy went on, ignoring him. And then when he was taking me home I would get him to drop me at a corner, up at the start of the Crescent, where all the rich houses are.

Didn't he wonder why? I managed to ask.

He did, love, said Aunt Lucy. And I told him it was because of my dad, my dad didn't want me riding with the lads. She began to laugh. And then one night it was raining to beat heck and I had no brolly and the boy didn't want to let me out to walk on my own. He was dead set on driving me home. So I named a street in the Crescent and he drove up it, all the while with a queer smile on his face, and I pointed to a house — they're all detached houses up there. I picked a grand one that had a double chimney. *Stop there*, I said to him, and he said, *I don't think that's your house, love*, he says. *Why do you say that?* I asked. *Because it's mine!* he says. (She collapsed into helpless laughter.) And here it was *his* house! I'd picked out his very house! Even Lois and Madeleine had to laugh, even Nan, who hadn't been listening, sent up her shapeless, childlike laugh. Oh, we did laugh! cried Aunt Lucy.

There was a little pause in the conversation. Pass Lily the sprouts, someone, said Aunt Lucy. Lois passed me the sprouts. While Aunt Lucy took a couple of leisurely mouthfuls, I sensed that the story had another chapter. And I was right, a sad chapter, signalled by a drop in Aunt Lucy's voice. This was just at the start of the Great War, she said. I kept going round with him until he was sent up. By then I was training to be a nurse. And then he died, poor lad, just before Christmas. One of his pals come to the house to tell me.

But that spring he sent you flowers, didn't he? prompted Madeleine.

Yes, he did, love, said Aunt Lucy, giving her a warm look. That year a lovely bouquet of greenhouse flowers come to the shop on my birthday, with no card to say who sent them, just the name of the florist. So I went round to the florist and they looked it up in their book and told me who they was from. And here it was him! Back in October, before he went to France, he asked me when my birthday was. And I told him April 14 and he went to the shop and ordered them. Fancy that! As though he knew he wouldn't be coming back, poor lad. So I decided to go and give my condolences to his mother. I asked my friend Sally to come with me and we went round. And it was his mother come to the door herself. But when she heard we spoke Lancashire she wouldn't let us in the door, she was that snobby.

It's not like that today, said Lois.

Archie's mother's having you over to Sunday dinner, then, is she? Madeleine said brightly.

Lois lifted her chin higher.

Ooh, I wouldn't be young again for a pension, sang out Nan. When I was a girl, my da smeared treacle all round the doorway so I couldn't hide in there and snog with my beaus.

Oh, Nan, he never! said Madeleine.

He jolly did! Nan cried, lifting up her head and looking at us fiercely.

They looked at one another with amusement and fell into eating. These were china plates we were eating off, white china plates with a rose in the centre, and roses climbed a brown wallpaper all around us, in both the parlour and the dining room. In the hall behind Uncle Stanley, in a framed picture, red-coated soldiers in a dark-panelled room leaned over a map. I picked up my silver knife and fork with hands still brown from the prairie sun and set to work cutting my own meat, watching my cousins covertly. *Lo-is, Lo-is*, I said in my mind, so I wouldn't disgrace myself by pronouncing her name the way we said it at home.

Finally Aunt Lucy lifted her face and said with a little tremor in her voice, This is just the age your Uncle William was when he left and went to Canada to live on his own. He was just the age of you girls, think of it. Going all that way to live among strangers, with just his cousin Boris to turn to.

Oh, the morning they left, I'll never forget it, cried Nan. She reached for my hand, her faded eyes misting up. The crowds of people and all the piles of luggage! *Goodbye, Dolly, I must leave you! God be with you till we meet again!* They had a band, you know. She lifted up her old, hoarse voice and sang, *God be with you till we meet again, keep love's banner floating o'er you, smite death's threatening wave before you; God be with you till we meet again.* She looked tenderly at us one by one as she sang, making her voice vibrate as though she were on a stage, and for good measure repeating the last line before she launched into her story.

The band was playing on the pier, she said, and they was all pressed together on the deck waving their handkerchiefs, our Willie right at the front waving to his mam. And we was waving ours and crying, and then the ship begun to keel over, and everyone started to scream, and they all run over to the other side. And then the ship almost tipped over that way! Poor lad, he nearly died before he even left the harbour.

They'd no ballast, said Uncle Stanley. They'd taken out the ballast and filled the hold up with colonists. Shillingford's brother was in the party. It was a ship built for seven hundred and they carried three times that.

No one had ever mentioned this to me, the ship almost tipping over. Did you see it, Aunt Lucy? I asked.

No, love, they wouldn't let me go to the port. And Hugh was likkle, our Hugh was just a baby. But I remember the morning Willie left. I can still see his face, poor lad, when he turned on the street to wave to me. Your Uncle Roland wouldn't even get out of his bed to say goodbye, he was that cross. He wanted to go to Liverpool to see our Willie off and Mother wouldn't let him.

Wouldn't *let* him! cried Nan. Wouldn't *let* him!! We was skint. Your da was buying his bootlaces one at a time, we was that poor.

So how did you send Uncle Willie to Canada? asked Madeleine.

Me Uncle Clive died, said Nan. He died and left us a few bob. He was a bachelor and he kep a little shop in Eccles, where he sold ribbons and buttons and such like, and lived above it. One day they found him at the bottom of the stairs, his neck broke. She leaned towards me and said in a fierce whisper, He took fits, poor soul.

Your dad was my favourite brother, love, said Aunt Lucy. I was only seven when he left, but I never forgot him. I had three brothers, and he was my favourite. I always thought he might come back for a visit one day and bring his wife.

Well, never mind, duckie, said Nan, patting my hand. He's sent you and that's what matters. And Boris never come back neither. What do you see of Boris and Trudy and the girls?

Trudy and the girls? I said helplessly. Joe Pye I was eager to talk about, but my nana didn't seem to remember him at all.

You girls show Lily the garden, said Aunt Lucy after the pudding. Nan and I will do the washing up. You girls go out and get acquainted.

Their house was the last house at the end of a steep street in the middle of Oldham, a semi-detached red brick at the top of a long row of terraced houses. It had a bow window in front and a fanlight over the door, and ragged roses still blooming against the iron railing in October. What was called the garden was a backyard covered with flagstones, the flagstones littered with husks fallen from a tree on the other side of the low stone wall. The garden looked out over an open space with a view of the hills. Madeleine called this open space Oldham Edge. Across the way you can see the Pennine Chain, she said. That's Yorkshire we're looking at.

Do you walk in the hills? I asked.

Not a great deal. Sometimes we go with Mother to pick whim berries. But George does. George walks everywhere. George wanted to walk home from Durham this term holiday, but Father wouldn't let him, he said he had to take the train. So he's not coming home at all, he's going on a tramp on the moors, to some dreadful wild place.

We wandered towards a red-brick outbuilding at the end of the garden, with a square window set into the bricks on its corner to look like a diamond. That's George's den, said Madeleine. Mother couldn't bear all his gear in the house, so they gave him one end of the potting shed. But slowly he's taken it all over. Father whinges about it, but he never did much potting anyway. She bent over and picked up a glossy brown nut that lay among the husks. In the catalogue of family features, Lois had got the best ones, yet it was Madeleine I found myself wanting to watch, for the listening tilt of her head and the play of expression on her face. On prairie roads in the spring little round potholes opened up and water collected in them and mirrored back the blue of the sky.

Madeleine's eyes were like that, two round blue pools in a face with no worry or pretense — just lively interest.

I put my face to the window of the potting shed. Inside among a lot of clutter I made out the unmistakable curve of a human skull. What is that? I asked.

I'll show you, said Lois. She flashed me a smile and ran back into the house. Madeleine frowned. She tossed the nut away and stood against the garden wall, pulling with both hands on the red-trimmed cuffs of her grey sweater. Are you in school? she asked, turning her blue eyes towards me.

No, I said.

They must let you stop earlier than they do us, she said.

You can finish when you want, I said. I stopped two years ago.

That's like Mother. She went until she was twelve and then Nana needed her so she stopped. She would never have been a nurse but for the war. She would have stayed a shopgirl. Or ended up in the mill.

Lois came back down the path carrying a long skeleton key.

Where'd you get that? Madeleine asked.

Never mind, said Lois. She stuck the key into the lock and opened the door.

George would have a fit, said Madeleine.

Bugger George, said Lois, stepping boldly inside. The potting shed had an earthen floor and smelled of clay like our cellar, but also of mould and paint. There's the skull, she said carelessly, picking it up. It's not real, although George will tell you it is. He'll tell you he found it in the cemetery in Hollinwood when the sexton was digging a grave. If you call him a liar, he'll back down and admit he got it from the stage manager at the theatre in Durham. That they had it for Yorick's skull.

But that's a lie too, called Madeleine from the garden, and they both laughed.

Torn, wanting to please both of them, I stood in the doorway, waiting till my eyes adjusted to the dark. Where *did* it come from? I asked.

He made it out of clay and paid them to bake it at the kiln in Failsworth. She thrust the skull at me. I'd never seen a skull, but it looked as I thought a skull would, although browner, especially with regard to its teeth. I put my hands behind my back. Lois and Madeleine laughed and Lois drew me farther into the shed. The shelves all around were crammed with jars of chemicals, chains with heavy locks at the end, fluted seashells, a stuffed bird with a long, pointed beak, masks with feathers on them, bones, a bow and arrow, a ship in a bottle. Hanging everywhere were drawings I couldn't make out in the dim light, charts or plans for buildings.

What a tip, said Lois. What a filthy mess. It's a wonder we don't have rats. And his bedroom is just as bad.

You can see George in every one of his phases, said Madeleine. When he was a junior chemist, when he was an architect.

When he was Michelangelo, said Lois.

When he was Charles Darwin, said Madeleine.

When he was *Erasmus* Darwin, said Lois, which was apparently funny in a cruel way.

He's not your real brother, is he? I asked.

Yes, of course he's our brother, Lois said sharply. He's been our brother since he was one day old.

It had been sunny when they'd picked me up at the port, but by afternoon, when we sat on the garden wall, a cold wind had packed clouds the colour of pewter tightly into the sky. I'm in

England, I thought, looking up at the fat grey clouds, homesick suddenly for the train, for the impersonality of the train on the first stage of my journey, when everyone was hurrying to different places on their own and I was invisible from both worlds, the world I'd left and the world I was going towards. Once I boarded the SS *Franconia* it was different: there we were all held in a little society in which it seemed I had to account for myself. Sometimes I thought the other passengers were piqued by my naïveté, and during the cool, sunny days while everyone strolled on deck I leaned against the railing and looked out to the horizon as though this were my habitual attitude, gazing across endless fields of rippling wheat. That's how I made my way across the ocean, playing the role of the unspoiled, forthright farm girl. One night in the dining room a man in a shabby brown suit talked about the drought on the prairies. It's a sign of the end times, I said boldly. It's in the Book of Revelations. There's a drought on the prairies every thirty years, said the man. It's a natural cycle. He didn't bother even to glance at me again. And then my longing for England was fierce, for England, where I could be someone else, although I didn't know then who that would be.

Now I was haggard with conversation, with seeing and being seen. We sat on the garden wall and they told me about their school, Ward Street Grammar School, from which Lois had been sent home twice for turning her waistband over to make her skirt shorter, and Madeleine asked me about my school and marvelled that students of all ages studied in the same classroom. I closed my palm over my thumbnail, which was black where I'd caught it in the hinge of the feed bin the day before I left the farm. The bruise had just begun its journey up my nail. My beautiful cousins lounged on the garden wall, stockinged legs crossed gracefully in front of them, feet in slight black leather slippers. What were your subjects? asked

Lois, and I thought of Miss Fielding with her hair wreaths. I was a stiff girl with a forced laugh, I became Gracie. Lois took the clip out of her hair and dangled her head forward to catch her hair up again, and Madeleine cocked her head towards me and said, Tell us about your brother. Is he very handsome? Is he very clever? And after a while I abandoned even Gracie, left her shivering on the garden wall laughing breathily; I became a pair of eyes a little apart, glazed with the effort of watching.

Then from the street in front of the house a car horn sounded. It was time to go to Nana's in another town, in Salford, where I would live. We all got up and followed the garden wall around to the front of the house to see Aunt Lucy helping Nan into the car. Aunt Lucy put her hand on my arm and said, Oh, lovie, you're freezing, and it was true, I was all clammy.

Don't you have a jumper? she asked.

I didn't understand that she meant a sweater and I said, I just have this suit and two dresses.

Well, we'll find you sommut, she said. My girls have all sorts they aren't wearing.

I'm going to ride along and keep Lily company, Madeleine said, climbing into the car.

By the time we were at the bottom of the street, rain had begun to bounce off the cobblestones. Nan dozed in the front as though she were asleep at the wheel, and from the passenger side Uncle Stanley steered the car expertly onto the main road. Outside a public house our headlights picked up a man with no legs on a low, flat trolley, pushing himself along with his hands over the rough stones, his head bent to the rain. Poor lad, sighed Nan, waking up briefly to the sight of him.

What happened to him? I asked.

The war, my uncle said. Lungs'll be dodgy too.

When I was little I used to play that I was *you*, Madeleine confided in my left ear. We always made you the brave one! *I'll be Lily-in-Canada*, I would always say.

She reached across the seat to squeeze my hand and I knew that I would be all right, that my terror sitting on the garden wall was just a fit of nerves.

It was dark by the time we rolled into Salford. Madeleine took Nan's key and unlocked the door of a narrow row house right up flat against the pavement and ran in to get the umbrella from behind the door. We scuttled in under it and Uncle Stanley carried my trunk upstairs. After they'd driven away, Nan and I took our hats off and I stood in the soot-stained kitchen, my father's kitchen. She put the kettle on and set cups and a sugar bowl on the table and turned towards me, squeezing my cheeks between her hands, crooning, Oh, they're lovely, aren't they! My grandchildren are all so lovely! They're the image of their nana, every last one of 'em!

My room was the boys' room in my father's day, his room. Narrow and dim and with a row of boxes lined up against one wall. I opened my trunk and a faint smell of home (of sour milk and dust and mothballs and mouse) rose from the folded things, along with the face of my mother, hovering self-consciously in the hall back at the farm, waiting for me to find the gifts she'd added to my trunk. I took them out, a new towel and facecloth, blue. A New Testament, with a motto from Ephesians inscribed on the flyleaf (*Put on the whole armour of God, that ye may be able to stand against the wiles of the devil*). I crawled into bed and lay on my stomach with my arms tucked under me because the bed was as cold as river mud in April. Boys passed under the window, their shouts gradually dwindling, and a bicycle horn hooted. A carriage went by, the horses' hooves hammering the set stones. I felt pity and chagrin and something that was almost tenderness for the girl I'd been at home. I was in England now, where the fires of hell had been dampened to wet cinders by fog and rain, where people went complacently about their lives, entitled to their songs and their small comforts. I lay in my narrow room and listened to the rain on the roof and the horses' hooves and thought of the sea, the vast swelling plain I'd watched from the deck of the *Franconia*, its restless, random waves no colour at all that you could name. The rain patted on the window and the sea washed over me, the unmanageable sea, and I sank into sleep.

2

I never met my granddad, but I recognized him everywhere, in the smell of pipe smoke, and the cribbage board, and the pile of yellowed *Manchester Guardian*s knee-high on the floor in front of the window. Nan kept thinking he'd just gone down to the Woolpack for a game of darts. At night she set her teacup on the newspapers as though they were a proper side table and settled herself in her chair by the window, and I got the wireless down from its hiding place and put music on (very low, so her neighbour Mrs. Crisp wouldn't hear and tell the inspector, as Nan had not bought a licence since Granddad passed away). But tears would begin to course down her cheeks, which already looked like the leaves of a book damaged by rain. So I would sit with her, because I'd nothing else to do. I'd want to ask about my father, and at first I did. Oh, he was a lovely lad, she'd say vaguely and start to tell me about him crawling through a hole in the wall into the next house, and then she'd get confused as to whether that was Willie or Hugh or Roland, or even her own little brother when she was a girl.

But every night she'd tell me about how Granddad's hand was cut off in the mill when they were engaged, and how her father came home and broke the news to her. *You get over to that hospikal,* he said, *and you take that ring off your finger and give it back to that lad. He can't be expected to support a wife and family now.* From the voice she gave my great-grandfather, I pictured someone stout and self-satisfied, the sort of man who enjoyed delivering bad news and managing its aftermath. But when Nan went weeping into Granddad's room at the hospital and saw his face white as the bedsheets, Granddad said (and his voice was so faint she had to lean her ear over his mouth to hear it), *You put that back on your finger, I'll show them.* And he did, love, he did show them! she would cry. We was never well off, but we was no poorer than the rest of them, and there was never an unkind word!

And then her tears would start again. Stories about Granddad would lead to stories about Isobel and Florence, my dad's two little sisters, who died in the flu. And these were sad too, so I would try to steer her to earlier days, to her father, a spoiled, artistic man (and here I pictured a tall, pale, romantic father, a different father altogether from the previous story), a man who never worked but went off on holidays with his snobby sisters and left his family without a bit of food in the pantry. But how they all doted on him! Her mother would boil him a chuckie egg when there were no eggs for the children, and he would cut the top off his egg and give it to whichever child had been good that day. He died soon after she was married. He was in the hospital, and she went alone to see him, and he asked her to fetch her mother because he wanted to be shaved. And when her mother got there he had died. So she was the last to see him alive, the very last. And she would tell me how his hearse drove by the Gaping Goose and the cellar men came out and stood in the street with their hats over their hearts. After a time she would say, Put kettle on, duckie, and so I made us a cup of tea and filled the hot-water bottles. Then I took the wireless (which was very heavy) and panting and gasping I climbed on a chair and pushed it up through the ceiling hole in Nan's bedroom to hide it, in case the inspector came round first thing in the morning. And then Nan came in from using the loo and planted a big soft kiss on each side of my face, crying a little and saying, Oh, pet, it is hard, but we'll manage, and we crawled between the clammy sheets in our two beds and went to sleep.

⚭

When Dad first came back from town with the news that another telegram had arrived, saying that Nana was in a bad way and was asking for me, my mother had scoffed and assumed he would scoff. Imagine plucking the one daughter out of a farm family in these hard times and sending her alone across the ocean. To look after an old woman she's never met! When there were scores of other relatives living nearby! Why don't they get one of Lucy's girls? I remember Mother asking. I get the impression that Madeleine may not be quite right, was what my dad said (a baffling comment when I thought about it now). Well, I've never heard *that* before, my mother answered.

My father just sat on the backless chair beside the house, scraping the soles of his boots with a stick. Finally my mother flew into a temper. For someone who thought Leithwood was too far away, she cried, you're awfully eager to send her halfway around the world! It was apparent that he had no intention of answering.

My father's implacable decision, something we had never witnessed before, threw us all into a tizzy. The morning I left, my mother's hair was neatly braided but the bun a little off-centre. But she had a new air of purpose. Don't forget that you are witnessing to them, she said to me at the station while Dad fixed the CPR sticker to my trunk. With everything you say and with everything you do. She had managed to find a logic for sending me — I was a missionary to a foreign land.

Well, we did go to church, didn't we? On Sundays when we didn't go to Aunt Lucy's in Oldham, I went with Nan to the service at St. Ambrose Parish Church. The church was dark and cold and smelled of mould and there was organ music and little benches for kneeling. In the jewelled windows saints knelt to have their heads cut off with swords, and two men laboured to stuff Jonah head first into the mouth of a large fish. Nan was not at all abashed that she went to church only if she had nothing better to do. There she sat, with a big orange silk flower pinned to her bosom (it had fallen off her hat that morning), savouring her own goodness for having put in an appearance at all. The vicar stood in a booth that jutted from the left front corner of the church, and while he declaimed in a voice that is never used in real life (which is something you could also say about Wesley Moore, of course), Nan rooted around in her pocketbook and gave me a humbug covered with fuzz. I sucked it through the sermon, hot saliva leaking down on either side of my tongue. God had not caught up to me yet and seemed no likelier to do so in the Anglican Church than anywhere else.

As we walked home we passed a humble hall that bore the sign PRIMITIVE METHODIST. Families streamed out, carrying Bibles. They were poorly dressed and had more children about them than God allotted to Anglicans. I recognized the signs of a more dangerous religion, but no one gave any sign of recognizing me.

※

Every morning we ate bacon butties for breakfast, and then Nan poured the bacon fat on the coals to make the fire burn better and set about making soup. *After the ball is over,* she crooned as she stirred, *after the break of morn, after the dancers' leaving, after the stars are gone.* Tin curlers dangled from hair the colour of turnips. I jumped up to catch one at the point of dropping into the soup. The smell of mashed pea rose from the pot.

Watch, Nana, I think the soup is burning.

She turned in my direction and lifted her tangled eyebrows. I was not to look away, but to let her lock eyes flirtatiously with me while she swayed and shuffled her feet, dancing with the soup pot. *That's why I'm lonely, no home at all. I broke her heart, pet, after the ball*, she sang, lifting the spoon from the soup and waving it like a conductor. Bits of green pea splattered the cooker and the floor. *Join in, join in!* her baton cried. Part of me wanted to join her, but the other part stubbornly did not and smiled patiently at her, as though she were a charming child.

In England young people were expected to be nervy and flitty and to go out pleasure-seeking, and Nan praised me to the heavens for putting the kettle on without being asked. When all on my own I took a knife and dug out the grey muck that had gathered around the base of the tap since my father was a boy in the house, Nan was not ashamed, not in the least, but cried, *Oh, you are a pet!* So I found I had a previously unrecognized talent for cleaning and asked Nan if I could buy some wax for the kitchen lino. Even my cousins noticed the new look of the place when they came up by coach for a half-holiday.

No doubt you'd have done as well, Madeleine, Lois said. She was wearing a beret that she declined to take off.

Too right, said Madeleine. I would have. Whereas you, Lois. Well! *Lois!* It was out of the question for *Lois* to come. Fancy Lois on her knees in Salford scrubbing the flagstones. Here comes Archie, rolling up Stott Street in his roadster. *Oh, it's Cinderella!* he cries. *I've found her at last!*

Nan reached for Madeleine's ear. She offered to knock my cousins both limbless. Then she sent us all out to the shop for a bit of bacon. I swung between the two of them up along the common where the plane trees grew, reduced to sending out clumps of pencil-thin twigs where their thick limbs had been brutally hacked off. Below us stretched row after row of identical roofs. Madeleine, I said when we came out of the trees. Madeleine, were you thinking of coming to stay with Nan?

Well, that's what Mother wanted. She was on at me about it from the time Granddad died. She didn't want Nan to be on her own. And then out of the blue Nana got the letter from Uncle Willie asking if you might come. Madeleine took my arm affectionately. Lucky Lily! Poor Lily! Oh, I love you, Lily-in-Canada!

I waited until Nan and I were cleaning up the tea things, after my cousins had boarded the coach back to Oldham. Nan? I asked then. Did you send my dad the money for me to come from Canada?

She was digging at a bit of egg burnt on to the frying pan. Why no, pet, she said. Did I heck as like! He paid your fare himself.

It was six o'clock and the lamps were lit. I stood still in Nan's kitchen, clutching a teacup in a damp towel. On the dark window in front of me the reflection of Nan's frowsy head wobbled and blurred.

At home it would be morning. An inch or two of snow would have fallen during the night and you'd see their tracks to the barn. They've finished milking. Dad is standing by the water trough. He's smashed the skin of ice on the trough, it's lying on the water in sharp triangles. He stands watching the mindless cattle sink their snouts into black water, three of them drinking at the trough while the rest blow steam and wait, governed by their bovine decorum. There's not much grazing in November, but he'll take the cattle out to the pasture anyway. He whistles for Chummy and sets off, his cap pulled down over his ears. I reach out and put a hand on his arm, stopping him. *How did you ever manage to do it?* I ask, and he shrugs and we look directly at each other, and I feel a wrench of love and wonder.

⚉

I thought of writing to thank him, but my mother often picked up the mail. The secret compact between my father and me was formal now: I'd been drawn into his wordless way of doing things — I could not even acknowledge this gift. I sat on the bed in my room (*his* bed, possibly), a blanket over my knees, and considered what it meant to be the beneficiary of his splendid resolve. To be the daughter he'd been paying attention to when she had no sense of being seen. Sent now to England to carry out his purposes, whatever they may be.

But in fact the days moved at a crawl and I was bored to a stupor. Had he sent me across the sea to spend my youth as a bit player in Nan's domestic dramas? Every morning before breakfast I was cajoled and flattered into going down the street to Baxter's shop to carry home four eggs and six slices of bacon, or an oiled paper with a pat of butter in it. *Our Lily,* I was called. (*She's off to the shops, our Lily, isn't she a pet?*) Poised to leave, I'd be pulled back into the house if the neighbour Mrs. Crisp happened to be outside, and I'd have to stand with my hat on and the little cloth change purse in my hand while Nana hissed, Oh, she's that eager to meet you, she's fit to be tied. But she shan't meet you, she shan't! This was all the consequence of a dispute in the Flat Iron Market over a hat that Nan fancied. Mrs. Crisp knew Nan fancied it, but she snatched it up and bought it herself, although it hung down over her ears and she wore it only the once. She's nasty! She's nasty! She's a proper devil! Nan would cry, her face darkening, clutching me by the arm until the coast was clear.

The autumn dragged by. Mist and fog rose up from the canal and mixed with the smoke from the factory chimneys,

146

and the leaves on the trees in Chimney Pot Park turned red and yellow and fell like bits of coloured paper to the grass. Laundry days we set up tubs in the kitchen and the whole house smelled of bleach because I was trying to whiten the sheets, which were a terrible grey because Nan had been washing them in the bathtub since Granddad died (and rarely enough at that). Market days we plodded up to the Flat Iron Market, Nan and I and Mrs. Grimshaw (the neighbour on the other side), so achingly slowly that I wanted to slump down on the cobbles while they went over it all again:

She knew you fancied it, love, it was wrong of her to buy it.

She's nasty, she's proper nasty! And she lies, Mary Crisp! You can't credit a word she says.

Well, she is getting on.

It's true, she's not the woman she was.

And me, I'm eighty-two, you'd never know it. *You'll never go*, the doctor says, *you'll never go, we'll have to shoot you.*

Mornings I watched girls my age hurry past in twos or threes, on their way to work or over to the Labour Exchange to pick up their dole. I stood by the window watching and longed for my real life in England to be revealed to me. In Oldham they talked about schoolmasters and parties and rides in Archie's roadster. And about George, who did not come home once all fall. When I went to Oldham on a Sunday, Madeleine showed me the advent calendar hanging in the front room, and it seemed to me that the little doors that opened to pictures of the Judean hills were there to count off the days until George came walking home over the Pennines.

So jump to Christmas, as that's what we were all waiting for (except for Nan, who was waiting for Granddad to come home from the pub, and Lois, who was waiting for Archie from Altrincham to show her that he cared). Jump straight to Christmas, to a snowless Christmas Eve with a thin skin of ice on the pavement, to Nan and me taking the coach to Oldham because Uncle Stanley was away with the car. To the coach climbing up High Street and coming around the corner by Buckley and Proctor's, where Lois stood alone in a smart plaid jacket, and across the street the Salvation Army laboured through "Oh, Holy Night." To a tall boy standing among them, not in uniform, not playing an instrument but miming one (a trumpet maybe), and as we stepped down from the coach and Lois greeted us, watch him execute a dramatic flourish and then lay his invisible trumpet on the top of a letter box and lope across the street to meet us. Knowing without having to be told that this was George, this tall boy with the overeager face was my cousin George.

They've asked me to join them, he cried. On a permanent basis. I agreed, if I could play the cymbals. But they've given the cymbals to a bloke from Old Man Road. To a Mr. John Fiddler. He comes from a long line of fiddlers, but he's made the leap to cymbals in one generation. I question the fairness of it.

George, Lois was calling sharply through all this, George! Shut your gob! Say hello to your cousin from Canada.

George, you cheeky devil, cried Nan, and he bent to kiss her and while she squeezed his cheeks and crooned over him he turned desperate eyes to me and said, Hello, cousin from Canada.

Now take the bags, said Lois, and he bent obediently and picked them up, swinging mine to one shoulder and Nan's to the other. He was still going on about the cymbals. *Showing off* is what we called this at home. I felt relieved when we started walking and Nan and Lois and I were all abreast and he had to fall behind, from where he continued to pipe "Oh, Holy Night" softly between his lips while we walked.

The house was full of people. My Uncle Hugh was there, my father's little brother, a middle-aged man with a bland, expressionless face, and Aunt Margaret. They had come from Liverpool for the occasion — a staggering undertaking, I was made to understand. There were also Mr. and Mrs. Shillingford, neighbours from down the street, and someone named Nettie Nesbitt, a tall woman who said, in the elaborate decorum with which she crossed her legs at the ankles and the care she took not to demand anything from anyone, that she'd been invited because she had nowhere else to go. Mrs. Shillingford sat in a wine-coloured hat that matched her velvet pumps and worked her way through a list of polite queries about the health of mutual acquaintances. My new aunt and uncle did not attempt to engage me in conversation, but I felt Mr. Shillingford's eyes on me, shy and avid, from the moment we were introduced. Finally he edged up to me and spoke. So does the name Hubert Shillingford mean owt to you? he said.

It sounds familiar, I said cautiously (for was it possibly his name?).

Me brother, he said. He were a Barr Colonist. Lives in Lloydminster. We had a card a fortnight ago. Only hear from him at Christmas. But it were all in the papers back then, what a trouble they went through. He gave a soft, apologetic laugh and sidled back to the settee, murmuring, Just occurred to me your dad might a knew him.

We crammed around the table and Uncle Stanley poured a glass of red wine for everyone, including Madeleine and me. We all pulled paper crackers and laughed when they popped, and little whiffs of gunpowder rose up through the smell of roast turkey. Everyone unrolled the flimsy paper hats that fell out of the crackers and put them on. Aunt Lucy passed around the highbush cranberry sauce I'd brought. It was a last-minute gift from Canada, decided on the morning I left, when my father was eating toast and pin cherry jelly. I wish we could send some of this along, he'd said. I recall Lucy did love jelly as a girl. So Mother had sent me down to the cellar to get up some jars. I'd brought pin cherry jelly, highbush cranberry sauce, wild plum jam, saskatoon preserves, and chokecherry jelly (although my mother protested at that, as chokecherries are an inferior berry hardly worth the cost of the sugar). Everyone at the table must have been a little shocked at all the big, flat seeds in the cranberry sauce, but they praised its delicacy of flavour.

I thought it would be nice to have a goose for Christmas this year, said Aunt Lucy, a yellow tissue hat on her fair hair. But when I saw the price of them I closed my pocketbook up with a snap.

When we was kids we et pot roast for Christmas, said Uncle Hugh in my father's even voice. We et pot roast and thought we was lucky to have it. Right, Mam?

When I was a gel we et tea leaf butties on Christmas and every other day, said Nettie Nesbitt. She flashed a smile after she spoke and flipped her tongue up to hide the spot of rot at the crack between her two front teeth, like an errant tea leaf.

George was crammed in beside her. Carotene, folic acid, manganese and potassium, he said. Although you'd be wanting protein. There were eleven of us at the table, and he couldn't pull his chair in all the way but reached forward to his plate with long, thin arms. I was filled with private hilarity at the paper hats and longed to catch his eye.

Last year we had a miracle for Christmas, I said. My mother wanted to make a Christmas cake and the hens had stopped laying. So in October we began to pray for eggs. And then the hens started laying again! Just four eggs, that's all they laid, but it was exactly how many we needed.

I wager your mother slipped them a little sommut extra

in their feed, Nettie Nesbitt said cruelly. We had hens when I were a gel and that's what we ud do. Buy a cup of flax, or some oats. Or boil up some barley, that ud do the trick. Before we knew it, there'd be a chuckie egg.

Must have made a change from the tea leaf butties, said Lois.

Stop staring, Madeleine said to George, for he had been staring at me since I started to talk.

For a colonial, she does have the look of an English lass, George said.

Of course she does, cried Nan. She's English through and through, is our Lily.

In spite of all temptations, George sang out, *to belong to other nations, she remains an English lass, she remai-ai-ai-ai-ai-ai-ai-ai-ai-ai-ains — an English lass!* By the last line his sisters had joined in and everyone was laughing and I was filled with shy delight.

After the pudding the men crumpled their paper hats and wandered into the hall and the ladies got up and moved to the parlour. I ended up on an upholstered chair at the archway to the hall, at the hinge between the two circles, and could listen to both, to my aunts in the parlour exchanging tender, inconsequential comments about the turkey and the pudding, to George cadging tobacco from Uncle Hugh. He bent over his pipe and the worldly smell of tobacco drifted into the parlour. Our Granddad's pipe it was — Nan had given it to him. Above their heads the red-coated generals, the festively dressed generals, leaned over their map. Cruel that my father was so far away, that he couldn't stand in the hall in a tweed jacket and trousers, a pipe in one hand and a glass of whisky in the other.

The curtains were drawn, but on the fanlight in the hall you could see that the rain had turned to snow — it had begun to stick on the glass, piling up in each pie-shaped frame, like a Christmas message for Canadians far from home. I turned my head, looking first at the women and then the men. It could just as well have been them, I marvelled, it could have been them that signed up to ship to Canada instead of my father. Aunt Margaret and Mrs. Shillingford washing nappies in a sod shack, Uncle Hugh and Mr. Shillingford standing in front of a cutter in January, their celluloid collars peeping out at the necks of buffalo coats, paper hats from their Christmas crackers still perched on their heads.

Cold, eh? said Mr. Shillingford from the hall. He was a little man, and his eyes were set strangely high on his face, as though a child had drawn him.

Ain't it, said Uncle Hugh. It ud freeze the nose off a brass monkey. Not a patch on sixteen, though. Remember Christmas a sixteen? The bleedin' water?

It's the bleedin' rats I recall, said Uncle Stanley. The devils swimming down the line, trying to keep their whiskers dry. I can still see them. His voice dropped and I couldn't hear what he said next. They puffed on their pipes, they turned their shoulders to the parlour. *Some poor blighter's hand*, it seemed he said, and then he said something that had *rain* or *brain* in it, words just on the edge of my hearing.

In the parlour Nettie Nesbitt, released from her caution at that very moment, embarked on a story about bodice fasteners. She wanted them fancy dome fasteners, she cried, but they won't do the job for a full-figured woman. (*Cleaned out the whole thing*, it seemed Uncle Stanley was saying. Whatever he said the other men stirred with discomfort. Just then he glanced sideways through the arch and saw me, saw me listening, and his face darkened. He reached up a hand as if he were a police officer, as if he were pushing me back. *Keep your nose out of it*, he was saying, and I dropped my eyes, embarrassed.) Three times I took it apart and still she weren't satisfied, Nettie Nesbitt was crying, while Aunt Lucy let out soft, sympathetic clucks. She's still not paid me a penny.

Then Mr. Shillingford said in an ordinary tone, It makes you think, when you look at this lad here. A whole new crop for the next go.

He's of an age, our lad, said Uncle Stanley. I will grant you that. But age is not everything. Then I did dare to look back at them. I couldn't see George's face, but from his posture he was miming a middle-aged man, completely absorbed in his pipe.

In the parlour Nettie Nesbitt fell silent, now when it didn't matter. Nan dozed on the settee beside Aunt Lucy, her tissue hat perched on the nest of her hair like a bird about to take flight. Mrs. Shillingford gave herself over to her wine, and the second it was finished her husband tipped his head towards her and she stood up and Aunt Lucy brought their coats. They said their goodbyes and stepped out onto the front sidewalk, fussing with their umbrellas, adjusting mufflers round their necks. Then they embarked cautiously on their journey home, three doors down the row.

When they were gone Aunt Lucy went to the kitchen to make another pot of tea, and Madeleine moved around the parlour collecting teacups from the last round. Lois sprawled on the carpet, looking listlessly through the gramophone records. I took off my party hat and examined it. It was two sheets of pink tissue glued together and cut into a crenellated pattern at the top. It was not so much a party hat as a joking reference to a different sort of party.

Across from me, alone on the loveseat, Nettie Nesbitt sat with her chin in her big, bony hand. On the shelf above her head was the Blackpool tower done in white china, and a Queen Victoria plate, cracked in half and mended with glue. Everything had been swept and dusted for Christmas, all the clutter tucked away, showing how shabby the parlour was under its crocheted doilies. The cushions Nettie sat on were so worn that cords showed white along their edges. Framed in the doorway to the kitchen, Aunt Lucy bent over a drawer, wiping at something inside it. The glass of wine I'd drunk revealed the scene to me with all its baffling proprieties. Sadness rising in the silence, people doing ordinary things with a secret intent I could not decipher.

Suddenly, in the archway to the hall George was looking over the bowl of his pipe at me, smiling cryptically with his puckish old man's face. His hair stood up in tufts all around, defying the shape the barber had intended for it. His eyes were the same slate grey as Uncle Stanley's and half of Lancashire. He blinked eagerly, trying to hold my gaze, and I looked away in confusion.

3

I saw Mrs. Grimshaw's hat outside our living-room window and opened the door before she knocked. No coat? I said.

Oh, lovie, it's just one door to the next, she said, stepping over the sill and plucking off her hat. She was an old bird, a bottom-heavy chicken hopping into the henhouse, her legs grown skinny with age and a scalp like a pink rubber bathing cap showing through her hair. Forty years your nana and I've been side by next, she said, batting at the feathers in her hat. Forty years I've lived here. Me sister died in the front room, and me husband died in the bedroom, and me mother died in the loo. It don't bother me none, death don't mean nothin' to me. She set her hat on the sideboard and plopped herself down in her usual corner of the couch. I'm eighty-two, me. You'd never know it, would you? *You'll never go,* the doctor says, *we'll have to shoot you.*

I stooped and looked anxiously at my hair in the peeling old mirror above the sideboard. New Year's. I was going alone on the coach to spend the night at Oldham, there was to be a party. Mrs. Grimshaw was to spend the evening with Nan and I'd filled the cookie tin with something special for their tea.

So our gel's flittin' off, is she? said Mrs. Grimshaw as Nan came in. She's flittin' off and leavin' us on our tod. She reached for my hand, pressing a toffee into it. I was just saying, dear, I was just saying to your Lily, I've buried three sisters and three brother-in-laws, and I woke up one morning and me husband was layin' in bed glarin' at me. Wasn't he, dear? Your nana seen him, pet, I come and fetched her. He was layin' there glarin' at me, he was stone dead, his kidneys give out in the night. But the doctor says to me, he says, *You'll never go*, he says, *I'll have to shoot you.*

There, love, said Nan, giving me a kiss. Are you warm enough? And don't let Stanley put you on the coach tomorrow. There'll be all sorts about, what with the holiday. You tell your Aunt Lucy he's to drive you home.

Madeleine met me at the coach. I'm *so* glad you've come, she said. Lois is in a right state. First Archie said he was coming, and then he said he wasn't but hinted at some posh party in Hale Barns he wanted to go to, and so she blubbered, and then he said, Oh, all right, he would come, but she doesn't believe he will. And he didn't ask her to Hale Barns, did he?

There were guests in the parlour already, but we climbed the stairs to see Lois. She was sitting on her bed, her face tragic. Look, look! she cried, stretching her legs out in front of her.

Yes, said Madeleine, leaning towards the mirror and raising her lipstick to her mouth. You have smashing legs. Everyone agrees.

My *stockings*, cried Lois. She dragged us over to the window, where light from the west still fell, and put her legs out theatrically one at a time, lifting her skirt to her garters.

I don't know what you're on about, said Madeleine.

Like heck you don't. *Lily?* They're different shades, aren't they? This one is *orange*. There — look — you can tell from her face! I'd like to know what's happened with the pair I bought last week. What have you got on, Maddy?

Madeleine stepped back out of the light. Never mind trying to strip my stockings off me, she said. It's first up, best dressed.

Oh, I can't stand it! Lois cried, gesturing beyond her legs to the heap of clothes on the bed, the water-stained wallpaper, her tawdry life. I'm fed up to the teeth with all of this.

Come off the perch, said Madeleine. Who'll be looking at you? Archie won't be here, and no one else cares. Let's go down, Lily.

In the kitchen Aunt Lucy said, The young folk are all out-side. I followed Madeleine into the back garden. At the sight of ten or fifteen boys and girls my age standing on the flag-stones and sprawled on the garden wall, my heart began to pound. George did a fanfare with his imaginary trumpet — he'd conjured me up as a party diversion. My full attention went to my shoes, not the hated tie-up farm shoes that had become as painful to me as a deforming birthmark, but the black-patent pumps I'd found in Nan's closet and asked to wear. Everyone called hello. You've come a long way! a kind girl exclaimed, and I understood with a stab that the patent shoes were *worse*, they were the cheap shoes an old lady might wear in a pathetic effort at glamour, and furthermore they were out of style. I couldn't speak and then the moment to speak was past and still I stood frozen. Finally they stopped looking at me and conversation drifted back to the long hike George and a mate named David had taken that day.

You lot are bringing on the war, you know that, one of the boys said. They'll think we're fit.

Not Monty, a girl cried. Monty's doing his bit for peace. Monty spent the day on the Bull's Head ramble.

It was a tramp and a jolly hard one, said Monty. He held his cigarette low, and smoke leaked from his mouth with his words. We walked six miles and the only pubs we could stop at were Bull's Heads. We had rules, and we kept to 'em.

How many did that leave you? someone asked.

He grinned. Four.

A small, thin girl stood with the boys, listening with a fixed smile. She wore a trench coat cinched tight around her tiny waist. It was dark in the garden, and the yellow light from the kitchen window fell on her amber hair. Madeleine pressed meaningfully against my arm and raised her eyebrows. That's the girl George fancies, she whispered. *Imogene.* But *she* fancies David.

Another girl, a very large girl, leaned in and put her arms around our shoulders. Stop your whispering, she said, unless you wants to tell me too.

We were talking about *her*, said Madeleine, tipping her head. My future sister-in-law there. I was just telling Lily.

Oh, God help us! moaned the large girl, collapsing against Madeleine. She was Jenny, from next door. She wore a felt cloche hat with a swooping feather, which she'd bought for three shillings sixpence in town. Her coat was also new, a Christmas gift.

You've got *fur*, said Madeleine, touching the collar.

Watch that! Jenny shrieked, jumping back. It's genuine monkey, that! she cried, going off into gales of laughter. Just that afternoon she'd been to a fortune teller, who read her palm and told her she'd be meeting an older man with red hair who would take her away in a ship. This was obviously her brother who lived in Guernsey, so she tried to get her money back, but the gypsy just offered to give her a different fortune. The rotten tinker! cried Jenny in her big, rough voice. She tossed her head gaily at the boys by the shed. She wanted to dance: she executed a few steps, thrusting her big chest forward.

Fetch the gramophone out, Maddy, somebody called.

Dad won't let us, Madeleine said.

Well, put it up to the window, then. They're not using it.

Jenny led a gang inside to set up the gramophone. In a

minute there was a commotion at the door and two boys came out. Carrying Lois, her arms and legs flailing. She was wearing slacks. Bloody Christ, she cried as they set her upright. Get your filthy hands off me.

The girls by the garden wall exchanged looks. Lois stared boldly back. I say, you're a dead lot, she said.

Just waiting for you, love, said Monty.

Well, I'm here now. Look at you! What a pack of tea grannies! Let's do something. Let's play kippers!

Kippers! everyone laughed. Just then the kitchen window was hauled open behind Lois. Jenny's hat feather appeared in the opening. Requests, Jenny called. Requests, ladies and gentlemen, let's hear your favourites.

Seriously, said Lois, ignoring her. Enough standing around.

All right! George cried, springing up. We'll play kippers. Seriously. Lily shall be *it*.

Not Lily, said Madeleine, taking my arm protectively. Lily won't know it. You made it up, they don't play kippers abroad. And she won't know the hiding places. From inside the house, a man's voice crooned, *Blue moon . . .*

All the better, all the better, said George. She'll spot new ones. Lily, it's just like hide-and-seek, but you'll be the first hider and not the seeker. When we find you, we all squeeze into your hiding place until only one is left looking. We pack in like little fishies. So choose a place with a bit of room.

They groaned and laughed, but eventually they buried their heads in their arms or leaned against the wall and started counting in chorus. I stood frozen until George raised his head and caught my eye. Get off, he said.

I ran around the corner. There the garden wall passed very close to the house. I climbed it and then, using the drainpipe for footing, I scrambled up onto the roof and lay flat on the cool hard roof tiles. The music faded and the counting stopped. I could hear the lorries out on the motorway climbing the hill into town. Above me the clouds glowed greenly with the reflected light of Manchester. In a moment I heard the crowd spread out. Some of them passed just below me. A boy said something like, *You're a right cow*, and a girl said something back (*I'll give you a thick ear-O*, it could be). I knew I would never be able to talk like that, in that quick, wry, sidelong way. But I lay on the roof and made a mental list, my New Year's resolutions: I would wear lipstick. I would learn to pin my hair up in front. I would buy shoes — I had the pound note Aunt Lucy'd given me for Christmas. *I will, I'll do it*, I vowed, *before I ever see any of them again. And then they'll forget what I was like when they first met me.*

It was George who found me. I heard him walking along the top of the garden wall and then the scuffing of his shoes on the drainpipe. For a moment he was silhouetted against the sky and then he stepped over me and eased himself down beside me. Inch up a little higher, he whispered. Your feet are peeping over the edge.

We lay side by side. Lady Mab and Sir William on their tombs, George said. You won't have seen that yet. It's at Wigan Pier. In the parish church. Like Ferdinand and Isabella.

He was so close I could smell the ale he'd been drinking, so close I couldn't bring myself to turn my face towards him. Sir William's got his legs crossed and his eyes open, he said. Whereas Lady Mab's *praying.*

He put his cold hand over mine and brought my arm up to my chest. Like this, fold your hands in prayer, he said. Lady Mab took a new husband when Sir William was away fighting in the Crusades. Then he came back. She had reason to pray.

Someone walked below us and there were shouts out on the Edge. They'll never find us, George whispered. No one's ever hidden here before.

I folded my hands in prayer. Above us a slanted moon floated free of the clouds. I wish I could mount my telescope up here, George said. Funny what a difference a few feet makes. What's the moon like in Canada?

Different, I said. In Canada it's blue. I dared to tip my face towards him and he laughed a silent, open-mouthed parody of a laugh. His breath hung above his face in the damp air.

Is this roof *stone*? I asked, after a minute. My legs were freezing.

It's slate. It cost a bleedin' fortune. If that lot climbs up here Stanley'll kill us. Let's get down. They won't check round this side of the house again.

We climbed down. There was a corner between the garden wall and the shed. We sat side by side against the house with our shoulders lightly touching. David and Monty found us and squeezed in, and David passed a flask to George. Others found us and we had to stand up to make room. Jenny pressed her way in, grumbling. A ragged song started up in the house. Aunt Lucy's company was singing. *It's a long way to Tipperary, it's a long way to go*. By now the moon had sunk over the roof of the shed and it was dark. We stood with breath in-held, a little pod of sweat and smoke and damp wool in the cold air. Oy! a girl hissed. You've burned me. Laughter telegraphed through the crowd. Tobacco smoke drifted over us. Quit that, the same girl said. You're going to knock us over!

Is anyone actually looking for us? asked Monty, not bothering to whisper.

Maddy's out in front, said Lois.

After a while we heard Madeleine opening the garden gate. Okay you lot, she called. I know where you are. There was a long silence. Then we heard her voice again, a little farther away, a strange, plaintive cry. Barley! she cried. Barley! Someone leaned back against me and the whole mass of bodies teetered, and then I was off-balance, held upright by the group, my arms pinned between other bodies, one of my dreadful shoes lost. We were a pile of laughing bodies on the ground then and no one tried to get up. Something was caught against my leg — it was a hand, the fingers cold and intentional. It slid along my leg, disembodied cold fingers stealing upward under my skirt with a private message to deliver. They were rooting for the soft skin at the top of my stocking, for the inside of my thigh. Then the whole body of us heaved and the hand was pried loose and with shrieks and laughter we disentangled ourselves and scrambled to our feet.

When I was back in Salford the next day I asked Nana about George, who he really was, how Aunt Lucy had come to adopt him, and she told me that some poor girl had borne him in secret and left him on the steps of the vicarage in Oldham. Aunt Lucy and Uncle Stanley had been married for three years with no sign of a baby, so the vicar brought George to them, and then before long Aunt Lucy had started a baby herself, the way women will.

Was he left in a box? I asked.

I believe so, she said.

What sort of box? I asked.

She thought deeply for a minute. I believe it was borax, she said at last.

The first anniversary of my granddad's death approached. The turning of the year to the pale green of spring had not carried Nan further from Granddad's death — it had brought her closer. Every morning she woke up mournful. Often she was awake before it was even light. She put her teeth in and went down to light the cooker and make herself a cup of tea, which she drank sitting in the kitchen, waiting until a decent hour (six o'clock) to climb the stair, calling hoarsely, Wakey,

wakey, rise and shine, where's our pet, where's our Lily? Come on, Lady Do-Nowt, rise and shine.

It was a small-enough space I had, just a narrow bed with a row of boxes crammed in beside it, and I surfaced from sleep to see her shapeless form hovering by the bed, a cup of weak tea in her hand (I didn't like milk in my tea at all, but she wouldn't be told). The tea and cheer were just a ticket to get into my room. Once in she sank heavily onto the bed and squeezed me up against the wall, and what was preying on her mind came out — she reverted to her grieving. She'd been paying into a burial club called the Funeral Friendly Society, but now that Granddad was gone she was worried that there wouldn't be enough for her. I'll go down to the office and inquire, Nan, I murmured, trying to hang on to my sleep.

And she didn't want her things sold, she didn't want the people from the terrace pawing through her things, Mrs. Crisp and that Irish woman from number seventeen. I'll tell Aunt Lucy, I said. Nan, don't worry. She sat and looked at me, her faded grey eyes hooded by her eyelids as if to save energy.

There's a wee sum in the building society, she said. But I don't want it touched. It's for you, for you children here, and for Roland's in Ireland and Phillip in Canada. Not a lot, mind. She poked me in the hip. Don't think you'll be rich, lady. We was never well off. But we was no poorer than the rest of them, and there was never an unkind word.

By then I'd pulled myself into a sitting position against the wall. Nan, I said, I wish you'd stop fretting. You're *fine*.

And then she roused herself and squeezed my cheeks and said, Oh, well, pet, there's life in the old doll yet.

※

But really Nan asked so very little of me. She asked that I be charmed by her songs when she could manage to sing them and pat her hand when she wept. That I not flinch away when she squeezed my cheeks and kissed me. That I respond on cue. She didn't ask to know who I really was. She'd taken in all she could take of other people through her long life, and by now if what they gave her was real or pretense, she couldn't care less.

And so I had a kind of privacy I'd never had in my life. I paid my tuppence at the library in the precinct and fell into reading, lying on my bed in the afternoons, pretending that I needed a nap and trying to lure the cat in to keep me company, feeling her pelt slip across the muscles of her back when I slid one hand into her soft fur, trying not to dig too deep because that would drive her away. Nan would climb the stairs calling, What's this, then, Lady Do-Nowt? Lying a-bed while the sun's shining? and then her snoring would start up like a pump that needed oiling, and I'd spend the afternoon on my bed, turning the soft, worn pages of books all rebound in black-painted cardboard, books named after girls and women. *Jane Eyre. Betty Trevor. Lorna Doone. Emma.* Even *Alice in Wonderland,* which Madeleine adored. Or I put my book down and got out the new black slip-on shoes I'd bought with my precious pound. I put them on and stood for a minute with one heel tucked into the arch of the other foot, the way Ruth and Imogene stood after the hiding game on New Year's (close to the boys, their bodies almost touching, Imogene laughing up into George's face). Then I crept down the stairs and pulled on my coat and slipped outside, carrying my book. Usually I walked to the bank of the Irwell where holly and blackberries and other vines were knit together into a picturesque fence and a fringe of chimneys poured smoke into the air. Sometimes I walked all the way out Moor Road to Kersal Moor, where (my nana told me) my father used to walk with his mates. Across the moor I saw the square white house that I'd decided must have been Joe Pye's. One day I would walk out there and ask. One day, when I had more time. At the gate to the moor was a hexagonal stone building with its windows shuttered, and I sat down on a stone step outside it. Robins hopped along the grass (smaller than our robins), and sparrows with dapper black and brown markings (bigger than the sparrows at home, which we called English sparrows). If it was dry I read for an hour before I walked reluctantly back.

When I came in towards tea time Nan would be up from her nap. You're like a coiled spring, you, she'd say peevishly, You can't sit still. Always out and about, every minute of the day. Some days she was too mournful to complain. Tears oozed from her as though her skin were permeable. Ignoring the dirty floor in the loo (which she was too short-sighted to see), I plunged into the jobs that signified good housekeeping on Stott Street: colouring the flagstones with the donkey stone, polishing the stove all over with black leading. Appeased, she asked me to pin up her hair, and I stood behind her coiling tin curlers into neat rows while she sat sipping milky tea at the table. I sponged scabs of dried pea soup off her blouse, I pinned a shawl around her shoulders. I was Alice, tending to the White Queen. Nothing would ever happen.

Then something did, something arrived in the mail, a petition from my former life. The envelope was addressed in my father's small, pointed writing:

> Dear Lily,
> When I picked up the mail in town this week, this letter was there for you. Your mother would be happier if I threw it in the fire. His family are city people and don't know the Lord and there doesn't seem to be any future in it.
> We were happy to hear from Lucy at Christmas.

They are very fond of you. I hope Mother is in
good health. Give her my best regards.

Fondly,
William Piper

A sealed envelope was folded inside, addressed to me. Its
return address was

R. Bates
27 Rue Argyle
Montreal, Quebec
Canada

Inside was a single sheet, dated almost two months before:

May 4, 1937

Dear Lily,
    You'll be surprised to get another letter from me
after all this time. Especially since you didn't
answer the first one. Are you still in this earthly
realm? I haven't heard about a bunch of Christian
farmers mysteriously disappearing from the
prairies, so I guess you must be. I saw Charlotte
last week and told her I was writing to you. She
told me not to pester you. But she sends her
regards. She's almost a nurse, she'll finish her
training in June.
    You and I had fun, bringing rain down in the
middle of a drought. Now that Dad's back in
Ontario counting his shekels I never go west. If I
did I'd come and see you. I'd like to see first-hand
what's happening with the Farmers Unity League.

I'm supposed to finish at McGill this year. I'm not
working as hard as I should be (as you can tell, I'd
rather write letters). Last Sunday I had a grand
time at a mock convention at the Labour Temple.
I played the part of Leon Blum, and others were
Mussolini, etc. etc. There was a lot of shouting and
too much beer consumed, and people wandered in
from the street to watch.

I'll be looking for work in a few months. It's not
like it is on a farm, where sons follow fathers onto
the soil. As hard as it was through the drought, at
least it was an honest labour, each man working
for his family and his community.

Come the revolution!

Russell Bates

This letter was written in a bold hand in blue ink on lined
white paper. I held it and could hardly credit the reality of it,
having long ago shifted Russell Bates from my memory into
my dreams. My own idiocy that day came back to me, my bare
legs covered with sand, my ridiculous makeshift bathing suit.
The watermark larger than me soaking into the car seat.
Christian farmers mysteriously disappearing from the prairies.
Heat collected around my eyes. Whatever was I thinking,
telling him that? He'd said he was starting university in
Montreal that fall, and I remembered asking, What will you
be when you finish? and he said, What will I *be*? so I heard
what a child's question it was. Our conversation played out
relentlessly in my mind:

How about you? You going to be a farmer when you grow
up?

Women don't farm.

No? What's your mother do?

She's a farmer's wife.

Oh. Well, maybe that's what you'll be.

I don't think so. And that's when I said, The Lord will probably come before then. I meant to say this tartly — I meant him to understand the way I both believed and didn't believe it. But he turned his narrow eyes in my direction, he asked in that humorous way, Is that the same as hell freezing over? and I had nothing clever to say to that. In a breathless, anxious voice I launched into explaining it, the last terrible battle, the horses wading up to their bellies in blood. We were up on the Lookout at that point and he was looking down at the village below us and he asked me the name of it. When I told him, Nebo, he said, That means *heaven* in Ukrainian. So, hey — you're living in heaven. You don't have to wait for Jesus to come!

I tucked the letter away. It was written to recall me to mortifications I'd put behind me. I was not going to answer. Anyway, in his own indirect way my dad had asked me not to. I did think about Russell Bates, though, the way he appeared every three or four years like a comet barrelling across the sky — or one of those birds that pop out of a clock, startling the heck out of you and making a racket before the door slams shut on it again. I thought about him, and one night I dreamt I was walking down the street and saw him walking towards me, his sturdy body all bundled up in a winter coat and scarf. I opened my eyes with a gasp. And then I lay furious that I'd yanked myself awake before I spoke to him, before I had the chance to ask, *Why are you writing to me?*

On Sunday I took the letter to Oldham and showed the last part to Madeleine, fussily folding the top of the page over, which of course increased the intrigue. She read it curiously. *Leon Blum.* You should ask George who that is. He's bound to know. She looked at me a minute with a smile, but she didn't ask.

And then something else happened, something for Nan. Edward VIII had gone away with his wretched bride and the coronation of the new king, King George VI, was set for May 12. There would be a parade with marching bands and tableaus wheeled down the street on wagons. The May Queen would be crowned the same day (as a local allegory, I assumed) and a tree planted in the common. A flushed old man from the Salford Lads Club, so bowlegged that he couldn't stop a pig in an entry (this was what Nan said), took up money for fireworks and Nan gave him sixpence. He bought his Roman candles from Mrs. Baxter as he had the money and stored them in a leaky tent in the garden. Two days before the coronation they were all ruined by rain. Mrs. Baxter told us. Mrs. Baxter herself had ordered from the BBC a pictorial map of London and a tiny lead replica of the royal coach and horses, so that as you listened to the coronation on the wireless you could move the coach along the London streets.

On May 11 Nan and I walked up to the precinct to see the decorations. A banner reading LONG MAY HE REIGN hung at the end of our street. After being knocked legless before Christmas by the abdication, Nan was well satisfied. There'd a been none of this bother for that gormless wonder, she said. It was Edward VIII she meant. We stood at the window of the post and telegraph office and admired a picture of the new King and his lovely wife and his two lovely daughters. Anyone could see it would be different with him.

When I woke up on Coronation Day it was colder than usual, and I burrowed the icy toes of one foot into the warm bend of the other knee. Then I realized with a shock that it must be very late and that Nan had not started the stove. I got out of bed and pulled my skirt and sweater on and crept across the hall to her room. The door was open a foot and she was still lying in bed. The motionless ridge of her legs under the cotton bedspread filled me with foreboding and I was suddenly terrified of opening the door. Then I heard a breath and I gave the door a push.

She was lying on her side, facing the doorway. The room was filled with the rough sound of her breath and then a silence, and then another — like the sound of someone breathing under water. Her lips had collapsed inward and her face leered against the pillowcase, where her drool had formed a dark circle. Her eyes were not quite closed. The space between the lids was blank, as if her pale irises had faded away altogether. But her vagueness was gone, she had been pulled into something that caught her attention. The expression on her face was of blunt surprise.

Except in animals I had never seen death. The dread I felt was a dread I'd known only in dreams, and instinctively I stepped backwards into the hall. In the long silence after a breath I turned and ran, pounding down the stairs, shoving my feet into my shoes at the door. Mrs. Crisp was sweeping the walkway, and I saw her surprised face turn towards me. There was no telephone on the street and so I pelted all the way to Mosley Lane and burst into the shop, the bell clattering above me. Mrs. Baxter heard me and pushed aside the blanket hanging over the door to the back room. She was wearing a smock and her hair was in curlers.

What's the trouble? she cried when she saw my face.

It's my nana, I said. I can't wake her.

I'll call the doctor, said Mrs. Baxter. She went into the back and I could hear her on the telephone, and when she came out she was tying a scarf over her curlers. He's on his way, love, she said. You mustn't go back on your own. I'll come with you.

When we got back to the house Mrs. Crisp was still in the street. I've shut the door, she said to me severely. You run off leaving it wide open. All sorts could of walked in.

Thank you, Mary, said Mrs. Baxter tartly. She pulled me into the entrance. You wait here, love, she murmured. I couldn't tell him the exact number. You wait right by the door where he can see you, and I'll see to your nana.

So I waited by the door, so frightened, so grateful, tears dripping down my cheeks, so relieved that I didn't have to go in and hear those rough, laboured breaths, didn't have to stand in that room in the terrible silence between breaths, avoiding those vacant eyes. Mrs. Crisp and I waited together. She bent down to pick up her milk, looking at me darkly, wiping the bottle elaborately with her handkerchief. The coal man came with his horse and cart and I shook my head at him and so did she and he moved on. Finally a hansom cab drove under the LONG MAY HE REIGN banner at the top of the street, and the wait was over.

4

Two days after King George VI glided out of Westminster Abbey with his scrawny neck in a spasm from the weight of his crown, my nana was buried from St. Ambrose Parish Church. Her coffin was carried into the church by neighbours wearing Great War uniforms, their bellies straining against the buttons of their jackets. Men who grew up with my dad on Stott Street (Robert Hodgkins, Basil Milgate and others whose names I didn't know), wearing twenty-year-old infantry uniforms because that was all they had by way of dress clothes. I walked with my cousins behind the coffin. It was all achingly poignant. The organ music, the handful of white-haired neighbours singing, *The day thou gavest, Lord, is ended, the darkness falls at thy behest.* The sun falling through a ruby window onto the lily wreath Uncle Roland wired from Ireland. The vicar with his silver hair and gleaming white robe proclaiming in a cultivated voice, *I know that my redeemer liveth, and that he shall stand at the latter day upon the earth* ... And then the line, *And though after my skin, worms destroy this body, yet in my flesh shall I see God*, and in the turn of a sentence it all fell away and I was hurled forward into the endless pathways of eternity, where the worm dieth not and the fire is not quenched. I saw with a lurch of my stomach that it was all empty — the piety on the altar boy's freckled face manufactured, the robes and candles and coloured glass just a pageant to keep the truth at bay, and I bent my head and held hard to the varnished wood of the pew in front of me. Furious tears burned in my eyes. Nan was never saved! It would have been more honest to bury her under a tree in the common. Or in the market, under the brick walkway of the Flat Iron Market with a bit of bunting strung over her grave.

⁂

I hadn't been able to bring myself to ask whether Nan was already dead when Mrs. Baxter went up to her room on Coronation Day, or whether she died some short time later. I'd waited in the kitchen for a long time after the doctor arrived, listening to the murmur of their voices above me, and then Mrs. Baxter came down and put her hand on my arm and said, Let's go back to the shop, love. You can telephone your auntie, you can tell her it's over. All I'd felt was a huge relief that I'd escaped the moment of death. But by the afternoon of the funeral, terror and shame had overtaken me, and when I saw Aunt Lucy in the kitchen putting teacakes on plates I began to cry. Between sobs I blurted out an approximate sin: that I'd told Mrs. Baxter I couldn't wake Nan when really, I'd been too frightened to try.

Oh, my dear, she wouldn't have woken, said Aunt Lucy, pulling me towards her soft shoulder. She'd had a stroke, lovie. You did just right to go for help. But the real dimension of things had been revealed to me, the meaning of the astonishment on Nan's dying face, and my terror stayed with me, pressing down on me when I moved or spoke, the way the damp cold will batter at you if you dare to move in your bed. Nan had believed in God the way she believed in the King: that he obliged us all by existing and doing his bit to keep the sun rising in the east and the trams running up Liverpool Street, but his person had no real bearing on hers. And I'd never tried to witness to her, never once. I hadn't mentioned the Lord except that one time at Christmas dinner when I'd alluded to one of his miracles, in a way that could have been dismissed as a joke. I'd spent the whole autumn focused on my own pleasures. So I let Aunt Lucy embrace me, and cried some more, but her comforting words did not touch me.

After the burial there was a tea served in the parish hall for the neighbours in Salford, and then we came back to Oldham and poured tea again, for Aunt Lucy's neighbours. Gradually they left, and Lois and Madeleine curled up on the sofa, silent and tired. They'd known Nan all their lives, but my own particular burden was of a sort not easily shared. I walked restlessly through the house. It was dawning on me why this had happened, that God was using this means to bring me back to him. Drastic, yes (I felt a wave of vertigo at the thought, a lick of the old despair), but it was always like that with God, things never were proportionate.

※

A lantern burned in the potting shed window, and George's head was bent over his workbench. I knocked, just twice, leaving off the last knock so he could ignore me if he wanted to. Without a word he reached over and opened the door from where he was sitting, as though he'd sent for me. I stepped across the sill into the yellow light of a kerosene lantern and smelled earth, rust, turpentine, bird nests.

The workbench of the potting shed was high, for standing, and sitting in front of it, George looked like a gnome at work. He seemed to be making something of a lump of brown clay. Had enough of Anglo-Christian burial rituals, then? he said. The lamplight darkened the shadows under his eyes.

Are you making another skull? I asked.

Well, well, so cynical and so young, he said. He stood up and pulled an oilcloth over the clay before I could see what it was. My sisters' influence, no doubt.

I smiled awkwardly at him. How long are you staying home?

I'm going back on the train tomorrow. I've got exams next week. I should be studying now, I suppose, but attention must be paid. In death if not in life.

You don't think we paid enough attention to Nan?

Me, I meant, he said. Not you or the girls or Mother.

Well, you're not home very much, I said. Why don't you go to university in Manchester?

I didn't get a scholarship to Manchester.

You're studying history?

In a way. I'm hoping to go into paleontology.

I lifted my chin, the way Lois always did. I wouldn't ask. He offered me his stool, his shadow, broken against the shelves, gesturing hugely.

No, that's all right, I said. I stood hugging my arms. Do you care if I look at your things?

Go ahead, he said. He held the lamp up for me.

This was still a potting shed, with clay pots nested under the workbench, and trowels hanging from pegs on the centre beam. But new rough shelves had been put up with aluminum brackets, and they were crammed with the paraphernalia I'd seen when Lois unlocked the shed. Hanging right in front of me was a chart of the heavens with the familiar constellations. Beside it was a diagram made up of circles, one inside the other. The planets were embedded in these discs like gems in a ring.

They're *spheres*, said George eagerly, following my eyes. Crystal spheres. As they revolve they put out music. Only the pure of heart can hear it. You must have studied Kepler?

I don't think so, I said. George pulled another chart out of a heap of books on the workbench. In this one the orbits of the planets had geometrical shapes traced between them.

Kepler calculated the ratio of the distance between planets, said George. The ratios parallel harmonic keys, which is kind of amazing.

Was there actual music?

How would anyone know? But mathematically there could have been. That was the point. He pushed his glasses back on his nose with his middle finger.

Where would heaven be? I asked, looking closely at this map of the cosmos.

Heaven? he said, amused. You're asking on behalf of all medieval souls?

Then he saw my tears start up, and there was a moment of acute surprise between us. He looked tactfully away and began to rifle through a stack of papers. I wonder what I have here, he said, kindly. For images of heaven you have to go back a lot earlier. I don't know if I have anything. A lot of my copies of etchings are in Durham.

He took a long time looking through his papers while I wiped my cheeks with my sleeve, and then he pulled out a large sheet of manila.

Well, there's this.

It was a picture of the Garden of Eden drawn in a circle. The heavens made a border around it, like the rim on an ornate tea plate. And God leaned over the plate, and the sun rose behind him.

I like this, said George, pointing to an orb in the heavens. It's the moon. Look how it has God's face. It's a little duplicate image of God keeping watch over the world. It's sort of interesting that they'd portray God like that, because the moon waxes and wanes.

Where did this drawing come from? I asked.

It was the frontispiece to the first Lutheran Bible. I copied it by hand.

I stared at this testy old man with tousled hair peering down over the garden where Adam and Eve walked with their naked front sides turned decorously away.

It was drawn in the early sixteenth century, said George. See, it says here.

He pointed to a legend at the bottom of the page, but my eye was drawn to the signature beneath the legend: *George Oldham*. Their family name was Sheffield.

That, he said, catching my questioning look. That's in the tradition of foundlings.

We stood close together, looking at the drawing. I felt my grief and guilt lapping inside me — I felt swollen with emotion, the way you feel full of sickness when you have the flu. And I felt something new, astonishment: I was almost off-balance with amazement. I'd never longed to know a boy like George because I'd never dreamt that such boys existed.

The door opened and Madeleine poked her head into the shed. Mother says to stop mucking about and come inside. George, Mr. Shillingford wants to see you before he leaves. Go upstairs and wash up first. She spoke as though he were a child. He held my eyes for a minute and then he tucked the oilcloth more closely over whatever he had been moulding and held the door open for me, and we followed Madeleine back to the house. As we crossed the garden under the gaslit Manchester sky, I understood why I'd come all the way across the ocean, the other reason, besides saving Nan: I'd come to take George seriously.

The day after George left for Durham, the rest of us drove to Salford to get my trunk and to clean Nan's house.

Nana said she didn't want her things sold, I said in the kitchen after breakfast. She told me almost every day. She couldn't stand the thought of the women on the street pawing through her things.

Well, we'll bring it all to the Tommyfield here in town, said Aunt Lucy. No one knows her here. What else can we do? I'm not burning the lot.

It was strange to go back into the silent house on Stott Street, to smell its old, mixed smell of fry-ups, ashes-of-roses dusting powder, mouldy boxes, stale pipe. I was cautious, looking into Nana's room. Someone, Mrs. Baxter probably, had made the bed up neatly and tucked Nan's grey felt slippers with the backs trodden down just under the fringe of the yellow bedspread.

I gathered up my things and packed up my trunk and stood in my dad's room for the last time, looking through the flawed glass at the view it afforded of the back garden wall, and then I went to help Aunt Lucy in Nan's room. We had to sort through all the junk I'd never attempted to clean up while I lived there: jars of face cream dried into cracks, boiled sweets all gone solid in their bag. Tangles of worn cotton stockings with stiff, dirty feet. An open tin of bright pink Gibb's toothpaste with a film of dust on the surface. Hairpins in crumpled brown paper. Granddad's bicycle lamp that we carried when we went out to the loo in the night. In a box of jars and bottles I discovered the recruiting pamphlet — the paper that sent my father to Canada — still wrinkled from the puddle where my granddad found it.

Garbage would go straight to the tip. Uncle Stanley rolled two barrels in for it and we filled them both. A man came in a van, and his boys began to carry out the furniture and all the boxes. Mrs. Crisp watched from her doorway. Mrs. Grimshaw stood on the curb arm in arm with Aunt Lucy, holding the cat. I buried me three sisters and me three brother-in-laws and me own husband, she said, but I never thought I'd bury your mam. I never dreamt your mam would go before me. Never in all the world.

On the ride back to Oldham Aunt Lucy's tears stopped dripping by Failsworth and she set herself the job of cheering us up. She turned around and patted my leg. All right, then, love?

I'm fine, Aunt Lucy.

My own girls wouldn't of done *half* as well with their nana as you did. Would you, girls? Lois and Madeleine gave her thin smiles. Well, it's true, I'm afraid, said Aunt Lucy. You would of been a dead loss, both of you, whingeing about missing your friends, and wanting to take the coach home every second day to see them. Lily was a real brick, not a word of a complaint. Although when you first come, love, I have to say I wondered. What a silent little thing you was when you first come. *Heavens*, I said, *what have we got ourselves into!* Didn't I, Stanley? *What have we got ourselves into?* I said.

What *had* they got themselves into? There I was with my trunk in their spare room, a big, healthy girl with an appetite for pork roast, apples, and bread and butter with brown sugar, bereft of any ambition she could openly admit to, scandalously ignorant of social niceties, as well as of Kepler, Ferdinand and Isabella, and the wave of Fascism creeping darkly across Europe. (War? I'd said to Madeleine after the New Year's party. Between who?) An eager, self-conscious young woman with a savage battle between God and his enemy ready to flare up at any moment in her heart, less than a shilling to her name, holes in her stockings and chilblains on her toes, dreading the moment someone would say, *When will you be going back to Canada, then, Lily?*

For the time being we had the task of getting Nan's things

sorted out and sold, and as Madeleine was still in school for almost a month and Lois had her exams, Aunt Lucy and I did it. On dry days we carried boxes out to the flagstones in the garden and set about cleaning. *Set not your affection on things of this earth, where moths and rust do corrupt and where thieves break through and steal*, that's what I'd always been taught, but really it was the *things* that lasted, Nan's smiling china terrier with its clumps of china hair outlined by a glaze of dirt, the silk pansies they gave her at the factory the day before her wedding, turned brown with age. The biscuit tin full of hair curlers with her hairnet stuffed on top, strands of pale hair tangled through it. It was all still here, but she was gone.

Everyone must take a memento, Aunt Lucy said, standing in the midst of it all with a scarf tied over her hair. For herself she took the photographs. For George she picked up a blanket, because it was almost new and his dormitory at the university was so cold. Madeleine wrinkled up her nose and took the china terrier. I took the Barr Colony pamphlet, of course, and things I thought my father might remember: the biscuit tin from the kitchen and the milk pitcher that Nan'd said was a wedding present. All the time I worked I thought of George, thought there must be something that would please him more than a cheap new blanket. Then in one of the boxes I came across our granddad's hook with its aluminum stump and leather strap, lying among his folded clothes like part of a pirate costume. I knew better than to ask. With my heart racing at my own daring, I rolled it in a towel and smuggled it up to my trunk.

Uncle Hugh came down from Liverpool and he and Aunt Lucy went to the solicitor's. Eighty pounds to each of you, Aunt Lucy said when she came home. Everyone was amazed at what you can put aside by asking the butcher for bones and buying your smalls at the open market. I sat at the dining-room table in one of Lois's old jumpers, afraid to meet Aunt

Lucy's eyes now that I had the money to buy my passage home. Then she put a hand on my shoulder. I'll write to your dad, love, she said. And we'll see what's to be done.

In July a letter came from my dad to me, saying, *Your Aunt Lucy asked if you would like to stay in Oldham and go to school with Madeleine. The money from your nana and granddad will pay for your uniform and books and keep you in pocket money. We know you will help out to pay for your board, you've always been a good worker.* Although I had not dared to pray for this to happen, I did pray then. I went outside and looked out over Oldham Edge and said a two-word prayer: thank you.

And so I was set the task of discovering how to live with a new family. They made no efforts to explain themselves (because of course everyone was the same, and when I wasn't the same they turned their eyes tactfully away). Manners, I had to learn. And the art of conversation. And tenderness. Aunt Lucy would sit on the bed brushing Lois's hair, chatting all the while, and then reach for me. (How were my mother and I with each other? I couldn't recall, those times were blank.)

That summer George was off in Dorset with his professor, Dr. Acworth — off *digging*, as they put it, at Charmouth, on the sea. (There's a tip off Middleton Road, said Uncle Stanley. If he's that desperate to dig.) Six or eight times a day I walked by his open doorway. I was allowed to go in; one of our chores (which Lois and Madeleine loathed) was to run a feather duster over his shelves. I stood in his room and thought of him sinking into waxy dreams in that bed, his long legs folded like a grasshopper's. Cautiously I opened cupboards and drawers, but most of his private things were gone. It was only on the open shelves that you could see George, and I stood and looked hungrily at the junk piled there, trying to guess what George would have to say about everything, the starfish that would not be just a starfish, the arrows with some sort of skin on them, the etching of a gigantic flea, all hairy legs and tiny praying head.

Meanwhile Lois was busy. When her exams were over she took a job on High Street as a telephonist — she'd had enough of school for the moment. She spent her pay on having her hair done, she bought smart new frocks and scented hand cream, she grew more beautiful by the day. She scarcely spoke to me. I didn't take this as a personal slight: she was like an athlete training to be the fastest runner in the world, her focus was absolute. The object of this unswerving ambition was *Archie*, an ordinary young man with a smile that hinted of nothing beyond it. Jolly good, he said, and A wee bit nippy out. But he drove a little green roadster, he had the Greek symbol of a posh school woven into his tie and apparently he had better vowels than the rest of them. At times I thought Lois was having us all on, but she gave no sign of this.

All through August, Aunt Lucy made Madeleine sit with me in the afternoons and go through her Third Form textbooks: algebra, geometry, French, English grammar. When it got close to September she went to see the headmaster at Ward Street Grammar School, and then I was taken to the school to be tested, in through the massive central doors of a red-brick building. Someone called a proctor, an extraordinarily tall girl with glasses that magnified one eye beyond the size of the other, took me into an empty classroom. You may sit where you fancy, she said, as though this was a significant concession, and handed me a booklet of foolscap and a slate on which was printed:

Discuss the British Empire's contribution to world civilization through her colonies.

Then she left and closed the door behind her. This question had been generously designed for me, with an eye to the debates that must take place nightly at tea all over the colonies. It required me to write about Canada, a notion that had become more and more flimsy as the months went by. After the first day, my Sheffield relatives had never asked, and home had shrunk in my mind to a miniature farm built for children, or a tiny sepia photograph in a leaflet from the Ministry of Agriculture. I stared at the question on the slate and a drift of debris floated into the examination room (chicken droppings lying like manna in the dust, the flat, wrinkled stream of cream shooting out from the spout of the cream separator. The image of my mother flinging potato peelings from an enamel basin into the pigpen. The pig with its two front feet in the trough, munching on something hideous, the red afterbirth of a calf). All of it too squalid to conjure up in words.

I sat wretchedly fixed on the word *colonies* for a long time and finally I dipped my pen into the bottle of ink Madeleine had lent me and began to write:

> *Near my home in Canada is a Hutterite colony,*
> *where we take our oats to be milled. Everyone in*
> *this colony dresses the same, mainly in black, and*
> *the women wear head scarves of dotted fabric.*

But I knew as I wrote that my admission into Ward Street Grammar School was doomed with this tack. I struggled to recall a map in the Grade Eight history text at the Nebo School — the head of Queen Victoria floating off the coast of England, with black arrows reaching like octopus legs from her neck to various corners of the Empire. Afraid to cross out what I'd written, I attempted a segue:

*The colonists who came from England to the
Canadian prairies in 1903 were not so sensibly
dressed for the perils that lay ahead.*

I was still on the follies of the Barr Colonists when the tall girl came back and asked me to surrender my booklet and led me from the room.

Why they accepted me into the Fourth Form I never understood. I can only assume that the master who read my essay was some sort of anarchist. Whatever the reason, Ward Street Grammar School, with its polished wood floors and high windows, with its gowned masters and piles of poetry books bound in red cloth like hymnals, was one of those extravagant gifts life gives you sometimes, the first token of which (the harbinger of joys to come, I wanted to call it as I read *Macbeth* the first week) was the uniform, radiating so much promise simply hanging from a hook in Aunt Lucy's spare room that even now when I stand in a dry goods store and finger a bolt of merino in that particular shade of dark blue, I feel a throb of pleasure move down the back of my legs.

5

Leon Blum? said George. Who's the bloke who wrote you this?

Just a friend, I said. A boy from Montreal. Our banker's son.

Lily has a beau, said Lois. She's a dark horse, that girl. She's been here more than a year and this is the first we've heard of him.

He's not my beau, I said. I might have wanted Lois and Madeleine to believe that he was, but not George.

Lily's friend is a Marxist, said George, looking up from the letter. That's what this is all about, and shame on you lot for your ignorance.

He's a *banker's* son, said Madeleine. He won't be a Marxist.

Most Marxists *are* bankers' sons, said George. That, or landless gentry.

What are you doing? I cried, for he had pulled a little notebook out of his pocket and was beginning to copy Russell's address off the envelope.

I just want to see if any of the lads here know him. There's a Marxist group meets in Bardsley's. In the bookshop. Monty's been.

How could they possibly know him, all the way over here? cried Lois. Oh, you are a git.

He's going to write to him, said Madeleine. That's why he's copying the address. Lily, stop him. He's going to take your boyfriend on as one of his pen pals.

Don't, I said to George, and put out my hand for the letter. George scribbled fast and then popped his notebook into a pocket and folded up the letter and gave it back. Don't write to him, I said.

It's nothing to do with you if I do, he said.

It's everything to do with her, you cretin, cried Lois. Madeleine grabbed him and I helped her and we pulled him down onto the floor. I could smell his scalp and his shirt, which was not as fresh as it might had been. While he writhed on the carpet we took the notebook from his pocket and ripped the address out of it.

George was home for his autumn half-term (which was the week after ours) and the whole house woke up. Even when he just sat in the parlour reading, he had the knack of turning everyone into more of what they naturally were — he refined their essence, you might say, making Uncle Stanley darker and more terse, filling Madeleine with gentle mischief, turning Aunt Lucy into an exact younger version of her mother, all songs and sighs. Or maybe it was just me he changed: he turned me into someone who breathed through her pores, who watched. Watched him especially. Standing in the front hall fiddling with the strap of my satchel, I watched him sunk in a parlour chair reading, irritation with the argument of his book playing across his pale face, his middle finger pushing his glasses up the bridge of his nose.

On Saturday night Archie came to pick Lois up and carry her away in his little roadster, and the rest of us — Madeleine, George, George's friend Monty, Jenny from next door and me — went to the pictures on Horsedge Street. Afterwards we tried to go into the Hartford Arms, and the proprietor called across the bar, Oy! Come back when those lasses are grown, so then we walked back home and George picked up two big bottles of Uncle Stanley's stout and we went out through the garden and onto Oldham Edge, where we passed the bottles of sour and yeasty stout back and forth. Below us lay the tangled yellow-green strands of the streets of Oldham, and the dark bulk of the mill where Uncle Stanley worked, looming like a parliament over the town.

It's *ever* so bright here compared to home, I said, hearing how English I sounded.

Oh, it was dark here once, said George. Back when hyenas roamed the moors.

Hyenas? I laughed.

He started to answer but Monty was beside me and I couldn't hear him for Monty growling and pretending to pounce on my neck.

Leave Lily be, Jenny cried. She flung her arm around my shoulders, and her hip bumped against mine. She lifted up her voice and sang out over the hills,

> *A north country maid up to London had strayed*
> *Although with her nature it did not agree.*
> *So she wept and she sighed and bitterly she cried,*
> *How I wish once again in the North I could be.*

Up to London? I asked. Instead of answering she launched into the refrain. *For the oak and the ash and the bonny ivy tree* . . . And while she sent the words out over the Edge in her raw, melancholy voice, we followed the wandering brow of the hill away from the town. It had been a cloudy day, and soon the sky was dark above us, and the lights of Oldham just a pool twinkling distantly below, the stars fallen into the valley, the constellations of the street lights disintegrating.

Off somewhere on the dark slopes sheep bells clanged. The moor was full of movement and shadows, a darkness made up of things, not the absence of things that made up the bare darkness of the prairies. My dad would know this. He must have walked like this when he was young, with stout or cider singing in his head, not exactly here maybe, but on paths very like it through the rough gorse. A north country lad. They think of themselves as *northerners*, I marvelled.

Jenny's song trailed off. We tramped on in single file, no one talking or laughing now. Oldham had entirely fallen away — we were trekking through a vast wilderness, we would come soon to the end of the footpaths and the end of man-made light. We'd been brought together with no common language but with a brave common purpose, with George as our leader. He walked nimbly through the gorse, his head bent like a crane's. He took us up and down along the Edge, holding back bushes to let us pass through. I'd managed to shake Monty off and I fell in behind George, and where the path rose steeply, he turned to take my hand. His fingers were thin and cold, they telegraphed urgency. I scrambled after him; light and joyous and sure-footed. *Oh, the oak and the ash and the bonny ivy tree*, I sang in my heart as the fog gathered in my hair.

I would happily have followed George until dawn, but Madeleine said she was cold and so we turned back. Crossing the garden on the way in, I felt a hand take me by the wrist. Don't go in, George mouthed, his lips barely moving. While Madeleine walked Jenny to her door and Monty rolled a last cigarette, I stood against the shed and waited, cradling my arms against the cold, feeling my hand burning with the imprint of his hand out on the path (his hand that had slid up my leg at the New Year's party). I stood trying to contain my heart thudding painfully in my chest, seized by the realization that love (which had sent me to this dark moor) was about to claim me at last.

We stepped into the potting shed, and I ran my fingers through my damp hair. George fumbled around and a match flared up. He was lighting the lantern, and so I saw that it was a declaration I was about to receive, not a kiss. He set the lantern on the ledge beside the skull and we stood facing each other, blinking in the sudden light.

I want to show you something, he said. He reached for a brown paper bag lying on the workbench and fished something out of it. Here, he said. Look at this.

The stone he pressed into my hand was oblong and black. I was so taken aback that I almost dropped it.

It's *dung*, he said. Fossilized hyena dung, from the caves at Kirkdale. That's in Yorkshire, not far from here. They found the bones of five hundred hyenas in those caves! And the remains of lynx and lions and bears. Can you believe it?

It's a stone, I said, setting it on the workbench. Everything was a little distant, as if I were looking through a wash of water.

Well, that's because it's fossilized, he said, picking it back up and bobbing it in his hand. It's coprolite. If you cross-sectioned it you'd find bone splinters inside — bones of all the animals the hyena was eating.

It looks like an ordinary stone to me, I said. My heart had slowed its pounding.

Well, yes, he said. He eyed me warmly. The fossils made it hard for people to classify things. Early on, I mean. Everything was stone. They were finding stone fish in the rocks. And so they didn't have a clear line between what was organic and what was mineral.

Maybe there is no line, I said. Rock can grow.

He bent down from his height, his face suffused with thought. Okay, yes, he said. Stalactites, I suppose. Or coral. A lot of people think coral is rock.

Rock can grow in your body, I said, thinking of Mrs. Feazel. Gallstones.

Yes! he cried. Gallstones! He laughed, he was delighted by the thought of gallstones. Gesner classified gallstones as gems — like pearls. Conrad Gesner — you haven't heard of him? He set out to classify everything — stones, shells, fossils, animals. This was in the sixteenth century. But then he died in the plague. In Zurich. So just to amuse myself, I'm working on the index for his encyclopedia. Look, these were his categories. He pulled a folder stuffed with papers off the shelf and opened it. On the top sheet was a list of headings:

On Stones Resembling Aquatic Animals.
On Objects Resembling Human Artefacts.
On Fossils Reflecting the Qualities of the Heavens.

And, simply: *Problematica.*

The light from the lantern wobbled and I bent closer over his chart. Starfish, I said, recalling the specimen on the shelf in his room. How did he classify starfish?

I seemed to be participating in this discussion, but really I was not, for the worm of romance had entered my heart.

So it wasn't George's hand that crept onto my thigh when we were all fishes pressed together by the shed. In a flash I discarded the hand, tossed it out of my heart with a shudder. But the night we walked on Oldham Edge was as memorable as if I'd been given the kiss I longed for. I had tasted romantic hope, and then been thwarted. And this thwarting, this wound to my vanity (a tiny wound, after all, for I hadn't let on what I was thinking), had a more potent effect on me than a kiss would have had, hardened my resolve to make of George what I wanted him to be.

I moved that night into a period of my life where every single new thought led swiftly back to George. I was with his family — every encounter was a chance to learn more about George. I'd sit on my bed reading and Uncle Stanley would appear in my doorway as if he'd stepped off a colour plate from a military history — it was Legion night, he had his puttees wound round his legs. He had my shoes in his hand and thrust them at me. I'd left them in the downstairs hall, apparently. Apparently that wasn't allowed. I got up and took them from him and he turned and walked heavily back down the stairs without a word. From my bedroom door I watched the crease in the back of his neck disappear around the landing, watched him with interest. How had a man like Uncle Stanley ever come to raise a boy like George?

※

My Uncle Stanley fought in the Great War and was wounded at the Somme. He was in a hospital in France for a long time. It was just a flesh wound but it turned septic, and finally they brought him back to England. By then Aunt Lucy had left the linen shop and trained as a nurse, and she was working at the military hospital in Manchester. When they brought him in she was in the storage cupboard with a friend, bent over a letter a soldier had written to them both, and the Sister had to call for five minutes before she heard her and came out with her rosy face all covered with apologies.

Stanley Sheffield was handsome and well spoken, but there was something peevish about him. Aunt Lucy never saw this as who he was. She put it down to the misery he was in, the fleas he had brought with him from France and the smell of putrefaction rising from his bandages. The nurses were used to peevishness and just jollied the boys along. Shortly after he came to the hospital the papers were full of talk of a negotiated peace, and he asked her for help in getting what he needed to write a letter, and then had her post it to both the *Manchester Guardian* and the *Times* of London. It was a one-sentence letter: *Reading your newspaper today I discover that I have lost the use of my right leg so that Mr. Woodrow Wilson can demonstrate his beneficence to the Huns.* He had not lost the use of his leg, that was just a bit of rhetoric, but he did fight the infection for months and months before the wound finally healed over. When the infection went away and the petulance stayed, my Aunt Lucy said the war had changed him. Why would a tall, dark-haired, well-educated young man from a good family turn that sort of face to the world otherwise?

He was an only child, raised in Birmingham, the son of an actuary. He said *hospital* and *bottle* properly, so you had to appreciate the independent good sense he showed in marrying the daughter of a toll keeper. But there was a diffidence in Aunt Lucy that might have made him think he could reshape her. If so, I think he must have been thwarted: her diffidence was not a lack of definition, it was who she was. She was artless and unthinkingly kind. Why she was drawn to him, that's another matter. By then she was twenty-four. With so many of the boys gone, it must have been like playing musical chairs, you grabbed the one nearest you and were glad of it, especially when the one nearest turned out to be a handsome man with a bit of money. They were married soon after Stanley got out of the hospital, even though the war was still on. Stanley thought he would go back to France, but that's not where they sent him. They assigned him to Lyndhurst as a drill master for the wretched boys and middle-aged men they were sending up by then.

After the armistice he took his discharge, and his uncle helped him get a place as an overseer at the mill in Oldham. Oldham was a step up for Aunt Lucy, a mill town but a more vigorous one than Salford, with a bustling market. Far enough away to feel she had her own new life and close enough that she could take her kiddies to see their grandparents. She was ready for that, so ready that she never had the nuisance of a monthly period as a newlywed. But she lost that baby in the third month, and after that, three years went by with (as Aunt Lucy put it) no sign of nothing. She'd escaped Nettie Nesbitt's fate, but now she feared the Shillingfords', bending politely over other people's prams in the street, eating Christmas dinners with your neighbours because you had no one around your own table, growing thinner year by year instead of stouter.

Then one morning after Stanley had left for work, a knock came at the front door. It was the vicar and his wife. The wife was holding a wee baby wrapped up in a towel. It was tiny, just born, and its face was as red as a brick. Lucy invited them in and put the kettle on, and the vicar told her that the baby had been born the night before to a local girl. Aunt Lucy asked who the mother was. She's a girl from a good family, the vicar said, just a little errant in her ways. Maybe we'll leave it at that, he said. The baby was fussing then, and the vicar's wife asked Lucy if she wanted to hold him. Lucy put her finger to his mouth and he started to suckle it. And so she said she would keep him until Stanley came home from work and then they would make up their minds. There was a woman on the lane with a baby, and when the vicar and his wife had gone she went straightaway to borrow what she called a "bokkle" so she could feed him properly. She'd told the vicar she would have to ask Stanley, but by the time Stanley got home, she was that stuck on the little flamer that Stanley didn't have much of a say in the matter. It still broke Aunt Lucy's heart to remember George with his thin little hands trembling in the air, making silent shapes with his mouth, and to think of the girl walking shakily down the street at dawn with her baby wrapped in a towel to hand him over to a stranger. People can say what they want about a girl like that, said Aunt Lucy, but it takes a lot of pluck.

She didn't drink *lye*, I said. She could have killed herself before she got too far along. I was sitting at the table eating a poached egg.

Aunt Lucy looked at me, startled. Oh, lovie, there's no need for that, she said. She stopped as if to catch her breath and regarded me, troubled. That girl didn't just leave her baby on the steps of the orphanage, the way some do, she said finally. That's what always struck me. She cared enough to knock on the vicar's door, and she told the vicar that the baby was to be named George.

✠

It was breakfast when Aunt Lucy told me about this, after George and Monty had gone off on a ramble. She'd been making scones and she'd ground to a halt once she launched into the story of George. She reached for the teapot and poured herself the half-cup stewing in the bottom.

That'll be cold, I said, getting up. I'll put the kettle on.

I was that stuck on the little flamer that your Uncle Stanley didn't have much say in the matter, she said again. Not that he doesn't care for him like a son, she added vaguely. He cares for George like his own son, does your Uncle Stanley.

Do you know why the vicar brought him to *you?* I asked.

She stood up then and turned the dough out onto the table. Oh, it's a small parish. Everyone knew I wanted a baby, I was crazy about babies. And they couldn't keep him, the vicar's wife was sick. She had a growth. Aunt Lucy touched her floury fingers to her left breast. She died before the year was out.

I let a little minute pass. Then I asked, Did George always know?

If I'd had my way, he wouldn't know to this day! Aunt Lucy said. She patted the dough into a huge disc. But Stanley was all for telling him, and one day when he was taking him back to St. Michael's he did tell him. And then he come in the door

194

that night and says, *Well, I've told him.* I was that vexed with your uncle, I was fit to be tied! And I couldn't see the poor lad then till he come home at half-holiday, and I thought that was hard. But by the time he come home he was just playing the fool like always. You know the way our George is.

She reached a glass down from the shelf and began to press it into the dough. Maybe it's for the better. It's a miracle he hadn't heard it before from someone in the town, there are always those who love to tattle.

※

In literature we read "Pied Beauty." *Glory be to God for dappled things* — . It was a list of all patchy and freckled and variegated things: the hide of a cow, a mottled sky. I pulled a sheet out of my notebook and began to copy the poem, raising an absorbed face now and then to where Mr. Ballard paced at the side of the room with an unlit cigarette in his fingers, droning on and on about Gerard Manley Hopkins's attitude to the Catholic Church. *Rose-moles all in stipple upon trout that swim,* I wrote, *Fresh-firecoal chestnut-falls; finches' wings.* I would take it to George. It was a category for Conrad Gesner: *On Dappled Things.*

Then the class was over and I slipped the page into my notebook and moved with the crowd to the refectory. I didn't wait for Madeleine, I was too hungry. I squeezed into the middle of a long table, pulled out my sandwich and began to eat, and then to gag on a piece of paper in my sandwich. I pulled it furtively out of my mouth and scraped the liver sausage off with a bread crust. The paper was transparent with grease, but I could make out two pencil images: a robed woman (a *figurehead*, it looked like, from a ship) and a clock reading four o'clock. Then I understood: it was not a figurehead at all, but the statue that stood up on the ridgepole of the Public Library on Union Street, tipping ever so slightly towards the street. *Don't go*, something inside me said, but I knew I would go. Madeleine was not in the corridor after class, but Jenny was. Will you stop in and tell Aunt Lucy I have to work at the library? I asked. I won't be home for tea.

I set off walking. I could see him when I was still a long way down the street: he was perched on the stone balustrade of the library. His long legs dangled over the edge, as though he were sitting on a bridge looking down into water. I made as though to walk right on past, and he jumped down, staggering a bit, and caught up to me, clamping his hand on the back of my neck and turning me around, steering me back in the direction I had come. We walked half a block up Union Street like that and then he dropped his hand and we walked along quickly and in step, keeping pace for a ways with the trolley car hauling itself up the street, dodging an old woman holding an open umbrella up against the blue sky, dodging a boy on a bicycle.

I was waiting for him to slow down, to turn towards me, to say something in his reedy voice. All I could manage was, Fancy running into you like this, and he smiled one of his sardonic smiles, one that said, *Clever*, and we walked faster and faster. Then we were in the shop district on King Street and I was walking on the inside, nearest the shops. I could see myself in the windows striding along in my blue uniform, my satchel slung over one shoulder, and I was stirred by the glamour of the scene, my long hair lifted by the wind, both of us as tall and slim as we ought to be for such a picture, our figures against the moving automobiles and the ornate doorways on the other side of King Street. And still he didn't talk, and the desire to provoke him rose up in me and what I did when we were almost to the top of the street was whip around a corner into a narrow passageway and press myself against the stone wall. He turned back around to find me — he was almost off-balance — and I reached for him with my free hand. I could feel how thin his waist was, almost nothing to hang on to (I can still picture his startled look as well), and that's when I stretched myself up to his face and kissed him.

I can't say whether he kissed me back or not. I don't know how he reacted after the kiss, because then there was no looking at each other at all. We broke apart and started walking again the way we had come, down King Street and up to the Mumps Bridge, where we stopped and watched the traffic on the motorway beneath and he reached down and picked up a handful of cinders and drizzled them over the railing. Then I pressed myself between him and the railing and turned my face up to his and we kissed again, longer this time, long enough for me to be aware of a figure brushing past us on the sidewalk and the honking of horns on the bridge. Then we turned in the direction of home, and I told myself that I would remember the Mumps Bridge all my life, and thought with excitement about the person brushing past us, imagining how it must have looked to him. We walked more slowly now, along the motorway at first and then up Manchester Street, past the Gardener's Arms, where the sign creaked in the wind as we walked under it, past the Ling Far Chinese Restaurant with its smell of frying shrimp, past the Working Men's Hall. Maybe he had in mind to take me somewhere or show me something (he must have done when he dug my lunch out of the icebox and planted a note in the liver sausage), but I'd showed him what his real plan was. If his silence on our way out was aloof, his silence now was stunned, bashful, gobsmacked.

I'll go in ahead. You wait a while, I said when we were at St. Peter's Church, which was about a five-minute walk from home. I stole a glance at him. He seemed about to say something, his expression was troubled, but before he could, I broke away from him and hurried up the street, just glancing back once to see that he had turned up Clegg Street to walk home the long way. I ran in alone and climbed the stairs and put my book satchel and hat in my room, and then I came down to the kitchen, full of exhilaration, and started peering into crocks and cupboards to find myself some tea.

Tomatoes, I said to Madeleine, who was sitting in the kitchen. How do we get tomatoes at this time of year?

They're hothouse tomatoes, said Madeleine. She had her books spread out on the table. Mother was feeling rich. She pressed the tip of a pencil against her chin. What was Otto von Bismarck's tactic for the unification of Germany? she asked.

George would be the one to ask, I said. Where is George, anyway? I added, bold as brass. I wasn't half as clever as I thought, because if someone had seen us together all I was doing was creating suspicion. But by the time George came down to the kitchen, just as I was slicing a tomato, you would never have dreamt that we had clapped eyes on each other that day. There was no holding my eyes just a second too long, no quick sideways smiles. Lois wandered in and attacked him about the mess in his bedroom, and to provoke her he told her about a debate held at the university on whether women have souls. Then he went off to play chess with Monty. In my bag was the sheet with "Pied Beauty" on it, terribly crumpled. After I crawled into bed it took me a long time to shake the last few hours, a long time to get back to the Mumps Bridge, the traffic rushing by us, and the sensation of his thin, cold lips.

⁂

For all Madeleine's talk about Imogene, George had no experience with girls. This was my impression then and time has borne me out. His only acknowledgement of what had happened was to take me further into the labyrinthine passages of his mind, which in real terms meant allowing me to visit him in the shed. There in the bleak light of a late October afternoon he sat on the stool, inking the lettering onto a diagram of Celtic adze heads, and I examined more of the charts and posters pinned along the wall.

I saw a chart that I took at first for a family tree, expecting to see my own name and those of my cousins on it, but the tiny figure at the top was labelled *Homo sapiens*, and interestingly, a sloth rather than an ape was man's most immediate ancestor. Beside it hung a poster of shells, of their designs and patterns. *E conchis omni*, a large legend read.

It was the motto Erasmus Darwin had painted on the door of his coach, said George.

I looked at him uncertainly. As a general rule I did not dwell on my lack of Latin.

Charles Darwin's grandfather, he said.

I've never heard of him.

I worshipped him for a while, said George. When I was in Fourth Form. I read everything about him and by him. He wrote his science in rhyming verse. In couplets. *Organic life beneath the shoreless waves, was born and nursed in ocean's pearly caves.* That sort of thing. People think evolution came from Charles Darwin, but his grandfather was there long before him. He knew that it happened, he just didn't know how.

George was my cousin, which let me into the shed where the skull grinned on the window ledge, and he was not my cousin, which let me drop my hand carelessly to his shoulder when he sat on a stool at the workbench and run the back of my fingers along his neck. I don't believe in that sort of thing, I said. In Genesis it says that God created the earth in six days.

You're a Methodist, he said, ignoring my hand.

No, I said.

Quaker, he said.

I don't even know what that is.

What then?

We're just Christians.

Well, you must be low church. Evangelical. You accept the Bible as a scientific text?

I guessed I did. I toyed with the bristly hair at the nape of his neck.

Well, the fossil record presents you with a bit of a problem. There is a theory that God planted fossils in the rocks when he created the world. In 4004 BC. October 22, was it? I've seen a Bible with the date in the margin. They figured it out from calculating the genealogies. Back in the sixteenth century.

I said I was glad they'd found a use for the genealogies.

You should read *One Hundred and One Obscenities in the Bible*, George said. It's a book a chap at school showed me. Onan spilling his seed and that sort of thing. It was Bernard Lowe's. He left it in the refectory and it was pinched, otherwise I would borrow it and send it to you.

Then his voice went up a tone. Maybe it's not the thing, in any case, he said, moving out of my reach.

Think how unhinged he was by my touch on the back of his neck, to say something like that!

⚸

After he had gone back to school, a letter came for me from George. No one in the family was at all curious: he was my cousin (and he was, after all, George). And they were right not to suspect, because it was not a love letter, not even really a letter but a list entitled *One Hundred and One Challenges to the Hebraic-Christian Creation Myth*. There were only nine points, but the list ended abruptly at the bottom of the page, to show that George could have kept going. The points were all about the age of the universe and its size, the vestigial vertebrae in the tails of birds, that sort of thing. This was the last one:

200

9. The Second Law of Thermodynamics: everything is sliding towards meaninglessness, randomness, silence and stillness, and this trend is impossible to resist. (Of course, this law can be used to refute evolution as well.)

Standing in the hall with George's letter in my hand I was distracted by the sight of my face in the mirror. Leaning forward to examine a tiny swelling in the middle of my chin, I had a momentary, dizzying glimpse of dark eons of time like the pages of a big book and myself a tiny dot somewhere near the end. My mind slid towards this prospect and then slid away again, slid back to the pimple on my chin and the smell of chips frying in the kitchen, to my garter belt riding annoyingly halfway down my belly, my new hair clip gleaming in the hall mirror. This is not to say I believed the world was created in a week in October 4004 BC. Rather, I accepted without thought that it came into being on June 18, 1920, the day I pried open the door of a cave and launched myself into it.

6

George was a collector of facts, theories, curiosities (both natural and man-made), blueprints, artifacts, small ironies, words. No find took precedence over any other — he disdained the organizing principle. He was a joyful, generous, insane collector, endlessly curious and undiscriminating. He pored over Jenny's box of matchbook covers and David's list of steam-engine numbers with the same avid interest he showed in his own crowded shelves.

Did he *like* me, or was I just that most rare and precious of all resources, an admiring audience? I studied him for evidence of *need*. His voice was a bit shrill in a group, and he had a habit of telling people about thirty percent more on any subject than they wished to know. You could see him monitoring this, trying to find more amusing ways to talk. You could see him offering his eccentricity up to his friends as a joke, pleased with his success when they laughed at him.

But it did seem he had a special regard for me. He seemed to consider me his collaborator. It was my spectacular ignorance that qualified me — I was a savant of the ingenuous question. Everything I said seemed to advance his thinking. I called this love. I have no idea what he called it.

Not that England was the ideal romantic staging ground. England was mildew and the black smell of the Dettol you used to beat it back. It was fog and chilblains and mushy peas and a certain shade of greenish-yellow enamel paint in every room. Signs nailed over public lavatories explaining proper technique with the flushing chain. It was all about marshalling resources for the coming storm. My Aunt Lucy joined the Women's Voluntary Service and spent hours of every day sewing cotton bags with drawstrings that soldiers could use to keep their things together and tidy while they lay wounded in the hospital. Her friend Nettie Nesbitt came over one day and saw the bags. Nettie Nesbitt was a seamstress, she made her living sewing. I know you mean well, love, she said to Aunt Lucy, but with all respect, these won't do. She was inspecting the bags, tossing the ones with poorly executed corners into a pile. Aunt Lucy seemed to see the logic in this and set to work picking the seams out while Nettie Nesbitt sewed them up again, biting loose threads off with her big, crumbling teeth. Day and night they sat in the parlour, where pink roses climbed up a brown wallpaper, working on those bags, *planning* for a time when lads would need something to keep their boots in, after their legs were blown off. I found it strangely cold-blooded. And dangerous, the way everyone was intent on imagining themselves into a war.

From Durham George sent me sketches of the Norman cathedral. From Charmouth he sent me sketches of the fossils he was finding, his room at Mrs. Slater's lodging house, Cornish Ellen who served their tea. He wrote to me almost every week, and he wrote to Russell Bates. One of his letters had this PS: *Russell says hello!* He never would tell me how he got the address. Likely he just remembered it, he'd put it into one of the overstuffed drawers of that brain of his. I was responsible for bringing them together and I could only assume I was at the heart of their correspondence. And I don't put this all down to conceit. They had a code name for me. It was *Phoebe*, a rustic maiden in Shakespeare.

The fact remains that I had the confidence to write to George but not to Russell Bates. I modelled my letters after George's. I wrote out the passage that drew me to Richard III (*Sent before my time into this breathing world, scarce half made up*). I wrote him little vignettes and even sketches of the people at school, my literature master, who chewed on the sleeve of his robe when seized by thought, the clever Rutledge sisters. Everything I wrote alluded to a significant moment in my life: what I felt when Mr. Ballard read out of *Middlemarch*: *Miss Brooks had that kind of beauty which seems to be thrown into relief by poor dress*, looking directly at me as he read it (although of course he had seen me only in my uniform). Or how I felt sitting alone in the study hall when the Rutledge sisters came in, how I counted three beats so that I would produce a smile at precisely the right moment, the way they walked right on past without glancing at me.

I was at Ward Street Grammar School for two years before the war started, and I arrange those years in my mind by George's visits home, by his three visits. Christmas of 1937 he didn't come home: he accepted an invitation to the Derbyshire estate of a classmate Aunt Lucy described as countrified. Either I was of no importance whatsoever to him, or I was so important that he was too shy to come home. It was spring before I saw him again.

April 1938
For three months in the spring our ages lined up: George was 19, Lois was 18, I was 17, Madeleine was 16.

Madeleine and I were still in school when George's term ended. He came home for a week before he went off to Dorset.

He was taller and thinner than I remembered and (I suppose it must be said) not quite as handsome, not really handsome at all. His hands were shockingly chapped and so were his lips. The inside of his shirt collar was a waxy yellow. We went to the pictures the first night with his old gang, and I could not connect the George in my mind to this gangly boy throwing a laugh back over his shoulder. But I knew that would not stop me. Something in me had decided on him, and I was not going to be put off by details.

The next day, Sunday, we went out walking on our own. He wore his tramping outfit, tweed knee britches and long socks. He talked the whole time about Charmouth. He'd brought me a belemnite. It was a fossil, a smooth cylinder pointed at one end, like an oversized bullet. It was a warm chestnut brown.

They used to find them all over, he said, just lying on the ground. People called them thunderbolts. They thought they marked the spot where lightning entered the earth. People kept belemnites in their houses to protect themselves from lightning.

Because lightning never strikes twice? I asked.

So they hoped, said George. I slipped the belemnite into my pocket and fingered its polished length as we walked.

By the end of that walk, George was slouching beside me talking in my ear. In spite of his height his natural posture seemed to be with his chin almost on my shoulder. After tea I went to his room and sat on his bed and we talked some more.

You two have become such pals, said Aunt Lucy when I came downstairs. She didn't look directly at me.

I had no intention of kissing George again: any overture had to come from him. But when three days of that precious week had gone by without him so much as taking my hand, I took his while we walked. Then I stopped walking and leaned against a tree and looked up at him through my lashes, and finally he had no choice but to bend and kiss me, something we accomplished with greater skill than we had shown previously. No one had taught me this sort of behaviour, except possibly Bette Davis. And then we walked home, past the piano factory and the crockery works with broken crockery embedded in the front pavement, past dripping hedges — our conversation stopped in its tracks, awkwardness settling onto our shoulders with the evening mist.

At tea the next night Aunt Lucy said, I think we should put our two schoolgirls together. Lois is working all hours, it's hard for her to share. Let's move Lily while we have George here to help carry things.

So I became Madeleine's roommate, and so I realized that Aunt Lucy knew. I bent my guilty face over my trunk and dragged it down the hall to the girls' room, and Lois carried her clothes on hangers over her arm to the spare room. Madeleine was pleased and Lois was thrilled, but I wanted to go to Aunt Lucy and cry, *I'm sorry, I'll behave, I'll behave.*

Christmas 1938
The whiff of gunpowder rising from paper crackers.

Aunt Lucy saying, I thought we might have a goose this year, but when I saw the price of them . . .

Polished green holly lying on the mantel on its thorny points.

Nettie Nesbitt sitting herself down at the table and holding the blade of a silver knife up like a mirror to check her lipstick.

Me in a new ivory blouse with my hair twisted into a French roll. Uncle Stanley bending over to wind up the gramophone and taking me by the waist as "The Blue Danube" started up, leading me deftly across the parlour towards George and then right on by, saying into my ear, You stay away from that lad.

That lad's nowt but a brain on a stick. You'll waltz like a washing-machine agitator if you let him teach you.

A long hike with George, who stopped on the edge of an open field near Rochdale to set his compass on a rock. You won't see compasses like this much longer, he said. They're busy putting compasses into cigarette lighters and tunic buttons. The thought of war makes inventors very happy.

I've never really grasped the point of a compass, I said.

Well, no, you wouldn't have, would you. It's behind the crystal.

I grabbed his hand, I tried to twist his arm behind his back. We walked along the edge of a plowed field that tipped slowly into a gully, where trees stood with their trunks in mist, as though they grew out of air.

Changeling, I said in bed that night. I keep wanting to call George a changeling. But I guess that's the opposite of what he is. In a way a foundling is the opposite of a changeling.

Why do you keep going on about it? cried Madeleine. You talked about it last night at tea. How do you think that makes Mother feel? He's just our brother. She rolled furiously over in her bed.

I'm sorry, I said. You're right, it was really stupid. I am sorry.

I rolled over myself, pressing my hot face into the pillow. I was too tired to sleep. We'd walked so long that day that when I closed my eyes I saw stubble dusted with snow. I saw the poplar bush we went into, a bush just like home, although the slender trunks were green with the moss that covered everything like thin green paint.

When Madeleine's breath deepened I sat up in bed, propped on my pillow. At home there was real snow, and on the kitchen table the picked-over carcass of a hen from the chicken coop, killed and plucked and cleaned the day before, and instead of me at the table, my brother's new girlfriend: Betty Stalling with her white-blonde hair. I looked sleepily at the dark shapes on my bedside table: my gifts. Books, and a hairbrush like Lois's lying loosely in gilt paper. Maybe they'd have had gifts at home as well, they got a crop off in the fall. Maybe my dad would be wearing a warm new flannel shirt. They'd have been to church. There was so much snow — maybe they took the cutter. When I was little I always longed to ride in the cutter. I could see them in it, Mother and Dad in the back, sitting with a quilt over their laps, my mother holding her hat on with a mittened hand. Betty and Phillip in front. All their faces are calm, expectant. Phillip has the reins and they dash across the field, leaving two clean lines carved behind them. It's King and Dolly pulling the cutter. The sky is filled with snow, big ornate flakes hanging motionless in the air, and on the clouds above them Jesus levitates, wearing a frock coat like Isaac Barr.

May 1939

I had been in England almost three years and I had never been to Blackpool, so in the spring of 1939 Aunt Lucy took Madeleine, Jenny and me to Blackpool for our term holiday, and George, whose term had just ended, came out to meet us, bringing his friend Monty, the one Uncle Stanley called his Bolshie mate.

The spring of 1939. Of course, now when you hear that phrase it has a particular meaning, and even at the time it did not feel like an ordinary spring. In March we heard on the wireless that Hitler had annexed Czechoslovakia, and then in April the Lords debated conscription in the house, and in the end they voted to conscript twenty-year-olds. Within a week there was a poster in the post office: *WE NEED THE 1919s*. As far as anyone knew, George was born on January 4, 1919 (that's what they'd always put down as his birthday), so it felt like hard luck. Although if George had a birth certificate, no one knew where it was. Aunt Lucy cried when she heard the news.

What chance does he have if they take him right at the beginning? she said.

When I wrote I asked George if he was afraid. He wrote back that he did not believe there would be a war. He believed that England and France would make a pact with Russia so that Russia could help to hold Poland against the Germans. This would happen before the summer was out, he said, and the conscription notice would be cancelled. He told me that George Bernard Shaw was of this opinion, and that, by the way, so was Russell Bates. And so I believed him, and felt above everyone's constant nattering about the war, and thought just about our holiday as we clacked along in the train past fields where black-faced sheep lay facing all in the same direction the way cattle will, and white gulls stood in the fields facing east as well like some species of domestic fowl. The train ran under dripping bridges with ferns growing on the ledges and through tunnels built of brick, not carved through stone as in Canada. As we approached Blackpool Aunt Lucy offered sixpence to the first to see Blackpool tower, the way she'd always done when the kiddies were young, and Madeleine won because she knew where to look.

This was Blackpool, the mill worker's dream: a red-brick town of terraced houses just like every other. Except that the moss on the rooftops was mustard-coloured and dribbled over with white gull droppings. And the hydrangeas tumbling over the walls (last year's rusty hydrangeas) were huge, as big as Nan's tousled head and about the same colour. It was the sea air that did it, and the sea air that brought people out by the hundreds to have a photograph taken on the beach when it was far too cold to bathe, sticking their heads through an oval hole in a propped-up painting of a Victorian bathing costume. Hotels lined the waterfront, mile after mile, but we stayed in lodgings with a lady they had stayed with before. The wind blew without pause and sand was carried all the way up to our street, two blocks up from the sea, where it lay like drifts of brown sugar on the pavement.

In the afternoon Aunt Lucy drank tea with the landlady, and we girls went down to the waterfront and took our shoes off and walked out onto the sand. The tide was out and we walked a long way, holding our skirts and watching the water seep into our footprints. The water in the tidal pools was warm with sun, and the wet sand shone like satin. That sparkling blue strip on the horizon was the grey sea I had seen from the deck of the *Franconia*.

Oh, I love the sea, I said with a sudden change of heart.

Huh, said Jenny. Good thing you can't see what's in that water. There's Germans right there. Right under that there water in their U-boats. Sally Higgins was dancing on Central Pier at high tide and she and her mates all seen a periscope sticking up watching them.

Oy, you out there, called Madeleine, lifting her skirt and flashing her knickers to the sea.

When we turned back, two boys were coming towards us across the sand, knapsacks slung over their shoulders, and a voice called, Die schönen Frauen mit der rosy cheeks! It was George and Monty. Madeleine ran to meet George.

Did you get it yet? she asked, meaning his conscription notice.

Nein, he said. Nicht. Nussing.

Monty came up to Jenny and me and kissed us both in an elaborate, European way, crying, Wonderbar, wonderbar! *That 'un can see through a keyhole with both eyes*, was what Uncle Stanley said about Monty, not just as an ordinary, general insult (which it was, in Oldham) but because his eyes were set so close to the bridge of his nose. But I liked Monty for his eager woodpecker face, and thought he liked me. Die schönen Frauen haben salt on zer lippen, Dr. Goebbels, he said when George came up.

So then George kissed us too, Jenny first, and then me. Ja, Herr Goering, sie schmecken vom Salz, he said. Sie schmecken wonderbar.

We walked back up to the boardwalk and wiped our feet with our handkerchiefs before we put our shoes on, and Jenny took the rubber sealer rings she had slipped over her sleeves and stretched them back onto her feet to keep her slippers on. The boys kept up their German foolishness all the way back to the lodging house, and Jenny held on to the strap of Monty's knapsack and sang as we walked. When we crowded into the hall we found Aunt Lucy still sitting in the parlour with the landlady. Look what the cat dragged in, she said, pulling George down to kiss him. You're coming home with us, aren't you, love?

Nein, he said. I can't. Dr. Acworth needs me in Charmouth by Tuesday.

He dropped his knapsack by her chair. Your dad wants a word with you, Aunt Lucy said.

He ignored this. Have we missed tea? he asked. I'm famished.

When we arrived back in Oldham without George, and Aunt Lucy reported that he'd gone to Dorset to wait for his conscription notice, Uncle Stanley kicked at a dining-room chair and knocked it over. The barmy little git, he shouted. He's not got the brains he was born with.

Bloomin' heck, Stanley, said Aunt Lucy, picking up the chair.

Maybe there won't be a war after all, said Madeleine.

We can always hope, said Aunt Lucy. We can always pray. That's all we can do, really, is pray that the good Lord won't put us through that again. Sit down, all of you. Your tea's growing cold.

Our tea — head cheese and barm cakes — lay already cold and pallid on our plates.

Maybe we'll make a pact with Russia, I said, pulling out my chair. Russia could move into Poland and help to hold it.

Oh, *aye*! said Uncle Stanley. That would be clever. Let's put a fox in the henhouse to guard the chickens. Who's put that in your head? George and that Bolshie mate of his?

No, I said hotly.

You know what a Communist is, don't you?

Yes, Uncle Stanley, I do, I said, for I knew what was coming. But he leaned over the table anyway and gave me his verse about the fellow with yearnings for equal division of unequal earnings, and then went on to tell us about the organizer at the mill who went to Tenerife on everyone's union dues.

What Uncle Stanley wanted was for George to join up before his notice came so he could join the RAF: it was the future of the armed forces. There hadn't been an RAF when Stanley enlisted, but if he had it to do again he'd have served in the Royal Flying Corps instead of slogging it out in the trenches watching his mates being blown to bits. George had been to university, he could be an officer in the RAF and he would be set up for life. George, however, declined to enlist because his first choice in any case was the army or the navy. The army because he liked the derivation of *infantry* — it called attention to the use of children as cannon fodder. The navy because of the daily tot of rum. I dare say George's reasons were designed to inflame his father, although no one had the nerve to pass them on to Uncle Stanley.

It was all very hard. If anyone had to do the killing eye to eye, it was the Tommies. *Horrifying* to think of George peering through the sights of a rifle at a boy who may have been one of his pen pals! — horrifying even if you knew it would never happen. Madeleine and I lay in bed and thought up the sort of job George could do if there was a war. He could work as a code breaker. Or he could polish up his German and write the leaflets England was dropping from planes over German fields and towns, exposing to the Germans the wrongness of their ways. He could be a correspondent, sending news back from the front. Or even a cartoonist. Every day the *Manchester Evening Herald* ran a cartoon of Hitler as a beer-swilling Bavarian peasant. George could do much better! Or, if England was invaded (and everyone said it would be this time), he could be a double agent, waiting for the Germans on the beach and swinging his arm up from the hinge of his shoulder in a Nazi salute, and then he could lead them out to the moors and into a trap.

I knew where he was at every moment during those three days in Blackpool, but he had many thoughts in his mind besides me. I began to despise him for his scrutiny of the seaweed at low tide, for lecturing Jenny on the parts of a sea urchin and taking her with him into the kitchen to fry some up, for wading out by North Pier to examine the crustaceans growing on the piles while I was walking on the beach alone. For his bony frame and his unbecoming walking shorts, for the yellow tinge to his skin, for the goatish bulge of his Adam's apple, and for the way he laughed, the exaggerated way, as though he wanted things to be funnier than they were. How like the White Knight he is, I thought, and I put on lipstick and tried to act the way I would act if he were nothing to me. When he cast me a quick glance it was as though the beam of a bicycle torch passed over me and lit me up for a second, just for the second before the torch moved away. I hated him for that too.

On our third and last night in Blackpool, when I had pretty much turned to stone, Aunt Lucy set out to teach Madeleine,

Jenny and Monty to play bridge, and George said to me, A bit of air? I leapt up and we put our coats on and went out into the windy streets. We went down to the seafront at Central Pier, where Lois first met Archie when he came with a friend to watch the shopgirls dance. Everything was shut down. They'd even closed the entrances to the piers, and so we walked along the beach, along where the donkeys trudged at high tide, the wind plastering my hair to my face and snapping at our coats. He kept his hands in his pockets, and I dared to link my arm through his and felt him pull me closer, and it was enough, enough to chase away all the last three days and make everything between us true again.

There was no moon and no stars. The wind reminded me of home, of walking in a dust storm, and I narrowed my eyes to slits. The sky was black above us and the beach a different black and the dark ocean chasing itself back and forth beside us a third. We came upon a closed chip kiosk and took shelter beside it. We were both shivering. I was wearing my foolish black slippers and I bent and shook the sand out of them. I turned my face towards the sea and felt spray on my cheeks. In front of us the lights of North Pier tossed on the water in a chain of wobbly yellow globes. Beyond them, men wearing German uniforms and crammed into steel capsules sped through the heaving black water. Where would George and I be if this notion of war had not intruded — what would be filling his thoughts?

In spite of the cold he spread his arms out against the chip kiosk, as though he were measuring it. Make a dandy bratwurst stand, he said.

What — you mean you think they're going to win? I said. I teased his jacket open and moved inside it.

No, he said. That's not what I mean. His shirt was untucked and I felt his warm, thin back. Then he twitched violently away from me, he whirled around and began to walk backwards up the beach, singing in an outlandish German accent, *There'll always be an England, while there's a country lane....* Humiliation throbbed through me, burned my eyes so that I could hardly see.

The Royal Hotel was at the corner where we came up onto the street. Wait, I said. I leaned against the window and emptied my shoes again. Inside, a foot away from us, a woman with bare arms sat in the golden light of the dining-room chandeliers. We plodded in silence up the side street towards our lodging, sand scuffing under our shoes, and I followed George into the stale air of the hall, with its blue-striped bedroom wallpaper and a torn orange lantern hanging from the electric light. He wiped his feet on the scrubbing brush nailed to the floor, and I tapped mine against the door frame. There were two chairs in the hall and I sank into one. If only we could talk, that was all there was left, and in the morning he would be on the train.

George, the girl who undertook to talk for me said breathlessly, I've been thinking. You might be all right in the Air Force. You could be a navigator. You could spend your whole day reading a compass. You would be good at it.

You're right, I think I'd be okay, he said, bending his head to dodge the lantern.

But maybe they won't catch up to you, the girl said. She held her coat on her lap, her hands marbled from the cold, ugly and red, and she crossed her legs, willing him to notice how long and slim her legs were, hating her thick lisle stockings, the way they accordioned at her ankles. Maybe you won't have to go at all.

I think I will. They're taking lists from the universities. Or they might just issue a general call for all the 1919s to register. He finally lowered himself into the chair opposite.

So why don't you just enlist? she asked.

He sat thinly with his legs crossed. Red blotches stood out in his white cheeks. Oh, I don't know how to say it, he said. Have you ever heard of Julian Huxley? I wish I had time to read everything he wrote. He was so brilliant. His grandfather was Thomas Huxley, you know, the scientist who defended Darwin. The man who coined the word *agnostic?*

He looked at her questioningly. She stared back at him, she stared her disappointment.

Agnostic, he said. It's one of the best words there is. Once he found the word, you could be one, you weren't limited to being either a believer or an atheist.

Julian, she said, meaning, *Get on with it.*

Yes, the grandson. Well, in *The Science of Life* he writes all about evolution in the modern age. How it used to be biology that shaped evolution, but now it's culture. We make choices, we don't grow hard shells like a turtle, we invent them, armour and weapons, that sort of thing, and they give us an evolutionary advantage. Although whether it's an advantage to the species in the long run is debatable.

She reached a hand up to her head and felt the grains of sand the wind had left on her scalp. Is this why you won't enlist? she asked.

I guess partly.

And then Jenny came out to the hall. She looked at them with her sharp, irreverent eyes and said, There's cocoa in the parlour, and they got up and followed her in.

※

He did write to me from Dorset. He did not allude to how awkward things had been between us. It was clear from his letter that he had put the war out of mind as well — he was coming at the problem from a different angle.

Charmouth, 28 May 1939

Dear Lily,

Mrs. Slater's son is home this week and takes supper with us and is very interesting. He's Exeter-educated and he has so much local lore to put together with it, of the days when curiosities lay all over the beach for the taking. He says the local chalk-diggers called belemnites <u>pencils</u> — a new one on me. They used to roast limestone here to make quicklime, and every time we pass the forge we picture them feeding intact ichthyosaur skeletons into the flames — a scene Ned Slater swears he witnessed as a boy, although I doubt it.

The field we pegged today is what they call a belemnite battlefield. It looks just like an ammunitions dump. They're all immature specimens, about two inches long and the exact brown of brass bullet casings. Dr. Acworth thinks it was a spawning ground. If so it might teach us something new about how they reproduced. We waited most of the day for the photographer to come to take pictures in situ. I used the time to make a charcoal sketch.

What is odd about these shells is that they're finely etched — like they've been exposed to acid. Here's the theory that popped into my head while we waited all afternoon: it was stomach acid. These belemnites must have been swallowed by a large marine reptile (a dyspeptic ichthyosaur?). It couldn't digest the casings, it puked them out, and that's our belemnite battlefield! Vomit and dung — my life's work. Now to convince Dr. Acworth (i.e., that it was his idea in the first place).

217

You must be sitting your exams this week.
Take a good pen. Try out the one I left in the top
drawer of my desk. Also, if faced with a question
you don't understand, write with authority about
something else.

Pax,
George

7

For months my mother's letters had featured Phillip and his girlfriend, Betty Stalling. They'd been engaged since Christmas, and he'd been going to Burnley to take his high-school equivalency so he could get into the Air Force if there was a war. But still I was startled when she reported on their wedding, I couldn't seem to keep the two of them together in my mind. In my mind Betty stood in a row of motherless girls, a nine-year-old with an earnest face and a thin white braid hanging down each shoulder. On the off-chance that this news was true, I took two pounds out of my account at the building society and bought a fine black enamelled tray with red birds on it as a wedding gift. The woman in the shop on King Street helped me pack it up for shipping.

In June a letter came from my father:

> *We're looking forward to you finishing school.*
> *Your mother is poorly and Dr. Ross can't seem to*
> *say what the trouble is. Betty is a big help, but*
> *your mother would like to see you home.*

Lying on my bed after tea I read the letter again and decided that this was a ploy that could and should be resisted. I was longing for Sixth Form: for *Othello. Paradise Lost.* The French Revolution. And the French subjunctive, that intriguing mood that would equip me for expressing doubt and desire on the Champs Élysées. When they got over this war idea, when Madeleine and I went to Paris. Within a week I'd come up with my own ploy and wrote back:

> *Uncle Stanley and Aunt Lucy don't think it would*
> *be wise for me to travel this summer with things so*
> *uncertain. If I could finish Sixth Form, I could*
> *teach after I come home.*

And then I went on to tell them that I'd had an essay on the life of George Eliot published in the school magazine. (*I wonder who that fellow is?* I pictured them saying to each other.) All designed to show my mother I was out of her reach, and it seemed to work, because it was a long time before I heard from them again.

※

That summer Stanley was named to the ARP — as an Air Raid Precautions warden. He would do this on a volunteer basis until war was declared, and then he would leave the mill. Aunt Lucy was not in favour. He already had varicose veins from wearing puttees in the last war, and all the ARP wardens did was walk. Nevertheless he wound his puttees on and went to the first ARP meeting, where they gave him a coupon to pick up a blue overall, a tin helmet and a whistle at a depot in the precinct. After that first meeting he set to work making wood and canvas shutters for the windows. The window over the front door, the fanlight, he painted black.

This war will be fought in the air, he said.

Oh, Stanley, that's ever so ugly, said Aunt Lucy. What will we do afterwards?

If there's an afterwards, said Uncle Stanley with satisfaction, we'll break it out and get another.

Uncle Stanley rolled sticky tape over the fanlight in a cross-hatching pattern. Then he fished a little screwdriver out of his pocket and took the glass face off the mantel clock. The mirror in the front hall had to go as well. (You girls won't be primping, he said. You'll have better things to think about.) All of these deadly missiles he packed into a crate destined for George's shed. Then he went down to the shops and picked up a new bucket and a jute bag of sand. If a bomb landed in the hall, we were to hold the sandbag in front of our faces as a shield while we ran up to it. The bucket was for water to put the fire out if the sand didn't do the trick.

Aunt Lucy said we should each have a new frock while you could still get fabric for that sort of thing. Her own was well advanced and Nettie Nesbitt came over to hem it. It had a full skirt with buttercups sprinkled over it, and the bodice was pale green like willows in the spring. Talking around the pins in her mouth, Nettie Nesbitt told us about working at the munitions factory at Chilwell in the Great War and how the sulphur in the TNT turned her skin yellow. I was just as yellow as that, she said, picking out a bright patch at the centre of a buttercup in Aunt Lucy's skirt. She was only sixteen at the time, younger than all of us girls. She was called a canary.

Oh, my poor dear, said Aunt Lucy. Well, you'd never know it now. You have skin like a rose (which could not have been further from the truth). Aunt Lucy stood on a kitchen chair, her own face flushed pink from the cry she'd had that morning, revolving slowly while Nettie crouched below her. When Nettie got round to the beginning again she stuck the last of her pins into the pincushion on her wrist and sat back on her heels and sang,

There's no uniform so dinky
As the girls' munition blue
She's working hard for the coming home
Of the boys at the front so true.

Dinky? laughed Madeleine from the floor, where she lay on a carpet of the *Oldham Chronicle*. She caught my eye and made a droll face. Listen to this, she said, bending over to read out: *Sir: I wish to call the public's attention to the grave risk posed by individuals of Teutonic origin residing in our midst. Allowing such individuals free access to bicycles and roadway maps is the height of folly and a threat to the security of the British people.* Mr. Schwartz at the pharmacy! she cried. He has a bicycle.

Oh, they do go on, said Aunt Lucy, still standing like a queen on her chair. Nobody living in Blighty today would side with the Germans.

Don't you believe it! cried Nettie Nesbitt. She hoisted herself to her feet and looked passionately about. There was them working for the Huns right in Chilwell. In 1916! Why do you think our lads had such a wretched time at the Somme? Their shells was duds! Not one in three would fire proper. It was them devils at Chilwell lost the war for us.

No one bothered to correct her. Aunt Lucy put her hand on Nettie's shoulder and stepped down. I've enough to plague me without being frightened of my own neighbours, she said. She had a glazed look, as though she'd been sitting up all night at the bedside of a dying loved one. Everyone was waiting. I could not be afraid the way Aunt Lucy was because I had no idea what was coming. None of our ways of seeing this was right — that's what I felt. If you see the funnel of a cyclone twisting across the fields towards you, you don't have any idea what you should fear, but you know that it will teach you.

That summer was as hot as home. We girls went around with no stockings. Out on Oldham Edge there was a breeze, and I tried to get Madeleine to bring her embroidery hoop and work outside, but she would not, she said it was common. I went out alone, walking through the prickly gorse, sweat trickling down from my hairline, and looked out at the dry brown Pennines. Remembering snow, a fantastic notion, the wetness and coldness of it, the way it blew into a sculpted frozen sea my last winter at home. I thought of snow and one night I dreamt of it, the field between our place and the Feazels' lying glistening in moonlight.

Madeleine and I spent the summer playing cards at Jenny's next door, doing little jobs for Aunt Lucy, and sometimes working at the WVS depot, sorting clothes for evacuated children. And I wrote to George. George usually wrote on Sundays, as they did fieldwork every day until dark and then they had to catalogue everything. He sent me a hand-drawn cartoon in which a girl picks up a belemnite and says, *Oh! It's a fairy finger!* and farther down the beach a military officer picks one up saying, *Ancient artillery shell.* It was labelled THE BELEMNITE: A CRYPTIC CURIOSITY. My own belemnite sat on the window ledge of the room I shared with Madeleine, a talisman against lightning. I thought about this cartoon, about what George was trying to say about the war, whether it was something we invented because it fit the way we thought about things. But you couldn't say we invented Hitler, obviously.

In August George's notice came, and Uncle Stanley managed to reach him by telephone and he said he'd come home from Dorset by train. We'd worried so much in advance that it was almost a relief to have it settled. Now we could all get on with doing what had to be done.

Poor lad, said Aunt Lucy. They won't know what to do with him.

He's just the sort they like, said Uncle Stanley. He'll be a testament to the army's powers of transformation.

It was a Thursday when he got home, the first week of the trial blackout, and we girls went to the station to meet him just after tea, before it was dark. Monty met us there and sat beside me on the bench. He had escaped conscription by two months, and at the moment he was working at the brick works. He was in a mood. There were boys in uniform all over the platform, holding their shoulders with a new importance, and he looked sourly at them and said, Playing at being their dads.

What about you? I asked. Going to sign up?

I don't know, he said. I'm holding off at the moment.

In the winter he'd wanted to go to Spain to fight the Fascists, except that his dad was poorly. I knew that, so I thought he wasn't opposed to being a soldier. Well, England didn't pitch in then, did she? he said. This anti-Fascist fervour is all a bit sudden. So I'm waiting to see if I'll pitch in now. I'm waiting and watching, but so far I haven't noticed myself signing up.

He sat close to me with his arm along the back of the bench. I hear your beau's a Party member in Canada, he said. What does he think? Does he see this as an imperialist war?

He's not my beau, I said.

Then the train pulled in with the blackout blinds already down. When George got off he made nothing special of me, so I made nothing special of him either. His friend David was there in his new blue RAF uniform and we all walked up Union Street and David got us into a canteen. There was a gramophone, and the place was crammed with people dancing.

Monty pulled out a chair for me with an irritating, proprietorial manner, so that simply sitting down on it made me feel as if I were surrendering to his designs. Then as soon as we were seated he said, How about it? and so I got up again to dance with him. He grasped my waist firmly and held me close to him, and under the guise of offering me dance instruction, insisted on pressing his leg between my legs the whole time. Every time I turned around all night there he was, wanting more, and I was forced to sit down and say I was tired. Imogene Miller, the very thin girl I first saw at their New Year's party, the girl whom George was said to fancy, appeared and stood by the table, lifting her chin and pulling on a cigarette.

I *adore* your frock, said Madeleine, who had a bright spot on each cheek from the cider.

Ta, Imogene said, blowing out smoke. Her dress was black with jet at the neckline.

So that's how we dress when we're ruined, said she, said Monty.

Sod off, said Imogene. She wandered away and then I didn't see her again and I couldn't see George. Across the table a girl named Ruth was fighting with her boyfriend. Her eyes were brimming with tears, she had a fixed smile on her face. You're horrible, you are, she kept saying, smiling and weeping while he drank his ale and stared out into the crowd.

Where's George? I said to the table. I want to dance with George. I was drinking cider too.

You can't be sweet on George, a boy named Harry said. He's your cousin. It would only end in tears.

It would only end in circus freaks, someone said. They all laughed and Harry tapped a drum roll on the table. The lights dimmed and the master of ceremonies announced a novelty dance, the Blackout Shuffle.

He's not really my cousin, you know, I said.

Anyway, Charles Darwin *married* his cousin, Madeleine cried. He would know, wouldn't he?

Dance with me, said Harry, so I did, their words drifting away into the smoky air, and when the bell clanged in the dark and we had to change partners I stepped blindly into the nearest arms and it was bloody Monty. Then the lights came up and George was back at the table with David and it turned out they had walked up to the Chinese restaurant to buy cigarettes because the canteen was all out. The canteen was closing then so we crowded out into the black street. It was a moonless night and the buildings made black, hulking shapes against the sky. Everyone was walking with heads tipped up, staring at the stars. To me it was an ordinary starry sky, but to everyone else it was a marvel. My heart was aching with longing to be walking with George. All the while whoever was beside me walked me closer and closer into the wall and then pushed himself against me and before I quite knew for sure that it was Monty, he had clamped his hands around my bottom and was breathing beer into my face, trying to put his tongue in my mouth. Get *off* me! I cried, shoving him away.

Oh, you don't half fancy yourself, he said bitterly.

Back at the house Madeleine was comforting a girl huddled crying in the hall. It was Jenny. She raised her head and stared balefully at me over Madeleine's shoulder. I was trying not to cry myself. I went out to the toilet and when I came back in Jenny had gone home and George had gone out again with all the boys, so I went to bed.

The next day George took the coach into Manchester to report. He went to a huge depot, where he lined up with a lot of other boys singing, *It's a long way to Tipperary*. He said it felt like a film set for a movie about the *last* war. He was made to stand for two hours (most of it in his underwear) before a doctor came and asked him to pee into a bottle, listened to his heart and checked his arches. *I've seen better bleedin' soldiers crawl outta cheese*, he heard an officer say as he was getting dressed — not about George personally (he thought) but the whole lot of them. He passed the medical and was sent home again because they weren't ready to take him into basic training.

Why call him up for nothing? said Madeleine.

They learned a lesson last round, said Uncle Stanley. By the end they had no reserves. Nobody except the midgets and the maimed.

Every day planes flew in formation over Oldham from the Manchester airfield. Huge ear trumpets were set up over London, they said, turned to listen to the sky. Near the end of August we all queued up to get respirators in tidy white cardboard boxes with carrying strings. Dinky, Madeleine and I called them. Boys in the service wouldn't get their masks until basic training, but George and his friends stood out in the garden wearing ours, making rude noises in the soft rubber around the snouts to irritate Uncle Stanley. As ARP warden, Uncle Stanley had to inspect all masks on the street once a month and issue a little chit to show they were properly maintained. He came back from an ARP meeting and read us a notice about a chap in Rochdale who'd been taken to court for throwing his mask into a yard and cracking the visor. Stanley himself bought a red storage tin with *Take Care of Your Gas Mask* on it. And he had a new electric lamp with a little hood over it for walking the streets during blackout, a lamp that cast an eerie blue light. I don't know whether he bought that lamp or they issued it to him. War had not been declared, but the shops were full of that sort of thing. All the while we were musing about the idea of another war and declaring it insane, factories across England were busy building fighter planes and respirators. Even at the time this struck me as a very bad sign: who would work to find another way after they'd made all this gear?

The question, of course, was whether there was any other way. George thought so, and he knew a great deal that Uncle Stanley did not know. He was standing in the Hartford Arms all night with Horace Maxwell, a reporter for the *Oldham Chronicle*. George knew that ambassadors from London were travelling up to Russia at that very moment in a steamship called the *City of Exeter*, on their way to make a pact with Russia. He knew that in a show of unconcern the prime minister was fishing in the Highlands, sending his friends fresh salmon in dripping crates of ice. George drew in more and more information, and saw so many angles to every question. He would quote George Bernard Shaw and Karl Marx and Neville Chamberlain and Julian Huxley. By the end of every argument he'd be trembling with eagerness, talking too fast, and Uncle Stanley would hitch himself testily around in his chair and pour another drink of stout with his disgust evident in the very way he held his tumbler. He had nothing but what they said in the Gaping Goose and his own self-evident truths. Then on August 23 it was *Germany* that Russia made a pact with. So Uncle Stanley was the one who turned out to be right.

Finally George got his summons, for September 1, and went to pick up his uniform in Oldham. It was rough khaki cotton, a mockery on an educated lad, as Uncle Stanley said to Aunt Lucy out of George's hearing. He had to report to a different depot in Manchester to pick up his insignia. I was the one who went to Manchester with him, and spent an hour waiting in Albert Square while he was in the queue. That was the one time we had together. That night after we got back Aunt Lucy sewed his shoulder flashes and insignia on, and Uncle Stanley borrowed a camera from a chap at work and we took pictures in the garden. Lots of other boys came by. A couple of airmen, looking so smart in their blue shirts and ties. Wilf, a mate of George's from Durham, the only one of his old mates going with him into infantry training. Lads who hadn't been away to school and spoke a shrill Lancashire. They stood together outside smoking and laughing, joking that they were attracting Zeppelins when they lit up in the garden at dusk. While they were there George seemed thinner and paler. His face was monkeyish — there was something *eager* about his cynicism, and I was glad when they left.

All that last day of August Aunt Lucy's tears dripped. She kept a hanky tucked in her bosom. It's *Failsworth*, Mother, said Lois. He'll be home more often than when he was in school, more's the pity.

In the morning Uncle Stanley and Lois said their goodbyes and left for work. George was wound up, jittery. He'd made himself up a case of books, although he didn't bring them out until Uncle Stanley was gone, so he must have known he'd never be allowed to take them. Aunt Lucy stood in the hall and shook her head at him. Pick one, she said.

Take a notebook, I said helpfully. You can write your own. You can write poetry.

I think it's all been said, he said. Then it was time to walk him to the coach and then time for him to get on the coach. He embraced each of us, the underarms of his uniform already black with sweat. It was me he embraced first in his stiff way, but I was all right with that, we'd had our trip to Manchester. Then he was gone, and Aunt Lucy stood on the sidewalk and said, I wish Hitler could see that lad. It might bring him to his senses. Then she took our arms and we walked home. When we got to the house she said, He's sure to be home for Christmas. This year we *will* have a goose. Will there be geese, with a war on? Madeleine asked, and Aunt Lucy said, No, I suppose not.

He left on the eight o'clock coach, and he must have been in the battery when we heard on the wireless that Hitler had invaded Poland. That was a Friday. On the Saturday, in spite of the heat and to calm herself, Aunt Lucy made a rag pudding. On Sunday morning she picked the Michaelmas daisies that had bloomed so early because of the hot summer and put them in a jar on the table. Then she put on her new green and yellow dress and, although Uncle Stanley didn't want to leave the wireless, she made him go to church with her. Madeleine and I were sorting out our things for school, rooting around in the bookshelves to find the books Lois and George had used in Sixth Form. A lady was giving a program about how to cook with tinned food, and suddenly her voice was cut off and the announcer said, This is London, and the voice of the prime minister came on. We both stood very still in the middle of the living-room carpet. Neville Chamberlain reminded England that he had asked Hitler to withdraw from Poland. I have to tell you, he said in his thin grey thread of a voice, that no such undertaking has been received and that consequently this country is at war with Germany. Now may God bless you all. May he defend the right. Then they played "God Save the King," and we kept standing because it didn't feel right to move around or sit down during the anthem.

He's declared war, said Madeleine in a small voice, and I thought how funny it was to put it that way. There's Mr. Chamberlain standing by his desk in his morning jacket. He's just taken a telephone call, his face is grim. There are children, maybe, playing outside the leaded window of his study, but he can't see them or the bearded seed heads of last spring's clematis hanging over the casement. He stands with his hand still on the telephone receiver, cornered into saying something unequivocal. So he says it. War! he declares.

The next day the papers were full of the SS *Athenia* being torpedoed by a German U-boat and 112 passengers dying, and what I thought was, Well, they won't be able to make me go home now.

8

Jenny knocked over a can and something rolled around in the dark. What in heck was that? she said.

It's corks, I said. Uncle Stanley put them here. If they start bombing we're supposed to put them in our mouths. So we don't bite our tongues off.

Funny he bothers, said Lois. He's sure to like us better that way. We laughed like maniacs. It didn't matter, not even Uncle Stanley expected Germans to be walking the streets listening for noise, not at this stage.

We were under the stairs, where all the junk had been cleared out and cushions and blankets piled. Madeleine was gone with Aunt Lucy to the air raid shelter at the bottom of the street. Aunt Lucy wanted us all to go, but I said I had a sore throat, and Lois had just washed her hair, so she settled for Madeleine. Aunt Lucy felt it her duty as wife of the ARP warden to go and to model the right attitude. She kept a tin of barley sugar in her bag for the kiddies. She kept a scarf handy to tie over her curlers when the signal sounded. Imagine someone getting caught in a bombardment because they've stopped to fuss with their hair, she said. The shelter was cold and smelled of wet jute from all the sandbags stacked around. If we had to stay into the night, there would be the moist snores of elderly strangers and the fretful voices of children waking up confused and scared. So when the ARP warden walked up the street turning the handle of his rattle like a hurdy-gurdy, Jenny just came over to our place and we squeezed under the stairs. It didn't matter: these were practice air raids.

Jenny wasn't mad at me, she was over Monty. She'd met a sailor from Portsmouth at the canteen. His name was Joe and she'd known him for three days, and just that morning he shipped out to the North Sea. She sat with her big legs folded under her, looming over us in the dark. She wore her father's pomade when her hair was unruly, and it filled the little space under the stairs with the smell of apples.

Joe was a right pest last night, she said. He wanted a little sommut to take with him. That's how he put it. *Come on, love, just a little sommut to remember you by*, he says. But I said, *Right-o, you'd be leaving a little sommut behind, more like. That's what I'm afraid of*, I said, *it's what you'd be leaving behind!* This war suits the lads to a T, don't you think? She passed us over a little bag of boiled sweets. What about Archie?

What about him? said Lois, taking a sweet.

When's he leaving?

Next Tuesday.

You watch. He'll bring his da's car this weekend. More room in the back.

I don't think so, Lois said stiffly.

I told Ma I was joining the WACs, Jenny said. But I was just winding her up. Girls look vulgar in khaki, don't you think? That's what everyone says. Friday I'm going back to the canteen. With Sally Higgins. *She's* joined up, did you hear?

I don't know Sally Higgins, said Lois. How would I hear?

Come with us, said Jenny, poking me. Monty won't mind.

It's not Monty she fancies, said Lois. Lily's in love with a boy from home.

I can't go Friday, I said. I'm going to the music hall with my auntie.

And then we heard the ARP warden, Uncle Stanley or the other one, coming up the street ringing a handbell for the all-clear.

All the rest of the week I magnified my cold, although by then my throat was sore only if I thought about it. Secretly I hated George Formby. So in the end Aunt Lucy took Madeleine and one of her friends and I lay in bed with a hot-water bottle. After they left I heard Lois going downstairs in her high heels, and then I heard Archie in the hall. Their two voices went back and forth, and then the door slammed and the house fell quiet.

I lay in bed and thought about George. This was what I'd been wanting, the house empty so that I could think about George. George had been moved from Failsworth. He was somewhere on the moors, at a place he called Fetlock Fields. All day the captain blew his hunting horn and they charged across a meadow thrusting Great War bayonets into a row of straw-filled Germans hanging from low gibbets, with the sergeant screaming, Shove it in 'is adjectival gut. Twist the adjectival thing! *Adjectival* was George's word, it took the place of something else. They were taught to scream as well, they had to practise it. They threw rocks in lieu of grenades, pulling imaginary pins out with their teeth. *It's a joke from the last war,* he wrote, *but we actually spent Wednesday digging a slit trench and Thursday filling the adjectival thing up. Nothing but chickenshit day after day, it's designed to make you long for combat.* He signed off, *Auf Wiedersehen, George.*

※

I'd spent those two weeks before he went to Failsworth in an agony of wanting to know where I stood with him. During the day Uncle Stanley had him working at the ARP depot and at night there was always someone around. When he went into Manchester to pick up his insignia, when Aunt Lucy said I should go along to keep him company, I was almost faint with happiness. I wore my blue poplin dress with the gored skirt and borrowed a cameo pin for the throat from Lois.

Is it true that you fancy Imogene? I said as soon as we got on the coach.

Yes, he said. We were secretly married in March. He looked at me with disgust. He didn't touch me until we got off at Piccadilly Gardens, but I knew from the way we sat on the tram that things would be fine between us.

At Piccadilly Gardens he laced his fingers through mine and we walked close together up Portland Street towards the town hall, through the press of people. We went to the post office, where an old man gave us his place in the queue in respect of George's uniform, and we looked into the library in St. Peter's Square. Then we drank coffee in a café on Deansgate Street. He had until four o'clock to report to the depot, so after the coffee he took me into the Manchester Art Gallery, where Darwin and other famous intellectuals lectured when it was the Manchester Institute. It was in the Roman style, with columns in front. He wanted to show me a famous painting he thought I might know. He dragged me into a gallery and I was taken aback to see that he was right, I did know it. There, in a little painting shaped like a church window, was Jesus from the cover of a Sunday-school book, knocking on the door of someone's heart.

A *woman* posed for this, George said. The artist used Christina Rossetti as his model for Jesus' face.

An ornate lamp spilled yellow light over Jesus' face and

there was something confiding about the way his small hand hovered over the door. I looked warily at the familiar bearded face, which struck me as sad yet reconciled, not like any woman I had ever seen but not like any man either.

Then we spent a long time looking at a frieze George remembered, casts from the Parthenon. It was a strip of writhing, muscular forms, some with the hind ends of horses and some just human. It depicted the battle between the centaurs and Lapiths, George knew it from Ovid. The Lapiths had invited the centaurs to a wedding, and the centaurs got drunk and tried to make off with the bride. Ovid had an eye for detail, for ripped nostrils with jellied brains oozing out of them. George had read it in Third Form and said that all the boys loved it. George pointed out how the weapons were the goblets and candlesticks from the banquet table and the antlers that had decorated the walls.

Why would you study that? I asked.

Isn't it obvious? he said. It was the turning point of Western Civilization. The victory of civilization over barbarism. Order over chaos. Athens over Persia.

That's what I had to remember now that George was gone: standing in the lobby of the Manchester Art Gallery, under the big, square skylight and the four big lamps, looking at the centaurs and the Lapiths braining one another with candlesticks, and then standing in a doorway at Piccadilly Gardens after George had been to the depot, kissing while we waited for the coach, him reaching out and pulling me into an entrance, the way I had the first time with him. The height of him, the furtive dart of his tongue into my mouth. Him reaching for me at last, as though the war had taught him desire.

I turned off the lamp and lay in the dark. There was a half-moon, I knew without looking out the window. But the blackout curtain was pulled, and I lay in bed in the dark and wrote to George in my mind. *Must I be interested in all of this?* I asked him. *Or is it enough if I'm interested in you?* Finally I knew I wouldn't fall asleep and I got up and went to the window and opened the curtain to let in the moonlight. I sensed right away that there was someone in the garden. Straight below me, in the corner you could see only from our bedroom, Lois was perched on the garden wall, embracing Archie, who was standing with his back to me. He seemed to be leaning into her, moving rhythmically against her. I could see her slender, white legs on either side of him, bright in the moonlight, and I felt understanding creep over me, starting deep inside me rather than in my brain: it was like coming across an engine room that accounted for a secret humming you could feel through the whole building. She had her face turned up to the moon (her look was preoccupied, as though she had to concentrate, brace herself), and I saw that she was not really embracing him but holding up his trousers.

I backed away from the window, afraid to draw the curtain again in case she caught the movement in the corner of her eye and knew I'd seen. I lay back down on the bed and found that I was crying, and I cried for a long time, giving myself over to my tears, drawing them up the way you draw water from a well. I had no idea why I was crying. Then I heard Lois come in, and I got up and wiped my face on my undervest and pulled the curtain across and finally I fell asleep.

The next morning was a Saturday, but Lois had to work and she came down dressed to the nines as usual and stood at the sideboard drinking her tea. I was at the kitchen table in my dressing gown. She finished her tea and set the cup on the drainboard. Then she took a little mirror out of her purse and touched up her lipstick and ran a finger over each eyebrow. I'm off, she said. Feeling better? She put her hat on, a new hat in the design of the artillery caps the lads were wearing, and clicked down the hall in her high heels without waiting for an answer. On some ordinary day she'd made a leap, an unimaginable leap like the movement of fish to land, and no one had been any the wiser.

⁂

Meanwhile Madeleine and I kept going to school. Some of the masters were gone, and some of the girls had left to enlist or take jobs, so our classes were the same size they'd always been. There were never any boys there anyway. Our English literature class was in the afternoon. As it started we'd pull the blackout curtains so that we could put on a light, and in the hiss of the gaslights we would sit and knit, knitting long mufflers of khaki wool, while Mr. Fox read *Don Quixote* to us. Mr. Fox usually read T.S. Eliot to the Sixth Form, but he said the war had rescued us from the twilight of modernism.

By the end of that first nine months, though, it was clear the war was going to be one of those things that failed to live up to expectations. As Jenny said, it was just as dull as peace. Worse, because the lads were gone. Our neighbours who'd moaned about having evacuees in the house moaned now that the ungrateful sods had sloped back to London. Uncle Stanley, however, saw no reason to lower the guard. He came home from an ARP meeting and showed us how to seal the fireplace all around with sticking paper so poison gas couldn't pour down the chimney, although we couldn't keep the seal up all the time because it was cold and we needed the fire.

Who *thinks up* this sort of thing? I laughed. They think German soldiers are dragging ladders up the streets and blowing gas down the chimneys? With no one noticing?

Uncle Stanley took me by the arm and sat me down on a chair. Does this war strike you as a bit of a joke? he said. Do you find poison gas funny? He pressed his face so close to mine that I had a disagreeable view of the inside of his nostrils.

Maybe you should have a talk with some of the lads who were at Passchendaele, he said. They'll tell you how funny it is, that's if they have the breath to talk at all.

He let go of me and turned back to his sticking paper. The Jerries have a chlorine *bomb* now, flower, he said. They've moved beyond canisters. Apparently your intelligence is not keeping you up to date!

What I hated most was the *flower*.

By *your intelligence* of course he meant George. Who knows what George knew. His letters had become sporadic and very strange. The censor had finally caught up to him — most of my letters and Aunt Lucy's as well arrived with parts of them painted over. I got one letter that was entirely blacked out, even the *Dear Lily*. Whatever could he have been writing about through the whole letter? Once he wrote to me in Latin, what appeared to be one of his lists. His regiment had finally formed, the 71st Searchlight Regiment of the Royal Artillery. Everyone had leave, but George didn't come home then or at Christmas; Uncle Stanley got notice that he'd been subjected to a disciplinary cancellation of leave. They were outside doing Morse code drills with a heliograph (this was an instrument you could use to signal with flashes of light), and he used his turn at signalling to play the fool. What he signalled was *Gott mit uns*, which was apparently what the Kaiser's soldiers had inscribed on their belt buckles in the Great War. It was considered very serious: he was put on charge for prejudicial conduct. Madeleine found this part out later from George's friend Wilf.

When he finally got leave, when I came in and saw him sitting at the kitchen table with his strange short haircut talking to Aunt Lucy like a sane individual, I almost cried with relief. Wilf was there with him and he got up politely to greet me, but George didn't get up, he just raised his hand in a two-fingered wave. I swear he was thinner, if such a thing was possible. His hands were chapped raw. He had dark notches under his eyes. I admired the shine on their boots and they told us there were two schools of thought: polish and then water and then polish, or oil, then polish, then Vaseline. George favoured the former and Wilf the latter. On their buttons they used jeweller's rouge. They weren't at Fetlock Fields any more. They'd been at a port somewhere for landing exercises. They'd learned to scurry like crabs down a scramble net. In the dark, everything in the dark. We sat and drank tea, and Aunt Lucy asked George for his ration book and Wilf started to laugh and George told her he'd lost it playing poker. She asked him when he was going to stop being such a silly apeth. This was the sort of conversation George always had with his mother, and I wondered if he seemed the same to her. To me he seemed very different, wary and contained.

Taperlegs, Wilf called him. While Aunt Lucy was up at the stove Wilf leaned towards me confidentially. He's in Company E, our lad, he said. He's in Company E and still they're calling him Taperlegs.

What's Company E? I asked.

It's a company of ectomorphs, George said. Tall and thin, he explained when I didn't respond.

They assign soldiers to companies by *height?* I asked. What's the point of that?

Wilf leaned closer. Saves measuring, he said, when the coffin makers and diggers are called in.

George jabbed him with an elbow. It's for parade, Lily, he said. We parade by company, and when you're standing on the pavement watching a parade it makes a better show. The whole column swells as it comes towards you and gradually tapers off. Impresses the hell out of the crowd. *Crikey! What a god-damn efficient marching machine!*

240

That can't be true! I cried. The army wouldn't care about something like that.

No? said George. What would they care about?

Why, they care about winning, I said, and they both laughed.

⚔

Wilf was the only friend from Durham University that George had in his regiment. He had coarse yellow hair and an impudent face, like a turnip with wedges cut out of it. He was going to stay in Oldham for his leave because he lived too far away to go home. They tipped their kit bags out on the flagstones, and Wilf showed me his helmet, the shiny little mark on its rim from a bullet.

You were *shot at?*

In a training exercise, he said. We had to do an obstacle course through Dannert wire. We were wearing full gear, and the goddamn officers were firing on us. Turned out it was live ammo — but we didn't know that at the time, did we, Taperlegs?

Oh, it was cracking, lad! said George. Adventures in the Woods Perilous!

Goddamn Dannert wire, said Wilf.

What is Dannert wire? I asked.

Barbed wire. It's coiled so you can just unspool it, it saves putting up fence posts. It's made in Germany. Nasty stuff. There's Dannert wire full of rotting sheep from here to Bishop Auckland.

Remember Jammer? George said to Wilf. Jammer was down at the Albert Docks in Liverpool and he saw a German merchant ship unloading Dannert wire. This was the end of September.

We were at war in September, I said.

Well done, missy! said Wilf. We were at war. We were well at war and we needed that wire!

241

They weren't going back empty either, said George. They were loading up with black pudding.

That's just one of the stories people like to tell, I said.

Oh, little Lily, mein Liebling, said Wilf, and they put their heads together and sang a song in German, a song that had my name in it: *Wie einst, Lili Marleen-a, Wie einst, Lili Marleen*. Love, even the Jerries are dreaming about you, Wilf said when they'd wound down.

I cocked my head at George. What was it you sent me in Latin? I asked.

He shrugged. It was just a translation of our DRO. I was confined to barracks for three days. Had nothing to read.

Why? What had you done?

The fuckin' NCO made me do an extra shift in the mess hall. Then he called inspection in the barracks and I didn't have a chance to get my gear ready. The fuckin' fucker fucked me over.

Adjectival's fallen by the way, I see.

Fuckin' right it has, said Wilf humorously. A lad in khaki talks like a toff, they think he's one of them fuckin' plants. Like the nun with the hairy knuckles who was spotted on the Clapham omnibus.

I stood on the flagstones, proud. They'd *never* talk like this in front of Aunt Lucy or Madeleine.

Other mates had the use of a flat in Manchester and came over daily. It was a conspiracy to keep George and me apart, a conspiracy of boys in khaki coming in and out of the back garden singing "Lili Marleen" and flirting with us girls, Aunt Lucy's head moving in the kitchen window, Uncle Stanley standing in the doorway with his pipe, Lois and Madeleine plying George with tea and cocoa. He never has a minute to himself, poor lad, said his mother, but George said he was used to it. Even if you wanted to go to the infirmary you had to stand for an hour with a dozen other Tommies with the trots. I hung around on the flagstones, brazen as a streetwalker. I leaned against the shed going over what I especially wanted to say to him, which was, *Don't let the war change you. If the war changes you, the Germans will have won, no matter the outcome.* As far as I knew, this thought was original to me. But there was no time for George to work on his Gesner encyclopedia, no time to walk on the moors. The boys in khaki were jittery and badly behaved. In George's shed they tacked a notice stolen from a public lavatory: FLIES SPREAD DISEASE. KEEP YOURS CLOSED. A boy I'd never seen before fell against me in the hall and expertly squeezed my breast, with people not ten feet away. I stumbled into the kitchen and George looked at me with his clever eyes, George, who never had been one for the direct gaze.

Their leave was over on Sunday, and on Friday night I was walking across the garden and heard a tap on the window of the shed. Then the door opened. George leaned out of the doorway and handed me a folded paper. I opened it and a card fell out.

> *Miss Lily Piper is cordially invited*
> *for a private audience with Private G. Taperlegs*
> *Suite 21, 48 Whittle Road (off Addington Street), Manchester.*
> *At her convenience Saturday afternoon.*
> *The hiring of a hansom cab from*
> *Piccadilly Gardens is advised.*

George had closed the door of the shed — there were two boys inside with him. I climbed the stairs to my room, my knees trembling.

Saturdays Madeleine and I always went to the depot, so that's what I did, I spent the next morning at the depot. Around noon I found Mrs. Tupper and told her I was poorly and was going home. She gave me a look that said what a poor showing this was. With a war on, the look added. But I just left and boarded the tram to Manchester and all the way there I thought about George. Two Georges had come home for leave. One was the crude-mouthed Tommy, all slang and bravado. The other was the clever cynic. Neither of them was real — you could see it in George's eyes, in the fixed way he delivered his lines. But the real George was still there, and I was going to meet him. I felt a dark excitement rising. I fixed my eyes on the window and a thought I could not dare to think lifted itself into my mind and I said yes to it, *Yes*, I said, and kept my eyes on the glass without seeing the streets skim by.

I got off at Piccadilly Gardens, but I did not hire a taxi to Whittle Road. I knew where Addington Street was; Aunt Lucy had taken me to the dentist there and I knew I could walk. I was afraid of showing up at the flat early and finding George's mates still there. So first I sat on a bench and ate the sandwich I was carrying for my lunch. I had in mind to buy George a gift, something to remember me by, so after I was finished eating I walked up Market Street. The shops were open, but their display windows were boarded up or sandbagged and you had to step inside to find out what they sold.

I finally went into a men's shop called Mayberry's and saw leather gloves fanned in a display case. Gloves would be the thing for his poor sore hands. For your dad? the shopgirl asked. She was a beautiful girl like a film star with dark eyebrows and her hair bleached almost white. No, I said, hesitating. Oh, for your sweetheart! she said. She reached under the counter and brought out a pair of fine leather gloves. She said they were called calfskin, and they *were* the very colour of a Hereford calf. They're not making this sort of thing any more, are they? she said.

They had a strap with a tiny buckle at the wrist. I fingered the leather, admiring the narrow seams and the cunning little piece that was fitted in to accommodate the thumb. The shopgirl pursed her lips and looked out over my head, and I knew she thought I was too simple to appreciate them or too poor to afford them. All right, I heard myself say, I'll take them. They were a shocking price for someone too poor to hire a cab, they were almost a quid. She wrapped them in dark tissue paper and tied a string around them and I put the package in my purse.

Then I walked back down Market Street and turned up in the direction of Addington. All along, doorways were sandbagged, and at corners the street signs fixed to buildings were buried behind the sandbags or taken down to foil the Germans. I walked up to a corner that looked familiar and turned right but the quarter was a tangle of narrow winding roads and I was very soon bewildered. As I walked I thought ahead to meeting George. I was glad for the gift. Having something to give him would ease the awkwardness when I arrived. He had given me several small gifts, but I had never given him anything. Not even our granddad's hook that I'd saved when we cleaned out Nan's house. When I moved into Madeleine's room I was frightened she'd see it in my trunk and think I was totally barmy, so I'd hidden it in the linen cupboard. Aunt Lucy'd found it and said, Bloomin' heck! Whatever is this doing here? There was a drive on just then for aluminum, they were collecting people's jelly moulds and pie tins, so she sent Granddad's hook along to be melted down into whatever it was they use aluminum for in a war. So that was a gift I never gave him, and it was just as well.

I began to need to go to the bathroom, urgently, it was all

I could think about, and then an inhuman sound like a *bleat* penetrated my thoughts and I followed it down a lane, and coming around a corner I found that I was back at Piccadilly Gardens and that the noise was coming from a newsman on the corner, jangling the change in his pockets and emitting a single raw syllable — *News!* — every five seconds. There was a public lavatory in Piccadilly Gardens and I went into it. It was freezing and stinky, but I didn't have much choice.

Back out on the street I suddenly felt distaste at the thought of the gift. It came to me standing on the pavement that the gloves I'd bought would not please George at all. There they lay in my purse, limp scraps of calfskin — it was their very fineness that appalled me. They were something Uncle Stanley would admire. And could George even wear gloves that weren't army issue? Maybe he could, but I didn't know, I had no idea how things worked. I saw painfully that this gift was a dreadful mistake — it put everything in jeopardy. I turned and ran all the way to the shop. There were other customers in the shop this time and I had to wait. I can give you a credit note, the shopgirl said coldly, not looking at me. That's the best I can do. So although I almost never came to Manchester and never bought anything in shops as fine as this one, I had to take a credit note.

I was not far then from Albert Square, and I walked to it and sat on the bench where I'd sat the day George and I came into Manchester. I sat watching the pigeons with their red feet stepping over the pavement, thinking about that day, the way everything had unrolled, so easily, so unthinkingly. I remembered running out of the post office with him, wearing my blue poplin dress, the tide of indulgence and longing that followed us from the people waiting in the queue (because we were tall and walking in step, because there was war coming). I'd snatched it up, turned my profile to it, and then I'd come out of the post office into the light of the sky, blinking at the brightness, and a convoy of lorries thundered past. I turned away from the noise and found myself looking into a dark passage at a soldier slouching there with his girlfriend, nuzzling her bosom. He was jawing her breast with an open mouth, the way a fox will jaw a goose egg. She wasn't laughing. She just stood with her head tipped obligingly against the wall, her face turned towards the street. She was wearing a blue poplin dress too — it was such a popular shade of blue, a sort of uniform. She stood there in the dark and I stood in the bright sunlight, in the petrol fumes and roar of engines, and then I looked back to see George gazing at me. Not tenderly, but studying me as though I was a subject of genuine curiosity to him.

Albert Square was not far from the Manchester Art Gallery and sitting on the bench I remembered going with George to see the picture of Jesus. I felt a sudden need to see it again, now, as I stood at the gate of my life. And so I got up and walked quickly in the direction of the art gallery. Its pillars were banked by sandbags, but the door was open. I went up the marbled stairs inside, past the centaurs and Lapiths roiling in the lobby, trying to let my feet take me to the painting of Jesus because I couldn't even recall what floor it was on. I could not call up Jesus' face, just the covert night scene, a pale green moon revolving behind his head, or perhaps it was his halo. His hand, his gesture at knocking, the hand that spoke of an intimacy with the heart he was visiting — although there were dried stalks and vines in front of the door to show it had not been opened for some time.

I walked through two floors of the empty gallery, listening to my own footfalls. I did find a white room that seemed to be the same room, but either it was not, or the picture had been taken away. Instead of Jesus there was a huge, gilt-framed painting of a woman lying on a bed in a lacy white gown. A lace cap was etched on her forehead like frost on a window.

Beside her stood her husband in a fine black costume. I saw immediately that the woman was dead, her features white and heavy. And that a third figure, a woman in a black gown sitting at the foot of the bed, was *the same woman*. This woman's face was alive with sorrow, she leaned her temple against her hand, a witness to her own dead self.

Back out on the street I walked blindly up towards Piccadilly Gardens. Darkness had fallen while I was in the art gallery and there were no lamps to hold it back. Massive buildings rose up out of the ground on either side of me, like cliffs thrusting up out of the paved city, and faceless figures moved in the black doorways. On the street there was still a bit of light from the sky, but a lorry with no headlights loomed up in front of me and I dove back to the pavement and stood against a pile of sandbags, trembling. I tried to turn my thoughts away from the picture, but I could not, I could not resist its details, the woven reeds on the floor, the husband's hand, resting on a skull that sat on a stand beside the bed — as though he'd reached down to steady himself and the skull was what his hand encountered. I started walking again, trying to shut my mind to the face lying on the gleaming satin pillow, the waxy, bloated heaviness of the dead face. So changed, so impossibly changed, so certainly the same woman. I trudged over the uneven stones and near Piccadilly I heard the newsman's bleat again, longer now, he was calling *Final News!* I heard the newsman and hopelessly I turned up the street I'd taken when I got off the tram at noon. I was in a desperate dream, a familiar one, distractions drawing me away from the urgent task at hand. But it was not until I stepped into a pub to check the time and saw that it was well past six that I realized the distractions had been devised by myself alone and that I was not going to meet George.

9

Both sides were praying, but apparently England was God's favourite. At first when France fell all they talked about was so many men getting out of Dunkirk in those little boats — the divine miracle of it. People said the Channel was calmer that day than mariners had ever seen it. But really, it was a shocking defeat, France gone and all the weapons and lorries England had managed to build over the last year smashed up and left behind. A boy I knew by sight, Ruth's boyfriend, was killed, and Uncle Stanley had a nephew lying in the Royal Victoria in Hampshire gravely injured. People now said that the Germans had four planes for every British plane, and the insane fact that England had lost the war began to press itself into our brains, although you couldn't say so out loud because you could be fined for spreading alarm and despondency. Daily we were told to expect the invasion. Archie was stationed in Wales with the RAF and he told Lois that the citizens in a village along the coast had collected soup plates and buried them in rows on the beach so the Germans would think they were mines being uncovered by the tide. By the end of June the Channel Islands were occupied. Jenny had a brother in Guernsey, and suddenly there was no mail in or out. In

Guernsey, it was rumoured, German soldiers roasted and ate the carrier pigeons belonging to English families, killing two birds with one stone, you might say. It was close, close.

Madeleine and I left school in June with no attention paid to our leaving whatsoever, and began to spend all our time with the WVS, working mostly in the donations depots. Going back to Canada was out of the question: the Germans had started to bomb Liverpool. Two weeks after that the Blitz started and then of course London was all on fire. It was a flaming target they could see from the other side of the Channel, so after that there wasn't much point to the London blackout. We hadn't been bombed yet, but each public garden and commons had a big wagon with a winch on it, and when the air raid siren went off a crew came out and put a fish-shaped barrage balloon up to foil enemy bombers. As we ran to the shelter we saw them hanging in the air over Oldham, the whole scene looking like a children's story of the future, of the day the fishes take to the air.

I did not write to George, and he did not write to me. The night I left him waiting alone in a flat in Manchester he didn't come home at all. He just rolled in to pick up his kit an hour before he had to get on the train on Sunday. Aunt Lucy didn't have the heart to be angry. I didn't see him, I had gone to deliver some sewing to Nettie. He missed his next leave. He was confined to barracks again, but Wilf dropped in to see us. Wilf said George had asked him to deliver a message: to tell us that he declined to submit further correspondence to the scrutiny of morons. I felt as if someone had clouted me, my cheeks burned with mortification. He means the *censors*! said Wilf. Christ, Lily!

I remember the maple trees along the Edge that fall had black spots on every leaf, like a leopard's. I remember bushes like saskatoons with round leaves, but bearing white berries that murmured poison. I remember how hard we worked, how greasy our hair was, how starved we were for comforting food, how we dressed in whatever came to hand in the morning. It didn't matter, it didn't matter what we were. All the longings we held for ourselves, all our hopes for things to be a certain way, were pressed down to a little glowing nugget and put to the side, buried in a hat box in the back of a wardrobe. I remember Madeleine lying face down in her bed and crying about their cousin in Hampshire, who had a brain injury. I sat beside her and stroked her shoulder.

I can't cry in front of Mother, she said when she sat up. You're such a pillar of strength, Lily.

Oh, Madeleine, I said, shaking my head. I couldn't say what I was thinking, that in a funny way those days suited me. It was a relief to just do what was expected of you, to be free to be good. Or maybe it's that I was more prepared than most. I never had imagined the future as an ordinary, flat road running off towards a vanishing point. This was the world as I knew it, a fearful struggle between good and evil.

It was the last four years that began to seem unreal, the unconscious days when I lived only for romance. Strangely, it was then I began to think about home, to worry about my father, that he was (to use Nan's term for it) *taking fits*, something my mother's letters never hinted at, but they wouldn't, would they? Home came to me freshly while I sorted through barrels of mouldy clothes at the WVS depot: the barn, where the dry, dusty hay and the moist, rotting manure were two strands of the same smell, my father's cheek resting on the breathing side of a cow while he milked. The path the cows had worn deep into the turf of the prairie. Thinking about walking with Dad to the pasture, I sorted shirts, walking back and forth between rows of garment stands in the damp old depot. My mother I could only really picture in an uncharacteristic moment: when she laughed, like the day we were picking saskatoons and she made her hair into a horsetail to drive away the flies. No one in our family made a sound when they laughed, but Mother's face would crumple and her eyes would stream as though laughter were so alien to her face that it completely dismantled it. How pretty she must have been as a girl! Before the light in her face was put out. By things never being quite what she wanted them to be. *By me* I thought as I dumped out a crate of flattened shoes. By my nature being something she was bracing herself to resist, by my turning out as she had feared from the moment I was born or even before.

It seemed my father loved me, but my mother's attitude was based on a clearer grasp of who I was. But who was I, what was so bad about me — what was the sin that stained me as a child, when Satan used me to distract listeners from the word of God? I could see the hungry little girl I was, the fidgety, yearning child. *I never did anything that bad*, I protested to myself, *I never did anything.* And this seemed very true, it still seemed to be true: I saw how careful I was not to do anything, not to have a self that anyone could lay hold of or blame. Better a series of gestures, better no self at all than a self who would be held responsible. And that took me to my long afternoon on the streets of Manchester, to a shame I turned away from.

Aunt Lucy asked us gently to pray for George, but I didn't even try. I was free to be good, but I couldn't pretend to pray. That particular canopy over the world, I saw now, had been dismantled and packed away. It wasn't George's science that had done it and it wasn't even the war. It had started before that, as long ago as George saying, *Oh, you're low church* (the way he said of Russell, *Oh, he's a Marxist*), putting a name on the thing, making it one thing that others looked at from the outside, the way the prairies were now one thing and not the whole world. Or before that: it was seeing the ocean, its mind closed, indifferent to the ships plowing along its surface and the ships rotting below with skeletons bobbing in their cabins. It was the size of the world, so much bigger than I'd imagined when I signed on to save it. And it was people such as Aunt Lucy, who were kind to me because they were kindly disposed, with no thought of attracting God's attention.

Prairie turf with all the sand dug out from under it, that's what my faith was like. As for the moment when it did collapse, I could picture myself out walking alone on Oldham Edge and seeing the face of God in the clouds with rays of sun shooting out behind him. A petulant, disagreeable face, like in the frontispiece from the Lutheran Bible: things have slipped beyond him. I look at the face of God and then I'm distracted by my thoughts and look away. A breeze blows across the moors, and when I look up again it's rearranged the clouds a little. The face is slanted, distorted, as though God's been stricken by palsy. And then the face blurs a bit more. The next time I look up it's gone, the clouds are just white clouds against a sky the colour of harebells, and I'm still walking along the Edge, a cold wind biting at my ears and, laid out at my feet, the fields along the Yorkshire border, where a batch of new conscripts in straggling columns charges at scarecrows.

They started evacuating people from London again, and Aunt Lucy got notice we'd be hosting *four* and she was to go down to the church hall to pick them out. All us volunteer girls were issued tin helmets and put on a rotation to patrol the roof of the hospital one night a week, watching for incendiary bombs and raising the alarm if one landed. Jenny and Madeleine were placed on the first shift. That same day, September 15, George came home on a forty-eight-hour leave — news everyone heard with heavy hearts because it meant this was his embarkation leave, his regiment was finally going to see action. By the time he made it home with two mates they'd had a fair bit to drink and there were just eighteen hours left (although I don't think that was entirely their fault, it was hard to get transport).

I stood in the kitchen and we said a grave hello to each other. I had nothing to say by way of explanation; silence was the truest thing I had.

It was Wilf and their new mate Tom Tipperton whom George brought with him. Tom Tipperton was known as Tommy the Tommy, or as the Tool. Madeleine offered them some bread pudding made with powdered egg and he said, Don't mind if I do, and before she could serve it he picked up a spoon and started eating straight out of the dish.

Madeleine smiled gently and reached down saucers for Wilf and George. You're a machinist, then, are you? she said to Tom. In peacetime?

I don't get you, love.

Well, I thought from your nickname.

They all laughed. Tell the lass, Tool, said Wilf, and George said, Tom was caught in the bathhouse in a state of priapic lubricity.

Tommy opened his wide mouth, displaying a quantity of chewed bread pudding, and screamed with laughter. Pricky lubricky, is that what you call it? he screamed. Is that what you had the night they debagged you?

Madeleine stood resolutely by the sideboard and asked if they'd like to have their tea with us that night, seeing it was their last night and they were on their own. But Wilf said they were planning an outing for their last night, to a riding academy in Manchester.

There's a riding academy in the *city*? Madeleine said, and Wilf and Tom acted as though they were choking and ran out into the garden bent over double with laughter. George stood by the window drinking his tea. Several of his fingernails had been broken almost halfway down, they looked ever so sore.

To get him to look at me, I said, Have you seen any of the bomb sites?

Yes, he said. He did look at me then.

Imagine bombing civilians like that! I said.

It wasn't intended, George said.

What do you mean?

The first time, he said. Back in August. They were after the air base at Thameshaven and in the blackout they missed it. So then Churchill bombed Berlin. And now they're retaliating for that. He tipped up his cup and finished his tea. Although, when it comes down to it, he said, we were the first to bomb civilians. At Westerland on Sylt. Back in January. Not that there's much strategy involved, from either side. They dump their payload and hope for the best, and then the citizens on the ground dream up the strategy.

He put his cup on the counter. On a different point, he said, have you heard from Russell Bates lately?

No, I said.

Last I heard he was in hiding, George said. It's quite the thing, what's happening in Canada. They've outlawed their Communist Party. Do you know which other countries have done that? Germany. Italy. Japan.

Is that a fact, I said. We looked directly at each other and I saw something measuring me, a look I was familiar with, but not from George.

His mates had come back in. Taperleg's talking politics, said Wilf. We're going to have to have a chat with the captain when we get back.

By tea Tom and Wilf were gone, but then Aunt Lucy came back with our evacuees, only three as it turned out, a Mrs. Whitelaw and her two children, so then *they* were there for tea. Mrs. Whitelaw talked through the whole meal about the bomb that fell on their terrace while she and the children were in a shelter under the railway bridge and about the terrible cries they heard from under the rubble of their neighbours' house when they went back in the morning. It was the G-R-A-N-D-D-A-D, she spelled, while her children watched her intently. *Wouldn't leave,* she mouthed to Aunt Lucy.

When she finally took the kiddies up to the attic Aunt Lucy turned to George (who had not uttered a word all through tea) and took his hand on the table. Can you say where you've been stationed, love? she asked.

He said he hadn't been stationed anywhere, he'd spent the last month driving back and forth over the south of England, pulling a field cannon, a twenty-five-pounder that was brought back from Dunkirk against orders.

What is the sense in that? Madeleine asked.

Look, Auntie Mabel, cried George in a high, false voice, *there goes ANOTHER one of them big guns! If that nasty Mr. Hitler tries anything on — we'll give him what for!*

Uncle Stanley shoved his chair back from the table. You never change, do you? he shouted.

He had to make sommut up, said Aunt Lucy soothingly. He can't say what they're really up to. Forgive me, love, I shouldn't of asked.

⁂

After tea George wanted to go down to the pub to have a word with his mate Horace, his newspaper friend. Just for an hour, he promised Aunt Lucy. When he was gone we turned the wireless on for the six o'clock news. London was bombed that day in broad daylight. Wave after wave of German planes filled the sky, a hundred planes coming over and then a hundred more, and then the RAF came out and there were dogfights over the Strand. Buckingham Palace was finally hit. Then Madeleine was truly frightened about rooftop duty, but we all said, no, it's probably better, the planes will be down tonight.

I put on my mackintosh and walked out with Madeleine

and Jenny just as darkness fell. They went down the street wearing their tin helmets and I stood breathing in the damp air, watching until they disappeared into the darkness halfway down the street. The mill was down there, but it had vanished. The houses were closed and shuttered, everyone had given up their torches and lanterns, the valley'd been given back over to the fog and the hyenas. I wondered what George would have to say about the news from London. I needed George, I longed for George to reach into his storehouse of theories and tell me what this was. But George was so determined to see what nobody else saw — could he even see what *was*?

A figure came up the street, a soldier. He was very close before I knew for sure that it was George, although from the height of him I thought it must be. He must have stood in a doorway, let Jenny and Madeleine walk on by without greeting them. But I was right in front of the house and he couldn't avoid me.

Well, if it isn't young Phoebe, he said in his reedy voice from the other curb.

You're home early, I said. I waited the way you wait for a stranger who's hailed you on the street, not knowing what might come.

Horace is off on his beat, George said. Still he stood on the other curb, he seemed to be gathering himself. Finally he detached himself from the shadows and crossed towards me, walking with the deliberation of a conscious drunk. Horace is off, he said, up the dark streets and down them again, jotting things down in his little book. All the news that's fit to print, that's what he's writing. The rest he saves for his mates. Ply him with cider and out it all comes!

He stood breathing ale in my face. I guess you've heard? he said. Quite the day, eh? Our Horace was on the blower with a chap from London. He said it was a cracking show! All the

London brokers out on the pavement waving their bleedin' briefcases and cheering. You could have charged admission! But it's all free in war, eh! He cackled at that and I felt a twist of fresh loathing for the way the Tommies talked. I took a step backwards and he tipped closer, trying to get me to look at him.

Here's a story for you, Lily-in-Canada, he said. It's a story from London, Horace told me. It's about a Dornier and a gallant little Hurricane. Do you know the Dornier, Phoebe? It's a great big German bomber, the Dornier, a brutal machine, its payload could flatten St. Paul's. But this Dornier was crippled — one engine was pouring smoke! And a Hurricane spotted it and darted in for the kill. What a moment, eh! What a David and Goliath moment! And quite the show as it turned out, a better show than anyone expected. Because — guess what? The Hurricane was out of ammo! Our brave little Hurricane had no fuckin' firepower left. He'd shot his wad, the poor perisher, he had nothing left, nothing but his bleedin' British pluck to draw on.

George dug his fingers into my shoulder. His beret was stretched down over his old man's skull. So what do you think he did? What do you think he did, Phoebe? Come on, cudgel thy brains!

I've no idea, I said. I stood against the curb. My throat hurt with the effort of holding back sobs. I'm not really interested in combat stories, I said.

Not interested in combat stories? he cried. Oh, Lily, mein Liebling, I wonder what you are interested in?

George slipped his arm around my shoulder and started walking me back, through the little iron gate and across the front garden. I wonder what it is you'd like to hear? he said. Because I will talk, Lily, I will tell you what he did, this plucky, barmy little pilot. He rammed his *plane* into the Dornier! That's what he did! He had no firepower left so he turned his plane into a goddamn weapon in mid-air — *four tons of steel at two hundred miles an hour*. That's *war* for you, that's the beauty of war, war is the father of invention.

We were by the house by then, where the house turned its long side to the moor. George leaned against the house and then his legs buckled and he slid down the wall. I slid down too and crouched beside him. We sat shoulder by shoulder in the little space between the house and the garden wall under my bedroom window, where Lois had perched the night before Archie left. The moss was soft under us. They should have lain down here, I thought. George leaned his head against his knees with great weariness. I tipped my head back against the wall. I could smell the autumn smell of earth, I could smell rain hanging over us. There were no sirens or searchlights, no lorries drumming along the motorway. Do you remember hiding here? I asked, touching his arm. When I first came? When we played that game at the New Year's party?

Oh, I remember, he said. He took my hand, he held it loosely and lifted it, he pressed it against his hot forehead. I remember all right, he said. But it's not the past you want to dwell on. That's well over now, there's other things crying to be thought about. This, for example. You think my story's finished, don't you? You think that's all there is. Ordinarily you'd be right. But it's not over. That's the thing about this war, there's always worse to come.

George dropped my hand, sat up and turned his head towards me. He lay his face against the bricks. Be glad I'm here to tell you this, Lily, he said softly. You'll never read it in the paper, you'll never hear it on the wireless. It's about the German pilot, the bloke in the Dornier. The RAF fighter downed the Dornier, but he didn't get the pilot. The pilot dropped out on his chute. He managed to get himself out and he came down in Kennington Park. You know Kennington — it's been famous for a hundred years, the Chartists made it famous. This German bloke came down on the common in Kennington and everybody saw him out of their kitchen windows, floating down past the chimneys, and there was a great commotion, everyone running out of their houses to look. All the gentle people of Kennington, coming out to see. They couldn't believe their luck! Their own German pilot in their own back garden — their own personal Hun! And then they ran back in to get their kitchen knives and pokers. They took their knives and pokers to him and killed him. They killed him! Beside the cricket pitch in Kennington.

And then he scrambled to his feet and snatched up my hand. Total war, lass, he cried. Total war this time, that's what the old men said. Why leave it all to the boys in blue?

He started to run then. My legs moved on their own and I let myself be pulled along like a wooden toy, past the shed and across the back garden, down the ginnel and out into the open field. It was raining and I couldn't tell the darkness of the sky from the darkness of the earth, but he had played there all his life, he knew the ways and he pulled me along, squeezing my hand so I thought my fingers would break. *The bells of hell go ting-a-ling-a-ling, for you but not for me*, he sang as we ran. Out on the Edge he stopped for a minute and pulled me close to him again with an arm around my waist and said in my ear, They cut up his parachute and took pieces of it home for souvenirs. About the disposition of his body I have no information.

I said, George, I'm going back, I'm cold, we're going to catch our death. But he started running again, holding my hand even harder and singing in a harsh, exultant voice, *Oh death, where is thy sting-a-ling-a-ling? Oh grave, thy victor-ee?* and then he said, Watch there. But it was too late — my foot plunged into a hole and I sank down onto the rough, wet gorse. He dropped beside me and began to kiss me then, pushing his tongue like an eel into my mouth and sliding his cold hand boldly up my thigh, groping under my skirt. I was crying and I pushed him away and scrambled up and ran, trying to sense the path with my feet. I could hear him behind me in the dark, singing like a maniac while I ran blindly towards higher ground. Rain wet my face, rain ran down the neck of my mackintosh. I blundered into a low thicket and shoved and lurched my way through it, blackberries clawing at my legs, and then I couldn't hear George and I was on open ground again. Ahead of me were two thin bands of light, an ill-fitting shutter it must have been, and I ran towards them and collided with a low wall — the garden wall of our own house.

10

That night, September 15, was the first in weeks that no air raid siren rose in the sky over Oldham, but — except for the evacuated children and maybe Mrs. Whitelaw — nobody in the house seized the chance for a real sleep. It was two in the morning before Archie left, and then Aunt Lucy and Lois sat with Lily for another half-hour before they went to bed. But Lily still couldn't sleep, and finally Lois got up with her again and they were in the kitchen making a cup of tea when George's mates dragged him in. It was about five o'clock by then but still dark, and Madeleine and Jenny had not come home, they were still watching on the hospital roof. It was Tom Tipperton and a different mate with George, a soldier they didn't know, and they used George's key and came in the back way, George with an arm slung around Tom's neck, looking very ill.

Crikey, Tom was saying, we had the devil finding the place in the dark. Lad-o wasn't much help. You have to see he makes the train at ten. He needs a few hours' kip.

A bath, more like, said Lois. You *stink*. She gave a little kick to George's shin as they lowered him into a kitchen chair.

Couldn't even spend your last night in! Mother's been *sick* with worry. You were needed.

He's had a rough night, the poor perisher, the other soldier said. Prolly picked himself up a dose.

Lily leaned against the kitchen cupboard, feeling the tin edging of it under her palms. She was not crying, not then, but her grief weighed on her like a new, chafing garment — a heavy buffalo coat, hot, stifling, something that encased her, something to be carried and borne, without it really altering what she was inside. *George will have to take notice now* was her thought (a thought she would recall with such shame) as Lois reached for her and said, Something's happened. Poor Lily's had — and Lily dropped her head forward and started crying, not bothering to blot her tears. Lois passed her a handkerchief and said something Lily didn't make out. And then with her tears the truth of it came to her again, the way it had come freshly two or three times through that long night, like stumbling across an accident. She turned her face away from it and saw George, his head buried in his bent arm on the table, his shoulders shaking. Tom said, Jesus, Taperlegs, get a grip on yourself, and then she heard the low foreign sound of George crying, and felt him reach for her hand, and knew that he thought her grief had something to do with him.

When Lily came in the night before, shaking the rain off her mackintosh, they were all sitting in the living room waiting for George. They all looked at her and she said, He was out on the street a while ago — I expect he'll be right in.

Uncle Stanley was off on his route, but Archie was there. He was on leave too, and Lois sat beside him on the couch holding his hand. They had stayed in because of George, and they sat in the living room with the wireless turned on low, and George didn't come in, and everyone was annoyed, everyone's anxiety was taken over by irritation, by hurt. At least it's a dark night, said Aunt Lucy, thinking of Madeleine on the rooftop. Archie tapped his pipe against the ashtray and they sat on in the living room without turning the lights on so they wouldn't have to put the shutters across. The smell of cabbage hung in the air, and Lily sat still on the couch, feeling George's rude, frantic hands on her thighs, and Mrs. Whitelaw began to tell her story again with new detail to justify the retelling: how piercing, how terrifyingly close the whistling shells were as they clung together in the shelter, and how she *always* took her blue china clock to the shelter but had left it behind that night in her haste. Distracted they all sat and watched through the lace curtains as the postman came up the front garden with the second mail (as though he were part of Mrs. Whitelaw's story, as though he were bringing news of the bombardment). He was very late, and he rang the bell, which he didn't normally do. Archie was the one who got up to open the door, revealing a small, uniformed man standing with a yellow telegram in his hand, like a boy playing the part of a postman in a music hall skit. Mrs. Whitelaw was still talking and Aunt Lucy looked at her to say, Excuse me a moment, and got to her feet and raised her hand to her throat. It was the moment Aunt Lucy dreaded and expected (although who would have expected it while George was at home?). But then it turned out not to be that moment at all, it was a rehearsal for it, for whenever it would come: *Miss Lily Piper* was the name the postman read out. Everybody stood up, including Mrs. Whitelaw. Archie brought the telegram over to Lily. She took it from him, looking at Aunt Lucy with wondering eyes while she opened it, surprised but not frightened, still protected by something she'd not ever thought about before (her belief that nothing real could happen to her in this world), and tipping the telegram up to the light of the window she read the inscrutable words: DAD PASSED AWAY SEPTEMBER 13TH STOP FUNERAL THE 16TH STOP BOOK PASSAGE HOME STOP MOTHER, and she passed the telegram to her Aunt Lucy, shaking her head. They've made a mistake, she said. It's my mother who's been sick.

There were only three ports open in all of England, but Liverpool was one of them. Uncle Stanley managed to arrange her fare for the end of the week. Normally this would have been impossible, but after the sinking of the *Arandora Star* in July, passengers cancelled by the hundreds. Outgoing passage was still considered safer than incoming, although what with the nightly air strikes in Liverpool and London and with George and Archie shipping out, no one dwelt much on fear for her safety. Stanley would have driven Lily to Liverpool, but they couldn't get petrol. So in the end she said goodbye to her aunt and uncle in Oldham and Lois and Madeleine went down to Liverpool with her on the train. Sitting beside Madeleine, with Lois across the aisle, she took the telegram out of her handbag and read it over. Her mind snagged on phrases like AWAY SEPTEMBER and STOP MOTHER and she still couldn't put aside the thought that they'd misinterpreted this message, that really it said something else. She passed it to Madeleine and asked her to read it again. Madeleine read it and looked at Lily with her smooth face full of sympathy, and then she leaned closer and sat with one hand dangling over Lily's shoulder, patting her from time to time all the way there.

There was Liverpool, the big stone buildings at the waterfront she'd marvelled at when she arrived four years before, and the two ungainly birds like wild turkeys perched on the top of one of them, one facing the water and the other facing the land. But barrage balloons floated above them, silver against a sky black with smoke. The Mersey was as full of traffic as a motorway, ships back from Dunkirk pockmarked with patches of red lead. All over the head of the river, the burnt-out hulls of ships stuck up out of the water — left like skeletons guarding a cemetery at the very spot where they'd been torpedoed, left to foil U-boats stealing up the Mersey to plant more mines. Her ship, the *Manchester Division*, was already at dock and boarding. It had been painted grey all over and had had two gun turrets mounted to its foredeck for this voyage. Uncle Stanley had come back from the shipping office proud of having arranged Lily's passage on this particular vessel, as on its maiden voyage in 1918 it had rammed and sunk a submarine off Flamborough Head. He made much of how safe it was, but Lily knew that in spite of her ship's historic prowess there were numerous ways she could come to a bad end during the voyage. George might think her ignorant, but she knew there were still mines in the Mersey, she followed the news enough to know that. And once in open water the *Manchester Division* might be torpedoed by a submarine, as the *Athenia* or the *Arandora Star* had been. Or a cordon of Messerschmitts might come droning over the horizon and drop a bomb on its deck. But Uncle Stanley told her there was safe passage across the Atlantic every week: those were the ships you never read about in the news. Mr. Shillingford had seen an aerial photograph of a naval convoy and he sketched it for Lily, the ships laid out in a diamond pattern the way a boy playing war might arrange them on the rug. He was very kind about it, drawing a tiny figure labelled LILY on the deck of a ship safely in the middle of the pack.

She had not said a proper goodbye to George and she knew she would never see him again. While Lois dragged the trunk over to the baggage area, Lily said to Madeleine, I'll never see him again, I know it, and Madeleine misunderstood and thought she meant her father, and said, He's safe, in a better place. Madeleine held her and patted her the way Aunt Lucy would have. There, love, she said. It's not so far. The war will be over and once you've put your mother to rights you'll come back to us. Or maybe we'll come to see you. Wouldn't that be a laugh, if we all came to Canada? When Lily started sobbing again she said, You're upset because of your dad, and who can blame you. Then Lois was back and gave her a kiss and it was time to board. At the top of the ramp, she looked down at the faces turned up to the ship, she scanned them for a spot of colour, and there was Madeleine's red scarf. But she saw it for only a second, and then it was lost in a sea of khaki.

Book Three

Up in cabin class the Barr Colonists would spend their days playing chess and bridge and musical instruments. On Sundays they'd sing, *And did those feet in ancient time walk upon England's mountains green?* but during the week it was other questions they mused over — *Where have you been walking, shepherdess?* or *Why do you weep, dear willow?* Below in steerage my dad and Joe slept in the smell of horse manure (the ship had been a troop ship in the Boer War), and when they weren't sleeping they played cribbage and poker with Bantam Bradshaw, a handsome, well-proportioned miniature of a man who took every step as though he were bobbing in a ring. He'd been to the Boer with the Bantam Regiment, and the song they sang over and over every night was one that he taught them:

> *In the fight for England's glory, lads*
> *Of its world-wide glory let us sing!*
> *And when we say we've always won,*
> *And when they ask us how it's done,*
> *We proudly point to every one*
> *of England's soldiers of the King!*

Even after they arrived in Saskatoon they did their best to maintain the lines, pegging a section off for cabin class. But they were all in the same sort of tent, ridiculous bell tents the Dominion Immigration Department put up for them, and there they squatted for days, torn between a desire to get to their land (which the homestead office assured them did exist, although Isaac Barr had never laid eyes on it) and a fear of being two hundred miles from a rail line. They were waiting for the luggage train, which never came. Scarlet fever broke out. The government agent was doing his best to get them moving, but they resisted. They resisted entering into any relations with the government. Those who had Union Jacks flew them, those of both classes.

Here Joe Pye becomes the modest hero of his own story for a bit. He compared section, township and range numbers with everyone he talked to and finally he found his neighbour, a man whose paper read 36SE-49-2. Playfair, his name was, a cigar importer from London who was rapidly going through his best collateral, a case of wonderful Cuban cigars. I picture Playfair as a soft-fingered, talkative man. He asked Joe into the beer parlour and over a small glass of whisky they agreed to team up. The next day he came by the single men's tent wearing jodhpurs and took Joe to see a team of chestnut geldings he'd set his heart on. The team cost four hundred and fifty dollars. While they were leaning against the stall, Playfair's wife appeared in the doorway of the stable holding her baby. When he asked her what she thought, she just looked at him and said, *Oats?* Her first name Joe Pye did use: it was Amelia. Joe could not imagine how Amelia and Playfair had ended up together, from either point of view — the last person a braggart wants to be with night and day is a woman who can break a situation open with a word.

Finally Joe Pye walked out of town, where there was less speculating, and bought an ox team and cart from a Doukhobor farmer. The oxen cost a hundred and eighty dollars and could live on grass. With their cart piled high with gear and the six Playfair children, Joe and the Playfairs set out for the west a few days before most. The oxen were young and tenaciously drawn to sloughs — apparently they understood only Russian. The whole area was as level as a lake on a calm day, and covered with light scrub and waving grasses. You can see ten miles ahead of you on the prairies — a long day's journey on an ox cart. The sky must have seemed twice as big as an English sky and bluer than heaven, the same white cloud painted over and over all along its lower edge, as though a painter had been cleaning his brush on the side of a bowl. Sloughs fringed with blonde grasses dotted the landscape, navy blue sloughs where the sky had been boiled down to ink. Joe said that they walked most of the day because the pace of the cart made them frantic. They walked and they camped on their own, avoiding the government camps along the way, where colonists caught scarlet fever and dysentery.

The *colonists*, Joe said, as though he were never one of them, one of the pretend farmers leaving Saskatoon in the spring runoff, in a cart top-heavy with rolled-up Persian rugs, crates of china, English saddles, cages of pigeons. (Didn't they lose all their luggage? I asked. That were the pianos, Joe said. The bathtubs and feather beds. They was on the train that were lost.) Criminally ignorant of domestic animals, tethering their horses to bushes the size of a cabbage and spending days wandering the prairies looking for them through opera glasses. Tying the halter to a wrist and being dragged to their death when the horse bolted. Leaving a team in harness for the whole trip because they wouldn't know how to put the tack back on if they took it off. Leaving dead horses to rot on the trail, their flesh torn open by scavengers. Falling into sloughs and alkaline flats (four wagons stuck at once in the same bog), and watching Isaac Barr gallop past while they struggled up to their waists in mud (or so they claimed). Plunging into the slough again when a grass fire roared by, standing up to their necks in water while the whole triangle between the Battle and the North Saskatchewan burnt up. Floundering on with no more small game for their suppers, no more forage for the oxen, convinced that the fire had been started by a spark from Isaac Barr's roaring campfire.

All these stories were about other people. Joe and the Playfairs did better than most: they had left early while the trail was still reasonably firm, and they got there ahead of the pack. Joe borrowed a compass and they set out to find their claims. The night they arrived was a soft evening — they must have felt like Adam and Eve in the Garden of Eden. His estate would be named Matilda Court, Playfair told Joe, in memory of his mother. While Playfair was showing Joe Pye where he'd put the cricket pitch, Amelia strung their canvas from the cart to a single tree and put the little kids to bed under it. And then someone rode by and told them they were two miles off. They set up camp three times before they got it right. Who would have guessed you need to calibrate a compass differently in Canada?

※

I linger over the rest of it, a love story, Joe Pye building a house for the forthright Amelia, while her husband found every excuse to spend the day at the colony headquarters (it appeared he was what Reverend Lloyd called a *liquorite*). Sod was for peasants, as oxen were, but what else could Joe use? They built the house by trial and error and with the advice of equally ignorant neighbours, and they hired two Cree men to thatch the roof. Joe liked working with sod, nestling each brick grass-side down into the wall, strong and limp and tractable like the pelt of a small animal. All they had to buy was the door latch and hinges. For light they worked three pickle jars into the wall, like portholes in a ship.

When winter came Joe slept on a palliasse on the Playfairs' earthen floor, amazed at the feeling of living in a burrow. The cold settled in, the colonists lost toes and earlobes, and an orphan brought to the colony by a missionary froze to death. It was Joe who ventured outside to hunt — they lived on jackrabbit stew. As the sod shrank with the cold it was Joe who dug up frozen earth and thawed it on the stove to fill cracks in the walls. Joe taught the kids to play cribbage, which Amelia liked because it was all arithmetic. He bought them a dog. He worked at being unobtrusive, a skill that came in useful all his life.

What was Joe's one indulgence? It was the mornings, when he could have got up first to make the fire and instead lay on his palliasse with the dog curled beside him and waited for Amelia to slip around him in her long flannel nightdress and shawl, waiting for the moment the kindling would flare and light up her pure profile bent over the stove in the dark shanty. Of course he didn't tell me this. I put the whole thing together from the way he said *Amelia*.

Joe was finished with the Barr Colony in less than two years. The weather was fine the second summer and the Playfairs bought two cows. And then one spring morning, with no fanfare, Playfair himself died on the path to the outhouse. Joe was on his own quarter-section by then, sleeping in a tent. The oldest boy came over to tell him. The boy had his mother's steadiness and he didn't cry. With all the gruesome things that could have taken Playfair in this wilderness, it appeared he'd died the way he might have on a London street: he'd had a heart attack. Amelia was friendly with the neighbours on the other side, and everyone helped with the burial and pitched in to seed the twenty acres they'd broken the year before. Joe thought she'd go home, but she didn't seem to want to, so he just turned up morning and night to do her milking. Then one night I picture her stopping him at the door with one of her looks. *You think you've found yourself a ready-made family,* she'll say. She won't say the second part (*Well, I'm not having it*), but he walks home almost blind with shame. He had no idea that's what he was after, but as soon as she says it he knows it is true.

None of the things he fancied about farming in Lancashire applied to Canada, but by that second summer he'd developed an unexpected affection for his claim: for the thick, spicy turf with its tangled grasses, the smell of the sage and wild onion, the tiny, nameless flowers, different every few weeks. The meadowlark's amazing song (*I left my pretty sister at home,* Amelia's little girl translated it). He had to break his claim if he wanted to hold it, break it open so the birds would be forced out and the Russian thistle moved in. In the end he didn't have the heart for it. He had something wrong with him that summer, a hernia I think, and couldn't do much heavy work and never did get started on a house. He was surviving by collecting buffalo bones off his land and selling them to be ground up for fertilizer. Then it started to get cold again and he couldn't see himself turning up at Amelia's door. One day in a mood he walked the twelve miles into the colony headquarters (by then it was Lloydminster in honour of Reverend George Exton Lloyd, in honour of his not being Isaac Barr). He went into the homestead office and asked if he could transfer his claim to Amelia Playfair's son. The clerk probably knew that the Playfair boy wasn't more than fourteen, but he let Joe Pye do it.

On his way out of the district Joe stopped in at the Playfair house and left the claim paper made out to Harry Playfair in the latch of the door. He left the team for her too, a larger gesture than he wanted to make but he couldn't bring himself to ask her to buy him out. It was one of those brilliant sunny days of late fall. The dog bumped at his hand in welcome. Amelia might have seen him out there, a telescoped version of Joe Pye in her porthole window, but she didn't come out, that part I'm sure about.

⚒

My dad was in Canada for ten years before he saw Joe Pye again. All that time Dad worked in the green belt that runs across the middle of the prairie provinces, where spruce trees grow like quills all the way from Lake Winnipeg to Peace River. The lumber camps tended to be in lowlands, in monotonous, insect-ridden bush relieved only by swamp. It was easy to get work, though, and he could save a dollar a day, he could send money home. There were a lot of camps and he moved often. Because, because.

It was the strangest thing. When he had one of his spells, when he fell into it, he was always seized with *recognition*, in this strange, rough country was swept back to a place where his true self had been before, to a terrible memory of leaves trembling against white sky, of following a doomed trail through bush, the squalid weeds with their white seed heads, the smeared toe of his boot sinking into mud. And then he was gone into the echoing silence, taken away. The place he surfaced to, after a lost time, was an *alien* place, a world without names, where he had to lie motionless until he recognized the brown shape lying in front of his eyes as his *hand*.

He couldn't predict when it would come, nor could he resist it. The most he could ask was that he be on his own when it happened. What I think he must have dreaded most was the way people looked at him afterwards: as though they had never seen him before either — and the sensation seemed to last longer with them than it did with him, never really went away. Once when he came to under a threatening sky, he just got up and started walking. He had no idea where he was. He

277

could see everything with uncanny clarity, but he wouldn't have been able to tell you it was trees he was walking through. It was lucky he had Saturday's pay in his pocket and his knapsack stuffed with his lunch, and that he came across a road and had the wits by then to follow it. He could just as easily have headed straight into the bush. He never went back to the camp — he just held his sore tongue on the floor of his mouth and picked the moss and twigs out of his hair and kept walking.

That became a way of doing it. It was the way he left three or four crews, including Peace River, in his seventh or eighth year. The trail he followed south had been etched in the prairie turf by the buffalo and deepened by Métis freighters and settlers in ox carts; it led past Lloydminster, where, he knew, the Barr Colonists had ended up. So he went into the post office and asked after Joseph Pye. The postmaster remembered Joe for his name. He laughed and said Joe Pye had left the district a long time ago. William stood on the boardwalk for a while, wondering whether Isaac Barr was still holding a claim for him. He looked through the window into the dry goods store, at the pretty young woman measuring cloth behind the counter, but he didn't go in. In his mind the girl in the green travelling suit had gone back to England some time ago. A Dr. Hignell had hung his shingle on Main Street, and my father, riding on what was left of his resolve, paid two dollars to see him. It was the first time he had ever asked anyone about it. The doctor was matter of fact. He said there was no cause of it but birth and no cure for it but death, a cure my dad might be able to stave off for a while by avoiding sharp-edged tools, machinery with belts, stairways, and bodies of water. There was an asylum in Battleford where he could go if he had to, but he shook my father's hand and said he hoped it wouldn't come to that.

And the wish seemed to take, because my father had some good years after that. He worked his way south and got a job in a general store and eventually moved on to the store in Burnley. One day he was weighing out navy beans for the CN conductor when Joe Pye walked into the store looking for tobacco. He was on a threshing crew working its way north from Burnley. On Sunday he hitched a ride into town, carrying his crib board, and spent the day at the kitchen table where my dad boarded, regaling my father with tales of the Barr Colony and Isaac Barr's chicanery. Neither of them ever raised the question of where Boris had ended up (except once, when there was a story in the paper about a man who dressed up as a lady and robbed a bank in Lethbridge, and Joe Pye said, "So he's still in the Dominion then, our Boris").

When my dad's fits started up again he couldn't just leave. There was my mother by then, and the whole thing started to weigh on him in a different way. I keep wanting to say (about everything: his marriage, his life in Canada), *He never imagined it would be like that*, but honestly I don't think he imagined very much of anything. I don't think my father had the habit of building a world in his mind and sending some version of himself ahead to try things out; it wasn't something he did. So he wasn't always having to reconcile himself to the way things turn out. But he knew what people generally don't discover until something terrible happens to them: he knew things drained of their meaning. What it is to open your eyes to a world you've never seen before, where every ordinary thing around you is blank, as senseless as a word you've ruined by saying it over and over a hundred times, turning it into babble. As I stood on the deck of the *Manchester Division* the first morning of the crossing home, what I wondered was whether this is the truer world, heaving grey waves with nothing of me in them, the blunt iron prow pushing through water intent on its own secular purpose. Whether meaning is just something our eyes bring to things, when what we should be straining to see is the nothing that was their real meaning all along.

1

When we pull in to Burnley, the train overshoots the station and has to grind its way backwards to unload the passengers. I've been on my feet since the whistle sign a quarter-mile back, watching a dark speck in front of the station materialize into Phillip. Bracing myself on the platform between cars, I'm carried past him, and then past him again in the other direction, while he stands looking at the train with his mouth slitted open, squinting against the rising sun.

Dad did not have a seizure and topple from the loft. He did not fall face first into the river. It was blood poisoning. Phillip tells me this as we drive along the section road towards home, my trunk in the back of the Ford and my suitcase at my feet. Dad was cutting wood near the river. He'd just sharpened the axe, and somehow he nicked his leg just above his boot. Three days later his leg swelled up and he was full of fever. So they laid him in the truck and took him to the hospital in Burnley. But half an hour after they got him there, he was gone.

Dad always said a *dull* blade is more dangerous, I say. I dig through my bag, but I seem to have left my handkerchief behind on the train. Did you let Joe know? I ask.

You tell me where he is, I'll let him know, Phillip says. On either side of us stubble fields lie like rough carpet. We're shuddering over washboard, I'd forgotten washboard. Phillip just drives. It's taken me twenty questions to get this story out of him.

When the truck pulls in to the lane, the screen door slams and my mother comes slowly across the yard. She's not terribly changed, but she moves as though she's walking through deep water. I go to meet her and she starts to cry and plucks at my blouse spasmodically. Her hair is paler, a pale apricot, but still in a coiled braid. Behind her comes Betty, my new sister-in-law, an apron tied high above her stomach. No one wrote to tell me she was pregnant. I say hello, but I don't kiss her. Just a few hours back on the prairies and I know better than to try to give her a hug.

I stand by the Ford and breathe in the air. It's September, but the yard is lusher than I've ever seen it. Look at the grass, I say.

Green all right, says Phillip.

A short-haired brown dog nudges its nose against my thigh. This is Blue, says Betty. You won't have met Blue. He's a rascal! Look, he's trying to say hello!

It's just breakfast time. They've made baking-powder biscuits for breakfast in my honour, and put out two kinds of jam. The floor is different — they've covered the boards with linoleum. Red, with a pattern of curling grey feathers. On the counter sits the Elizabeth and Margaret Rose tin I sent home. We sit down and bow our heads. There's a little pause and then Phillip says, Lord, bless this food to our use and us to thy service, amen. My mother holds her head bent after the grace in her own private prayer. Afterwards she doesn't look at me and I feel the old dark ache. And there is the old sour-sweet smell of the cream separator and the bitter smell of boiled coffee. The clock with its scraping hand; I'd forgotten about that clock.

I want to linger over this scene, picture it from a vantage point high in the southeast corner of the room, the way a watcher perched on top of the cabinet would see it, or the two little princesses looking serenely off their biscuit tin: the daughter returned from abroad, a young woman wearing wide-legged navy trousers, an elastic belt with a red metal buckle, and a white cotton blouse (terribly creased, though she did her best to freshen up in the yellow light of the station washroom in Winnipeg), red lipstick on her mouth and her hair pinned up in that new way so the waves stand high in front. She's twenty — a glamorous age, she's always thought — but life is not about her. There's her mother, suddenly a widow because an axe fell two inches awry. There's the white-blonde sister-in-law lifting her cup consciously to her lips, only nineteen herself, and a baby at that very moment drumming its heels against her spine. And the brother, the brother with a farm and a sick mother and a pregnant wife to look after, stolidly working his way through his third biscuit with jam. No, life is not about the daughter, although she is twenty, and (for all she's just lost her father, and is shaken by his absence at the table that day and his grey jacket and cap gone off the hook by the door) she yearns for someone to say, *Well, what a fine young woman you've grown into, Lily. And how was your voyage?* But no one says it; even this moment, the morning of her return from a long stay abroad, is not about her.

⁂

So I sit below the clock with the bent minute hand and break open a warm biscuit, and what I say is, Have a lot of the lads from here signed up, then?

There's a moment of strange chill and then Betty blurts out, Phil has signed up.

Phillip swallows his biscuit and takes a long drink of coffee

before he finally says, I got my papers in August. RCAF. *RCAF!*
So much pride in the way he says it.

Who's supposed to keep the farm going? I cry.

Had my call-up last week, he says.

It was *supposed* to be last week, corrects Betty in her exuberant child's voice. He was supposed to report for basic training on September 20. But after the funeral he called them and told them what happened, he went to Feazels' to use the phone, and asked for the number on his call-up letter. The man on the phone said they would likely give him time to get things sorted out. And then he got another letter saying he has until October 20.

He could get a compassionate discharge, says Mother. She gets unsteadily to her feet. All he has to do is ask for one. He can say his father's passed away and his mother's sick and he has a farm to run.

She's hardly eaten, but it seems she's done. She shuffles off into the living room. She is thin, so thin, but she was always thin. Phillip smears butter and jam on the top of another biscuit, not bothering to split it open. Dabney's going to put the crop in next year, he says. Harry. I've rented to him.

What if *he* decides to enlist?

Already tried.

And?

Wouldn't take him.

Why not?

Heart.

What's wrong with his heart?

Nothing. Just a heart murmur. He's fine.

But, Phillip, didn't you try for a discharge? I cry.

He tips his chair and teeters on its back legs the way he's always done, and then he turns his face and looks straight at me. Why shouldn't I have my chance? he asks. You had yours.

None of this serving King and country business for Phillip.

Betty's cheeks turn pink. She gazes at him, her tear-filled eyes saying, *Isn't he outrageous? Can't you see why I love him so?*

I can hardly speak. What about Mother? I ask at last, dropping my voice.

She's been mad at you for a long time, he says. Now she can be mad at me.

⁂

Back in my room I open my trunk and start to unpack, shaking out my two frocks and hanging them in the wardrobe, spreading my other clothes on the dresser and the bedstead to air them. I take out Nan's milk jug that I saved for Dad and the tea tin full of George's letters. George's belemnite I put on the window ledge, the way they did, for luck. My bedroom has the sad familiarity of things you remember in your bones, not in your mind. I couldn't have told you the colour of the walls, for example, but I see now they're whitewashed plaster — yellowed like newspaper that's lain in the sun. Dead flies have collected between the two windows and I fling the inside pane open and use my washcloth to wipe them up. As I turn back to the room I'm jolted by a sudden glimpse of Dad in the corner of my eye, walking across the yard with Chummy, wearing his overalls and big rubber boots. I fling the cloth down and dart out of the house through the veranda and hurry with trembling legs to the barn. The door slides heavily aside and the dry hay and damp manure smell fills my nostrils. It's dark, but I know at once he's not there. The barn's changed, it's been shortened — someone's built a crude wall with planks halfway down, just past the loft opening. There are only four stalls on each side now and they're empty — Phillip's taken the cattle out to the pasture. A cat, a grey cat I know, stretches at my feet. The pitchfork leans against a manger, and the gloves Dad wore are stuffed into the Y joint of a beam. Above me birds clatter in the loft. I stand for a minute in the dim light with a cat pressing itself against my ankles and try to see my dad. Milking, as he did every morning and night. I can see the whole business of it, the way he flipped a pail over to use for a stool and settled himself on it, reaching for the udder that hung like part of the cow's insides fallen out. The din of milk pounding into the bottom of the pail suddenly muffling when he got a fast double rhythm going. His cheek is pressed against the cow and his eyes are hidden by his cap.

It's the middle of a sunny morning, but my mother is lying on her bed when I go back in. I will be the one who talks about him, I think fiercely at the bedroom doorway. She's lying on her side, her long pale hair loose, clutching a balled-up handkerchief. I see she's crying, and then I feel pity and something else, surprise at what a child she seems to be, a tired, hardused child. I sit beside her and put my hand on her rounded shoulder. She reaches up and presses my hand. Finally I ask, Were you with him at the end? This makes her cry harder.

The doctor was in the room, she says finally, rearranging her hanky, looking for a dry spot. And the nurse was nowhere around so he had to go out himself to get what he needed, some medicine, I guess. And then he didn't come back and your dad's breathing was very bad and I was worried so I sent Phillip to see if he could find the doctor and finally I went out myself. And when we were out in the hall — sobs shake her and she can't finish. He went so fast, she chokes out at last. No one would think it could happen that fast. If I'd had any idea I would have made him go to town the day before. It was just such a small cut, you'd never have thought anything about it.

I sit there for a long time until her sobs subside. She lies with her cheek against the pillow then, looking straight ahead. Her window is closed, but the sounds of the farm seep in, Betty's high voice, the rooster strutting out by the bunkhouse. The dog whines and the screen door bangs.

How about you? I ask. Are you feeling pretty bad?

Oh, it's no different from how it's been. I'm not in any pain. I'm just a little clumsy. I need a lot of help around the house.

I should have come home sooner.

Yes, you should have. She sits up and wipes her mouth with her hand, and then dries her hand on her skirt. Then she locates her handkerchief on the bedspread and blows her nose. She straightens the collar of her dress and smoothes her apron. Her face is defiant. *This is grieving*, her gestures say, *a rough business, but don't think it changes anything.*

Dad, I say. Was he mad at me for staying in England?

He never would be mad at you for anything, she says. She says it with the old bitterness, but I do what I want with it, I take it as a gift.

* * *

I arrived home in late September, the same week that I left in 1936. Autumn has resumed as though it's the same autumn: the prairies have a will to make those four years a dream of someone else's life.

It's going away that's supposed to be a voyage of discovery, but for me, coming home is. I learn that our fall is a very brown affair, bereft of splendour, and that in Manitoba everything is weighed down by the weight of the sky. The buildings are low, the trees don't aspire to be much more than what a child can throw a rope over. I understand now that our roads are straight because there's nothing for them to go around. Wandering out to the yard that first morning, I discover that in a prairie garden asters and marigolds are planted in military rows made straight by unwinding a spool of binder twine tied between two sticks.

Phillip is working hard to get ready to leave. He's sold the cows to a farmer at Shadwell and cancelled the cream contract. He's already shipped half the cattle and then cleaned out the barn. It was an amazing crop, Dad's last crop, a bumper crop, but the Wheat Board quota is only five bushels an acre, so for now it will sit in the barn. That's why they built cribbing across the back half — so we can use it for a granary. We're going to keep one cow for our own use, so in that first week home I go out every morning and help with the milking. The second day my hands are so stiff I can hardly hold my hairbrush, but it soon gets better. Molly, I tell Phillip, is the one I want. I've picked Molly because she's small, and my forehead fits neatly into the hollow of her hip, and the size of her freckled teats is right in my hands. She's not the best producer, but he can't be bothered to argue. He has three grieving women on his hands and I'm at the bottom of the list. He nudges me off the stool and sits down and manages to get almost another pint of milk out of her. You'll have to do better than that or she'll dry up on you, he says. How amazingly like our Uncle Hugh he is, our uncle he's never seen.

If he really is going to leave, we have a lot to do. I take the Ford out on the road and practise driving, and when I have the hang of the gears I drive to the low, long town of Burnley and park at the town hall and pick up my driver's licence. While Betty tends to the house and makes the meals, I clean up the garden and Phillip cleans out the well. He also rebuilds the pigpen, deworms Molly and cuts and hauls wood until we have a pile the height of my waist running all along the north side of the house. We go to town together and open a bank account jointly in my name and Mother's. A truck comes from Shadwell and loads up the rest of the cows, and the farmer hands Phillip a roll of worn bills. We stand in the yard and watch the truck drive off and then I put out my hand for the money. I'll deposit it, he says, shoving it in his hip pocket. Phillip hasn't changed in the slightest, except that he's about fifteen percent larger in every proportion than when I left. When Phillip was a small boy he looked like a big-headed little man and now that he's a grown man he looks like an overgrown boy. I feel a familiar tingling in my foot, the urge to kick him in the shin.

So, I say. Do you think they'll let you stay around until Betty has the baby?

I don't know, he says. I guess they'll do what they wanna do. He has a look about him I remember from the sign-up days in England: the proud, surrendered glow of someone who's attached himself to an absolute power, like a courtesan just chosen by the king.

I'm going to take Mother in to the doctor's, I say. To see what I can find out.

Good luck, he says, turning and walking back to the barn.

And he's right, she won't go. She says she's been and he told her everything he can tell her and she's not going to bother him again.

I haven't heard what he has to say, I say.

Well, I'm not going in with you, she says, fiery. I'm not a child. He said I should come back in six months and that's what I'll do. If there's anything I think you should know, I'll tell you.

She's standing by the window and I can see her making little adjustments to keep her balance, the way you might if the floor was tilting under you.

What did he say it is? I ask.

He didn't say. It's just one of those things that happen sometimes. He said I should eat raw egg whites.

I make an appointment with Dr. Ross without telling Mother and I go on my own. I don't really know him, I was never sick. His hair is longish but immaculately shaped (*I'm a professional man*, it says). And he wears a ring with a polished agate in it. He has an office full of solid oak furniture, like a city doctor's, but the picture on the wall is of a prize Charolais bull.

It's hard to predict, he says, but it doesn't look as though she has the galloping kind. He tips his chair back, as though he's taking a break from work. This is, what, two years?

The galloping kind?

She's got the symptoms of MS, he says. Has no one told you?

I ask him what this is. Can you write it down for me? I say, and he sits forward and prints the two words on a sheet of paper, printing upside down so I can read it, as if to demonstrate a boyhood prowess.

What is it? I ask, staring at the words.

No one is quite sure. It might be a hardening around the nerves. A buildup of plaque. That's one theory.

Have you told her?

I may not have mentioned the term to her. Sometimes it just makes it worse, attaching a long name like that to your troubles. You never know how it's going to go. There are people who go on for decades with just a little wobble in their gait.

If it does get worse what can we expect?

He stands up and pulls a book from the shelf and flips through the pages, reading silently for two or three minutes, and then he sits down and reads out: *weakness, numbness, tremor, incoordination, pain, slurred speech, loss of vision, bowel and bladder dysfunction, paralysis, dementia.*

Could I take a look? I ask. At what else it says?

He puts the book back on the shelf. He doesn't bother to answer this, and I see just how absurd I've made myself.

Is there anywhere else I can take her? I ask.

What's the point? There's nothing anyone can do. Nothing. That's all they'll tell you in Winnipeg. Save yourself the trip. He tucks a cigarette into the corner of his mouth and bends his head over the flaring match. I suppose you could get your people to pray, he says, his eyes mocking me as he shakes the little flame out. He doesn't mention my dad.

In our spare, clean kitchen I talk about England, no doubt I bring it into every conversation. It's not that I'm trying to impress them. Without thinking about it, I call the boys *lads*, and the truck the *lorry*, and a sandwich a *butty*. Don't start the whites until I get my knickers, I say to Betty on laundry day. All of that has to be packed away along with my trunk. Any hint that there's more out there, a world different to this one.

On a warm day Gracie comes over and we take kitchen chairs outside and sit in the yard. Gracie's short bangs lie pasted to her forehead, each clump indented by the clasp of the tin curlers she wore to bed. I think of the way she used to skate, in little stiff steps like a cat walking on ice, the socks she wore over her hands because her mittens were too short to cover the long wrists sticking out of her sleeves. And the way she smiled at me, love aching in her eyes, a half-inch of pink gum gleaming at the top of her teeth. She's wearing a baby blue cotton dress now — it could be the dress she wore when we were fourteen and dreaming about going to the Burnley fair. But she's changed, as much as I have. Something — disappointment maybe — has displaced her willing spirit. It's more striking than if her nose had suddenly grown into a different shape.

One fall Madeleine and Jenny and I went to York for the day, I say. We went by train.

Betty and Gracie glance at each other. In England I advertised Canada every time I opened my mouth. Now I discover that I have an English accent.

Was it nice? Betty asks.

Very nice, I say. It has an old wall around it, York. You can walk on it. Silence sets in. They know there's a world out there, drawing Phillip and the other boys away, but they don't know what to ask. They're like I was, on the ship in 1936.

Did you ever see Mr. Churchill in England? Betty asks finally, making an effort.

No. But I did live in Oldham. That's where he was first elected to parliament.

Phil and I heard his speech on the radio, says Betty. *We will fight them on the beaches, we will fight them in the mountains, we will fight them in the fields*, that speech. He has such a funny way of talking.

That wasn't actually Winston Churchill. It was an actor impersonating him.

How do you know?

George told me.

No mail from England. They must be writing, but for the time being there's no mail. I take old letters from George out of the biscuit tin and read them in bed at night. I examine the name and address on the envelopes, tracing the uneven, spiky letters with my finger, trying to feel the energy in George's hand, hear the sound of my name in his mind as he wrote. I don't write to him, except in my mind. I have all his letters, but the only ones I read are the early ones, from Durham and Charmouth.

Charmouth, 16 July 1938

Dear Lily,

   Six o'clock, still waiting for our tea. Mrs. Slater is starving us on purpose. This morning when Ellen came in to serve breakfast she looked like a cross between Cleopatra and a frightened rabbit. Turns out she has conjunctivitis in one eye and the nurse at the clinic told her to lay off the face-paint, so she gobbed up only the good eye. Mrs. Slater

would have let her stay but we made a big stink
about the contagion. So now Slater's on her own
and she's paying us back! Me stomach thinks me
throat's been cut, to quote our mutual granddad.

I'm sending you a drawing of the Oxford
belemnite. As you can see, the creature apparently
had two parts. The thunderbolt fossil, like the one
I gave you, was just its tail (which it used as a
buoyancy chamber). A stony cone sometimes found
in the same areas was actually the room where the
creature lived. So they've identified two fossils
in one stroke. A clever solution. But inelegant,
wouldn't you say? We almost never find the
phragmocone part. Apparently they're more
fragile. I do have one I bought in a curiosity shop.
It's in perfect condition. Interestingly, there are
growth rings in it, like a tree trunk.

Lily, could you keep watching Bardsley's for
a couple of books for me? I really need them but
I can't afford to order them new. I'm sending you
a pound. If you need more, ask Mother to lend
the rest. Some of them are pretty old, so Bardsley
might pick them up at an estate sale. In fact, you
could leave my list with him so he can keep an
eye out.

Pax,
George

And then there was a separate sheet with a list of the books, only one of which I was able to find.

⬡

Dad's clothes are too small for Phillip, and Mother wants me to clean them up and send them to the aid depot at Burnley.

All that's left are his three shirts and his work pants. He was buried in his suit. And then of course there're his heavy and light jackets, his Sunday shoes, his rubber boots. His combination underwear. His workboots. I wash the shirts and press them. I tell Mother I'd like to keep his light jacket. Tears well up in her eyes. She's been reading the *Burnley Herald*, showing me the ads for war bonds. I want it all to go to the depot, she says. It's all we have to give. I decide to slip the jacket out anyway and hide it. But she knows me. She follows me out to the kitchen when I carry the box and sits guarding it like a commissionaire until Phillip comes in to take it to town.

I go outside, trembling with fury. What she doesn't know is that I've found a pair of Dad's shoes, his house shoes, under the Toronto couch on the porch where he left them the last time he lay down for a nap. The shoes look different to me, cheap and shabby, not like his wedding shoes at all. I handled a hundred pairs like them in the WVS depot in Oldham. But the inside is finely polished from years of his feet sliding in. Each toe has made a distinct bed. When I slide my hand inside I feel the shock of intruding on his privacy. I wipe the dust from them with my sleeve and slip them back under the couch.

Three times a day we gather around the worn yellow oilcloth of the kitchen table. We begin each meal with grace, Betty full of conversation, my mother drooping like a wilted flower over her dinner, will and cunning and frustration chasing across her white face as frankly as they do across the face of a child. Some days she pulls her plate down to her lap and lifts her fork slowly to her mouth. We might be able to force her to eat, but she'll be damned if she'll enjoy it! Some days she gets up and shuffles into the bedroom in the middle of the meal, and we never know why. We just keep eating. I always thought it was just me that was wrong with my mother, but now I hold to the fact that there is something else. Sometimes I think about the particles of stone collecting like crystals on the endings of her nerves, and I think, I should be kinder, but I'm exhausted at the concept.

Alone I encounter my father, I come across him as I walk to the pasture. His fundamental kindness hangs over the path, it glistens on the bare branches of a poplar bluff. *Tell me*, I say to him. *This life — was it real to you? Did you see yourself here?* Maybe Mother and Phillip meet him too, maybe they hang their heads and let out their tears the way I do, when no one else is near.

The Sunday Phillip leaves we all squeeze into the Ford and go out to the cemetery. It's on a little knoll marked from a distance by a clump of spruce trees. Some of the graves have painted white crosses, some large stones collected down by the river. Others have proper granite headstones. My father's grave is a blank garden plot. It's flat to the prairie turf around it, not mounded. There's a piece of shingle stuck into the ground at the top end with PIPER written on it in ink. The colour's drained from the grasses around it, they're all just shades of brown and grey. My mother clings to Phillip's arm.

Going to be sunk in by spring, says Phillip. What was Norbert thinking?

Lily will have to arrange for a headstone, says my mother.

Above us clouds move in two directions — low, fat white clouds skim west, and high above, against the white sky, wispier clouds drift slowly east. Wind murmurs in the tops of the spruce trees. It's a bleak day; it's October, what other sort of day could it be?

Soon it's too cold to be outside with no purpose, and when she's not working she lies on her bed. The fossil George gave her sits on the ledge above her. The ancients were wrong about it, of course, it has no protective powers. She leaves her curtains open night and day. All she can see through her window is black branches of scrub oak against the sky, haphazard lines of ink on a white paper. When there's a wind the oak branches scratch at the window. Someone should go out and prune them, she thinks, it's what Dad would have done. Instead she does what George would have done, she looks *untoward* up in the dictionary. Whatever happened that night may have been *improper* or it may just have been *unfortunate*. Or it could have been both.

She had to hear the news from her mother — Aunt Lucy addressed the letter to both of them. Betty brought the mail from town, and Lily climbed the ladder from the cellar with the enamel basin full of potatoes to find that her mother had opened the blue airmail envelope and had the letter unfolded in her hand. She climbed up through the hole in the kitchen floor to hear her mother saying to Betty, She seems to be the kind of person who makes a fuss about things. You'd think he was her real son, the way she carries on.

Lily scrambled out of the cellar opening and snatched the letter out of her mother's hand. The first impulse of her eyes was to scan it, trying to snatch reassuring words out of the even blue lines. But Aunt Lucy's round script resisted her and she had to calm herself to start at the beginning. Aunt Lucy is sorry it took her so long to write and they hope Lily had a safe passage. They are all well, but feeling very anxious because of a telegram that came after she left, on October 20. It told them that George was missing. Then a letter arrived with the same information, that George was missing. Not missing in action. He was simply missing, he'd gone missing at sea, and his captain could not divulge the location or mission of the vessel at the time. There had been what he called an *untoward incident* during the night, not involving the enemy, and George, who'd been present for roll call in the evening, was not present in the morning. Lily read that they intend to conduct an inquiry. She read that Aunt Lucy wonders at times if he could have gone AWOL, but she knows he would never do such a thing and she can't really hope for it. He was like all the other brave lads, ready to do what had to be done, and there must have been some terrible accident. *We are trying to be brave too*, Aunt Lucy wrote, *but it's very hard not to know what happened. Lois and Madeleine are heartbroken but are trying to keep their hopes up. We know how much Lily cared for George, and are sorry to have to write to you with such bad news, dear, but send you all our love.*

Well, if he did drown, it's better than being shot in the trenches, Lily's mother was saying to Betty. The way my brother Franklin was in the last war. He got a shell in the stomach, and he had to lay in the mud for two days before they could get him out.

Lily stood looking out the window at the chickens pecking around the henhouse, and then Betty noticed her and brought her a handkerchief, handing it to her with a tender little moan. It's a miracle he didn't bleed to death, Mother said, and Lily went outside, lifting her coat off the nail in the porch and shoving her arms into the sleeves. She had known it all along, she'd carried this truth home with her the way you might carry a stone in your mouth: that she had let him down and that he was gone. She'd known it all along, but now that the letter had come she found she could hold it away from her, she could trudge in the usual way with her shoulders hunched against the wind, along the edge of a stubble field with broken stalks of wheat bristling the clods of earth. After she reached the corner and turned her back on the wind, she found she could even switch briefly to the other side: to where he was alive, where he had slipped through their fingers like one of the Romanovs, or Bonnie Prince Charlie, or the dauphin. He was making his way incognito over the cobbled streets of a village — not an English village, he never managed to blend in very well in English villages, but one with a rounded bell tower like an inverted bowl, and villagers with wooden clogs and their faces shadowed by cloth hoods. She saw a woman standing in a doorway with a little girl leaning against her skirt. The woman handed George a round loaf of dark bread. They exchanged some words in her language, and she smiled, and then he waved and walked off down the lane. He was wearing a felt hat Lily had never seen on him before, but he had his old walking stick and he walked the way he had always walked, in that same loose-jointed way.

Suddenly they begin to get mail from England. She goes to town on her own when she can and one day there are three letters from Madeleine. She takes them out to the truck and drives to the edge of town, pulling over onto the shoulder beside someone's spent garden, where broken carrots and dry cornstalks wait for snow. She checks the postmarks and opens them in order. The first one was mailed just three days after she left Oldham. Somehow Aunt Lucy's letter got ahead of it.

> *You've only just left and I miss you already. It was like having a real sister (don't tell Lois I said that). My legs are hurting like the dickens because — guess what, I have a job! Working for the Transport Authority! The day after you left it was in the paper that they needed conductors because they've doubled the tram schedule (not enough petrol to run the coaches). Mrs. Tupper said they were taking girls, so I went down to the office yesterday and I was hired. They gave me a uniform and put me to work that very morning. It's not bad, except for the lads who think a girl who will work on a tram is a certain kind of girl! Those lads need to realize that things are different now and we all have to help out!*

Lily has never known Madeleine to pray, but she says that they are praying for George. They believe they know where he was sent, although she can't say in a letter. *He had that queer idea about not writing last year*, she writes, *but now that the action has really started, I hope the silly apeth will at least let us know how he is.* Lily can hear her, the anxiety in her breathless voice, she can picture Madeleine's small hand pressed like a starfish on her breastbone while she talks. She lingers over this letter. It's hard to open the next, as if she will make this thing happen, as if it will happen in the little moment between her reading the letters, while she sits with sunlight milkily pouring through the dusty windshield.

Finally she leans her head against the window of the truck and opens it. Madeleine's handwriting is large and round and childish:

> *By now you will have Mother's letter telling you*
> *about the telegram. I wish we could have you*
> *here with us, Lily. Mother is wretched and hasn't*
> *slept since it came, but she is still going to the*
> *depot every day. It's easier to keep busy and feel*
> *you are doing some good. Archie's stationed in*
> *Bournemouth now and Lois went down to visit*
> *him. It's very hard to know what to do, we can't*
> *even have a service. We feel as though our hearts*
> *are breaking and I know you will feel the same.*

This must be the way women all over Europe have learned to say it, Lily thinks, folding the letter up with trembling fingers, that they feel as though their hearts are breaking.

The last letter is in a brown honour pledge envelope, the sort you can buy to ease the workload of the military censors. Madeleine has signed a pledge in a little box on the front: *I certify on my honour that the contents of this envelope refer to nothing but private and family affairs.* Inside she makes no effort to disguise names and places. She says that Wilf was home on leave and came to see her. He told her that the 71st Searchlight had been sent by frigate to the Orkney Islands to defend Scapa Flow, and that the night of October 16 they'd had engine problems and had to moor alongside the high cliffs at Duncansby Head. The officers were drinking in the stateroom and no one bothered to take roll call. The enlisted men were up on deck in the dark. George said there was a lunar eclipse — that was their pretext for being up on deck, the moon under blackout orders. There was a dreadful sea, and they were drinking on deck, and around midnight they got into some sort of scuffle. A private from Liverpool went over. They had grappling hooks and they pulled him out half drowned, but they couldn't put searchlights on the water to see if there was anyone else. But then when they went below, George's bunk was empty. When Lily reads this she can see the tilting, slippery deck, the dark, confused shapes of the men, the waves lifting themselves to the obscured moon, smeared with its orange light, and her image of George walking at dawn through the cobblestone streets of an ancient village melts the way a dream melts at morning.

About the disposition of his body they have no information. Some sediment somewhere will draw him in, some ledge of molluscs, he will take his chances with all the other curiosities. That's not what she thinks about, exactly, that or his dying. When her mind goes slack what's there is their wild run in the rain along Oldham Edge that last night. Always there, the way a book falls open at the page where the spine was broken. And then her mind takes her onwards from there, follows George back to the city, takes her remorselessly with him back through the streets of Manchester, to the flat on Whittle Road where his mates were drinking, and then down another lane to the house George went into later, the narrow staircase with a soil line on the wall from people reaching blindly for a banister, and a girl climbing the stairs in high-heeled shoes too big for her (it's Ellen climbing the stairs, for some reason she pictures Cornish Ellen, who cleared the tables at Mrs. Slater's in Charmouth), George following, misery ticking at the fringes of his mind (but mostly it's the ale he's feeling), and Wilf and Tom and that other boy gloating on the pavement below, laughing the moronic laugh that boys laugh over things that are not funny. George climbing the stairs to sign his pledge to a new way of being. She does not quite go into the room, her imagination lets her stop at the door, lets her roll over then and pull the quilt over her face. She knows him now, now that he is gone; she knows what was behind the elaborate ramshackle construction of his personality, that it was this one longing, to be like everybody else.

They don't talk about the news from England. Lily is aware of her mother watching her. She must know. Betty has a greedy, elevated look — she senses an opening, a wound. She's got a personal stake in Lily's spiritual condition: in her mind she was the one who led Lily to the Lord. One day Lily finds a page torn out of a notebook on her pillow:

> *Dear Lily,*
>   *Trust in the Lord with all thine heart and lean*
> *not unto thine own understanding. In all thy ways*
> *acknowledge Him and He shall direct thy paths.*
> *I am praying for you.*
>   *Your sister-in-law-in-Christ,*
>   *Betty*

They don't talk about the news from England and they don't talk about the war. It's far away, they hear it the way you hear the sound of the parade on the day of the fair, drifting intermittently out of town on the wind. Lily picks up a day-old *Winnipeg Tribune* in town. On the second page are the lists, seventeen names today. MISSING IN ACTION. MISSING AND PRESUMED DEAD. KILLED IN ACTION. Evidently a name can progress daily through the lists, as though to take families gradually through the stages of shock and disbelief. Only Canadian names, of course, but somewhere else there must be lists of the English, and the Germans, and the Italians. And the Russians — they're fighting in Russia now.

Deep in the night she swims to the surface, her arms flung across the mattress as if across waves, and she can't keep her pain in, it comes wrenching out of her. It's her mother who comes in the dark, clutching at the door frame and falling clumsily onto the bed. She pats Lily's arm, over and over. It's hard, I know it's hard, she says, her voice thick with emotion. We can't see a reason, but God always has a reason. A monster version of Lily leaps out of bed and yanks her mother to her feet, screaming, *Get the hell away from me*, digging her fingers into her mother's upper arm. Her mother is crying then too, with her mouth open like a terrified child, her head wrenched sideways by Lily's grasp on her hair. *Stay the hell out of my room*, the voice cries, a thrilling voice, plucking Lily out of the swallowing waves. But this is not what Lily does. Lily keeps her face against the pillow and all she actually says is, I'm all right, and after a few minutes her mother goes away.

Things happen in the night, but gradually, when sunlight twinkles off the scrolls of frost on the windows and the kitchen is full of the smell of coffee, the night draws them back in and opens a space in the day for ordinary pleasures. Betty is a great one for togetherness. She likes to make beds together, sheets floating down between them, she likes to stir while Lily pours. Before Lily went to England, she always wanted more talk in this house, and she has to laugh, remembering that. Betty tells them how many eggs she finds under which hen compared to how many she found last week, she tells them who drove down the road while she was walking across the yard. The less that happens in a day, the more she tells them. When she comes back from town she repeats both sides of every conversation: *And I said, We can't really use the whole thing, and he said, Well, do you want me to cut it in half for you? And I said, Sure, that would be good, and so he did, and then he said, Which half do you want? And I said, This one would be fine.* Lily can picture Phillip when he comes home with all his life in the war inside him, sitting at Betty's table and the handful of words in his mouth drying into peas.

Betty gets a long letter from Phillip — a mystery in itself to contemplate — and comes to the table with her face puffy from crying. He's applied to be an airplane mechanic and will be sent to Mountain View, Ontario, for training, and then no doubt overseas. Lily has her school atlas from England and she brings it out, but Mountain View is not listed in the index. Ontario is just a pale orange patch in a map of Canada. She shows Betty approximately where the CP line runs across Northern Ontario. Betty traces the line slowly with her finger, considering how close Phillip will travel to the Great Lakes. For the first time Ontario is finding a place in her mind, by the prospect of Phillip travelling across it. Lily knows the way these brides think. On the train from Saint John there were a lot of Canadian brides who had gone east to see their husbands off. They took her in, even though she declined to produce a story about her sweetheart: they valued her as an audience for their special knowing. Then he went to *Trenton*, they would say, taking a pull on a cigarette, *Valcartier, Petawawa, Shilo*.

Scapa Flow, she says to herself, thinking that George must have liked the feel of that name on his tongue.

Betty's bangs are cut straight across her forehead and her hair hangs in a long pale curtain down her back. She sits at the kitchen table resting her hands on her belly, and Lily stands behind her and braids her hair into two gleaming whips the colour of ripe wheat. Who taught Betty this way pregnant women have of hoisting themselves out of a chair? She's the same age as Lily and she thinks nothing of all of this, she never complains, her expression doesn't change when some sudden subterranean flailing lifts the cotton of her apron. Lily comes back from the barn and catches her hauling a pail of water in from the pump, swinging the axe over the chopping block. It doesn't seem to occur to Betty that she could ask for special treatment. The first Mrs. Stalling, Betty's mother, died in childbirth, when Rose was born. *Are you afraid?* Lily wants to ask Betty, but what good would it do to ask?

It takes her a long time to write to Madeleine and Aunt Lucy. She can't bring herself to say, *I feel as though my heart is breaking,* and really, there is nothing else. Every time she picks up the mail she sorts through it, breathing fast, but there's never an envelope with George's spiky writing on it. Every morning she goes out to the henhouse to feed the chickens, stepping over the sill because her dad never got around to building a step. Then she goes to the barn and holds the pitchfork where her dad's hands wore the handle smooth and pitches clean straw down for Molly. Morning and night she dresses up warmly, wishing for her dad's grey wool jacket, and walks out to the pasture. One cow could forage in the barnyard, but soon there will be snow and she won't be able to take Molly out, so for now she does it to remember her dad. She calls Blue and leads Molly out of the barn. She sees herself from the sky, a cow and a girl and a dog walking single file across the yard, like the premise for an Aesop's fable. In the evening when she goes to fetch Molly she cuts across the fields, holding the barbed-wire fence down to swing her leg over the way he used to hold it for her, breaking off a willow switch and slashing at the dry, leaning skeletons of Russian thistle. During the day she remembers her dad, during the night George.

3

The new year comes, 1941. There's no enterprise to make anything at all of this year, how could there be? I'm almost twenty-one. I'm five feet seven inches tall, I have blue eyes and brown hair past my shoulders, splitting at the ends because it hasn't been cut since England. I wear a blue sweater that was once Lois's, trousers my brother wore when he was half grown, with muslin blouses from England stuffed into the waistband. I have a wary, even-featured face, possibly severe, possibly interesting. No one cares, why should they? Lily and 1941 are going to roll on anyway. January, February, March, I'll squat cantilevered over the icy plank of the outhouse with my pee hissing down in its momentary passage towards steam and ice, I'll find a rusty stain on my underpants. Business as usual, while German tanks roll into Greece. I'm not consulted about this or anything else — I can't choose not to breathe.

※

As far as everyone around me is concerned, January 1941 is about William John Piper, born at nine in the morning on January 3, an infant only a mother could love. He's born in the Burnley hospital, and it's Betty's dad and sister who go in to town and bring Betty and the baby home to us. (First a widow and now a grandmother, my mother sighs.) The new nephew is comely enough, with fair skin and hair and a strong little body. But he has a rackety cry, like a badly tuned engine starting up, and his diapers have a smell beyond foul. Try to rock him and he stiffens and looks frantically away as though hoping for salvation from another quarter. They name him William, but five minutes with that baby reminds me my father's sweet nature is gone from this earth forever.

Now it's Billy who cries in the night and brings people hurrying to his side. He cries in the late afternoon as well, from the first sign of light fading until he falls asleep four hours later. After supper I take him. I show him the picture of his father on Betty's bureau, I sing him the song Joe Pye learned on the ship, shaking his little hand to its military beat. I'll be the one in charge of teaching him irony, I decide. He reacts to everything with the same outrage, letting out that terrible mechanical cry. I hold him warily. I keep expecting him to turn himself into a piglet and run away, I keep hoping he will. One evening when there's no wind I tie him into a shawl against my breast and go outside. As we walk down the road his crying subsides and his blue eyelids slide halfway down over his eyes and he turns his face up with his lips in a little pout. I'm happy for the warm weight of his body against my breasts and walk for an hour, not sure whether he's asleep or just dangling suspended over his grief.

By March he seems a little more reconciled to life, but Betty, wandering pale and puffy out of her bedroom for morning coffee, is not. March is about Betty, who's talking less and praying more. Phillip is gone. He saw his new son and then he had to leave, and Betty is inconsolable. March is three stories about Betty, the first of which I'll call *The Provocation*. This story begins when she spies me sitting cross-legged on my bed playing solitaire, and cries, Oh! and rushes from the room to conduct a fraught, whispered conference with my mother. Then, while I'm outside, my demonic playing cards disappear from my bedside table and a trash fire is set in the burn barrel. When I come in, the two of them are flushed and defiant, waiting for a confrontation. While they're waiting, prayer sessions begin in earnest, and further notes and religious tracts appear on my dresser. These I carry ostentatiously out to the burn barrel.

Secondly, there's *The Opportunity*, Betty's attendance at her sister Isabel's wedding to an Aussie airman. I'm not invited, but I do witness Betty trying to find a dress to wear, trying on all her old clothes over her new body, walking back and forth to look in the mirror in Mother's room, and in the end having to wear a maternity dress. She comes back from the wedding looking like a cat that's swallowed a bird. Everyone says hello to both of you, is all she says by way of report, as she picks Billy up from the chesterfield where he's at last asleep.

And then *The Leave-taking*, announced at breakfast the next morning. Betty has decided to move back home. Her father will come for her on Saturday. There's room for me now that Isabel's gone, she says. Her long pale lashes flutter.

Well, I know Phillip was hoping his son could be raised with the family, Mother says, and goes to her room.

But Betty hangs on. Billy seems to do better when we're there, she says, cutting her toast into fingers, her little morning ritual. He settles down faster at night. I don't know why. And I guess . . . I guess I sort of miss living with my sisters.

Betty hates her stepmother, and even with Isabel gone it will be an awfully crowded house. This is down to Mother, who never thinks of anyone but herself. The baby can be crying his lungs out and over the screaming we'll hear Mother: Could one of you girls bring me a cup of tea? But Betty won't talk about it.

She does come to visit, she brings the new catalogue and a letter from Phillip and we have a nice conversation. I ask her if she'll come out to the barn and hold the door level while I tighten the screws of the hinge. When I get her outside I force her to tell me why she left. I was just thinking of Billy, she says. It's not an atmosphere I want him to be in. I straighten up and stare at her, the screwdriver in my hand. You don't even close your eyes when we say grace, she says, her eyes round.

Then she looks away. And the sort of filth you read, I've looked into your books. Well, into one of them, but that was enough.

Which one? I can't help asking.

I don't remember the name, she says. She flushes. I have to think of Billy, she says.

There's a long pause, and then she looks up at me again, clearly terrified at her own daring, her blue eyes blinking rapidly. I hate the way you treat your mother, she cries. I feel sorry for her. Look what life is like for her. She's lost her husband, her only son's gone to war. And she's getting worse every day. She can hardly walk across the room. What's going to happen to her? Tears begin to drip down her cheeks. I feel *terrible* leaving her, she sobs, but I just couldn't stand it any more. I felt like I was going crazy. I know it's not right, what I'm doing. It's *selfish*, I know it's selfish. Phil's going to be so mad. I prayed and prayed for God to give me the strength to stay. And he didn't, it just got worse. So that must mean something, don't you think? Betty reaches for my hand. Maybe I can be more help if I'm not living here, she says. But don't worry. I won't tell Phillip the real reason.

Tell him whatever the hell you want, I say, shaking her off and turning back to the barn door with the screwdriver. Adjectival cow! I add under my breath.

So then Mother and I are on our own, and April and May and the months after are about us, about the way we make do.

Nebo Gospel Chapel, where my dad's funeral was held while I was packing up my trunk in Oldham. I like walking in, I like the moment when everyone standing in the foyer registers my high heels, the upsweep of my dark hair, my slim black skirt and the Haig tartan jacket Lois gave me because she didn't like the way it hung on her. It's red and yellow and it hangs just fine on me.

Mr. Dalrymple-the-church-planter is still there, tending his crop, although he seems to have lost his preoccupation with the Rapture. His belt's risen three inches closer to his armpits and his scalp's coming off in flakes like oatmeal. Other than that he hasn't changed much, but now I've seen a shark in a Blackpool aquarium and I recognize the *mouth* with its collapsed lips and inward-leaning teeth.

On Sunday mornings everything sticks to you. It's the effect of all that silence. Getting ready for church I saw my dad standing in the kitchen in his undershirt shaving, his braces hanging down over his Sunday trousers. That sharp moment is still there, and what I felt when I saw Mrs. Feazel in the entrance, saw how she's shrinking and darkening with age, her eyes getting sweeter and darker, like raspberries you're boiling down for jam. And what I heard in town yesterday, I'm raw from hearing that a ship full of children being evacuated from London was torpedoed crossing the Atlantic. It's an excellent badgering religion Mr. Dalrymple preaches, excellent for the Thirties, but now I want to hear what it has to say about this. We stand (why do we stand?) and Mr. Dalrymple prays at length that God will protect our boys and help them resist temptation and bear witness to the power of Christ for salvation wherever they go so far from home. That's it then: this business with fighter planes and U-boats and tanks is just a metaphor for the real battle, the battle for *souls* being waged in dance halls and canteens all across the Empire.

I open my eyes and look at the bent heads in front of me. None of us take it all in. We each have a little sliver of this war, our own little universe of suffering, but nobody has the whole thing. Except God, maybe. We sit then and I cross and recross my legs against the bubbly varnish of the pew, straightening the front pleat of my skirt. Maybe that's what God is. God is a mind that can comprehend the whole thing, the sheep starving in Dannert wire on the Yorkshire moors, each separate child falling burning into the sea from the deck of the *City of Benares*, old men crying out from under rubble in London and Berlin, chimneys standing in rubble all across Europe and all the boys in khaki in Stuttgart and Oldham and Kiev with knowledge in their hearts. I turn my head, fix my eyes on the white cross-hatching of the window, on the pale green fields beyond. In the fraught days of my salvation, I never really put it to myself, what it would mean if God were true — a mind that could comprehend the whole world.

The next week I roll up to the church and hear the gravel crunch under the tires, and I say, I'm not coming in. Do you think you can manage the steps on your own, or do you want me to help you? My mother turns her white face to me and looks at me with loathing for the power I have over her and says, Take me home, then. While I negotiate the turn onto the Burnley road she clutches the edge of the seat and keeps looking straight ahead, terrified someone will see us. She'd rather miss church, rather have people believe she's too ill, than appear in the doorway on her own and have to explain about me.

I've found myself in an alien life; she's found herself in an alien body. It would be clear to anyone which one is worse. Sometimes I feel a wave of shock go down my back when I see the way the flesh has dropped from her arms, how swollen her shoulders and elbows and knees look in her skinny limbs, like ball joints, which I guess is what they are. But pity is not love. Her body might change, but nothing else has. It's hard for her to know if she's here and breathing; it always has been. The only way she can tell is if she can get other people to do what she wants. And now we have to, because she's sick.

But I have my ways. I can furtively put three spoonfuls of cocoa into her cup instead of the two she insists on, I can bring the Hudson's Bay blanket when I know she wants the thin grey one. When she has to ask me to make a second trip, I can move in a way that shows her how demanding she is and how long-suffering I am. Or I can be scrupulously kind, another kind of cruelty. Not showing her my anger, which would be honest, never giving her anything real.

She hears from Mrs. Feazel that three ships transporting Canadian soldiers have been sunk. Phillip is safe in Ontario, so it has nothing to do with her. I guess a lot of girls will have to get used to being on their own, she says with morbid satisfaction. My stomach knots and I refuse to look at her face, which I know is lit up with the excitement of hearing news as bad as anyone could hope for. But really I feel a little thrill myself and I hold the moment up like a trophy — how cold she is! How cruel! I picture her as a little girl, sitting on the path swallowing stones, one of which eventually worked its way into her heart.

In June, when the nights are warm enough and the smell of lilacs fills the yard, I drag a big quilt smelling of mothballs out to the Toronto couch on the veranda, and that's where I sleep, in an old pair of Phillip's pyjamas. Before the war girls never wore pyjamas. That's what the war's done, one of the things. I fall asleep right away. But late in the night the song of the frogs down at the river falters and something touches me on the back of the neck and I'm awake, suddenly aware of a soldier standing in the yard, like a sentry, beside the old bed-springs. I open my eyes and sit up and look out through the screen. By the time I get my eyes focused he's vanished, but I know who it was. Not George. It was Wilf, waiting for me to wake up, wanting to talk, to tell me about the waves crashing on the deck of the frigate moored outside Scapa Flow. About the shrouded moon, the strange red light that fell from it. The moment when George slid out of his frame of vision, and the sick terror Wilf felt when this registered, the way he turned to climb down to the hold, turned away from the deck *knowing*. Crawled into his bunk (muttering, *Taperlegs is playing the fool*) — while every impulse in him cried out to do what he could not do: turn on the searchlights, raise an alarm, run to the stateroom and call out the officers. I know it was Wilf wanting to confess, wanting me to carry his sin, to add it to my own.

I know Wilf's sin, but he doesn't know mine. No one but me remembers me wandering the streets of Manchester that afternoon in some sort of cowardly funk, not going to meet George, not letting him know, too weak to know myself what I was doing. That day is only in my mind. There's a revised version of it that I've turned to more than once: me climbing the stairs to the flat on Whittle Road, the door opening the minute I knock. (A worn oriental rug on the floor, a blue velour sofa. A stranger's belongings, thoughtfully assembled for a lovers' tryst.) George at the door, the real George, wearing a white shirt and his hair standing in tufts. Give him his gift . . . a leather-bound book with gilt edging. Wait for him to say something. His face is strangely fixed; nothing comes. A sick feeling comes over me, disgust at this enterprise, so far from the marrow of truth.

I'll never know what I missed that day, the awkwardness, false starts, the faulty satisfactions. I'll never know what I missed and I'll never have it now. There's a difference between what I try to make true and what is. And I understand with a wrench that the dreams I'm left with are not much different than what I had when he was alive: I always made him up out of my own brain, I never really saw him the way I see him now, standing separate and apart, his mind teeming with ideas, scanning the world to see how one thing fit with another. I see him, the body he hardly inhabited, his long, thin arms, the nub of his Adam's apple rising and falling in his throat, his way of turning slightly away when you spoke, as though looking straight at you would compromise his listening. George, who tried, finally, to evolve, to fit into a different world, but couldn't do it fast enough. I think, He was and he is gone, I feel this like a pain in my bones, I lie rocked in it.

When the pain recedes a little I get up and stand for a long time looking out through the screen. At the lane curving out to the road, outlined by lilacs. The pump, and the rusty bedsprings propped up to keep the chickens out of the garden. The wagon abandoned on the lawn, quack grass growing up around its handle. Homey objects standing in their private, nighttime guise, no colour at all in the dark but gleaming with a light that they gather from the night sky.

4

In the fall there's no more sleeping on the veranda. There is
an extra hour of darkness, and then light filtering in around
my bedroom blind.

Early, while my mother snores gently in the next room,
I get up and pull clothes on over my flannel pyjamas. I steal
down the hall and out through the veranda and down our
lane. Stubble fields lie flat all around me. The sun is behind
the Feazels' shelter belt, but light from the east fills the sky. At
the road I cut across onto the field on the south side. Sparrows
twitter in the bluff along the river. They're English, those
sparrows. They were brought to the New World by colonists
and they don't migrate, they don't know enough to do it.
Otherwise it's a perfectly quiet fall morning — just me moving,
a tall girl walking across a flat Manitoba landscape at sunrise,
another transplanted species.

The sun's rising now, shooting bright shards of light through
the tree branches at the river. I stand and stare, brought out
here on an ordinary morning by an impulse I can't put a name
to. I'll never show this solitary landscape to George. I don't
know what he'd make of it, anyway. He was one for reading

backwards and forwards from things and England suited him so well, the way its past was scattered all over its surface. The crumbling town hall, held together by vines, the gigantic trees in Alexander Park like trees in the Garden of Eden, their massive limbs twisting upward like the limbs of naked wrestlers. There were initials carved in the trunks of those trees as high as a boy can reach, but they'd blurred, been stretched and thinned by the years.

I turn back to the yard. The cottonwoods in the yard shimmer in the rising sun, and beyond them the fields stretch golden brown. There's just one maple left, rotten and hollowed out with age, dead branches poking up from its crown. It's not the tree I used to perch in while I waited for my dad to finish chores — that one's been chopped down and burned in the stove. I stand at the edge of the lane and narrow my eyes, trying to catch this landscape giving itself away in the morning sun.

⋇

Harry Dabney ships some grain and drops off a cheque, and I come home from town with a new dress for myself and an Eaton's catalogue for Mother so she can pick out something new. I show Mother the balance in our bank book. She peers at the number in disbelief and declines to look through the catalogue. There are certain virtues you had to have in the Depression: frugality, self-denial, pessimism. You needed to shrink yourself down to what was available to you. These virtues are stodgy now, I decide, like cotton stockings. I try my dress on and check it out in the mirror. It's dark green with a white collar. She watches me sourly, denied the satisfaction of seeing hard times teach me what I declined to learn from her.

Look, I say, showing her the tag. It's made of *nylon*. They invented it for the war. You don't have to iron.

Phillip comes home around then for his embarkation leave: he's being sent overseas. He and Betty spend their days at the farm and our Gilmore cousins come over and we all sit around the kitchen table drinking coffee and talking about grain quotas and about the war. Not like the last war, Uncle Jack says. You won't be killing Huns, from what I hear, you'll be killing time. Billy sits on Betty's lap and gnaws at the edge of the table. Mother and Betty wear tragic faces. He's *ground crew*, for God's sake, the biggest risk he'll face will be driving a lorry on the wrong side of the road during the blackout.

After he leaves, Mother is keen for the mail and so I drive to Burnley at least twice a week. Madeleine writes, she always writes. Phillip is safe in England. He's visited Aunt Lucy's and given them all his ration coupons. She describes him as *nice but very quiet*. He's based in Dishforth, Yorkshire, he's servicing Lancasters. She shouldn't be telling me this. The military police are going to show up at Aunt Lucy's door one day and ask for Madeleine.

I go to the library and carry home bags of books. I stay up later and later, carving out a private time for myself in the night. One morning, bleary from lack of sleep, I hear the sound of artillery and go out to see a big grey Harvard lumbering over the shelter belt, dragging a canvas windsock across the sky. It will be from the air base at Burnley, out on a training exercise. Two little fighter planes dart around it like starlings around a crow, pretending it's a Messerschmitt. Puffs of grey smoke blossom around the windsock, and a second later I hear the bangs of another round.

My mother's put her coat on and joined me in the yard. Look at that! she cries. The drogue is right above us and you can see a dot of blue sky through a rip in the canvas.

How can they tell which pilot hit it? she asks. Her neck's cranked back and colour's surfaced in her white cheeks — the war is having its intended effect.

I don't know, I say. Maybe they'd train you to keep score. I'll take you out to the base and see if they want to recruit you.

The three planes bank over the river and drone back towards us. They've got roundels painted on their sides, the way RAF planes do. Archery targets. What is that — a taunt to the Germans? When the first training plane tips I see the little heads of two airmen in the cockpit and feel (not for the first time) surprised. I can't shake the notion that it's the machines fighting this war on their own. But there are miniature men up there. Prairie farm boys. They'll be smug, looking down at our farm tilting beneath them: up there in the cockpit they think they've stumbled onto something real at last.

I haul a chair outside for my mother and she settles on it eagerly. After that as long as it's warm enough she sits in the front yard whenever the plane with the drogue is out, watching the fighter planes training. At dinner she tells me all about it. It's like they say in England, *What did we do with ourselves before there was a war on?*

Fall passes, all fall I read, while Mother watches the planes and waits for news from Phillip, while the grass between the house and the barn freezes into a spongy carpet and our own modest version of the English sparrow gathers in the garden. Madeleine writes me that in Oldham the stars have gone out again because the night sky glows red from all the buildings burning in Manchester. *Oh, Lily,* she writes, *you would be shocked to see the corner of Oldham Road and Linacre Street, it's just a huge crater. Everyone tries not to dwell on it. At work we have to wear badges saying, DON'T TELL ME. I'VE GOT A BOMB STORY TOO.*

Here we still have stars. Here, across the river, coyotes yip like geese. Winter comes, the winter of 1942, and I lift my eyes from the black letters on a white page to see four crows working their way across a sky filled with snow. Hoarfrost collects along the steaming bellows of Molly's sides in the big, empty barn and I pile straw two feet deep into her stall to make a cozier nest. When Betty comes over with Billy, we can't let him crawl on the floor.

⚒

There are dances at the base in Burnley. The town is full of Aussies, and I have a fair idea how the evening would go, but still I toy with the idea of slipping out after Mother's asleep. Although she'd be bound to hear the Ford start up. I picture creeping in at two in the morning, beer on my breath and my lipstick nibbled away, to see her fallen on the step between the living room and the kitchen, one accusing eye open against the linoleum.

By now Betty's living in Burnley. She stayed only a month at her dad's and then Isabel's husband shipped out and Betty moved in with Isabel. So I stop in at Isabel's house in Burnley and ask Betty if she'd come out to the farm on Saturday and stay overnight with Mother.

Where do you want to go? she asks. Stupidly, I tell her.

I don't think Phil would want to see his sister at one of those dances, she says. Come on, Betty, I say. *Hope deferred maketh the heart sick.*

She looks at me, startled; she knows it's a Bible verse. I'm amazed myself sometimes at what is buried in my brain, at what comes out of my mouth. I could ask Gracie to stay with Mother, but I don't care that much.

⚒

I wish *Gracie* could meet a boy, I happen to say to Mother one day. She should move to Winnipeg. She should get a job at Eaton's, or take a secretarial course.

Is that what you're thinking of doing? she says, darting me a frightened look. She's sitting on the chesterfield knitting. It's

319

just squares she's making, for a shawl, for some missionary project. Afghans for Africans is what they have in mind.

Of course not, I say sharply. I'm not going anywhere. I'm going to stay on the farm and marry Joe Pye.

Joe Pye, she says, drawing her needle out of the last row and pulling at the tail of yarn so the last chain of loops disappears. He hasn't been by for ages. Since before the war. He's probably dead by now, the way he smoked. Remember how he wore his combinations all summer? When they were threshing and it was so hot, he'd take his shirt off and there he'd be in his combinations.

I turn away to the window. Joe Pye sitting on the backless chair by the back door, spear grass and thistle barbs sticking in his wool underwear, impossibly skinny. Watching us with affection, with his hands dangling between his knees. Watching his ready-made family. She's pronouncing him dead without a shiver! Oh, he'll be back, I say after a minute. Remember those old moccasins he wore in the winter?

You and Gracie will both meet nice boys one day, she says. This generous thought coming out of her mouth scares her a little and she tacks on a warning. You have to be careful, though, she says. You never really know a person until you marry them.

Dad was a nasty surprise, was he?

I never said that. But I had to find out what was wrong with him on my own and you'd think he could've told me ahead of time. I had to find out by seeing him fall down in the middle of the living room. Her face is stiff.

I don't remember that, I say. I move casually into the kitchen and pick up a damp rag from the table. Back in the living room I wipe at the window ledge. I think about the day I looked it up in the public library in Oldham, stood riveted between the stacks reading about excessive signals from cerebral neurons, about *déjà vu* and *jamais vu*. I open my mouth to tell her, but I can't risk squandering the moment.

It started when they were on the ship coming from England, didn't it? I say instead.

Where did you get that idea?

I don't know exactly. If it was happening in England they wouldn't have sent him. And I thought it might be why he went on his own up to the lumber camps as soon as he got here.

I run the rag over the upper sash. Really (but I don't tell her this) I gleaned it all from Joe Pye's stories. From my instinct for when Joe Pye was holding back. My mother is silent. She's flattening her new square onto the stack she's finished, lining up the edges.

Remember that time he fell down in the pigpen? I ask. You went somewhere the next day. Where did you go?

Now she's picked up her needles again and she's casting on for a new square, counting stitches. Once she has her first row on she says, We went to Winnipeg. We went into the big hospital there and talked to a doctor. I made your father go. So then we knew what it was. We never knew before that, he never once went to a doctor. I wouldn't let him go to Dr. Ross. You can't trust Dr. Ross not to talk.

She presses her mouth into a straight line and bends over her knitting. I stand with the rag in my hand. So. I have to cast off the doctor in Lloydminster, the genial Dr. Hignell hanging his shingle up in a boardwalk frontier town. I have to slip Dr. Hignell back into the American western I got him from, likely a picture I saw with Madeleine on Horsedge Street.

The conversation is finished. I rinse the dust cloth in a basin in the kitchen. This all started with a moment of panic about my leaving. But she's not thinking of me, of what I'll do. There must be a faint smell of failure in her nostrils from her enterprise in raising me, but my actual independent existence is not something she considers. No doubt she thinks mostly about the body she's found herself in, the cage she can't escape, the way her shaking hands slop tea onto her lap. And of small memories, old humiliations sending out their poisonous fumes, things no one else has thought about for decades. I stand with my hands in a basin of cold water and watch my mother frowning over her wool.

⬡

My Tucker grandmother had five children, and in the dance of her family my mother was the one without a partner. Agnes and Eva were princesses who ran into the bush after milking in the morning, dragging an old pillowcase of lace collars and high-heeled shoes for their court. Franklin and Morris were soldiers who played with sticks in the dirt under the veranda. But my mother was an orphan who hid alone under the rhubarb leaves against the garden fence, until their mother came out of the house and pulled her up by the yoke of her dress and made her collect the eggs and chase the chickens out of the garden. From the shadows of the barn eyes watched, the sad eyes of the plow horses and the piggy-dumb eyes of the sows in the wallow, but there was no one besides her who cared about the injustice of it.

Agnes was the one my mother longed to be. When she made a sampler she copied Agnes's exactly, embroidering the letters L N M O in the middle of the alphabet, a mistake Agnes had been too lazy to pull out, and everyone laughed when they saw it. Even the hired boy got the joke. Agnes had soft, full lips and a slow way of talking and it was Agnes she longed for, not Eva, who was halfway between them in age and had the same pale wavy hair as my mother and the same set to her mouth and was the one who had stolen Agnes's love. Eva was full of malice. She pulled Mother's underpants down once when all their cousins were in the bedroom changing so that

322

everyone saw her bum, she dribbled molasses in my mother's autograph album. At the supper table Agnes and Eva looked at each other with shining eyes and laughed and then Franklin and Morris pretended to share a secret joke too, but she had no one to laugh with and Agnes never so much as looked at her.

When Mother was about my age she worked as a hired girl for a bachelor farmer named Felix Macdonald, who lived on a treeless yard on the Bicknell road, a tall, stout man with black spots on his gums, who always came to the table stinking of the pigpen, never slipping his overalls off or even his boots. She lasted only two months. She always said it was too bad her hands had to get so coarse for nothing, although being a good milker was handy later when she and my father were shipping cream. She lasted two months with the smell of the pigpen at the table every morning, noon and night, but finally one day she dared to complain. The next day Felix Macdonald came in at supper and walked straight over to the table and dropped a kielbasa on my mother's plate, a fleshy red sausage like a stallion's penis. A sausage of the type my mother's family would never eat: he must have stopped in at one of the Galician farms to buy it. There was no wife in that house, just Mr. Macdonald's sister Frances, who sat at the table with her head down. My mother wanted to knock the sausage off to the floor, but she was afraid to move. And then he asked her if she knew why her family had sent her, *her* in particular, and told her that he'd asked for the homeliest sister, he didn't want his hired girl getting married on him. That was when she packed up her bag and left. When she got home she cried and told her mother angrily what he had said, and her mother got angry too and said, None of my girls are homely.

All this she tells me while we're sitting at the table one day. She's a little defiant about the big sausage: because she knows what it meant, or maybe because she doesn't quite know. I could tell her things from England, but she has that shame-faced, overconfiding air.

What did you do after that? I ask.

I went to work in town for the reeve's wife. That's when I started going to church.

What church?

It was the Presbyterian Church, she says. But back then they had a minister who was a real born-again Christian. I was saved in that church.

I think of my father as William, but even in my own mind I never use my mother's name. Well, it's Lily.

Warm weather has come to England. Madeleine writes that Uncle Stanley has lifted up the flagstones in the back garden and she and Aunt Lucy have planted carrots and turnips. Spend an hour in the garden, not an hour in the queue. Here worn and ragged patches of snow hang on under the trees on the north side of the yard. Finally it warms up. The robins appear and the spruce down by the river splay out lime green tips. The ducks come back and I walk over to the river after milking and watch them dragging silver wedges behind them in water as smooth and bright as mercury. In the pasture I find crocuses. There were crocuses near Foxdenton Hall, although they bloomed in September and October. They weren't indigenous to North England, they were brought back from the Crusades by the Knights Templar, who had learned on their travels to need saffron. That's what George told me. But these are our own, these are older than England's. They've developed their own furry little coats.

My mother sits where she sat all winter, watching the traffic on the section road through the window. I can't lure her out-side to see the peonies or the bleeding hearts. It's my fault she's not going to church any more, I think as I sprinkle the laundry and roll it up for ironing. She's going to sit in that chair the rest of her life, her legs fusing with the oak rungs. In the meantime I'm working hard to get the garden in. It's been a year since we've had a pig and the whole pigpen is a pit of rich, ripe compost. I carry load after load in the wheelbarrow and dig it into the garden and the flower bed. I plant corn, peas, beets, radishes, lettuce, onions and carrots from seed. I cut potatoes from last year into quarters, making sure there's an eye in each one, and drop them into holes. Turnips I refuse to plant; I throw the seed into the slop bucket.

The meadowlarks come back. One sits on top of a fence post by the pump and calls, *I left my pretty sister at home.* It makes me think of Joe Pye. I wish I knew what the little flamer is singing about, he said to me once, and I told him what it was I heard. Recalling Joe Pye in our yard is a powerful magic — the next day in town I hear news of him. He's up in the Interlake, working as a handyman at a residential school. Susan Dabney's auntie came to visit and mentioned him, and Harry Dabney told me. I'll find a way to visit him, I think. After the garden's in. I'll take the truck and make a day of it. I need to tell him about Dad.

Then one day I notice someone's built a little fire behind the barn. There are fresh ashes, a few charred pieces of split poplar that could be from our woodpile. Eggshells scattered on the ground like bits of broken china. I tell Mother when I go in. I've been thinking so much about Joe that I have the crazy idea it could be him, come back to occupy our yard in a different way.

It's a tramp, she says. She's used to tramps, they came through all the time in the Thirties. I wonder if it was our eggs he was eating? she asks. You'd think we would've heard someone in the henhouse.

That evening I climb up to the loft to get fresh straw for Molly. There's very little hay and very little straw left, and the straw's been rearranged, made into a nest. I climb cautiously up, calling, Hello? Hello? while Blue waits at the foot of the ladder, tail wagging. There's no sound so I pull myself right up into the loft. A newspaper lies in the straw. A tramp has come to kill us in our beds and carried a newspaper to read while he waited. I pick it up. It's a Winnipeg paper, the *Tribune*, dated two days before. He's on the move, heading west.

I take the newspaper back to the house and read it through. It's been a while since I've had news of the war. The list is posted on the third page. There are thirty-two names that day, if you include the category PREVIOUSLY REPORTED MISSING, NOW FOR OFFICIAL PURPOSES PRESUMED DEAD. Of course this is only for official purposes. Unofficially, families can think what they want. They can keep dusting his bedroom, keep storing little things up in their memories to tell him, keep waking up in the night, shaken by their disbelief. I pass over an article with the headline HEART OF COLOGNE SHATTERED IN HUGE RAID. It's not the sort of article I read any more. Instead I read the article beside it, a short piece that would have entranced George: about London, about the Roman bowels of London being exposed by the bombing. Too bad there're no archaeologists around to take advantage of it. I read the comic strips as well and then I fold the paper and put it in the kindling bin.

It's drizzling the next morning, not enough rain to do the garden good but too much to let me work outside. After I've got the fire going I tie a scarf over my head and pick up the milk pail. Halfway across the yard, I glance up at the barn just in time to see the shutter over the loft opening swing closed. I stop in my tracks and wait. No one comes out of the barn.

Blue, I call, and keep him close to me while I cross the yard. Inside the barn he starts barking his watchdog bark. Light falls weakly from the dirty windows to lie in squares on the aisle. I have to pause a minute inside the door before I make out the figure of a man standing in the aisle at the far end. Hello? I say and walk towards him. It's such an empty barn, only Molly moving restlessly in her stall with the weight of her milk, and the cats following me, crying for breakfast. It's a minute before I can clearly see the man leaning against the feed bin, his arms folded and his face full of the expectation of seeing me. I don't know who it is. Then my heart gives a sideways thud and I do: it's Russell Bates.

5

I drop the milk pail with a clatter and reach down to quiet Blue.

I thought you were never coming, he says. Aren't milkmaids up at the crack of dawn?

What *on earth* are you doing here?

He smiles and gestures, the way you'd say, *It's a long story.* He's wearing a plaid wool shirt in blue and brown, suspenders and a tweed cap. He was a good imitation of an adult when I last saw him six or eight years ago and he's a man for sure now, although of a different sort. You couldn't find me something to eat, could you? he says. I'm so hungry I can hardly see straight.

Well, sure, come on to the house. We haven't had breakfast yet.

No, he says. No thanks. Could you slip me something out here? Don't let anyone know I'm here, if you don't mind.

All right, I say, puzzled. I click my tongue for the dog and turn and walk back to the house, trying to move casually, as though I've forgotten something. In fact my knees are shaking. Mother is dressing. I can hear her moving around her bedroom all the time I'm slicing bread, buttering it in big swaths with the bread knife, breaking off a chunk of cheese. My jacket has huge pockets, and I wrap everything in a tea towel and slip this loose packet into one of the pockets just as she makes her way across the living room.

I thought I heard you go out.

You did, I say. And then I came back. And now I'm leaving again. I go out and let the screen door slam.

He takes the bread gratefully and offers me some, which seems overly courteous under the circumstances, but out of nervousness I do take a piece. We sit on a manger at the empty end of the barn, wheat spilled at our feet from last year, when the barn was a granary. He takes his cap off and I watch him stealthily. His hair is long. It's not the military haircut we're used to seeing and it's not the clipped city haircut he had before. Without being what you'd call dirty, his clothes look as though they could use a freshening up. He has a working-man's look — a bachelor's look: no woman is tending to him. The more I stare, the more I'm amazed that I recognized him, and wonder like a fool if I've made a mistake and he's a total stranger after all.

Sorry I couldn't manage coffee, I say, to say something.

No, this is great, he says. Excellent bread. Did you make it?

I nod.

I'm impressed. You can't be on your own here?

Have you been watching for a while? I ask.

Since yesterday. You knew I was here — you have my *Tribune*.

I did have it, I say. I read it last night and then I used it to start the fire this morning.

Best place for it. He takes out his handkerchief and wipes his mouth. Who's in the house with you?

My mother. But she never comes to the barn, she hardly steps out of the house. She's not well. And then I tell him that my father has died, that my brother has got married and gone overseas.

Charlotte's getting married too, he says. In fact, she may be married by now.

Aren't you in touch with her?

Well, yes and no. I was getting mail through a friend for a while, but the system broke down. I guess I should look for a chance to telephone her. I don't see a telephone line in your yard.

Molly moos, cranking her neck around to see what's keeping me. Astonishment at the sight of him starts to rattle me, my calmness is falling apart.

We're really close to the base, I say. There's training flights over the yard all the time. Not that they'd notice you from the air. You're probably okay. Unless someone sees you who knows you shouldn't be here.

He laughs. I feel off-balance, the way I did that sole afternoon we spent alone together, when I was clearly amusing him in a way I didn't intend. Well, I have to do the milking and get back to the house before Mother starts to fret, I say. Seeing you're *not* on the lam, are you going to come in and introduce yourself like a proper guest or are you going to keep lurking in the barn?

He reaches for my hand in a conciliatory way. He might look like a workingman, but his hand is as smooth as it was back then. Milk your cow and make some excuse to come back and talk to me. But don't tell anyone I'm here. Don't tell your mother or anyone else, okay? I'll wait up in the loft. No one's going to come up there, are they?

Sounds very cloak and dagger, I say. Sounds very quisling. But no, I think you're safe with me.

I can tell he finds this less than funny. I get up and brush the crumbs off my jacket and take the stool and pail over to Molly. I wipe off her udder with the rag hanging from a nail

on the wall and then sit down and clamp the pail between my
knees, leaning my temple against the hot, twitching wall of
her side where her hair swirls into her haunches, and start up
a rhythm of milk against the bottom of the pail. The whole
time he sits on the ladder to the loft, watching me. Through
the years I dreamt once in a while of meeting him again,
dreamt of showing him the new, urbane person I had become!
But there's nothing to be done about it, so I press my cheek
against Molly's flank and try to ignore him and when I finish
and stand up, he's gone.

✕

By mid-morning it's cleared up, an answer to prayer if I were
the praying kind, because it would have taxed even my
imagination to find an excuse to stay outside all afternoon on
a rainy day. After the chickens are fed and the kitchen is swept
up I slip into my bedroom and take stock: of my rough hands,
the dirt ground under my nails, of my brown face and loose
brown hair. I carry a basin of warm water to my room and
scrub my hands and face and then I put lipstick on, rubbing a
little onto my cheekbones as well, and pinning the front of my
hair into waves, the way I used to do in England. I look at
myself in the mirror for another long moment and then I take
the pins back out and wipe the lipstick off. He'd know it was
done for him. The mirror gives me back a tanned, oval face
with just a hint of rose where the lipstick was, a serious face,
as unfamiliar to me as his was. Then I go back to the kitchen
and build up the fire, peel the potatoes, open a jar of yellow
beans, and put a pan of little pork sausages in the oven. When
dinner is almost ready I walk out to the barn and poke my
head up to the loft. He's lying on the straw propped up against
a knapsack, reading a book.

Where were you when I did the milking last night? I ask.
My English accent seems to have returned.

331

I guess I missed you, he says. I'd gone for a walk. Foraging, actually.

Stealing eggs? I ask.

He laughs. That was earlier. You were out in the garden with your wheelbarrow when I stole the eggs.

I climb all the way up and show him from the loft opening where to meet me near the river. And then I go back and set the table. It's very strange to sit in the kitchen with Mother, under the clock that falters and dithers about declaring the morning over, and know he's out in the barn.

Are you going to have a nap this afternoon? I ask.

I guess I'll lie down for a while, she says. I don't like to sleep during the day because then I won't sleep at night. That's what she says every day, right before she tips her head back on the chesterfield and dozes off.

Finally I have the chance to pack potatoes and beans and a row of sausages into the Elizabeth and Margaret Rose tin and slip outside. He's where I told him to be, sitting with his back against an oak. Can we be seen from the road? he asks.

No, I say. I'm sure we can't.

You wouldn't mind checking for me? he asks. So to humour him I walk back and check, but you can see nothing. We're below the level of the road and entirely hidden by a fringe of poplars and chokecherries.

He's smoking when I come back and I sit beside him, putting the tin on the ground between us. He turns his cigarette sideways to look at it. Three left, he says, and then I'll be rolling whatever I find growing in the ditches. He takes pride in being in such straits, you can tell. You don't smoke? he asks.

No one has ever smoked in our house. Joe Pye used to smoke in the barn in the winter. He could burn the barn down as long as he didn't disgrace us by smoking in the house.

Joe Pye, he says, remembering. How old were you the summer we went for that drive? He reaches over and circles my ankle with the hand holding the cigarette.

I think I was fourteen.

I must have been seventeen. It was just before I went to McGill. And Charlotte was sixteen, I guess. Did I tell you Charlotte's graduated as a nurse? She's got a job in a surgical ward.

In a military hospital? I ask.

He lifts his hand off my ankle and takes a slow pull on his cigarette. Hard to believe, he says, but there are civilians selfish enough to take sick while there's a war on.

There's a road here we could take, but I refuse to go down it. I sit with my arms around my knees and look straight at him. He's thinner than he was at seventeen — his face is bonier, with deep parentheses around his mouth. He seems very changed to me, but then I'd spent only the one afternoon with him years before, and my memories of that day are so pawed over, so grubby with use that they're almost unreadable. But it seems to me that the biggest change is internal, as it is in Gracie: a cockiness is gone, or it's settled into conviction, some of the fun has drained out of it. And he's wary, it's in his mind I can't be trusted entirely.

How long do you plan on being here? I ask. If it kills me I won't ask him again why he's hiding.

I'm not in a very good position to plan.

I can't feed you forever without my mother noticing.

He shrugs and draws again on his cigarette. So don't feed me. He has a way of seeming to smile when he's not smiling, and it softens his words. Does anyone else ever come out to the barn? he asks.

Betty does sometimes. My sister-in-law. She brings her little boy out to see the cats. Just watch out when there's another truck in the yard.

We sit and he smokes and I watch the sunlight shining on

each separate moving leaf of the cottonwoods on the other bank. We sit side by side a few feet apart as though we've arranged to meet to watch the passing of the river. Dabs of fluff from the cottonwood trees ride east on the surface of the water, lit up by the sunlight. Khaki, that's the colour of the water: it takes its colour from the trees and sends back a light that reflects in moving ripples on the branches. Thistles have sprung up where the ice ripped the bank open in the spring, and a dark butterfly tries to settle on a thistle head and is thwarted by the breeze, carried past us with its wings motionless.

So how long were you in England? Russell asks.

Four years. I tell him about looking after Nan and then moving to Aunt Lucy's and going to school.

Why didn't you write to me? he asks.

George wrote to you.

He smiles. You're right, he did. That was so strange, suddenly getting a letter from this English guy I'd never met. He's quite the character, George. He's got an amazing mind, he's got a theory about everything. And then in other ways he's such a kid. He used to address my letters to *Master Bates*, he thought that was a real gas. I haven't heard from him in ages. I had to leave Rosamund Street and I guess he lost track of me.

No, I say. I raise my head to look at him. That's not what happened.

Oh, he says, and the word is a groan. Oh, shit. He doesn't ask me. He throws his butt like a dart into the river, and we watch it float around the bend. He doesn't ask me and I don't tell him. It's as if he's wearing Madeleine's badge: *don't tell me.* I lie back and lower the red screen of my eyelids down against the light. But the grass picks at me through my blouse, and I arch my back. When I open my eyes again he's eyeing me and I sit up, embarrassed.

Wild strawberries, I say, lightly touching the white flowers scattered through the grass. I'll come out in a few weeks and pick them for jam. They're so tiny, it takes forever. But it's the best jam in the world. I push the tin with the picture of the two little princesses towards him. Don't you want your dinner?

He lifts the lid and looks at his dinner with appreciation, picking a sausage up with his fingers to eat it in two bites. It would stab my mother in the heart to see me eat these, he says. It would send her to an early grave. It's a Jewish thing, he adds, when I raise my eyebrows. You have no idea.

Oh, maybe I do, I say.

That's right, your family is religious.

Yeah, I guess that's one way of putting it.

After a minute he asks, What about you? Still waiting for the Lord to come?

Naw, he stood us all up. We share a little laugh.

So you've totally given it up? No more heaven, no more hell?

I still believe in an afterlife, I finally say.

Really? Some plane of existence out in space?

No. Some plane of existence here. When you feel like your life is over.

Curiosity flickers in his eyes.

Well, it's a test of character, isn't it, the war? You start to see yourself in a different light.

Oh, I don't know, he says. Not the truest test. Something primitive kicks in. He sits with his back against the rough black bark of the oak. There's a grace to the way he sits, his hands dangling on his knees. *Konk-la-ree*, whistles a red-winged blackbird, lifting and resettling on a different reed. Suddenly I can't bear to have his eyes on my face.

I should get back, I say, and scramble to my feet.

Wait a sec, he says. You've got something all over your blouse. He stands too and takes my hand to draw me to him.

With his free hand he pulls three or four spear grass heads off my blouse and shows them to me.

I pluck one out of his fingers and stab him lightly in the upper arm. That's for you, I say. Nature's tooth and claw. It's been in the grass since last fall. Waiting for a city boy to show up. I smell his cigarette, the grease of the sausages, I see dark hair curling where his shirt opens in a V at his throat. I can't look at his face for the sunlight glittering off the water and the spinning poplar leaves. I have to go, I say. I'll bring you some supper when I do the chores.

Bring it later, he says, still hanging on to my hand. After your mother's asleep.

He's nowhere around when I lead Molly into the barn after supper. I don't see him and I don't sense him watching from the ladder. She's restless tonight, lashing her tail back and forth. Her teats feel more rubbery than usual, resistant. It takes me a long time to milk, trying to keep her tail pinned by my shoulder. When I finish and carry the pail towards the house, the setting sun is smeared along the side of the bunkhouse and light gleams off the bellies and forked tails of the barn swallows wheeling over the yard in their nightly roost. Everything is catching and holding the sun, conspiring to keep night at bay.

Mother is annoyed when I carry in an armful of wood. Who's for popcorn? I cry, cramming split poplar into the stove.

It's too hot, she says. It's far too hot. She sits on a kitchen chair watching sullenly while I open a lid in the stove and shake the popcorn basket over it. When the popcorn's done she ignores the bowl I give her. Don't eat it so fast, she says. You're just shovelling it in. I must have told you about the girl I went to school with who was so crazy about popcorn.

Yes, I say. You've told me.

Well, she choked while she was eating it, a kernel went into her lung. And it festered there until she died. It took three months. She was only fifteen, did you realize that? One of the Skinners from the Shadwell road. She would have been Susan Skinner's aunt.

I'm going to have a bath, I say. I may as well, as long as we have a fire. Why don't you have one too? You'll sleep better. Then she is thin-lipped with annoyance, not about the waste of water, but about the challenge to the principle of the Saturday-night bath.

I'll just have a little one, I say (thinking, If she gets too worked up she won't sleep). I'll just use the kettle and the reservoir. You're right, I shouldn't have built up the fire. It's too hot. But now we have the water so I may as well.

Afterwards in my bedroom the towel falls open and in the mirror I catch a narrow image, as if through a keyhole: a frank female torso like the most daring of the Blackpool postcards, the ones Monty found on a rack at the back of the store. Turning my eyes from the mirror I dry myself quickly and put on my cotton eyelet nightdress. The nightdress Aunt Lucy gave me for my birthday that hot summer just before the war started, the finest thing I own. The night air from the window is wonderfully cool on my skin. I don't let myself think about him, lying in the straw across the yard. It's not him pulling at me from the dark, it's something else, the self I'm going towards.

I wrap a blanket around me like a shawl and go out to the porch and sit on the Toronto couch, the tin with Russell's supper on the railing. Are you okay, Mother? I ask through the screen. Night, she answers, and I hear the creaking of her bedsprings. The sky is dark blue, it's as dark as it will get this night. Across the way a few late frogs chant in the river. It seems a long time until I hear the falling rhythm of her sleeping breath, the little disgusted huffs that mean she is asleep. Suddenly I can't bear it any more and I slip my feet into my shoes and start across the yard, still wearing the blanket.

There's a commotion of silver light behind the cottonwoods. Even now the moon may be leaning into the big, square loft opening. Blue wants to come with me. I bend over and scratch his ears. Home. Go home, I say. Through the thin cotton of my nightdress I can feel his cold nose against my thigh. *Go home,* I repeat, giving him a little shove. He stands in the middle of the yard, watching me. Clever, he's a clever dog, and he can't make this out at all.

The darkness of the barn is a kindly, lived-in dark, like the dark of a quiet bedroom, full of breathing and turnings: there are corners that are never out of shadows, even in winter when you bring a lantern to milk by. But the work you do in a barn you can do half asleep, by smell, by a thousand repetitions, your hands sliding along rails polished by other hands. Inside the barn the cats greet me, moving like wraiths around my ankles. I move past the lying-down prow of Molly's rump, to the square of moonlight the loft opening has dropped on the aisle. At the ladder I slip my shoes off, I drop the supper tin on a bench and clutch the blanket around me and begin to climb, the rungs pressing into the arches of my bare feet. Above me a dark shape kneels, and a hand reaches down and pulls me up.

6

Russell's story was not the sort of story I would ever have put together on my own, and my comments the morning I discovered him in the barn were stupid, offensively stupid, evidence of how ignorant I still was, how all the time in school, all the reading, all George's efforts to drag me into the twentieth century had not managed to let more than a few pinpricks of light into my dim understanding of the world. Of course I knew he was a Communist, but I did not give a moment's thought to what was happening to him from day to day all this time, in spite of George's reminders. When I did think about him it was to picture him thinking about me and wondering why I never wrote. I was bold as brass that first night. It was bravado, it came out of my indistinct grasp of what I was going towards.

Now it's not just him I have to hide, but my astonishment at the new force field I've moved into, at the light glinting off the kettle, the boiled beets throbbing in their red juice, energy dropping like mercury from my fingers while I scrape the plates into the slop bucket.

You're going to ruin those slacks working in the garden, Mother says as I clear the table after dinner.

They're already ruined, I say. I've been wearing them in the garden all spring. It's not the slacks, and she can't put her finger on what it is. Besides, I say, I'm not working in the garden this afternoon, I'm going to town. Do you want to check the list?

She bends over it and her lips move, but she's reading mechanically — suspicion is hammering at her concentration.

I take the list back from her. Bye, I say and go out.

He's waiting in the Ford, as we planned while I was doing the milking that morning. He's half lying on the passenger side, half crouching on the floor. This is a waste, he says from the vantage point of my right knee as I start the truck. I thought you'd be wearing a skirt. When I turn onto the section road he presses on my foot on the gas pedal to make me scream. Once we're well away from the farm he makes a move to climb onto the seat. No, I say. Get back down there. You have no idea how people talk.

I give him a couple of dollars and let him out on the blacksmith's road. This trip is for cigarettes, which I can't buy in Burnley without creating a sensation. He takes the money without protest or any hint of embarrassment — he just winks at me and starts down the maple-lined street in the direction I point him, an ordinary-looking workingman walking a packed dirt road. The people who see him will have to place him and they'll decide he's a Galician farmer without the cash to buy gas.

After I do my own errands I drive back to the corner by the blacksmith's and wait, reading my letter from Madeleine. Lois and Archie were married in June by Special Licence. Everyone pooled ration points so they could have a nice reception. *The wedding wasn't so different from what Archie's parents would have put on*, Madeleine writes. *You can say that for the war.* And then she tells me about the frock she wore, made from the

yellow and green dress Nettie Nesbitt made for Aunt Lucy at
the start of the war. It had such a full skirt they were able to
get two straight-skirted dresses out of it. *Father's taken down
the iron railing from the front garden*, Madeleine writes, *and
hauled it out to be salvaged for armaments. We have not had to
go to the air raid shelter since Easter, but every night we can hear
the bombing at Manchester. I'm used to my job and I like talking
to the people, but my legs still ache at night from standing so long.
Next week I have three days off. If you were here we could go
somewhere together.* And I think, I'll send Lois the credit note
from George's gloves, that can be my gift. I should have left it
in England in the first place. I wonder if they'll still honour it,
if the shop is still there. A bee buzzes in the corner of the
windshield. I open the passenger-side window and use the
letter to try to scoop it out. It dodges me and flies behind my
head and I ignore it. I'm overcome with drowsiness — somewhere between the grocery store and the post office my need
for sleep caught up with me.

Suddenly Russell's face is at the window. He climbs into
the truck with two paper bags. Besides a tin of tobacco he's
bought a newspaper, six bottles of beer and a dozen tins of
beans and canned meat.

You might get tired of feeding me, he says. I don't want to
wear out my welcome.

I start the truck and pull onto the road. We spin along, not
talking. There's no way back from the sort of conversation
we've had. I roll down my window and let in the spring smell
of alfalfa and the piping of red-winged blackbirds in the reeds
that have been resurrected in the ditches since the drought
ended. The road is empty all the way home and he stays on
the seat until we get close to the yard. I park the truck close to
the barn with the passenger side away from the house.

Wait, he says from where he's crouched. What are you up
to this afternoon?

I have to smile. Betty will probably show up, I say. You should keep an eye out.

I creep into the kitchen and put the things away. Mother's sleeping on the chesterfield. There's work to be done, most urgently hauling water out to the transplanted tomatoes. I stand in the quiet kitchen, the linoleum cool under my feet, and then I go to my room, where the thin white curtain breathes in and out with the breeze. I sit on the bed, up against the wall, my head stuffed with sleepiness. I sit like a brood hen over the night just past, not looking at it, not letting anything draw me away.

I don't know if I will always be able to recall what it was like in the loft that night. Maybe not, if I have a lucky life with lots more of the same. But when I'm an old woman, I'll still go back to the morning when I climbed down the ladder and walked barefoot across the yard in my nightdress, pale green light rising from the fields towards the dark of the sky, the trees secretly breathing over the house. The grass damp under my feet, a robin singing on the old bedspring by the garden, its song curling into the cool air the way a breath does. Blue lying on his side, not moving. I'll remember opening the screen door and stealing into the silent house, creeping along close to the wall to avoid the floorboards creaking, crawling into bed with my feet wet and grimy, pulling sleep over me like a blanket.

These are the things I filch from the house for Russell: a bar of soap (he has his own towel in his knapsack), a plate, fork and spoon (he has his own cup and knife), a pillow and an old quilt. The blanket I wore out to the barn the first night stays there as well. He's desperate with boredom so I start taking books out to him: *Emma*, which he abandons on the third page, Dickens's *Hard Times*, which he sinks into with astonishment and insists is a socialist tract. I bring him writing paper, a pen and ink. I steal a shirt of Phillip's. Candles or a lantern I refuse to bring because I have no wish for Mother to see a light in the loft and I don't trust him not to burn the barn down. Although of course he smokes in the loft, while we lie among the bars and arrows of brilliant sun that burn through cracks in the walls and pick out certain airborne dust specks and certain bits of trodden yellow straw to touch with gold.

This is the story: In 1938, he was living in a flat with a friend named Lennie, who was a member of a Communist youth club. There were a lot of soldiers coming back from Spain that fall, *Mac-Paps*, he calls them, and Lennie talked Russell into letting some of them stay in the flat until they could be sent home. The mornings Russell got up for classes he had to step over snoring bodies on his way to the door. They were mostly from Alberta, he said. They were Finnish. At first I thought he said *finished*, and he said they were that too, exhausted and discouraged. Groups of them came and went, different men sprawled over the living-room floor all that winter, talking all night and sleeping till mid-afternoon. By the spring of 1939, Russell had more or less stopped getting up for classes. He joined the Communist Party and took a job in a tire factory, where they were trying to get a union going. Then the government stepped up the harassment. At that point the police actually had a squad dedicated to harassing Communists, assigned to throw tear gas into meetings and to condemn buildings where the Party met. The Red Squad, it was called. Finally there was an Order-in-Council declaring them an unlawful organization. That Order-in-Council included Fascist groups too — that's what was really galling, that in people's minds they were one and the same. Lennie was picked up and taken to what Russell called a concentration camp. Russell happened to be out the day the police raided the flat. He knew the police would be back for him so he packed up a few things and left, went to a house in the suburbs, to the basement of some friends. And there he hid for almost two years. The two years I'd been back in Canada he was living in a cellar in a brick house in Montreal. Sometimes people brought him work to do, writing pamphlets arguing for a Second Front, writing newspaper articles under an assumed name. A couple of times he took the risk of going out to a meeting somewhere, in a barn or another house, once to a big meeting at St. Janvier. Finally he had to move on and he came west. He stayed in Toronto for a couple of months, with a woman who was selling her silverware one place setting at a time to help him and his comrades. She gave him money and he took the train to Winnipeg, tried and failed to arrange a meeting with some Communists there, and hitched a ride to Burnley. He found me without having to ask a single person for directions because he remembered the six-sided silo I showed him from the Lookout the day of our ride in his dad's car.

What would happen if someone did turn you in? I ask. We're lying near the loft opening, where I can see the road and the house.

I'd be hauled off to a concentration camp in Alberta. To Kananaskis, where they're keeping the German POWs. I'd be put in a cabin with a bunch of fucking Fascists, pardon my language. I'd have a bull's eye sewn onto my back so I could be shot on sight if I left the camp.

Are you serious?

I'm serious. I'd be bunked with Nazis and they'd know why I was there and they'd beat the crap out of me every night while the guards played cards.

But what would they say at your trial? I turn in his arms, observing by the way he holds my waist how slender it is.

There wouldn't be a trial.

So I don't understand how they could put you in prison.

I'd be charged with belonging to an unlawful organization. Or I'd be charged with sedition, exciting ill will, creating discontent. Either way, they wouldn't have to try me. We're under the War Measures Act at the moment.

What about the people who hide you? I ask.

Oh, he says. They'd be shot. Summary execution. He pinches the soft skin of my upper arm. No, my gallant collaborator, a wholesome farm girl like yourself, you'd be below their regard. Though they might start a file on you. It could have been nasty for Esther, where I stayed in Montreal, because she and Martin have links with the Party.

Russell casually pulls the blanket over himself, although he can't be cold. But it's not even that, he says. It's more that you don't want to give the bastards the satisfaction. When did the Germans invade the Soviet Union? June '41. So for a year now it's been Russia holding back the Fascists. And the feds are still chasing us down! Some people would rather see Germany win the war than have the Bolsheviks win it for us. At least the Germans believe in God.

This is interesting, but I suddenly can't listen, I come back to something.

What does *Esther* do? I ask.

She does typing.

Do they have kids?

Four, four boys.

Were they in school?

Three were. The smallest would be about five now. Esther works at home.

Russell launches into a long story about the husband, Martin, how the police broke into Martin's shop when he was out and waited for him to come back. He ran a press that was known to do printing jobs for the Party. While they were waiting the police pissed on the floor and started a fire in the stove with his antique printing blocks. Martin was taking his usual long lunch in a café somewhere. He was a big talker — that's what saved him from being picked up, how long he talked at lunch. Someone went to the café and warned him, so Martin went into hiding too, in the cellar of someone else's house.

So when was this? I ask.

I guess it was early in 1940.

Just after you moved into *their* cellar? I ask.

Yeah, I guess it must have been.

If you were safe in Martin and Esther's cellar, why couldn't Martin just stay home?

He couldn't *come* home. They were watching the house. We could see them, two swells sitting in a car playing cards. Esther liked baiting them. She'd walk out and ask them if there was some problem. Something the neighbours should know about. She'd offer them coffee.

So why did you leave? I ask.

It was just time, he says. Time to move on.

I feel hurt rise up in my chest and I sit up and start brushing the straw off my blouse.

Hey, he says, pulling me back, pinning me down. Never mind that. Never mind getting all huffy. He knows right away what I'm on about; that tells me everything. I wriggle an arm free and cover my face with it. In the dark I can feel tears stinging in my eyes.

Hey, Lily, he says.

What about in Toronto? I ask. The woman who was selling her silverware? Were you sleeping with her too?

She was seventy-six, he says. Mind you, she did have a bosom on her for an old bird.

He pulls my arm off my face. Think about it, he says. He props himself up on one elbow beside me. *Lily.* Before you get all worked up, think about how I've been after you for years.

Well, yes, I say, with a sob. What was that about? You didn't have the slightest clue who I was. You met me *once.* It was just stupid.

I liked what I saw, he says stubbornly. I had an impulse and I followed it. It's not a bad way to live.

He leans over me and toys with the hair on my temple. I watch him, I trace the lines around his mouth with my eyes. His face is blunt-featured, amused, kind. He is knowing and contained. He gazes back at me and I can't look away. Remember this, I say to myself. Remember how he thinks.

Betty comes. She steps into the kitchen, holding Billy and a plate of matrimonial cake for Mother. I offer to take Billy to see the cats to forestall her going out to the barn. Russell must have seen us cross the yard, because he climbs down the ladder and perches on it, watching us. Billy is fighting to get out of my arms. As soon as I put him down he sets off in a wide-legged run after the cats, who melt away before him. Blue nuzzles at Russell's knees, his tail wagging.

The kid's not a talker? Russell asks, reaching out to pet Blue.

Maybe under torture, I say. But normally all he says is *No! No! No!* And he barks. I crouch in front of Billy. What do doggies say, Billy? What do *doggies* say?

The last cat disappears up into the rafters and Billy starts to wail. I pick him up. He may not be barking this afternoon, I say, but the boy can bark. I'm standing close to the ladder and Russell runs his fingers over the fine skin behind my knee, stroking my bare calf. Is your sister-in-law likely to stay long? he asks.

A couple of hours, I guess.

Let's take off, he says. Think of an excuse.

On my way back to the house I set Billy down in the yard and go back to the well and draw up the honey pail of lemonade we keep there. And also two bottles of Russell's beer, which I carry over to the Ford and slide under the seat. The lemonade I take into the house.

Just two, I say to Betty, when she reaches down glasses. I won't have any. If you're going to be here for a while, I thought I might go to town.

Oh? she says, surprised, a little hurt. I had a nice long letter from Phil this morning. I was going to tell you all his news. She's cut her hair to the middle of her back and it's softer and wavier.

I won't be long, I say. I go back out into the sunlight, trying to shake off her disappointment, thinking, I should have told her how nice she looks.

⬩

I drive the truck west up to the Lookout, and stop about where Russell slid off the road that afternoon eight years ago. Remember this spot? I ask.

Too well, he says. This time he doesn't bother with coy little games to get his arm around me — he's behaving like a man too hungry to taste his food. He hasn't shaved in a couple of days because it's such a nuisance to heat water, and his beard is rough against my face.

Russell, I murmur. Let's get out. I open the door and almost tumble out the side of the truck. I walk around to the front and lean back against the hood.

This is what we call a major geological feature on the prairies, I say.

Pretty impressive, he says, following me without once looking at the view. He's wearing his plaid shirt, he's looking at me with frank intention, and in this light I can see the glints of gold in his hazel irises.

You know, that day when I was swimming in the river, I say. I thought you came especially to look for me.

Well, I would have if I'd known what I'd be finding, he says gallantly. I used to spend a lot of time just driving around, whenever Dad would let me have the car. I was always trying to get away from Loretta.

Loretta?

Charlotte's mom. My stepmother, I guess I should call her. So that day I guess I ended up at the river. And lo and behold, there was the beauteous Miss Lily Piper, her long legs sticking out of a fetching antique bathing costume.

My *legs,* eh? I say, grasping his hands that have gone straight for them. That's what you remember? *That's* why you were writing letters to me three years later!

Largely, he says humorously.

Men are so strange, I say.

What do you remember from when we met?

Outside the store?

Yes.

You weren't wearing a hat and you didn't have a tan line on your forehead.

My freaking tan line. Well, I find that stranger. He presses me back against the hood of the Ford, his hands grasping my backside, up under my skirt, his mouth on my breast, leaving wet marks on my blouse. This is to be a different version of what we've had before. Caw, caw, caw, caw, a crow cries from somewhere above us. And another four quick calls: caw, caw, caw, caw.

Hey, I say, pushing him away. Don't be crazy.

We get back into the truck and turn up the Parrots' lane, to where the abandoned brick house sinks into the yard, almost invisible behind overgrown lilacs and caraganas and willows. Russell's driving. He stops the truck behind the house where no one can see it from the road. The last time I was actually in this yard was for their sale, the Parrots' sale, and Russell was there then too.

The grass is almost to our knees and we leave a trail wading from the Ford to the house. The back door stands a few inches open. He pushes it farther and we step in. No one's lived here since the Parrots. An inch of dirt from the dust storms lies over the floor like a rug, patterned with curls of bird droppings and the wavy tracks of snakes. Thistles poke up along the edge where a floorboard is missing. There's still a stove there, with swallows' nests plastered all around the chimney. Pretty spooky, he says. He presses me against the crooked door frame and kisses me, if this urgent business of tongue and teeth can be called a kiss.

When we finally settle, it's in the grass between the house and the shed, we sink into the lush grass under a tree, breaking the grass under us, him pressing on me, silent, relentless. Beyond his shoulder green branches sway. From the tree above I see my legs against the grass, my panties around one ankle, my body displayed to the startled sky, skin white in the sunlight. He's pursued by something that hardly has to do with me — I can only retreat from it. It doesn't matter, the fact of it is the same. In a moment it's done, my body is marked inside and out. He rolls over and turns his face against the grass to look at me. He lies in his pleasure and I lie in mine, the pleasure of hearing his final cry. When we get up and pull our clothes on and wade back through the grass to the truck, we leave a nest behind us like deer do along the river.

7

The war shudders on. Headlines are printed, men in uniforms sprawl on the decks of ships, Russell and I lie in the loft with our legs entwined. We're hidden away so it doesn't matter. In a certain way you could say it's not really happening — but *it is*, I'm finding: here in the afterlife it's the hidden things that are real, the whispered secrets, my skin's surprise at his touch, the trail his lips leave on my breast, like the phosphorescent wake of a darting fish. Deep in piles of hay we nestle while my eight-year-old self watches from the rafters. Church in the loft! Russell finds it so funny. Where did the priest stand? he asks.

I gesture to the spot. Not a priest, though. Wrong religion. The pastor.

Well, I knew it wasn't a rabbi. He gets up and stands where Mr. Dalrymple's crude wooden pulpit stood and recites a long phrase in syllables I've never heard before, sounds made high in the roof of his mouth. I'm lying on a quilt sewn from patches of our old coats, sweat gathered like dew between my breasts. You know *Latin?* I ask.

Latin? Wrong religion, my dear. It's Hebrew. *Blessed be the Lord, the Lord is One.* He walks across the loft to me. His naked body is a white surplice, his tanned hands like brown gloves. He drops down in the hay beside me and rests his cheek against my knees. That's it, he says. That's all the Hebrew I remember. My mother wanted me to be bar mitzvahed, but it didn't happen.

Hebrew, Latin, Greek. I work my fingers through his damp hair. I wish I knew other, more cryptic words for all this, I wish I spoke in tongues.

⬥

Early summer swells into fullness and the hollyhocks tip forward with their flowers hanging like crumpled handkerchiefs. You feel the heat when you step out of the house first thing in the morning. On a hot afternoon our prying apart of limbs is a damp and sticky business. Before I go back to the house, to my life, my other life. To Mother knitting, or cleaning out the cutlery drawer, or just sitting on the chesterfield with her eyes bright with anxiety. After a time I have to face the fact that there's a new atmosphere in the house, Mother answering me in monosyllables and picking at her dinner, her face hard. Of course she's caught on, although I don't quite see how. All day she sits in the living room knitting her squares. The fighter planes haven't been training since last fall and I can't even get her out to the veranda. Sitting on the veranda you can be seen from the road. She doesn't want to remind people she's still here, so changed.

I'm fine, she says when I ask. She doesn't raise her eyes. My guilt makes me try harder. After supper I put two chairs in the front yard and try to get her to sit outside with me.

No thanks, she says. She's sitting on the chesterfield reading the Bible, a sure sign of trouble to be reading the Bible at that hour. At a glance I'd say she's somewhere in the Epistles of Paul. I try to recall what the Apostle Paul had to say about

352

deception, cunning, betrayal. About *fornication*. I bring two cups of tea and sit beside her.

Are you in pain? I ask.

No, it's nothing physical, she says. Her mouth is a straight, lipless line.

Well, what is it then?

Tears drip down her cheeks. Oh, I feel so bad, she bursts out.

Oh, Mother. Maybe you should try to see a doctor in Winnipeg.

She shakes her head.

I think you should. Maybe there's something they can do. Some treatment Dr. Ross doesn't know about.

It's not that, she says. We sit while the clock ticks off a long minute. Finally she lifts her eyes defiantly. I miss your dad. He wouldn't always try to avoid me.

What do you mean?

You'd rather sit outside in the rain than be in the same house as your mother.

I feel heat rise in my face. I'm restless, that's all, I say. I've always been restless. I've always lived outside in the summer.

You can't look at me, you can't bring yourself to speak to me. Every chance you get you take off outside, or to the barn.

Oh, Mother, I say. It's not that. It's not *you*. I'm not avoiding you. We *are* in a new place, I think, that she'd complain about this. I put my arm around her shoulders. She doesn't flinch away but sits very still like a frightened child and begins to cry in earnest.

That night I don't go to the barn, I go to bed when she does. I'll take her somewhere, I think, curling up on my side and hugging a pillow to me. After Russell goes. I'll take her with me when I go to see Joe. We'll drive up and stay by the big lake for a day or two. There must be cabins there. Suddenly I think of the girl in the green travelling costume on my father's ship. Was there ever any mention of a girl on the ship? I think now that there was not, that no one ever mentioned a girl at all. It was a nice bit of fancy, giving my father a different love, a love who looked, well, a little like me.

The fugitive in the loft tells stories about his father. Mr. Bates was one of those enterprising men who thought there was enough of him for any two women. He lived with Russell's mom until Russell was about eight and Stephen was ten, and he kept Charlotte's mother on the side. Loretta, who had been (of course) his secretary before she got pregnant with Charlotte. *Banker's hours?* Russell's mom would yell when he tried to slip in at midnight. *You call these banker's hours?* Russell gives his mother a Polish accent in these bits. They were living in Toronto then, and Mr. Bates was working at a bank on Spadina. Then he was offered the management of a branch in London, Ontario, and he had to choose which family he was going to take with him. And he picked them, Loretta and Charlotte.

That must have been *awful*, I say.

Russell draws on his cigarette and smiles his half-smile. No, it was better. It woke her up — what's the word . . . it has to do with science, with electricity? It *galvanized* her. Before she knew, before she really knew, she seemed half asleep all the time. It was like there was a slow leak somewhere and she couldn't put her finger on it. After he left at least we had our mother.

What's your mother like? I ask.

Oh, she's a bit of a character. The pleasure of the story he's going to tell creeps over his face. She likes excitement and she finally had a little drama in her life. She was actually the one who packed his stuff up when he left. She went over to Loretta's and banged on the door while he was at work. She was dragging a case of his stuff, the most embarrassing things. He had this truss thing for a hernia, and she dragged the freaking thing out and tried to show Loretta how to wrap it and work the buckles.

Did you see this?

No, but my mother gave me a play-by-play. And Charlotte was there.

I've brought beer up, and he gets up then and takes both bottles over to the narrow slot where the ladder is nailed to the loft floor. Our bottle opener. He cracks them open and comes back and hands me one.

You knew Charlotte then?

I got to know her that summer when I went down to London to see Dad. He tips his bottle back and takes a long drink and I watch his Adam's apple pumping the beer down his throat. I'll say this for Loretta, he says finally, wiping his mouth and dropping back down onto the blanket. Once the whole thing blew open she wanted Charlotte to know she had brothers. Dad would send train tickets, and she always made me welcome. Well, in her fashion.

Which is?

Well, how can I put it? If my mother is borscht, Loretta is consommé. He grins at his own joke, showing me his strong, even teeth.

So then you grew up with one parent, I say greedily, although I can see he's running out of steam.

He bends his head to light another cigarette, and I reach out my hand for the match and drop it into an empty beer bottle. Oh, it was all right, he says. She moved us closer to our uncles, she started going to synagogue again. She was free to make him the butt of her jokes. He always supported us, I'll give him that. A principled man. He thinks of himself as a principled man. As long as he handles *money* properly. Stephen never went to visit. Stephen's the principled one.

Russell lies back in the hay. I was always a little ashamed that Dad could *buy* me, he says. Send me a train ticket, and you can't see me for dust.

I lie beside him watching smoke curl into the dusty air. No, I say. I'm glad you're the sort of person who went to see his dad.

⟁

He wants me to come to Montreal with him. There's lots I could do, even if I'm not a Party member. I could be a fellow traveller — that has a nice ring to it. I toy with the idea of giving myself over, listening raptly from a seat in the front row in a crowded hall in Montreal, wearing a tweed jacket and the tie-up shoes I took to England. I try hard to keep my feelings off my face while he talks. Maybe there are situations where *imperialist running dogs* sounds like sensible language, maybe if you spend all your evenings in cramped rooms on hard chairs with comrades who talk the same way.

But I hold my little seedling opinions close to my chest. If he sees them he'll have them plucked out in a flash. I've joined the League of Esther, or whatever her name was in Montreal. Among the services I provide for Russell: Going to the Burnley library to ask for newspapers from down East (there are none). Stamping and mailing his letters (he writes a lot of letters). Carrying Mother's scissors out to the loft and trimming an inch off his hair all over, letting the brown pieces fall onto the straw. And, after he's been here a couple of weeks, delivering his mail. Unread — which, I might add, requires a lot of discipline, seeing as his letters all arrive addressed to me.

He's got two contacts in Winnipeg. He doesn't know these people, but he says he can stay with them, a family on Selkirk

Avenue or a single comrade named Al living in an apartment on Burrows. I'll take off by the end of the week, he says (more than once, at the start of different weeks). But he doesn't go. I keep slipping an extra piece of chicken or steak into the oven when I'm cooking dinner, I keep on with my double life. Two lives are more than most people hope for.

Mother stands in the living room for the longest time, looking out towards the barn. I'm peeling potatoes for dinner and I keep calling comments to her, trying to distract her. Finally I wipe my hands on the dishtowel and go out to join her. What are you looking at? I ask.

Oh, I was just thinking about your dad. He never did put a step at the henhouse door. For twenty years we've been tripping over that sill.

George told me that the Chinese build their houses without steps so the evil spirits can't walk in, I say. Maybe he was just looking after the chickens.

She holds on to the window ledge. She has the skin, beyond white, of someone the sun never sees, not even for the twenty seconds it takes to go to the outhouse. It was a mistake to buy a commode chair. She's using it all the time now, even during the day.

Your dad was slow at getting around to things, she says. Maybe it was part of his trouble. He fell down in the loft, you know. When we had church there. The men had to carry him out.

Fell down. That's our term for it. Suddenly I remember. I was standing in the yard crying and I remember them carrying him out. It's a scene from hell, three men carrying my father through the lake of fire, his body sagging between them. Was there a fire in the barn when it happened? I ask.

We never had a fire in that barn, she says. It was an evening service, it must just have been the sunset. Sometimes it looks like fire, the way the sun shines on the windows.

This was during the service? What did everybody do?

I didn't see it. You were being bad and I had to take you out, I had to give you a spanking. And then we were walking back to the barn and I heard the commotion and they were carrying him out.

I didn't realize everyone in the church knew all along, I say.

They didn't really know. They didn't know what it was. Her face twists with pain and her voice breaks. Mrs. Stalling started the story that he was a Pentecostal. From before he came to the district. They thought it was something to do with that. You know, the way the Pentecostals behave.

They thought he was speaking in tongues? I cry. When he had a seizure? They thought he was filled with the spirit? Suddenly I'm seized by longing, thinking of my father, his silence torn open by ecstatic words, his voice filling the loft. Crying out who he was, declaring himself, the swallows darting to the rafters in alarm. After a minute I reach for my mother's arm. She grips my hand. Her mouth is held in a grimace of emotion, a silent upside-down U.

Filled with the spirit, I say. Well, I think he was.

⁂

When you're naked in broad daylight, every subject is a confidence. I tell Russell about my dad, some things. I tell him about the Barr Colony. They wanted to come to the New World without really changing, I say. The man who led them made them think they were better than everyone else. I'm trying to confine myself to what I know for sure. Russell is more interested in the supply syndicate and all of Isaac Barr's other schemes.

It was a *Utopian* movement, he says. I've never heard of it, not this one from England. What were your dad's politics?

His politics? Oh, I don't know. He liked the King. One Christmas he managed to get a battery for Joe's radio so he could get up in the middle of the night to listen to the King's address. We didn't have an alarm clock, so he slept on the chesterfield with the thinnest of blankets — that's what he did, so the cold would keep waking him up.

Talk about conditioning of the masses, says Russell. Something floats up through the heedless warmth between us, something brown and murky, my distaste for his way of talking as though everything he says is the last word on the subject. I can't bear feeling this way. I run my hand down his chest to where the curling hair ends, feeling the soft sinking at the bottom of his ribs, and then I turn my face up knowing that this will bring his down to me and we will kiss.

We talk about the war, in our way, which is different from George's. It's one of our best subjects, the war, although Russell manages to make the Communists the centre of everything. He thinks, for example, that England and France let Germany build up arms in the Thirties in order to contain Russia. I don't argue. All his opinions are so worked out — they've been distilled in all-night debates with other men wearing braces, they're supported by covert sources of intelligence from all over the world.

He drags his knapsack across the bare boards of the loft and pulls something out of it to show me, a paper folded into the packet of letters and pamphlets he's hauling around. It's in George's familiar handwriting. A play script, or the first page of one, on a sheet torn out of an exercise book:

A British undergraduate encounters the Major
    on the esplanade.
MAJOR: *(hale, scarlet):* I envy you young chaps.

It's the life, the very life. Never happier than
in the last round.

UNDERGRADUATE: *(examining a cloud over the
ocean very like a whale)*

MAJOR: The last round was nothing compared
to this! We've got tanks, we've got RDF, we've
got the naval advantage.

UNDERGRADUATE: I reject the naval
advantage.

MAJOR: Total war this time. War at sea, war on
land, war in the air. We'll show the Jerries
what for!

UNDERGRADUATE: *(regards a cloud backed like
a weasel)*

MAJOR: Salute when you meet a senior officer,
young fellow.

UNDERGRADUATE: *(salutes)* Sir!

Where's the rest of it? I ask.

That's all he sent me, says Russell. Maybe it's all he wrote.
Of that particular play. He looks at me, bemused. Does it
make sense to you?

Yes, I say.

Well, I had to *study* the fucking thing, says Russell. *The
undergraduate salutes* — that must be George, when he gave
up and decided to enlist.

He didn't enlist, I say. He was conscripted. But he didn't
fight it. He just couldn't step aside from what was happening.
He saw himself a part of it, even if it was a terrible mistake. I
speak slowly because seeing something of George's has filled
me with emotion. Because what I'm saying is about Russell
too, Russell sleeping in a loft while other men are going
knowingly to die.

But he just sits and watches me with interest. Russell feels no shame about not going. He doesn't think he's part of it. He says, trying to be helpful, George must have just figured it was bigger than him.

No, I say. It's the politicians who think it's so big. They act as though the war is an act of God. As though there's no resisting it.

Hey, Lily, they *love* it! he says. Ever noticed how baggy their trousers are? That's so no one can see their woodies. Churchill's been walking around with a woody since 1937. Hell, since 1914!

He raises a toast. Let the warmongers fight the war! Conscript the bastards!

We clink our bottles together. Down with the Fascist imperialists! he yells.

A plague on both their houses! I cry.

I need to make everything up new. They were wrong about everything, George Bernard Shaw and Neville Chamberlain and Mr. Dalrymple and my shamefaced mother. Russell may be wrong as well. I need to figure everything out on my own, and one day I will. But right now I'm more interested in pinning Russell against the loft wall, running my fingernails over the muscles in his back and then smoothing out the scratching with my fingertips. The brides on the train from Saint John are starting to pop up in my mind, though, girls perched in the aisle, juggling babies and cigarettes and saying things in brittle voices they wouldn't dare say to their best friends. It all came back to sex. They'd just lived through a shipping-out leave — they had a bleary, worked-over look. There was a blonde girl about my age arguing that you have two safe weeks, with your period in the middle of them. That seemed like useful information and I stored it away. Of course, her system does not take into account the rainy days when I set myself the task of clearing up the old harnesses in the barn, or the days when Mother is unwell and sleeps right through from dinnertime until supper. I haven't worried because you can't worry and do what I've done. But when I think of it, she was very pregnant, the bride who said this, her belly button sticking out like a thimble in the middle of her stomach.

And then there was that other girl I rode beside, the girl who sat and jiggled her leg from Sault Ste. Marie to Port Arthur. In the middle of the night she got up to go to the bathroom and when she came back she saw I was awake. Don't ever get pregnant, she said. You have to pee every ten minutes. We started talking and we talked until morning. Doris, her name was. Her boyfriend had died in a training accident at Petawawa before she even had a chance to tell him. His name was Guy. He was French, a Catholic. She had a little diamond ring. She went to a jewellery store on her own and bought it as soon as she realized. I'm going to tell my family we were engaged, at least, she says. Not that we were. Not that he ever said a word about getting married.

When Mother falls asleep on the chesterfield in the afternoon I steal into her room and pull her underwear drawer open. The paper I'm remembering is still there, up against the back of her underwear drawer, yellow and cracked. I unfold it. There is the title, *Family Planning Aid*. As far in as possible? Ten minutes before? No wonder I remembered it. I slide it back into her drawer and go back to the kitchen, to where a roasting pan of cucumbers sits on the table. We're making pickles. The cucumbers are perfect for fancy dills, just three inches long. But they already have little nubs on them, like the black whiskers on an unshaven chin. I pour water into the pan and work the nubs off with my fingers in the clear, cold water, feeling the small pimple each one leaves behind. *Tannic acid. Boric acid.* I wonder who gave the recipe to her and if she used it. She must have, she must have used something. Boric acid, I think, is used for cleaning. Tannic acid maybe for tanning cowhides, that would make sense. I can't imagine doing it, it makes me feel sick.

⚅

One day she sees him in the yard. I tell Russell while we play rummy, sitting down by the river where there's a bit of a breeze.

She saw me? When?

At the pump.

What did you tell her?

I told her it was Harry Dabney. The fellow who rents our land. I told her he walked in from the road. I said his truck broke down and he needed water for the radiator.

Lily, you are a scary broad. I dread the day you have to lie to me.

I'm good at making them up. I'm not that great at delivering them.

Russell picks up a card and deftly reorders everything in his hand. While I was a girl memorizing Bible verses he was squatting in a Toronto alley playing rummy. He snaps a run of clubs, king high, on the grass between us without even bothering to look at me: he's won the game and winning is his due.

I wish you'd let me get your water, I say.

Well, you know what I wish? he says. I wish I could walk into the house and introduce myself. I'd tell her I'm in a bit of trouble and need a place to stay. She won't let on. She won't want the police out here. If I know mothers.

You don't know my mother.

You don't know your mother.

What do you mean?

You don't know your mother. Women never do. Women never really see their mothers. He has a clever grin on his face.

And why is that, do you suppose?

I guess they don't want to see themselves.

I give a sharp kick to his shin and then I roll away from him and down the bank. He doesn't react. He sits silently above me, smoking. I roll under a spruce, a big spruce. I lie among its knuckled roots in a bed of needles. I'll get sap in my hair, I think, but I don't care. This is the tallest spruce, it's the spruce where my father saw a lynx long ago. This is where he opened his eyes and saw the lynx watching him. Whatever it is that makes a lynx afraid of humans was gone that day.

My dad saw a lynx here once, I call up to Russell. You better watch out.

He doesn't answer. He sits there looking thoughtfully down the riverbank. I'm included in his gaze and I look silently back. He looks tired. The romance of living in a barn is wearing thin. He hasn't had mail for a few days, nothing to remind him he's a revolutionary. He should go, I think, for his own good. I'd be glad, I'd like a break from him. To find out what I'm feeling, just to drop a leg down and see if I'm in over my head or can still wade to shore. I study his face between the dark spruce boughs. He's more tanned than he was. He's been weeding the field plot where we grow potatoes and corn. He took it on because it can't be seen from the house or even really from the road, and when I tell Mother I'm weeding it we can be busy with other things.

He's still watching me. It's not just my body he wants. He wants my silence, he wants my moods, he won't leave me even a tiny place in my brain. I roll over, I roll out of the shadow of the spruce tree and press my face into the leaves and grass of the riverbank: poplar leaves, and that narrow beige grass with seed heads like tiny scythes, grass we walked on every day of my growing up but never spoke of because no one had ever given it a name. The blackbirds pipe and there's the constant electric hum of insects. I lie face down, I flatten my body into the tough, dry grasses and listen for a pulse.

There's a day when summer peaks. You don't always sense it the day it happens, but you know it the day after, as soon as you step into the yard. All that pulsing green is static, there's a stuffiness to the heat that tells you you're on the slide towards fall, that plants are starting to put their force into seeds and not into flowers. You tell yourself you're wrong, but out in the garden you see that the bottom leaves of the peas are drying yellow, and you have to take down the flypaper in the kitchen, carry it at arm's length out to the outhouse and drop it in a hole because it's black with dying and dead houseflies. And then you see spikes of goldenrod poking up out of the ditches and you know summer is well and truly over.

I decide to buy the ingredients one at a time, and on a morning when the sun is obscured by a haze of heat I ask the clerk in the grocery store for boric acid.

Boric acid? she says. Why don't you just use vinegar?

Mother said boric acid, I say.

Her eyes narrow in their wrinkly little pockets and I'm seized by the insane fear that we're talking about the same thing. Well, you'll have to try the drugstore, she says. We have Bull Dog Powder, and Blue Imperial, and Mrs. Stewart's Liquid, but we haven't carried straight boric acid for a couple of years.

Mr. Gorrie is still behind the counter of the drugstore, wearing his dark glasses. He's given no sign of recognizing me since I came back from England, but I feel my stomach tighten at the clerical bent of his back, the evangelical slope of his shoulders. *Into the fog with the rag-tailed dog*, I hum to myself, *ho ho ho and a bottle of rum*. He's weighing out a white powder for the woman beside me at the counter. Half a pound, she says. No, make it six ounces. Her singed yellow hair is familiar, and then she turns her head and I see it's Susan Dabney, our renter's wife.

Oh, Lily, she says. You haven't had Harry knocking at your door this morning?

No, I say cautiously. Should I have?

Well, I gave him enough sandwiches for ten men. But they'll be gone by noon. She has her little boy with her, and she reaches down and pries his hands one at a time off the glass counter. Can you manage an extra for dinner? I'd say send him home, but he's got the team.

Harry's working at our place today? I ask stupidly.

You didn't see him? she says. He started haying north of the river.

Mr. Gorrie adds another half-ounce to the white pyramid on the scales, and a tiny cloud of powder lifts towards his glasses. *Into the bog with the rag-tailed sog, into the bog, into the fog* . . . You know, I say to both of them, I just realized. I left Mother's prescription in the truck. I'll be right back.

I can see Harry as soon as I turn off the section road. I can't imagine how I missed him on my way to town. He's doing it the old way, with a team of horses. I stop at the edge of the field and wait until he makes his way up to the road and lifts one hand in greeting. The horses are already wet in their withers.

You've got a hot day for it, I call.

Sure do, he calls back and turns the corner. There's nothing to be seen in his sunburned face. No curiosity.

I park the Ford close to the barn, the way I have been lately. Russell's sitting up in the straw when I get to the top of the ladder. He's been sleeping. His face is red from the heat, wrinkled like a satin dress, his hair is damp. He's stripped down to his shorts. I know, he says. I saw him when he came. I guess I shouldn't be sleeping. Is he going to fill the loft?

Yes, but not today. He has to let the hay cure first. I lean on the edge of the loft, but I can't bring myself to climb up into the heat.

When, do you think?

A couple of days. Not long in this heat. But he'll be in and out of the yard to water his horses and I may end up feeding him. You'll have to work at staying out of sight.

Maybe I should just go now. I can't take much more of this.

Where will you go?

I'll go to town and hitch a ride to Winnipeg. I keep writing Al that I'm coming and then I never do.

We can't talk about it. The heat baffles us, it's so thick in the air that our words don't carry. Are you thinking tomorrow? I ask, although he's begun to cram his things, his letters and towel and tobacco, into his knapsack.

He'll be here again first thing in the morning, won't he? I'll go now, while he's over in the field and you have the truck out. I think I should just go now. He stands up and starts to pull his pants on.

It's cooler down by the river, I say. You could spend the day down there.

Lily, he's working down by the river.

Oh. I'm feeling a little dizzy and suddenly it's important to get off the ladder. Sorry, I say, I can't seem to think today.

I sit in the kitchen and drink a glass of water. Mother's lying on the chesterfield. She's loosened her hair and it floats above her on the cushions, as though she's sinking down into a lake. She has the afghan over her legs. How can you stand that? I ask.

The circulation to my feet isn't the best, she says.

Listen, I say, I have to make another trip to town. I forgot to drop off the eggs. I'm such a dolt. They're sitting in the truck.

She doesn't say anything and I feel relief that this charade may be almost over. I'm losing perspective when it comes to lies — I can't tell what's reasonable and what isn't. I go to my room and take a couple of bills out of the envelope I keep in my top dresser drawer and slip them into my purse.

I stop the truck on the east side of Burnley, near the highway. Russell and I sit in the Ford like any farm couple come to town, except that the woman is driving. We sit and look at each other. I have no idea what this is, so I have no idea how I should be acting. I wish you didn't have to go, I say.

Well, when it comes right down to it, I guess I don't, he says.

What do you mean?

Well, Lily. Let's not pretend I'm hiding for my sake.

I stare at him.

I'm ready to go to the house and introduce myself to your mother, he says. I told you that. You're the one who wants to keep hiding me.

I look out at the road.

It's true, isn't it? He nudges his knapsack with his foot. If you can't live your life around here you should leave. You could come with me now. I can hang around Burnley for a day or two until you get yourself sorted out. We could go to Winnipeg. I'd get work at the *Clarion*.

You think I can just leave Mother on her own? I say.

He makes an impatient little movement.

Well, what then?

Ask your sister-in-law to move back.

I can't do that.

Why not?

I don't answer.

What are you going to do? he asks me. You can't stay here forever.

I sit behind the wheel. I refuse to look at him again.

It's just going to get harder. She'll get worse. There are people who are good at nursing.

My mother wouldn't let anyone else help. She's too proud.

Well, maybe that's something she'll have to get over. A hayrack moves down the road with three children nestled in the back. They wave at us and I lift my hand in response. Lily, he says, and waits until I look at him. Lily, there are a lot of women like you who sacrifice their lives to look after others. It's unselfish and I admire it. But is it the best thing in the long run? As long as people work on their own like this, the system doesn't have to change.

I've just been called *unselfish*, this is not lost on me. But this is an artificial argument, it's not the argument of the moment. It's hard to breathe and I reach over to roll the window down, but it's already down. I feel sick to my stomach.

He reaches to the floor of the truck for his knapsack. I wonder if this is the best place to catch a ride, he says.

There's a train in an hour, I say. Why don't you just take it? I take the folded bills from my purse and hand them to him.

Thanks, he says. He lifts one hip from the truck seat and slips the money into his back pocket. By now I understand why he can take money from me so easily. It's not for him, not really. I start the Ford up again and drive to the railway station, where I park by the fence.

Listen, he says. I'll just go to Winnipeg for now. I won't go back east without you. So you've got some time to figure out what you're going to do.

How long, do you think?

I have no idea.

He doesn't want to meet my gaze. He's been glib, he knows it. He leans over and drops a neutral kiss on the corner of my mouth. The city's coming back to him — I can see his purpose and excitement and relief. He turns at the station door and waves. I start the Ford up and back crookedly out to the road. On the road I press my foot to the floor, wanting to get some breeze. At the first corner I turn up the Nebo road and head towards fall.

8

My deck of playing cards was seized and burned a year ago by the Inquisition. And Russell took his deck with him. I wish I'd asked to keep it, he'd have given it to me. I miss playing cards. The cards are dealt, the cards are played — all in ten minutes the game is up.

I find a stack of old calendars and cut them into pieces. I pick out sets of numbers and paste them to little pieces of cardboard. Mother would never play cards, but she doesn't realize that's what she's doing. I teach her a couple of games, including a calendar version of Old Maid. Do you have August 15? we ask each other. Do you have September 3? She's very good at it and beats me the first two games. All right, I say, that was best of three. You win, Joe Pye.

For supper I make her a chip butty. We still have a few wizened old potatoes and they're best for chips, they don't spit as much when you fry them. Remember how Dad always talked about the way they ate when he was growing up? I say. Chip butties and sugar butties and tea leaf butties.

Tea leaf butties, you and Phillip would shout, she says. Her speech slurs a little, as though she's had a couple of drinks too fast.

August has vanished, there's no getting it back. All that heat is gone, collapsed on itself like a plague that went too far and gobbled up its own food supply. The colour has drained from the grass, and yellow patches in the Manitoba maples draw your eyes to the branches that are dying. It's the season of Dieppe, that's all people will remember in the long run. But someone set the clock for harvest and no matter what else is going on in the world there's no putting off the harvest. The second crop of beans is finished, and the peas, and we're eating bright orange corn that no one except a fiend for salt and butter would consider eating. On the ground everything is drying up. It's the time for underground growth, for the carrots pushing wider into the earth during the night, the potatoes furtively swelling. Our best crop is unintentional, the turnips that came up as volunteers in the pigpen, where I kept throwing the kitchen slop even after I sold the pig.

Inside the house two women take their Saturday-night baths: the younger one tall and strong and healthy, spectacularly healthy, she has health enough for two. The older, her muscles shrivelling in retaliation, but retaliation for what? Her fingers are losing their range of motion, there's a hint of vindication in her face when she shows me. She can handle bathing herself, but she can't get in or out of the tub on her own. When she calls me to help her out, she struggles to hold a towel in front of herself like a curtain. She looks fearfully, defiantly over it at me. It's always there, Betty's question about what will happen to her. It's always possible that her life matters as much to her as mine does to me. This is what I think: that I have to show I can do this better than a Christian.

Finally she's dried and in her nightgown, sitting forward over a chair back with her head bent into a basin on the kitchen table. We don't wash her hair very often and a sharp smell rises from her scalp. I gather up the ragged ends and press them down into the water. The colour's stripped from them, the way it's stripped from the grass, and they resist the water. When her hair is finally wet it's like reeds rotting in the bottom of a slough. A handicraft of some sort: yarn I'm dyeing — that's what I have to tell myself.

Your scalp must ache, I say. Imagine what it would be like to have a man use your hair as a ladder. Do you know that story? Rapunzel?

I'm thinking of getting you to cut it off, she says. Her voice is muffled. I can't believe I've heard right, but I know better than to press the point.

Whenever you want, I say.

My own hair gleams like never before when I brush it, and high colour shows through the tan of my cheeks. I dry myself methodically. If I don't pay too much attention, maybe my body will *shut up*, stop sending me messages. There's a strange, metallic taste in my mouth. My breasts are heavy, the flesh of my nipples seems darker. There's also a sign I can count on my fingers, but it's the other things I brood over — they tell me more, the way a glance can tell you more than a word.

Every time I go to town I pick up a newspaper. On September 8 I read a little article I would never have noticed before and learn that some members of the Communist Party of Canada were released from Headingly Jail. A few days after that the names of the dead in Dieppe are released and start to fill the papers, page after page, day after day. Not too many Manitoba boys, although the blacksmith's son, Jimmy Thrasher, is one of them and everyone is talking about it in town. I don't buy the paper that day. How could you read a paper like that, what would you do with it after you'd read it?

I get letters. From Madeleine:

*We've been cleaning out George's shed. Mother
wanted to leave it until the end of the war, but
Dad wouldn't let it rest. I saved a lot of funny
things I couldn't bear to throw away. I'll share
them with you when you come back. I've had
another new frock. I have filled out, if I do say so
myself, and I had nothing that fit. Nettie's gone to
work at a factory in Leeds, so I had to do my own
sewing. I'm not much with fasteners. Every time
I put it on Mother has to stitch me into it and then
cut me out of it after. I guess that will keep me out
of trouble. Which leads me to my biggest news!
Lois is expecting at Christmas! She's feeling poorly,
no surprise there, but even Archie's mother is
happy about it and has been over to see Mother.*

So.
From Russell:

*I said I'd come back to the farm before I go
east, but there is so much happening here I never
figured on. A big party to celebrate Jake Penner's
release. He was held for over a year. But they're
still holding on to warrants for quite a few. I
assume I'm one of them, but how would I know?
I guess I could walk into a police station and ask
if they want to arrest me!*

*Actually, that may happen. I've had a letter
from Everiste saying that some of the comrades
down east are going to get together and turn
themselves in. They will probably do it in Hull.
Or Toronto. The idea is to force the hand of*

the police, see if there really is a will to arrest
Communists right now. (And to provoke a public
reaction.) Al and I have been talking about it.
I'd like to join my comrades, but we don't have
the fare to go east. So I am seriously thinking of
walking into the police station here. If they arrest
us here they might send us to Ottawa on the public
dollar. I don't think Al will go along with it in
the end. He has a big garden and he wants to be
around to get it all in, the carrots and potatoes,
etc. He's feeding half of Burrows Avenue.

If this works out, you might have to come
east on your own. You can visit me and smuggle
cigarettes in. I don't know what you want to do,
Lily, you never tell me.

I put the letters in a chocolate box on the window ledge in my
bedroom. A stony little cigar still lies there. *Lapides lyncis.*
When the scholars wanted a Latin name for the belemnite,
petrified lynx piss was the one they took up. It would be so
amazing to come across a belemnite in a sheep pasture, a tiny
talisman dropped from heaven. It was somebody crouching on
a rock on the coast of Wales who identified it as the chamber
of a mollusc. This was back in the nineteenth century, but
George was coy about that. He never really wanted to admit
it — the closing off of possibilities about the belemnite.
Problematica — that was his favourite category. It's not a
category that exists for Russell, I think, and I feel a stab of
longing for Russell, for his certainty. I think of one night,
a night I got up and walked barefoot across the yard under
a litter of stars and climbed up into the pitch-black loft without waking him, crawling clumsily through the straw in the

direction where he always slept until I bumped into him and felt the heat of his body and nestled in close, smelling cigarette smoke and perspiration. I always think about George in the night, I whispered. About the way he died. There was a long silence. Russell stirred and curled one arm around me. You never told me what happened, he said, his voice thick with sleep. So I did tell him while he lay still with his arm around me.

Were you back here when you found out? he asked.

No, I said. I knew it when I left Oldham. Before it even happened.

Oh, Lily, he said. You didn't. He propped himself up on an elbow then and tried to kiss me. You imagined something terrible, you were afraid. But you didn't know.

He was wrong, I knew, I knew. I rolled over onto my back then and pulled him towards me. I sank down into the dark under him, feeling his weight on me, turning my face away from his kisses.

Was he your cousin? he asked me after a time. Was he your lover?

No, I said. No, I said to both questions, he wasn't.

I stand in my bedroom now and roll the belemnite back and forth in my hand. It's a lovely brown, the very brown of the scrub oaks by the river. Polished, as though someone has taken a soft cloth to it. It's not a stony finger or a bullet casing, it wasn't made by magic and it wasn't made by man. It's a buoyancy chamber. Some little speck of an animal excreted it to keep itself afloat, millions and millions of years ago, halfway around the world. I stand in my bedroom with the belemnite in my hand and then I put it back on the window ledge.

⬦

I go to bed earlier and earlier, I sink hungrily into dreams. I dream that Mother and I get jobs. We're taking the train to work. She *has* had her hair cut — its waves peep out from the rim of a jaunty beret and her face is glazed and willing. I have no idea where we should be getting off. I get up at every station to see if it's our stop, but the train never slows down enough for me to tell. Then I'm walking back from the barn in my nightdress, being followed by a dog, a stray dog with shaggy fur tinged with rust. The sheets are tangled around my legs like ropes of seaweed. I kick them down to the bottom and lie under the scratchy blanket. I dream of a catalogue coming in the mail, its pages sticking together where someone spilled sweet coffee on them. Then I'm in St. Ambrose Parish Church in Salford. I'm walking up the stone aisle, squeezing past a big watering trough. (*It's for the baptisms,* says Nettie Nesbitt.) When I finally open my eyes the light is grey. It's the dawn of a cloudy day. I lie in bed for a long time, thinking about telling her.

I'll do it one evening when the sunset paints the underside of the clouds crimson. Mother will be sitting in the front yard where she sits to watch the fake air battles. I drag a chair out and sit down beside her. *Mother —* , I say. Her eyes turn up, fear rising in them. I tell her, in one clean and fearless sentence. I watch the rage collect in her face. She doesn't ask how this could have happened, with us alone on the farm these last two years. It's something I hatched up in my own sinful body, it's been in the cards since I was thirteen. *I want you to leave,* she says in a strangled voice. *Get out of this house. Now. Before anyone finds out.* She would rather lose me than face the disgrace. In fact, she'd love it if I left — the world would know me then, the sort of child she's always had to contend with: everyone would know my breathtaking wickedness. I take some pleasure in imagining this, I enjoy tearing down the fragile structure the two of us have been building.

The rooster is doing his best to wake up the henhouse. Mother's bedsprings creak. The sheets need washing — I smell myself on them, sweat, and the garden, and the yeasty smell of bread. I wonder guiltily when Mother's bed was last changed. I should get up and start the laundry, I think. *Or, I think*, dipping back into my story. *Or* maybe I don't tell her. Maybe while she's sleeping I just drag my empty trunk out to the Ford, and then gradually I spirit my things outside and fill it. On cue I get a telegram from Phillip. He's in Halifax, he's being sent home! He's been diagnosed with a *heart murmur.* I drive to town to pick him up. He gets off the train wearing his civvies. My trunk is standing on the platform — the station master unloaded it from the Ford. The whistle blows and I hand Phillip the keys of the Ford and board the train. Mother would rather have him anyway, she'd much rather have Phillip and Betty than me.

But then of course the train that brought Phillip home carries me west, that's the way it's headed. Where do I go in the west? — under that endless sky, with stooks of grain running to the horizon in every direction, and farmhouses just like this one, one every mile, red kitchen floors with their pattern of curling feathers from here to Edmonton. The train chugs doggedly on. I can't get it turned back east, to Charlotte, opening a heavy oak door to greet me, wearing her nursing cap — Charlotte who hardly knows me but is kind. Or to Aunt Lucy, reaching out to pull my head down to her shoulder, saying, *There, there, love, there's no need for that.* Or to Doris, the girl I met on the train whose boyfriend'd been killed. Suddenly I see Doris. She's wearing a trim business suit and red shoes. She's standing outside an office on a wide city street with a handsome little boy beside her. Her child, the baby that was just a thought inside her when I met her on the train. *It was hard*, the caption below this picture reads, *but you can do it.*

To Russell. In my mind I see the train come for me, but I can't get it turned back east to Russell.

It's cold now. I get up one night long after Mother's asleep and pull my clothes on, reaching in to the floor of the wardrobe where my winter clothes are piled and throwing on the first things that come to hand. I visit the outhouse and then I walk across the yard, out under the cottonwoods standing silver against the dark sky. They're always the last to lose their leaves. Their long roots go down into an underground stream, that's what my dad said. On the other side of the line of trees the fields stretch flat in the starlight.

I wade through the grass to the roof of the old chicken house. I used to sit there all the time before I went to England, I used to sit there and read the Bible. I climb up and lie back and stretch my legs out. Then I sit up again and hitch my jacket around to cushion my spine against the shingles. The air is cold, spiced with smoke from stubble burning on the other side of the river. This roof's at a perfect slant for lying to look at the stars. I tip my head back and narrow my eyes, and the tiny bits of light above me blur, jostling for space. Above me they dance, sending down their old light. They crowd into one another — that's the way it seems from here, but really there are infinite plains of darkness between them. I snuggle into my jacket, resisting the cold. Deep inside me my heart beats on unbidden. All through my body, cells go about their business, do their private, independent work. It's not a matter of thought: my thinking or not thinking will not affect it in the slightest.

We expect the threshing crew, but it rains. I run into Harry on the road. He rolls down his truck window to pass the time of day with me. He's grinning in spite of the rain. The *Farmer's Almanac* promises one big storm and then clear, dry weather for weeks. Anyway, he has the bumper crop of all bumper crops, he can afford to see it drop a grade.

It's raining so hard when I come in from milking that I wish I had a lid for the pail. I open the kitchen door and slide the milk in, standing in the porch to shake the water off my coat. There's an unfamiliar oilskin jacket hanging on the nail by the door. When I step into the kitchen, someone's sitting at the kitchen table. A brown-haired man, his hair shining black from the rain. Mother's standing by the stove. There's a bright red spot on each of her cheeks. Her hands are shaking with her agitation, but she's managed to put the kettle on the stove for tea. Or Russell helped her. And there he sits at our kitchen table, an amazing sight, with his broad shoulders and confident, friendly face. And how it must amaze her too, this Satanic figure from my girlhood, such a commonplace man after all, seemingly sober and wearing a grey cotton shirt. An ordinary grey shirt — it should look ordinary to her, it's Phillip's.

I stand on the rag rug and shake rain out of my hair, and when I feel as though I can speak I turn towards the table. Russell, I say. He rises up a little from his chair. It looks as though he's about to shake hands with me, but then he sits back down. He's wearing a ridiculous, elated smile. Hello, Lily. Nice to see you.

Nice to see you too, I say.

He was just travelling through, says Mother. Someone dropped him off on the road and he came to the door. While you were milking. She's fumbling to get the tea tin open and I go to help her.

Actually, I've been in Manitoba for a few months, Mrs. Piper, Russell says. But I'm heading back east now. I just wanted to stop in before I left. Russell keeps his eyes on me while he talks, and I stare back. I'm looking for something in his face. For whether he came to ask me for his fare to Hull, or for some other reason. Finally, without looking away, he says, Maybe before the tea is ready, I'll just use your outhouse. Out back?

Where else? I say. He goes out, lifting his waterproof off the nail.

Imagine that fellow showing up, Mother says when the porch door slams. Imagine him remembering you after all this time.

Yes, imagine, I say. I'm beginning to get my breath back. Of course, he did write to me while I was in England, I say. At least twice. I guess it's always possible that I wrote back.

She ignores this. That dog is not the watchdog he should be, she says. That fellow was right at the door before I knew. He said he knocked on the porch first, but I didn't hear him. I didn't hear a thing until he was right at the kitchen door. I wonder who it was that dropped him off? I asked him, but he didn't know the man's name. Whoever it was must have wondered why he'd be coming here.

She teeters over to the cupboard to get down teacups. He doesn't look much like his father, she says. Mr. Bates had a finer-featured face. This one is kind of broad across the cheekbones. His mother must be a Ukrainian or one of those nationalities.

I sit down in silence at the table.

When he comes back in he says, It's stopped raining. Do I have time for a smoke? He tips his head for me to join him, with an expression that will surely speak volumes to my mother, but she's staring at the cigarette he's rolled in the outhouse, rigid with fear that he'll try to light it in the kitchen. I should try to make this all seem natural. *I'll show Russell around*, I should say. But I can't be bothered. I just get up and stalk silently to the door and reach for my coat.

We stand under the overhang of the porch. The rain has slowed momentarily but water drips from the roof like vines.

He pulls me into his arms and kisses me. If you'd just shown up in the loft, we could have spent the night together, I say. (*You might have seen then*, is what I'm thinking, *you would know without having to be told*.) It's full of fresh hay, I add. It's very pleasant at the moment. Cool as well.

In a minute I'll be crying.

No, he says. No more of that. I've had it with living like a criminal. He lets me go and lights his cigarette. Anyway, your mother offered me a bed. She said I could sleep with you.

I bet she did, I say. Comes the revolution. We smile at each other. It's starting to rain again, it hadn't really stopped, and I pull my scarf up over my hair and nudge him back under the overhang.

Blue crowds under the overhang with us. Bloody dog, says Russell, grabbing his muzzle. He was all over me. Almost ratted me out to your mother. Eh, Blue? You missed me, eh, Blue?

I thought you were turning yourself in to the police in Winnipeg, I say.

Oh, that's a story, Russell says, letting Blue go and bringing his cigarette up to his mouth. I did try. I went to the station in the North End. The waiting room was full of thugs. Army rejects with bashed-in faces, and prostitutes trying to start a fight. A Sergeant Mike O'Connell was on the desk. *Communist, eh?* he says. *So why you telling me?* I told him about the Order-in-Council. I suggested he call the RCMP, get them to check their outstanding warrants. *It's a Saturday night, lad*, he says. He's about thirty himself and he calls me *lad*. Then he pulls a dollar out of his pocket and hands it to me. *Take yourself off to the pub*, he says. *Be glad you weren't at Dieppe.*

Russell can do a reasonable Irish brogue. His tan has faded, he's had his hair cut properly and he's looking cleaned up and full of life. When I kiss him there's the smell of cigarettes and the pepper taste of his skin.

Mother and I had supper before I did the milking, but Russell hasn't eaten, so while he drinks his tea I warm him up a meal of the leftovers we would otherwise have had for tomorrow's dinner. Roast beef, new carrots, new potatoes fried in butter. A saucer of sliced tomatoes and cucumbers. The meat was in the Elizabeth and Margaret Rose tin I used all summer to take food to him, and he leans against the counter and fiddles with it while he watches me cook. We've lit a lamp — strange for the kitchen to be so dark at this hour. Prairie cooking! he says when I put his plate on the table. Thank you, says Mother, as though she cooked it. She turns away so that she doesn't have to witness him starting to eat without saying grace and then she goes over to the cupboard to get him a piece of date cake. I can see him looking bemused at the sight of a thin braid that's wormed its way loose from the ball at the nape of her neck and hangs halfway down her back. He catches my eye and winks.

I know he's going to want another cigarette. Let's go sit on the veranda, I say when he's finished eating. I have never in my life seen Mother sit out on the veranda after supper. But he has these city manners. Can I give you a hand, Mrs. Piper? he asks. So she takes his arm and I go out ahead of them and straighten the quilt on the Toronto couch. She lets go of his arm at the door and manages to grab a corner of the couch, sitting at the end where my father's shoes are hidden. So I sit on the rocking chair and Russell eases himself down beside Mother on the couch. The wind is blowing from the northwest, so the rain isn't coming in, although when I reach my hand out I can feel a mist. Blue presses himself against my legs. He won't sit down because of the storm. He stands alert, on guard against thunder. The smell of his fur rises in the humid air. It's so dark, Mother says. You should bring the lamp out, Lily. I lean over to scratch the base of Blue's ears and wish her away. It's in my bones to wish my mother away, it's the calcium in my bones maybe, whatever makes them strong.

We sit and watch the storm. Thunder thumps in the distance. When lightning flickers you see the rain bouncing up from the lane, like hail. Russell takes his tobacco pouch and papers out of his shirt pocket and rolls a cigarette. I wonder if Mother appreciates the practice it takes to roll a cigarette in the dark. You wouldn't have an ashtray, would you, Lily? he asks. I get him a saucer from the kitchen. I can't see the expression on Mother's face when I hand it to him. It's so dark, it could be midnight.

Russell draws on his cigarette. The ember glows orange and lights up the planes of his face, the deep notches on either side of his mouth.

You're not enlisted, says my mother.

No, says Russell. At the moment I'm a member of an illegal organization.

She doesn't ask. It's as if she didn't hear. My son is in England, she says. He's an airplane mechanic with the RCAF. He was an AC2, but he's had a promotion, he's been promoted to LAC.

What does that stand for? asks Russell.

I couldn't really say, says Mother.

Russell takes another drag and I can see he's smiling his sardonic half-smile. The storm was in the west, but now a sheet of lightning flashes in the south, lighting up the fringe of trees along the river. Then a bolt cuts its way across the sky, fibres of light on either side of it. A few seconds later the thunder comes. I wonder, when artillery guns go off, whether you see the flash of fire before you hear their thunder. Probably not, they'd be too close to you. Apparently if lightning strikes close enough you can smell it, ozone George said it was, hanging in the air the way cordite hung on Union Street after a bombing.

My husband's family is from England, my mother says.

So I understand, says Russell.

From Salford, County Lancashire, she says. Her uncooperative tongue makes it hard for her to get this out. Where is your family from?

He knows what she's asking, but he's not offended. My mother is a Polish Jew, he says. Her family left Poland in 1910. My mother was about twenty. I guess they were lucky. They were luckier than anybody knew at the time.

Lightning cracks across the sky again and Blue yelps. In the Bible lightning is God's arrows, thunder is his voice. This *could* be the end times, the final battle; maybe the faithful have been snatched away without our noticing, leaving us, just us on this narrow veranda, with nothing but a ragged screen between us and the lashing rain. There's another flash and we light up as if we're in a photograph, captured in an unthinking moment. The three of us here in the damp autumn air — Russell with everything he's sure of, his solid body shrouded by curling smoke, Mother and me with our secrets: she's caught in a moment of attention, her white profile turned towards Russell and an expression of uncommon interest on her face; me, I'm balancing on the rocking chair with one leg curled under me, my hands tucked into the sleeves of a tartan jacket. And if so, if that was the Rapture, I'm relieved, glad it's over, glad to be abandoned to this world.

ACKNOWLEDGEMENTS

Quotations from *The Pilgrim's Progress* by John Bunyan are from the Dodd, Mead & Company edition (New York, 1968). Biblical quotations are from the King James Version. Lyrics to "I'll Fly Away" by Albert E. Brumley are quoted with permission of Brumley Music Group.

Among many sources on the Barr Colony, I would especially like to acknowledge Lynne Bowen's *Muddling Through: The Remarkable Story of the Barr Colonists* (Douglas & McIntyre, 1992), and among sources on the two World Wars, the work of Paul Fussell. George's parody of "Oh, death, where is thy sting?" is cited in *The Great War and Modern Memory* (Paul Fussell, Oxford University Press, 1975). Numerous and varied accounts of the unfortunate airman falling into civilian hands in Kennington are found in Internet and print sources.

Thank you to the Manitoba Arts Council and the Canada Council for the Arts for grants that provided essential time to write. Thanks to everyone at Anne McDermid and Associates Ltd. and to my editors: Patricia Sanders for crucial advice in the early stages, Heather Sangster for judicious copyediting, and especially Bethany Gibson at Goose Lane Editions, who has been unfailingly responsive, insightful and encouraging. Thanks to Robert Kroetsch and my group in the Novel Symposium at the Sage Hill Writing

Experience, and to friends for their astute readings: Connie Cohen, Heidi Harms, Faith Johnston, Susan Remple Letkemann, Hazel Loewen and Christina Penner.

I want to express my appreciation to Dr. Janice Ingimundson and my gratefulness to my family, whose gifts — my mother's love of reading, my father's love of the prairies, and my mother-in-law Betty Dunn's wonderful Lancashire stories — have found their way into this novel. Special thank you to Bill and to Caitlin, for their love and for making room for this work in our home.